Augury Answered

PHILLIP MURRELL

This is a work of fiction. Names, places, and events are all work of the author's imagination. Any resemblance to actual events, organizations, locations, or persons, living or dead, is completely coincidental.

Copyright © 2019 by Phillip Murrell

All rights reserved. This book or any portion thereof may not be reproduced or used in any manner whatsoever without the express written permission of the publisher except for the use of brief quotations in a book review.

Printed in the United States of America

First Printing, 2019

ISBN: 9781096096191

This book is dedicated to my bonus parents, Jimmy and Rosie. Not to be confused with my in-laws, Jim and Rose, to whom this book is also dedicated

CHAPTER 1

A **young girl** chased a small frog as it hopped away from the threat she posed. The girl squealed with delight as she cornered the green amphibian alongside her house. The frog pressed against the sturdy brick wall of the large plantation home. With delicate caution, she moved her pale and freckled hands on each side of her prey. The frog had ceased moving and remained still as the child wrapped her small fingers and held it tight.

"Murid! My sweet, where are you? Murid, it's time!" a woman shouted from the doorway of the two-story, brick home.

"Time to meet my prince," Murid said to her new pet before releasing it. The frog hopped away with the eagerness expected of nature, now that Murid offered it a safe passage back to the swampland surrounding her home on this sunny afternoon.

"Murid! Come here!" the woman shouted again.

"Coming, Mother!" Murid replied.

Murid smoothed the front of her dress. Her muddy appearance would likely displease her parents. A princess must always be presentable. They'd told her this many times in her life. She was seven-years-old! She didn't need constant reminders like she was just a little kid.

Murid sprinted around the corner and found her mother. Queen Colchi looked like an older version of Murid. The humid air surrounding their home in Soust, the capital of the kingdom, easily frazzled the full, red hair they both possessed. Each had beautiful eyes that people felt forced to comment about at every opportunity. Murid's deepest hope was for the freckles on her face to fade and reveal the beautiful unblemished skin her mother had.

Queen Colchi held out her arms as Murid ran into them. Mother and daughter laughed as Queen Colchi twirled the young princess.

"It would be too much to ask that you kept your outfit clean," Queen Colchi said.

Murid looked at the ground with only timid glances at her mother.

"I'm sorry, Mother. I saw a frog, and—"

"And you had to catch it?" Queen Colchi finished the statement for her daughter.

Murid kept her face on the grass that lined the outside of her home. Behind her, she heard the many servants and guards that protected her family milling about as they completed their tasks.

"I'm sorry, Mother," Murid repeated.

Queen Colchi sighed. "There's nothing we can do

about it now. You better hope your father is too busy showing off for our guests to notice."

Murid looked at her mother with hope. Queen Colchi winked at her.

"I won't tell him if you won't," the queen teased.

Murid giggled with her mother and accepted her outstretched hand. Mother and daughter entered their luxurious home and closed the sturdy, wooden door behind them.

Their home's entrance had a grand foyer. Elegant flowers lined the rails that ran along both sides of an exquisite imperial staircase. Murid knew it was *exquisite* because her father made certain to boast about it to everyone brought inside their home. Between her parents and many teachers, Murid had learned an expansive vocabulary. It was important to show people how intelligent she was. That way they would never take advantage of her.

Queen Colchi continued to grasp Murid's hand as she whisked her toward her father's private study. As they approached the room Murid seldom had access to, she heard the deep and commanding voice of her father.

"Please calm down. As always, you're overreacting, Viktor," King Haymel said to his guest. "The Corlains have enough land and resources. They won't continue to expand. We're safe enough in this frontier to avoid their overbearing rules and regulations."

"I'm certain there are many Namerian tribes who would argue your willingness to appease the Corlains will lead to regret," King Haymel's guest answered.

"We aren't Namerians, Viktor. The Corlains want

their stones and the secrets they hold. They don't care about the rest of us out here," King Haymel replied.

"Wrong again. My apothecaries are constantly ransacked and destroyed by the Corlains."

"Why?"

"Sick people are easier to control. If you heal those with ailments, then you become a savior. The Corlains lack many traits, but cunning isn't one of them. They *will* take what you have. We must fight them first."

King Haymel scoffed. He was about to respond to his guest's bold claim when Queen Colchi and Princess Murid entered his study.

"We'll continue this discussion later," King Haymel said. "Princess!"

Murid scampered away from Queen Colchi and thrust herself into her father's arms. He picked her up in a powerful bear hug and held her tight to his chest. King Haymel wasn't a physically intimidating man. He was only average height and build, but his mind was sharp. Murid breathed in his musky scent that consistently comforted her. She knew her father would always keep her safe.

As King Haymel placed Murid down, she looked at the other two men in the room. First was the speaker from the previous discussion, King Viktor from the northern country of Vikisoteland. King Viktor, like many of his countrymen, was a barrel-chested giant among men. He had a thick, brown beard and hard features. The only parts of him that one might label *soft* were his brown eyes. The brown was so deep they reminded Murid of mud in the fields outside her home after a thunderstorm.

The second person was a boy but significantly older than Murid. He was lean and tall but not nearly as tall as either king. A small mustache lined his upper lip, and the teenager constantly rubbed it with his right index finger. His name was Hafoca, Prince Hafoca. He was the *man* she would marry. Her mother had told her as much this morning.

"Come now, Hafoca, introduce yourself to your betrothed," King Viktor commanded.

Hafoca sighed. He seemed to want to keep his disinterest to himself, but the glances that King Viktor and her parents gave indicated he failed. Hafoca stood and rubbed his tunic. His outfit was clean; the soiled green gown that Murid wore stood out in comparison.

Hafoca stepped forward. Murid felt her father's hand nudge her forward to meet the man who would be the father of her own children. Not the silly dolls she played with as a child but *real* children. She'd asked once how to get real children. Her parents laughed whenever they remembered the question to this day.

Murid curtseyed before Hafoca. He accepted her small hand and kissed it after offering a slight bow.

"Princess Murid, it gives me immense pleasure to meet you today. I look forward to the day when we become one in the eyes of the gods. Mount Heilagt will rejoice in our union and welcome our children into their banquet hall," Hafoca said.

Murid easily kept herself from giggling. The Vikisotes believed in many gods, not just one. It felt odd to her, but her parents told her it was her duty to believe in them too. Even though there was only one God. Apparently, the Vikisotes didn't understand that yet. Her parents told her it was also her duty to try and get these people to let go of the old ways. It all seemed quite silly.

"Thank you, Prince Hafoca. I am honored that you will have me. I . . . I um."

"I will give you strong sons," Queen Colchi said to remind Murid of her rehearsed line. Murid knew her parents would have words with her later. She came late, dirty, and forgetful. Not even her mother would spare her a harsh scolding.

"Thank you," Murid said. "I will give you strong sons and obedient daughters."

Murid winced at the last line. Sons and daughters should be *both* strong and obedient. It made little sense to pick only one attribute for each gender.

The two kings and queen clapped as Hafoca placed a quick kiss on Murid's cheek. She felt happy, but only briefly, because she saw Hafoca nonchalantly wipe his mouth after the kiss.

"Splendid," King Viktor said. "What a beautiful fiancée. Don't you agree, Hafoca?"

"Yes, Father."

"Look at those piercing blue eyes. Red hair and blue eyes aren't something I've ever seen. Your wife will be the envy of all men."

Always the blue eyes. Her mother's eyes were a royal jade color, but other women had red hair and green eyes. More than one person had described his or her envy of the rare combination that Murid had.

"Yes, her *eyes* are lovely," Hafoca said.

Murid's head snapped to face Hafoca. His words were polite, but his own eyes lingered on her nose and cheeks. Exactly where her dense patches of freckles lived. It didn't matter how beautiful her hair, eyes, or mother were. People would voice their appreciation of these features while thinking about how ugly her face was with so many freckles. Murid felt the hot burn of tears forming. She willed them away.

Queen Colchi placed her hands on Murid's shoulders and moved her closer to Hafoca, who had backed away again.

"How about these two new lovers enjoy a leisurely walk around the estate?" she asked. "I'm certain Queen Katrin has recovered from her nap. I'll leave you two gentlemen to your discussion."

"Excellent idea," King Haymel said. "Don't get any ideas before your wedding night."

Prince Hafoca looked disgusted. Murid was unsure why.

King Viktor chuckled. "Yes, Princess Murid, would you please show my son where you practice your archery? Prince Hafoca has become quite adept at handling a bow and arrow."

Hafoca begrudgingly offered the crook of his left elbow. Murid accepted it but only because three sets of eyes were on her with hope and expectance. Hafoca led Murid out of the study, through the home, and into the open air.

The two walked in silence as Hafoca led her to where the targets waited. Murid had intended on being a thoughtful guide, but the teenager's long strides made it impossible for her to keep up without running. Murid took a few deep breaths as Hafoca examined the expensive bows laid before him by King Haymel's servants.

Hafoca observed the walls surrounding the ten acres protected inside.

"How many warriors do you have?" Hafoca asked.

Murid scrunched her face. "*Warriors*? Do you mean guards?"

"Where I come from, we don't have guards. Every man is a warrior first and ready to defend Vikisoteland from any invader."

"What about the women?" Murid asked.

Hafoca smirked. "We have shield maidens as well. Naturally, they're also prepared to sacrifice their lives. Until they become mothers, of course."

"That's exciting. Will I be trained as a brave shield maiden when I move to your country?" Murid asked with hope.

"Absolutely not!"

Murid looked down in embarrassment. Some sting seemed to leave Hafoca's voice as he spoke again.

"That is to say, you won't have to. You'll be a princess of two kingdoms, eventually a queen. No Vikisote queen should have to go into battle when she has heirs to raise."

"I suppose not," Murid said with downcast eyes.

"Hey, would you like to see something impressive?" Hafoca asked.

"Yes, please."

Hafoca posed in front of Murid with a devilish grin

and an oak bow straddled across his lap. Murid stared at him and waited. Nothing happened.

"I'm sorry, I don't understand," Murid eventually admitted.

Hafoca snorted laughter. "I thought you hailed from an intelligent family? *I'm* the impressive thing."

Hafoca posed again. Murid finally understood, though she would have used a word like *arrogant* versus *impressive*.

"Brilliant," Murid said with a flat voice and rolled eyes.

"No sense of humor, huh? Perhaps all those freckles stole the ability."

Hafoca laughed profusely at his own joke. Murid felt heat rush to her face. This time she had to blink repeatedly to keep the tears secured behind her eyes.

"Relax, Princess Murid. I'm only joking. You really do have beautiful eyes. I'm positive full hips will follow them. Now, watch this."

Before Murid could take offense again, Hafoca quickly fired three arrows into the target one hundred meters down range. Each arrow struck true in the center of the target.

Murid stood with her mouth open. She looked at Hafoca with complete wonder. She'd never seen anyone fire so accurately. Perhaps he did have a reason to boast.

"That was amazing!" Murid exclaimed.

"It was. I'm glad you agree."

"Will you teach me?"

"Why? I'm told you already know the basics."

Murid beamed with pride.

"I'm actually pretty good. Not as good as you, but my father says I'm better than he was at my age."

"Why don't you show me?" Hafoca asked.

He smiled as he passed the bow to Murid. She accepted the weapon and nocked an arrow. Murid steadied her breathing as she aimed for the same target Hafoca had hit. The distance was much farther than she usually attempted, but she refused to let Hafoca show her up. Her tiny arms trembled as she pulled the string back as far as she dared. She let loose the arrow and watched it sail. The arrow hit the hay target with a satisfying *thump*. Unfortunately, the arrow was inside the black portion of the target, indicating the minimum number of points. Hafoca looked quite amused by this.

He laughed briefly. "I'd hate to have seen your father at your age."

Hafoca laughed again. Murid threw the bow down and clenched her fists in rage. Hafoca only laughed harder. Murid closed the distance with him and swung a wide sweeping punch at her betrothed. Hafoca didn't even try to defend himself. He laughed even harder as Murid pounded him with insignificant punches. Eventually, Hafoca grabbed both of her wrists and held her arms still. Tears poured down her face as her frustrations overtook her. Her emotion appeared to transform Hafoca into a decent human being.

"I'm sorry," Hafoca admitted. "I keep forgetting you're still just a kid."

That label forced Murid to sniff. She *was* a child. She wanted to play, mostly about being a brave warrior, but *adults* kept telling her she wasn't allowed to enjoy juvenile delights. Her destiny meant something more for her than the average child.

"Do you forgive me?" Hafoca asked.

He lifted her chin with his thumb and forefinger to force her to face him. His eyes held sympathy. Murid sniffed again and nodded.

"Good," Hafoca said. "You came at me like a wild crick."

"A *crick*? What's a crick?" Murid asked.

"I guess you don't have those in this part of the world," Hafoca said while rubbing his chin. "A crick is a beast from Vikisoteland. They stand two-and-a-half meters tall and weigh well over five hundred kilograms. They have hairy bodies with long, poisonous claws, but their heads are scaly with a forked tongue. They stretch hoods around their heads moments before spitting a caustic venom that'll easily kill the healthiest of men."

Hafoca held out his hands as he detailed the beast. The description enamored Murid.

"Have you ever seen one?" she asked.

Hafoca put on his devilish smile again. "Not only have I seen one, but I've hunted and killed one. The pelt lines the floor of my bedroom, but the real prize is the venom gland. That venom is priceless to any military. Our warriors use it in battle against the Corlains."

"You've fought the Corlains too?"

Perhaps Prince Hafoca truly was a man worthy of her affection. She promised herself to give him the strong sons and daughters he would need to keep their future kingdom protected.

Hafoca exploded with laughter again. All Murid's

respect for him evaporated with each hurtful chuckle.

"You fell for it again! I can't believe you're the girl my children will have to call *Mother*. Run along and play dress up or something."

Hafoca turned his back and fired more arrows at the far target. Murid considered throwing a large rock at Hafoca's back, but she knew it would lead to more trouble than it was worth. Hafoca's shoulders continued to shake between shots. Murid screamed at his back and ran away.

Murid sobbed as she rushed through the courtyard toward the stables. All her life, Murid had enjoyed the smell and comfort of the stables. After seeing how horrible Hafoca was, she needed the familiar neighs and fragrant hair of her companion, Willow.

Willow was a chestnut mare. She was old by horse standards, but that suited Murid fine. Her age gave her experience, which meant it was safe for Murid to be around her, even when she had been a toddler.

Servants mucked the stalls surrounding Willow, but her stall was untouched. Murid had taken it upon herself to see to her own animal's needs. The servants were good people, but Willow was family. Murid grabbed a brush and stroked Willow's mane. Willow pressed her head into Murid's shoulder. Willow always seemed to know what to do to comfort the princess.

"Oh, Willow, what am I going to do?"

"Isn't that the question for us all?" a middle-aged woman asked.

Murid tensed at her voice. She looked back at the entrance. Gone were the handful of servants. None of them would likely have spoken to the princess without being asked a question first. Murid focused on the entryway.

Standing there was a woman who looked about forty years old. Her shoulders were wide, just like many women from Vikisoteland. Her hair was a pure blonde, almost white from its brilliance. This woman was beautiful, but she wasn't the queen.

"Who are you?" Murid asked.

The woman placed a hand over her heart and slightly bowed before Murid.

"My apologies. I'm Faida. I came with the King and Queen of Vikisoteland. I saw you run in here after speaking with our prince. Forgive me if I'm being too bold, but I felt like we should have a moment to talk."

"Why? Your king and queen have already made the decision that my parents agreed to. What would our conversation accomplish?"

"You're a very precocious young woman. I like that. You and I will get along excellently."

Precocious. That's the word adults used when they really meant *obnoxious.* It was the consequence of forcing more education on a child than playtime.

Faida approached Murid. Willow nudged her toward the stranger. Murid made it a point not to ignore Willow's instincts. She took this as a sign her friend approved of this woman from Vikisoteland.

Faida stopped a few steps from Murid. She bowed once more, but this time she made a goofy face when she stood erect again. The unexpectedness of it made Murid giggle.

"I knew there was still a child behind all that maturity."

Murid liked Faida. Her compliment felt genuine, unlike most she got from the dignitaries who visited her parents on official business.

"My parents say my destiny means I have to grow up faster than most," Murid said.

"Pish posh, what do parents know?"

Murid covered her mouth to keep from laughing too loudly. She'd never heard anyone say something even remotely impolite about her parents. Faida was braver than most adults Murid had met before.

"Who are you exactly?" Murid asked.

"I told you, I'm Faida."

"Yes, but what do you do for King Viktor and Queen Katrin?"

"It's not what I do for them, but what I will do for you."

"Which will be?"

"Among other things, I'll be your spiritual leader and personal servant."

"Oh," Murid said.

Her heart sank. She had plenty of servants. Just because one came from an exotic land didn't make her special. Murid already had servants from all over the planet. Some were even Namerians and Canfras.

"Don't look so disappointed. I'm a special kind of servant. I'm meant to teach you how we live in Vikisoteland. I'll teach you our culture, our traditions, our food; even our dances. Just wait until you experience your first Celestial celebration."

"What's *Celestial*?"

Faida's eyes looked misty as she spoke. "Celestial is the most holy of time. It's a three-day festival to honor Jorosolman. It's so holy, one should accept death rather than offend the gods by ignoring the festivities. I look forward to teaching you all about it, especially the presents."

"How about teaching me how to be a shield maiden?" Murid asked.

Faida snorted laughter. "I mention *presents* and you want to learn how to swing a sword? You'll do well in our kingdom." Faida chuckled again, then composed herself to answer Murid. "I'm not the best person to teach you those skills. I also doubt the royal family would like me to let you learn."

"Oh," Murid said, glancing at the straw-covered ground.

"But," Faida said, "if you keep it between us, I'm sure I can find someplace else to be when Olha trains you."

Faida added a wink after her statement. Murid allowed a mischievous smile to spread. She definitely liked Faida.

"When's our first lesson?" Murid asked.

"How about now?" Faida answered while patting a bale of straw.

Murid sat next to Faida as the older woman told her a story.

"Princess Murid, how much do you know about politics?"

"I know enough not to ask questions when others

speak of it. That's an easy way to be excused from the room."

Faida laughed. "I'm sure it is. Do you know anything about Corla?"

"Yes," Murid said matter-of-factly. "It's an absolutely evil country."

"It definitely is, but do you know why?"

"Because they're mean to everyone else?"

"That's a spectacular understatement. The Corlains are greedy, vicious people. They make demands on how each of us must live. They steal the resources from the lands our ancestors worked. They slaughter the innocent and any who stand in their way of global domination. I can say without exaggeration that there's no such thing as a good Corlain. Unfortunately, many people across Glostaimia appease the Corlain Empire. They bow and scrape and hope the pain won't be too much. This attitude has led to universal suffering for our planet."

"The Corlains can't be that strong, can they? How can they possibly control all of Glostaimia?"

"They shouldn't be that strong, but when you combine the indifference of the eastern countries with the subjugation of the southern countries and acquiescence of those in this part of the world, you can see why Corla controls so much."

"Why don't good people stop them?"

"Isn't that the million-coin question? Fear controls most. Impatience makes some who could be a threat to Corlain imperialism easily defeated. I like to believe a third option is why the good people wait to find their courage and their voice."

Murid leaned in with absolute fascination. Faida chuckled as she did this.

"I can see you want me to tell you."

"I would enjoy that very much."

"Have you heard of the prophecy?"

"The prophecy?"

Faida smirked to herself. "I suppose you wouldn't have. You don't know our gods, so you can't possibly know our prophecies. It was foretold by the gods that 'he who survives a violent massacre by foreign oppressors will lead his people to victory.'"

Murid furrowed her brow. Prophecies always sounded too general to her. Violent massacres happened all the time.

"Do you believe in the prophecy?" Murid asked.

"I must. My faith is the only thing that keeps my fear of being tortured by the Corlains at bay."

Murid was about to speak again when Willow started kicking inside her stall. Murid stood and looked at her horse. Willow continued to act erratically. Faida stood next to Murid. A noticeable rumbling in the ground became apparent. Wheelbarrows filled with horse dung rattled and tipped. Murid and Faida shared confused looks.

"What is it, Will—"

The wall exploding inward interrupted Murid's question. A wild pachymule revealed itself to be the reason for the destruction. The pachymule was easily four meters tall with thick, gray skin. Murid recognized it as a bull by the ivory tusks jutting out from not only its mouth but also surrounding the joints of all four legs.

The tusk wall made it difficult for predators to jump and snap at the vital arteries in its neck. Being male meant it weighed over seven hundred kilograms. It trumpeted a challenge out its long trunk. Willow never had a chance.

Murid covered her eyes in absolute horror as Willow was first gored, then trampled by the panicked pachymule. Murid screamed long before she realized someone was carrying her. Faida had the young princess cradled in her arms as she sprinted away from the pachymule. The wild animal seemed unconcerned with the fleeing humans.

Murid moved trembling hands from her eyes. Pandemonium surrounded her. Servants and guards ran around, attempting to corral the beasts. There were at least four charging through the front doors of Murid's home. People screamed next to mangled bodies. Murid stifled the vomit trying to erupt from her mouth as she saw the body of a young servant. Murid couldn't remember his name, but he was only a few years older than she. He often helped his mother working in the garden and never required punishment. She'd taught him discipline. His once innocent face was contorted into a depiction of pure terror. The impression in his back and spilled organs proved he was unlucky enough to have been crushed by a small pachymule.

"Faida! Bring the princess here!" King Viktor screamed.

Faida nodded and raced toward her king. Faida lowered Murid once she arrived. King Viktor briefly tapped her head, but soon his eyes searched for his own family.

"Father!" Hafoca shouted.

The teenager, with bow clutched and a quiver full of arrows, hesitated as a pair of pachymules separated them.

"Hurry!" King Viktor shouted.

Hafoca appeared to summon his courage before charging across a lawn that was once immaculate. Now clumps of mud littered the green grass. Hafoca reached his father. They embraced each other as the Vikisote guards surrounded the four.

The Vikisote guards pulled vials from pouches hanging on their leather armor. Each man and woman squirted a thick, clear liquid into their hands, then smeared the substance onto their faces and any other exposed skin. Murid scrunched her nose. Whatever the fluid was, its smell resembled minty urine. Why would anyone want to put the stuff on his or her face?

The Vikisotes drew weapons. They looked determined to fight the pachymules with nothing more than the swords and round shields they held. It seemed impossible.

"May I have some crick oil, Father?" Hafoca asked.

King Haymel shook his head as he added his own oil. "You know you aren't old enough. Soon, my son. Soon."

Hafoca clenched his jaw and turned his face away. His eyes locked with Murid's. "What are you looking at, brat?"

Murid opened her mouth to respond, but the sound of wood splintering drew the attention of Murid and her rescuers. She watched in horror as her home, the only one she had ever known, imploded. Only the brick exterior stood aloft, but several holes perforated it from pachymule charges. They were powerful animals.

"No!" Murid screamed.

She fought against Faida's steely grasp. The woman held her firmly. All Murid could do was watch as her world crumbled around her from multiple pachymule passes.

"Let me go!" Murid protested. "My parents were in there!"

"So was my mother," Hafoca said. "We must wait for it to be safe before mounting a rescue."

"How did these beasts enter in the first place?" Faida asked.

"I don't know," King Viktor answered.

"They came through the front gate, milord," a guard answered. "It was abnormal. They pushed their way past as one mind, then panicked once inside."

"From order to panic?" King Viktor asked.

The guard nodded to confirm.

"No!" King Viktor shouted. "It's a trap."

As if on cue, a loud *crack* quickly followed by several more echoed. The guard who answered King Viktor's questions fell forward as blood pooled from inside his leather armor. Murid noticed several holes. King Viktor lurched backward and held a hand over his left bicep.

Murid fearfully searched for the source of the attack. Standing by the destroyed portcullis was an army. A Corlain army. Their full plate armor shined brightly in the late afternoon sun. In fact, it was *too* bright. Most of the Vikisote warriors and castle guards were forced to cover their eyes. Murid covered her own eyes but peeked through her fingers at the advancing soldiers.

The intimidating Corlain soldiers had glaring armor that reflected the sun almost like a weapon. The only color visible on their armor was a thin, red triangle lens. King Haymel had once told Murid that the Corlains had the most sophisticated weapons, armor, and equipment in all Glostaimia. Their unique armor was principle among this military advantage. Despite most of the defenders being blind, Murid knew the Corlain soldiers comfortably saw what was before them because of the red filter they wore. Even at night, when their shiny, enchanted armor would transition to black, they could still see their enemies clearly.

Once again, Faida grabbed Murid and cradled her. Murid watched as the wounded King Viktor led Faida, Hafoca, and the closest guards away from the advancing intruders. Murid sobbed uncontrollably, burying her face into Faida's chest. She knew she should look for her parents, but she wanted the comfort that darkness provided at this moment. When she found her courage enough to peek from her "sanctuary," she saw the front line of Corlains with muskets had stepped aside to let those with halberds and broadswords slaughter the few remaining guards and servants.

"Take this, child," Faida said to Murid.

Murid accepted a small vial with a green liquid inside. Small black flecks swirled with the viscous drink.

"What is it?" Murid asked.

"Don't worry about that. Just drink it. It'll give you

courage as we find your parents and escape," Faida answered.

Murid nodded. She remembered what the adults had rubbed into their skin. It may have been strong, but here was the child version. The Vikisotes bravely fought the Corlains. Murid would try to do her part. With a single gulp, Murid downed the foul-tasting medicine. She waited for the courage Faida promised her to fill every gram of her being. Instead, she became sleepy.

We'll find them, Murid thought, as darkness overtook her.

CHAPTER 2

Two Dogs took a stealthy step as he brushed his long, dark hair from his eyes. He slowly placed his moccasin-protected foot onto a moss-covered rock. The green lichen complemented the green of his animal-skin footwear. Two Dogs was a prime specimen of a man. For thirty-two years, beginning with his birth, Two Dogs prepared his mind and body for greatness. He had broad shoulders complemented by well-defined muscles. Every woman in his tribe commented about his attractiveness when they thought he couldn't hear. Two Dogs was always listening, and he thoroughly appreciated the compliments from the fairer sex.

Ahead of Two Dogs was his hunting partner, Swift Shot. Although a few years younger than he, Swift Shot was the best friend he'd ever known. Like Two Dogs, Swift Shot was athletic, though her love of wrestling made her less beautiful. None of that mattered to Two Dogs. Currently, he appreciated her most for her superior hunting skills.

Swift Shot held up her right hand. Her left hand held a bow with an arrow already nocked. Two Dogs knew to wait for her to signal him to move again. He looked past her shoulder to see what lay in the open prairie ahead of them.

Two Dogs' heart fluttered when he saw the prey in the clearing. Past hunting trips, too many to count, had been disappointing. The mighty turklyo became more and more scarce as Corlains over-hunted the animals that meant so much to Two Dogs' Lacreechee tribe. Thanks to Swift Shot's keen tracking skills, a single turklyo grazed in front of them.

A turklyo was a large herbivore, but the Lacreechee wouldn't waste any of the animal. It had tough, green skin that would be used to make the moccasins and clothing the Lacreechee wore. Stretching ten feet long meant the tribe would craft new outfits. The six hundred pounds of meat would feed his tribe for two weeks. The armored shell on the animal's back would be suspended over another family's tipi and protect them from the occasional magically summoned hail storm. The children had to learn to control their power at some point. The beak would be converted into whatever tool the tribe needed next.

All the physical features of the turklyo had life-enhancing uses, but none compared with the bone plate on the crown of its head. The igsidian plate, often referred to as the stone, was a reflective black color with orange marbling running throughout. It protected the turklyo's head, but the Lacreechee people had a far more important use. Igsidian stones gave the Lacreechee magical power. All children in the tribe learned how to manipulate the power inherent in each stone. Some, like Swift Shot, became experts in elemental powers. Lightning, fire, frost; they were all easily weaponized to protect the tribe. Others learned to create lifelike illusions to confuse an enemy. A few felt it was better to learn intermediate levels from each magical school. Two Dogs' brother, Proud Wall, was a man trained in multiple schools.

Two Dogs looked at the mighty turklyo in front of him. Magical attacks were unwise when hunting; it led to wasted meat. Unless, of course, you learned protector magic like Two Dogs had. He clutched his tomahawk and knife. Each had a shiny black blade made from the Igsidian stone he recovered from a hunt when he was a young teen. He focused on the power that each weapon had. The blades glowed bright orange as he summoned an invisible, protective armor around his body. The igsidian embedded in his turklyo-skin shirt and leggings also glowed. Two Dogs felt his muscles tighten as his strength multiplied a dozen times. His speed only improved by a factor of four, but summoning this much magic took a toll. Exceptions had to be made.

Swift Shot glanced back at Two Dogs as his igsidian brightened to a warrior's level.

"Let me take the shot," she whispered.

The sound may have been quiet, but Two Dogs felt like she'd screamed. The turklyo must have sensed something. It quickly jerked its head upward and sniffed the air with amphibian nostrils. The female slowly retracted its head into the relative safety of its ridged shell.

Two Dogs smiled at Swift Shot. "Well?"

Swift Shot let out an exasperated breath at Two Dogs' mockery. She aimed at the hidden head of the turklyo and let her arrow fly. The turklyo honked to express its pain. Swift Shot's arrow snapped as the turklyo's head quickly extended from the shell. The enraged animal ran away from Two Dogs and Swift Shot. Two more arrows flew at its back. One bounced off the shell, the other plunged into the back of the knee on the left rear leg.

"I thought you were good at this?" Two Dogs teased.

"Just get it!" Swift Shot shouted.

Two Dogs could sense her annoyance with herself as much as she was pissed he could be such an ass, even when they finally found a turklyo again.

Two Dogs gave a mocking salute to his friend with the tomahawk clutched in his right hand. He chased the sprinting turklyo as he adjusted the grip on his knife to an inverted one.

The turklyo may have had a pair of wounds, but it was still a relatively quick animal. Swift Shot, or any other human who didn't have igsidian-enhanced physical abilities, could never catch the amphibian. Two Dogs laughed to himself as he closed the distance in under a minute.

"Where do you think you're going, big girl?" Two Dogs asked.

He dove at the turklyo and landed on the animal's

shell. His igsidian grew warm to the touch as both blades and all six stones in his clothing reached the brightest orange possible. His improved balance kept him upright on the shell as he gracefully walked along the animal's back. Once he reached the neck, he sat and allowed a leg to straddle each side.

"Thank you for your gift, Mother Turklyo," Two Dogs whispered.

He plunged his knife into the left side of the turklyo's neck; his tomahawk hacked just below the right eye. The turklyo honked again from this new round of pain. Two Dogs ensured his weapons were protected for the strain they were about to be under. With each blade firmly inside the animal, Two Dogs twisted clockwise. His increased strength made short work of the turklyo's neck. Cracking vertebrae echoed as the animal crumbled to the ground. Two Dogs jumped free. He executed several aerial somersaults before landing perfectly.

Two Dogs took a moment to gather his bearings. The turklyo was mere feet from entering the relative safety of the wooded forest that bordered the tall grass prairie. The igsidian stones in his weapons and clothing faded to their original black color with occasional orange streaks marring the surface. With the magic surrendered again, Two Dogs took in several deep breaths. His body shook as his adrenaline subsided.

Swift Shot caught up to Two Dogs. She was equally out of breath, but her reason was more basic. The short chase had taken Two Dogs a full mile away from where they had started.

"Do you always have to show off?" Swift Shot asked as she regained her composure.

"Every time. The tribe expects it of me now."

"Perhaps we should change your name to *Too Modest*?"

"Some already *do* call me that."

"If you make this about your dick again."

Two Dogs laughed. "Nobody would believe me if I told them it was twenty inches from the get go. I have to convince them it's a manageable twelve inches, then they get the surprise."

Swift Shot gestured to the open plain. "Mother Turklyo, please give your son Two Dogs a reason to pause before speaking. We mere mortals can no longer breathe when all the air goes straight to his head."

Two Dogs and Swift Shot clasped forearms as they good-humoredly laughed together. Their attention went back to their prey.

"That's a big one," Swift Shot said.

"Women tend to say that around me."

Swift Shot slapped Two Dogs on the back of his head.

"I meant we'll need the cart, the one you left a mile to the west."

Two Dogs rubbed his head. Swift Shot had hit him harder than most would consider polite.

"I guess I'll go get it," Two Dogs said.

"I guess you—wait," Swift Shot said.

Before Two Dogs could ask what was wrong, he got his answer. A second turklyo sprang from the tree line. Two Dogs quickly realized the danger he and his friend were in. The second turklyo was a bull. Not only did this mean it was three times larger than the female they'd killed, but it also came equipped with additional defenses. The male turklyo's shell was twice as thick and covered in spikes that towered two feet tall. It also had a four-foot tail that ended in a solid igsidian ball. The clubbed tail flicked twice before the turklyo charged.

Both Two Dogs and Swift Shot dove away from the stampeding beast. Two Dogs rolled into a fighting position to the left of the enraged animal. He quickly summoned his magical defenses back but with reduced limits. He hadn't recovered enough from his showboating earlier. Swift Shot would probably have words for him, assuming they survived.

The turklyo hissed at Two Dogs. It seemed to sense the threat Two Dogs posed. This distraction worked in Two Dogs' favor. Three arrows quickly entered the animal's large head. It honked in pain but didn't even look in Swift Shot's direction. Instead, it charged Two Dogs. Two Dogs hoped the magical shield he'd erected would be enough to intercept the blow.

The turklyo smashed into Two Dogs. Two feet before connecting with his body, an orange bubble flashed. Two Dogs sensed his barrier breaking, but it held just long enough to stop the animal in its place.

Three more arrows lodged themselves inside the turklyo's tail. It swung its weapon at Swift Shot, who barely jumped back enough to avoid fractured ribs. Two Dogs took the opportunity that Swift Shot created to swing both weapons at the turklyo's head. Mother Turklyo wasn't with him. The animal flicked its head back around and lowered it. Two Dogs' weapons connected with the extra thick igsidian plate. The shock was too great for Two Dogs to maintain control of his weapons.

The turklyo head butted Two Dogs in the center of his chest. All air promptly left his body as he smashed into the ground. The turklyo raised a foot and dropped it onto Two Dogs. He used the last of his magical strength to hold the leg off. Thousands of pounds of pressure strained against his own willpower. Two Dogs gritted his teeth as he fought for his life. Eight more arrows, the last of Swift Shot's quiver, sequentially pierced the animal's neck and head. Taken together, they were mortal wounds for the animal, but apparently the bull turklyo didn't know this yet. It continued to press against Two Dogs' hands, which had now collapsed against his own chest.

"Swift Shot!" Two Dogs screamed.

His friend was now on his left side with her tomahawk in hand. It glowed orange as lightning swirled around her left hand.

"Hold still!" she shouted.

"No!" Two Dogs screamed as he heard the crackling of her power. "I'm holding this thing."

"Arrogant man!" Swift Shot exclaimed.

His words must have convinced her. Instead of convulsing from bolts of lightning, the turklyo was blown from Two Dogs body as gale force winds lifted it off him. Two Dogs' igsidian stones stopped glowing merely a second after the animal was pushed aside.

The turklyo rolled several yards away. The wind

attack ended as Swift Shot prepared a fireball.

"We need the meat," Two Dogs said, wheezing.

"We need to live a lot more," Swift Shot countered.

Two Dogs couldn't find a flaw in her logic. He slowly stood. He held his tomahawk weakly in his right hand, but his knife remained on the grass and dirt. The turklyo faced the two Lacreechee hunters.

"One step and I blast it," Swift Shot promised.

Two Dogs just nodded. Red blood poured from the numerous arrow wounds in the turklyo's neck. The animal didn't move forward. It let out a painful honk, then slumped to the ground. It tried a single time to stand. After it fell again, it ceased moving. The two Lacreechee stared for several minutes. Each waited for the animal to lurch forward. Two Dogs couldn't believe that a bull turklyo was killed by only two hunters.

"So what do we do now?" Two Dogs asked.

Swift Shot didn't immediately answer, but she dismissed the fireball burning around her left hand.

"Why don't you check its pulse?" Two Dogs suggested.

Swift Shot looked at him incredulously. "Why do I have to confirm it's dead?"

"You killed it, didn't you?"

"What? We both did."

"Did we? It looks like every arrow you brought is sticking out of it."

"Yeah, well, you set me up for those shots."

"I mean, if you want to share the kill with me, I'll take it. Mother Turklyo knows I need more adoration from the tribe."

Swift Shot rolled her eyes. "We both did this."

"Fair enough," Two Dogs said. "But you did more. Therefore, you need to make sure it's dead. Nobody's going to believe the pair of us did this alone, especially if I end the story by saying 'I checked to make sure.'"

"You do tend to exaggerate," Swift Shot said.

"Exactly."

Swift Shot looked at the sky and screamed. "Fine. I'll do it."

She walked hesitantly toward the turklyo. It had been dead for at least ten minutes, but Two Dogs chuckled more than once at the slow pace Swift Shot took. Eventually, she reached the animal. She cautiously felt around its neck, then started ripping out arrows.

"He's dead," Swift Shot matter-of-factly stated. She smiled. "That wagon's going to be really heavy now."

"Damn it," Two Dogs said.

It took Two Dogs forty minutes to retrieve the wagon they left at the start of their hunt. His igsidian could have made it easier for him, but the unexpected appearance of the first bull turklyo had him spooked. He completed his task as a normal man to ensure his stamina was high enough to fight the second beast that resided in his paranoia.

"What took so long?" Swift Shot asked.

"I was taking in the sights. We missed some beautiful nature as we chased the female," Two Dogs answered.

"I'm sure that's the reason."

Now that Swift Shot was with him to provide area coverage, Two Dogs felt comfortable enough to use his igsidian to augment his strength. He hoisted the bull first, then the female turklyo. The wagon sagged from the combined weight, nearly a ton. Fortunately, Two Dogs could easily shift his magical focus to reinforce the integrity of the wagon. Next, he began the tedious process of hauling the wagon back to their camp.

It was mid-afternoon by the time the two hunters returned. It would have been faster if someone would ever agree with him to build a bridge across the Fraz River, but such was life. The children were the first to see them approach. They raced to meet Two Dogs and Swift Shot. As they saw what was inside the wagon, they squealed with delight. The older children raced ahead to be the first to tell the community of the amazing trophy the pair had.

"Mother Turklyo blessed Two Dogs and Swift Shot! They have a bull! They're the greatest hunters ever!"

Two Dogs wore a radiant smile as he heard the adults chastise the children for exaggerating. Even Swift Shot let a snicker or two loose as adults confirmed what the children had already told them. It wasn't long before other Lacreechee warriors took over for Two Dogs. Strong tribe members lifted the triumphant hunters onto their shoulders. Two Dogs' father, Owl Talon, approached him with their chief, Bright Stone. Though in her sixties, Bright Stone was the most formidable woman Two Dogs had ever met. When many could only understand the intermediate spells from multiple schools, Bright Stone had mastered all types of magic. She was an army unto herself as the dozens of eagle feathers in her hair attested. Two Dogs felt his heart quicken as she approached with his proud father.

"For the people, Chief Bright Stone," Two Dogs and Swift Shot said in unison.

"They rejoice," Bright Stone responded to their greeting. "I had to see for my own eyes what the children praised."

Two Dogs and Swift Shot stepped to the side as people pulled their wagon forward. Two Dogs felt immense satisfaction when he heard both Bright Stone and Owl Talon gasp at the pair of turklyos.

"The two of you did this alone?" Owl Talon asked.

"Yes, Father," Two Dogs answered.

Owl Talon and Bright Stone shared a look of immeasurable respect.

"Cooks, prepare a feast! Tonight, we award these legendary warriors another eagle feather!" Bright Stone announced.

Two Dogs swallowed hard to keep from letting emotion overtake him. Swift Shot seemed to do the same. He had two eagle feathers already, but one was simply for being born. Earning one with his best friend made it more special than the previous two.

"It's okay to cry . . . a little," Owl Talon joked.

Bright Stone and the rest of the tribe shared a laugh as Two Dogs and Swift Shot both took Owl Talon up on his offer. The hunters wiped their tears as Bright Stone indicated she wanted them to follow her to her tipi.

Inside the tipi, Bright Stone gestured for Two Dogs and Swift Shot to take a seat on the plush furs lining her floor.

"Would you two care for some refreshments?" Bright Stone asked.

"No thank you," Swift Shot said.

"Speak for yourself. You didn't have to drag that wagon three miles with a pair of turklyos pressing down on it."

Two Dogs greedily accepted the turklyo shell platter with fruit covered in honey. He selected a sour cherry dripping with sweetness. Two more rapidly followed the first. Two Dogs chewed obnoxiously as he announced his pleasure.

"Oh, that hits the spot," he said.

"You always did love your sweets," Bright Stone said.

Two Dogs grabbed a pear slice and slathered it in the errant honey lining the platter. This also went into his mouth with the minimal amount of chewing required not to choke.

"Why did you summon us, Chief Bright Stone?" Swift Shot asked as Two Dogs finished the last of the sour cherries.

"She wants to hear about the turklyo hunt, obviously," Two Dogs said around a large bite of plum in his mouth.

"I would," Bright Stone agreed, "but not now. We must speak of politics first."

The serious nature of Bright Stone's tone compelled Two Dogs to place his platter to the side.

"What do you need us to do?" he asked.

"I don't need to tell the pair of you that turklyos

are becoming scarcer because of the Corlains," Bright Stone said.

This was a true statement. Two Dogs' blood boiled at the mention of the Corlains. They took without concern for the people who had lived in these lands for centuries. Often, they didn't even acknowledge the legitimate claims to the land. There were murmurs among the tribe to attack the Corlains. Two Dogs suspected they may be more than just the mutterings of the young men.

"Did you see any Corlains on your hunt?" Bright Stone asked.

Two Dogs remembered none. He looked at Swift Shot to confirm he hadn't missed an obvious sign.

"No, Chief Bright Stone," Swift Shot answered.

Bright Stone nodded and let a small sigh escape her lips.

"This is good news," she said. "Mother Turklyo continues to bless us. The Azca people to our southeast were not as fortunate."

This information shocked Two Dogs. Swift Shot also seemed surprised by the admission.

"What happened to the Azcas?" Two Dogs asked.

"When did it happen?" Swift Shot added.

"Word reached us just this morning, after you had left for your hunt," Bright Stone answered.

"Are you telling us because we should expect to see them passing through our lands?" Two Dogs asked.

Bright Stone grimly shook her head. She seemed incapable of looking the young braves in their eyes.

"You misunderstand," Bright Stone said. "They

weren't relocated like the tribes before them. They were eliminated. The sole messenger died in our camp. Strong Cure could do nothing for him."

Two Dogs and Swift Shot also looked at the floor. Strong Cure was a powerful healer. If he couldn't save the Azca warrior, then nobody could.

"The messenger claimed it was the Black Cloud that attacked them. All Corlains are evil, but this unit shames their ancestors with their barbarity," Bright Stone said. "They defeated us in my youth."

"What?" Two Dogs asked. He leaned forward.

Bright Stone sighed. "I'm sure it hasn't gone unnoticed how much we move. When I was young, we raided the Corlains. We were too proud to back down. Owl Talon and many others aided me in defining our borders. It was foolish."

Bright Stone wiped her eyes. Two Dogs and Swift Shot remained quiet as she cleared her voice.

"Soon after, half our tribe had perished, and I was the new chief. We forfeited our land to the Corlains. It led to our troubles with the Esquit tribe. I'm sure you remember them."

Two Dogs instinctively rubbed the second eagle feather hanging from his hair.

"We can't move again! The Corlains decimated the Azcas." Bright Stone's body shook with adrenaline. "They continue to spread influence over Glostaimia. Not even their own are spared, I'm sure you remember the attacks in the swampland over a decade ago."

Two Dogs vaguely remembered the pale people in the swamp suddenly ending trade when he was a teen.

He brushed the thought aside.

"Did they steal the Azcas' igsidian stones again?" Swift Shot asked in a meek voice.

Bright Stone slowly nodded. "As always, the Corlains claimed that which Mother Turklyo meant for her chosen children to possess. The Corlains can't speak to the stones like we can, yet that doesn't temper their greed."

"What exactly do you need us to do?" Swift Shot asked.

"Anything," Two Dogs added. "You need only ask."

Bright Stone smiled. "I can always count on you two. After your feat today, you'll be leaders among our community. I want you to use that popularity. You must convince the people that we must fight. Not just our tribe; the other tribes must join forces with us. The time of appeasing the Corlains is over. They only understand violence, so we'll give it to them."

Two Dogs filled with pride. He was a warrior before all other things. Fighting was what he was best at; it was his purpose. The Corlains didn't scare him like they did so many of his neighbors. With Bright Stone's blessing, he would raise a war party and ambush the Corlain patrols along the ugly *roads* they continued to build.

"What about Corla's new leader?" Swift Shot asked. "Their own people can't tolerate a leader for long. The infighting proves they're sub-human, but could this one be the one to finally listen and leave our land and our igsidian alone?"

Two Dogs wanted to slap Swift Shot for asking such a cowardly question in Bright Stone's presence. He loved his friend, but if she couldn't grow some balls because of her gender, then she needed to grow a backbone instead. She had always been courageous on hunts, but warfare was something she seemed to want to avoid at all costs.

"It doesn't matter who their leader is," Two Dogs stated. "Chief Bright Stone has labeled them my enemy. They will die, with or without the aid of the other tribes."

"Not just the other tribes," Bright Stone said.

"What?" Two Dogs asked.

"We need the other nations as well," Bright Stone answered. "For decades they've attacked not only our people and Mother Turklyo's other children, but they've ransacked the other foreigners. In the twenty years since I've been chief, the Corlains have attacked the Vikisotes, the Francos, even those fools who lived in the swamplands. Those people could be powerful allies. We'll need them to defeat the Corlains."

Two Dogs didn't necessarily agree, but he knew changing Bright Stone's mind would have been more difficult than simply allowing the other nations to claim some of his victory. Swift Shot looked at the platter of fruit. She finally grabbed an apple slice and rubbed it through a pool of honey. She chewed as a silence hung between the trio.

"I feel I've soured your victory enough already. Get cleaned up. As soon as night is upon us, I'll personally award you another feather," Bright Stone said.

Two Dogs knew when he was being dismissed. He and Swift Shot stood as one and left the tipi.

Hours later, the night had enveloped the tribe. A large bonfire illuminated the painted faces of Two Dogs and Swift Shot. The full tribe, three hundred strong, surrounded the heroes. Many had full bellies of turklyo meat, a staple denied for more than a few dinners.

Bright Stone stood in front of the two friends. Each had an immense smile as Bright Stone held an eagle feather before them.

"For the people!" Bright Stone shouted as she held the feathers high above her head.

"They rejoice!" the tribe responded.

"Before you are two heroes of our community. Never in my long life have I heard of two hunters claiming a bull turklyo. If my stomach wasn't bursting from the flavorful filet I had for dinner, I still wouldn't believe it. If ever two warriors deserved this honor, it's Swift Shot and Two Dogs."

Many Lacreechee shouted war cries. Two Dogs stood straighter as he waited for Bright Stone to give him his prize.

"You will prominently display these feathers in your tipis. Show the honor to your home. Soon, you will add them to your headdresses."

Two Dogs and Swift Shot each accepted their feather. More war cries erupted from the assembled.

"Now, let's celebrate!" Bright Stone shouted.

The Lacreechee fully obeyed. Two Dogs and Swift Shot proudly accepted many congratulatory comments and embraces. Owl Talon gave a tearful hug, while Two Dogs' brother, Proud Wall, lifted him off the ground with his bear hug. Proud Wall was three years older than Two Dogs, but genuine pride trumped sibling rivalry.

"If I hadn't been busy this morning, I'd have been there to claim my portion of your glory," Proud Wall said. "Now I have to work twice as hard to earn a fourth feather. There's no way I let you stay my equal."

Proud Wall gave Two Dogs a good-natured slap on the shoulder. He must have used a little magic, because Two Dogs had to take a step to keep from falling.

"Where were you exactly?" Two Dogs asked as he rubbed his shoulder.

"Where indeed?" Owl Talon asked.

Proud Wall looked both embarrassed and caught.

"Did you raid?" Owl Talon asked in a fierce whisper.

Two Dogs' suspicions seemed confirmed. Proud Wall and his friends must have attacked some Corlains.

"Answer me!" Owl Talon demanded.

"Father," Proud Wall whispered. "Not here. Those people took our turklyos. We simply gave them a reason to go back to where they came from."

Owl Talon clenched his jaw, then observed the party. He shook his head. "I won't ruin Two Dogs' celebration."

Proud Wall let out a trapped breath. Two Dogs also exhaled.

"Don't think we won't have words tomorrow. The Azcas may have paid for your actions!"

A few faces from the tribe watched the stern family

conversation, but the beat of drums made it unlikely any heard it.

"I should let you go. Bird Song doesn't seem inclined to wait much longer for your attention," Proud Wall said, obviously attempting to change the topic.

Two Dogs followed Proud Wall's pointed finger. Standing on the opposite side of the bonfire was Bird Song. She was beautiful. Not the most beautiful woman in the tribe, but the most beautiful to Two Dogs. Her figure always enticed him. Her smile religiously made him babble. It was her voice that captured his heart. She sang better than any person or animal he'd ever heard. Her voice could make a mountain cry. Despite the seriousness of their conversation, Two Dogs suddenly felt the urge to excuse himself.

"I've seen that look before," Owl Talon said, though he still glared at Proud Wall. "Before you give in to your second brain's wishes, I have something for you."

Proud Wall genuinely smiled with his father as the older man presented a necklace to Two Dogs. It had five long, brown claws separated by four polished discs of igsidian. Two Dogs swallowed his emotion as he grabbed the expensive jewelry. He completely forgot the tense moment shared with his family.

"More igsidian?" Two Dogs asked. "This belongs to Swift Shot. She saved my life."

"So we've been told," Proud Wall said.

"You didn't think this was the best part of the bull's tail, did you?" Owl Talon asked.

Two Dogs looked confused until he followed his

father's pointed finger. Swift Shot swayed to the beat of drums while juggling a pair of cups, likely containing corn ferm. Sometimes she drank more than was appropriate, especially at a party. The drinks clearly weren't what Owl Talon intended him to focus on. Slung across Swift Shot's back was a quiver. Even from this distance, Two Dogs could see the glint of several igsidian stones lining the opening at the top. Approximately a dozen arrows poked out.

"You made her a return quiver?" Two Dogs asked incredulously.

Return quivers were unheard of. The amount of igsidian necessary made them a vanity that few warriors felt comfortable accepting.

"It took some convincing from Bright Stone to make her keep it, but you yourself admitted she did most of the work. She deserves Mother Turklyo's share of the igsidian tail," Owl Talon explained.

"I understand," Two Dogs said.

He truly meant it.

"I believe we've delayed you long enough," Proud Wall said.

Two Dogs smiled at his family and walked to Bird Song. Owl Talon firmly grabbed Proud Wall's arm and pulled him away. Two Dogs wished his brother luck. Then again, the bastard hadn't invited him on the raid. He deserved whatever punishment their father had in store.

Two Dogs refocused his attention on Bird Song. As he neared her, Swift Shot intercepted him. She swayed but caught her balance as she held a pair of clay cups, presumably holding corn ferm.

"Try some of this," Swift Shot said as she thrust one of the cups into Two Dogs' hands. Swift Shot downed the contents of her mug and blew out a powerful breath. "That burns."

Two Dogs smiled and swallowed his own drink. The fermented corn drink seared his throat. The potency of the beverage forced him to cough more than once.

"Do you make it stronger every time on purpose?" Two Dogs asked.

Swift Shot nodded. "Yep. You need that liquid courage to speak with Bird Song."

"I've never needed liquid courage to speak to any woman and you know it."

Swift Shot ran her finger inside her cup. She licked the drops that came out with her digit.

"You better make your move . . . or I might," Swift Shot said as she sucked her finger clean.

"Thanks for the warning. Do I need to fawn over you about your reward?"

Swift Shot angled her body for Two Dogs to see the luxurious gift.

"You noticed, huh? I tried to refuse it, but I'm pretty okay with Bright Stone twisting my arm," Swift Shot said.

"I'm sure you are. Have you practiced with it yet?"

Swift Shot poured another cup of corn ferm.

"I'm not in the right state for target practice." She giggled ridiculously as she finished another shot of corn ferm in record time.

"That's probably for the best. Now, if you'll excuse me."

Swift Shot giggled again as Two Dogs continued toward his target. Bird Song saw him approach and smiled.

"I was wondering how long I'd have to wait tonight, now that you're a living legend and everything," Bird Song said.

"I asked if you wanted to come," Two Dogs responded.

Bird Song laughed. "Yeah, and listen to you and Swift Shot trying to one up each other all day? No, thank you. Though it would have been great to have seen Swift Shot save you . . . again."

"She doesn't save me that much," Two Dogs protested.

Bird Song scoffed. "Keep telling yourself that."

"I could, or I could take you to my tipi and tell you something else?"

Bird Song smiled devilishly. "And tarnish your reputation with the tribe? I would never do that. All the women will want you now. Someone will have to make an honest man out of you."

Two Dogs inched his body closer to Bird Song. He rested his hands on her hips and pulled her close.

"Someone like you?" he asked.

Bird Song smiled. "Perhaps."

"I like the sound of that, but if you want to make me honest tomorrow, you're going to have to do something dishonest with me tonight."

Bird Song smiled again. She grabbed Two Dogs'

hand and pulled him along to his tipi. She yanked him to the floor quickly and had her turklyo-skin dress off before he had time to place his newest eagle feather on the altar at the back.

"What happened to being dishonest?" Bird Song asked.

"Let me do at least one thing right tonight. My father would condemn me otherwise."

"I'm sure you would find a few choice insults of your own."

"Probably, but I have better ideas of what to do with my mouth right now."

Bird Song leaned back on the furs lining the tipi floor. The central igsidian plate glowed to provide both light and warmth as the lovers admired each other. Two Dogs removed his turklyo-skin shirt and pants, then leaned into her.

Two Dogs woke with a fright in the early morning hours. His unexpected motion disturbed Bird Song, but she didn't sit up. Owl Talon snored loudly on the other side of the tipi.

"What is it?" Bird Song asked between a pair of yawns.

"Shh. Something's wrong," Two Dogs answered.

His warrior sense screamed at him to investigate. It wasn't quite dawn; pale moonlight shone through the opening at the top of Two Dogs' home. He reached for his clothes and quickly threw them on. He pulled the necklace he received from his family earlier out from inside shirt and allowed it to rest prominently on top.

AUGURY ANSWERED

"What are you doing?" Bird Song asked. She was more alert now.

Two Dogs wrapped his belt with tomahawk and knife around his waist.

"I don't like this. I'm going to check outside," Two Dogs answered.

Before Two Dogs opened the flap on his tipi to exit, he heard the war cries of a few Lacreechee men. Two Dogs quickly drew his weapons. Loud cracks and pops sounded outside the tipi.

Bird Song stood on the furs that had been her bed. She looked apprehensive. Owl Talon leapt to his feet, suddenly completely awake.

"Those are muskets!" he shouted.

Muskets? Two Dogs had heard the word before but never seen one used. Only the Corlains had muskets, which meant—

Musket balls penetrated the turklyo-skin walls of his tipi. Both Two Dogs and Owl Talon dove for cover. Bird Song wasn't as quick footed. She screamed out in pain as multiple musket balls pushed through her left arm, throat, and twice through her stomach. Two Dogs was too slow to catch her as she crumpled to the floor.

"Bird Song!" Two Dogs shouted.

Two Dogs grabbed her body. Her eyes stared blankly. Her head slumped backward in his arms.

"Bastards!" Two Dogs shouted to the Corlains ambushing his village.

Owl Talon grabbed his war club, the ball at the end made of solid igsidian. He grasped his younger son and pulled him back to his feet.

"We fight first, then we mourn," Owl Talon said.

Two Dogs nodded his understanding. All of Two Dogs' igsidian burned bright orange as he prepared himself. Owl Talon formed a ball of frost around his right hand. Both men charged outside the tipi. Owl Talon was first. He only made it two steps before the line of Corlains by their door opened fire. As Two Dogs understood it, muskets were exceptionally inaccurate. The reason only Corlains used them was because their army was the only one large enough to have enough soldiers to make the gunfire accurate by volume.

Flashes of orange lit up the space around Two Dogs as musket balls hit his magical shield. Owl Talon wasn't as fortunate. Several shots passed through his body, and he collapsed at Two Dogs' feet.

His father's body, mixed with the raw emotion of Bird Song's death only moments before, ignited Two Dogs' well known fury. He assaulted the squad of eleven men. His enhanced speed and strength made him a difficult, nearly impossible, target to track. He wouldn't be able to keep up this effort for long, but these men would not survive the night. Two Dogs swore that to the souls of his loved ones.

He took a moment to find the Corlains. Their armor was pitch black with the small exception of a narrow red triangle on their helmets. If not for the full moon, the Lacreechee would have had little chance of even seeing their enemy. Fortunately, Mother Turklyo had given them some assistance. Two Dogs watched as the squad who killed his father reloaded their weapons.

The other thing Two Dogs knew about muskets

was how slow they were to load. While the Corlains fiddled with their weapons, Two Dogs attacked. Only nine of the Corlains had muskets. The two on the ends of the rank each held a broadsword and a shield. They stepped forward to engage Two Dogs while the others readied their weapons for another volley. Two Dogs rolled under the swing of the leftmost soldier. He thrust behind him with his knife and embedded it into the spine of his foe. He stood as he turned and buried his tomahawk into the neck of the same man. With his improved strength, he kicked the man into a pair of his companions. The trio fell to the ground, one dead. The other two soon joined him as Two Dogs rapidly stabbed them.

Two Dogs parried the attack from the other melee soldier with his tomahawk. The force of Two Dogs' block made the Corlain lose his balance. As the man fought to regain his footing, Two Dogs decapitated him with a single blow.

"Two Dogs, defend!" Swift Shot shouted.

Two Dogs knew instinctively what to do. He dismissed his strength and speed to summon a protective cocoon of magical reinforcement. Soon after, a turklyo-tipped arrow surrounded by flames slammed into the ground. It exploded with lava and scattered the remaining Corlains. During the explosion, the arrow disappeared with an orange flash.

Swift Shot ran up to her friend. An orange flash behind her demonstrated why it was called a *return* quiver. The arrow she had just fired was once again nestled in the gift Owl Talon gave her.

Two Dogs uncurled himself from his defensive position and readjusted his magic to give himself an advantage over the magic-blind Corlains. Swift Shot briefly hugged Two Dogs as she reached him.

"Thank Mother Turklyo," Swift Shot said.

Two Dogs pushed her away. It still wasn't the time for mourning. Two Dogs surveyed the battlefield. Many dead Lacreechee littered the battlefield, but twice as many Corlains joined them. The Corlains seemed to have split up into numerous small fighting units. These squads had infiltrated the village and attacked without provocation. Two Dogs witnessed magical feats of every school, but the Corlains had the numbers. At least a thousand must have attacked their community of three hundred.

"Where's my brother?" Two Dogs asked.

Swift Shot shook her head. "I don't know. I think he was protecting the children on the west side of camp, but the Corlains are everywhere. Many tried to escape. Hopefully, he was one of them."

"Not my brother. We need to find Proud Wall and Bright Stone. Few can erect the barriers we need to survive their muskets."

A piercing war cry interrupted the chaos. Two Dogs and Swift Shout followed the sound to see Bright Stone lead a charge with the warriors specializing in protection magic. Their target appeared to be the leaders of this Corlain unit. There were small skirmishes between squads of Corlains and small groups of Lacreechee braves, but several hundred Corlains stood in rank and file. These soldiers were Bright Stone's objective.

The first rank of twenty soldiers fired their muskets at Bright Stone's party. Orange flashes lit up the sky as the Lacreechee continued to charge. The first rank took a knee and reloaded. The second rank now fired. This led to the same result of the first rank. When the third rank fired, a pair of Lacreechee fell over, dead. The Corlains attacked like this for six ranks of soldiers, then the first rank stood and fired again. Bright Stone's warriors were decimated. Only she and three others survived. Their magic was strong enough to hold any amount of musket balls, for a time.

"We must help them!" Two Dogs shouted.

Swift Shot didn't respond, but she nocked three arrows at once. She aimed high and arched the arrows into the left flank of the main Corlain position. Lightning arced through the formation as the bolts chained throughout the enchanted metal armor the Corlains wore. Dozens dropped to the ground and convulsed.

"Keep it up!" Two Dogs shouted as he charged the formation from the left.

Bright Stone and her few remaining warriors collided with the formation. Bodies flew as she blasted them with wind. Others shattered as they turned to ice from both Swift Shot's arrows and Bright Stone's fists.

As Two Dogs charged the formation, a group of Corlains caught his eye. They had different uniforms than the others, colorful outfits made of cloth. In front of them was a long, gray tube on a pair of wheels. Upon closer inspection, Two Dogs saw three more groups of men had a similar object. The men seemed to fuss with the strange object as they pointed it toward the village. Two Dogs followed the direction to the target. It was Proud Wall and two dozen children.

Proud Wall had a magical barrier surrounding the children that stayed orange from the constant assault it was under. Many Corlains hacked at the limits of the shield with axes and broadswords. A few of the children huddled in fear, but most fought like true Lacreechee warriors! They cast simple elemental spells that passed through Proud Wall's barrier. The children weren't trained enough to be effective. Most Corlains hit ignored the elemental power. A few took a step back after impact, but their armor had enough enchantment to protect them from juvenile power. Suddenly, the Corlains ran away from the children as one unit. This perplexed Two Dogs.

Two Dogs came back to the reality of his situation by a thunderous noise. He stepped back and rubbed the ringing in his ears away. When he looked back at Proud Wall's position, his heart shattered. Inexplicably, Proud Wall and the children were dead. They were more than dead; their bodies had been ripped asunder. Two Dogs looked back at the strange Corlains in their colorful uniforms.

The open ends of the long tubes smoked as the men pushed the objects, which were clearly weapons, back into position for another attack. With the deaths of Bird Song, Owl Talon, and Proud Wall, Two Dogs no longer felt any emotion but unabated rage. Perhaps a dozen Lacreechee were still fighting. Bright Stone was alone in the main group, but the fight still seemed even.

However, his fury was entirely directed at the men with the doomsday weapons.

Two Dogs summoned nothing but strength and speed. He breathed heavily, but he had more killing to do before he could meet Mother Turklyo. He sprinted toward the first group of men and leapt twenty feet into the air. The men seemed unaware of his presence. A single Lacreechee was easily overlooked. That mistake cost the Corlains dearly.

Two Dogs landed with a tomahawk in one man's skull and a knife slashing a second's throat. He made short work of the remaining three men. Mother Turklyo gave him additional strength. He hoisted the large weapon and, with some effort, tossed it toward the next position. Two men were crushed between the weight of their weapon and the one Two Dogs had thrown.

Two Dogs slaughtered the men. All twenty were dead before a second volley of death had been loaded. The man Two Dogs assumed to be the officer-in-charge was the last to taste Two Dogs' blade. He allowed the man to cower as he advanced on him.

"Please, I have children," the officer begged in the guttural trade language common among outsiders.

Two Dogs scoffed contemptuously and answered in the distasteful tongue. "You just murdered children, and now want to hide behind them?"

"They were combatants," the officer argued.

Two Dogs knocked the hat off the trembling man. He grabbed a thick handful of brown hair. The man shrieked and blubbered as Two Dogs jerked his head backward. Although he had intended to scalp the man, with his emotional state and enhanced strength, his blade cut through the man's skull instead. The top two inches of head and brain dropped onto the ground. The man continued to scream, so Two Dogs chopped his tomahawk into the unprotected organ staring at him. This ended the officer's suffering. Two Dogs pushed the body to the side and breathed heavily.

As he summoned his magic, it occurred to Two Dogs that he no longer heard battle sounds. Swift Shot's arrows had ended. The wounded had silenced. Dawn exposed its earliest rays of sunlight. Two Dogs looked forward as he saw Bright Stone lean against a caged wagon. She didn't move, but from this distance it was hard to tell if she was dead. Unfortunately, Two Dogs could easily determine that several dozen Corlains stood around her body. They stabbed her repeatedly with spears.

"Bastards!" Two Dogs shouted.

The Corlains turned their attention to him. Two Dogs saw movement inside the cage. A person stood and an orange light shone.

"Fallen Lacreechee, your spirits have not wandered far. Take your revenge on these murderers!" the woman shouted.

That sounded like summoning magic. Two Dogs' suspicion was confirmed when ethereal yellow bodies rose from the fallen Lacreechee citizens. They immediately charged the remaining Corlains. Ghost warriors were fearless but not invincible. Many *died* a second time as enchanted Corlain blades passed through them. However, now the numbers were in the Lacreechee's favor.

They eliminated the final Corlains and disappeared.

Two Dogs surveyed the battlefield that was his home only an hour earlier. He dropped to his knees and wailed at the sky. He was the last of the Lacreechee.

CHAPTER 3

Murid swung her sword with maximum force. Despite fifteen years of intense training with her adopted people, Egill easily parried it away with his axe. The force of the block sent Murid into a spin. She felt the flat side of Egill's axe plant itself on her bottom and shove her forward. Murid sprawled into the mud. A cool morning wind added to the indignity. Roars of laughter came from the Vikisote warriors observing from the fence lining the training pit. Dozens watched as Murid once again failed to score a single point against her teacher.

Murid immediately stood and swung three slashes at Egill. He backpedaled as he intercepted each blow. He taunted her by only using one hand to wield the massive axe he held. Despite Murid's best attempts, she couldn't overcome the advantage his brawn provided.

Murid overextended herself with a thrust. Egill ducked under it and swept her legs out from beneath her. More laughter roared as Murid once again spat wet dirt. She felt the full weight of Egill resting on her back. She strained to force him off, but he outweighed her by at least sixty kilograms. Egill didn't move.

"Do you yield?" Egill asked.

He stood and allowed her to roll onto her back. Egill looked sympathetic as he offered her a hand to pull her up from the muck. Murid graciously accepted it. She observed Egill after she stood but kept ahold of his hand. Egill was a man in his mid-forties. He had a salt and pepper beard that hung to the middle of his chest. He had once told her it was to hide his numerous scars, though that may have been a joke told to a child. Regardless, he had far too many scars to count. In fact, most looked so severe that Murid could barely believe this man was still alive, let alone the captain of the Vikisote guard.

"I never said *yes*," Murid said as she tried to strip Egill's axe from his hand.

It was a foolish attempt. Egill seemed to have anticipated Murid's underhanded trick. He practically laughed as he yanked back on his axe and pulled Murid into his waiting knee. She gasped as his body connected with her solar plexus. Once again, Murid found herself on the ground, hacking up phlegm.

"I taught you better than that," Egill scolded.

This time, Murid stood unassisted.

"I'm sorry, Egill, I know that was sneaky. If you ain't cheating, you ain't trying," Murid said.

"You think that's why I'm upset?" Egill asked. "There's no such thing as dirty fighting. I'm upset you were so sloppy. Every one of us knew you would try something so obvious."

Egill gestured to the surrounding warriors. The dozens who witnessed another embarrassing defeat nodded knowingly. Thankfully, it was only a few dozen and not the full three thousand warriors who made up King Viktor's army.

"I learn something new every day," Murid said.

"Yes, but it's been over fifteen years since we began training you. I'm beginning to wonder if Olha was thorough with your initial lessons? Perhaps what you think is something new is simply that which you forgot when you were seven?"

Many Vikisote warriors laughed, but a stern look from Egill reminded them they should get back to their own training. The men and a few shield maidens paired off and went back to their drills.

"I thought she showed remarkable improvement," Hafoca said.

Murid turned to face her fiancé. He was much more than the fifteen-year-old who had tormented her when they first met. Now a man beginning his thirties, Hafoca had evolved into someone whom Murid usually respected. She felt this regard would ultimately turn into the same love he professed to her daily.

"Thank you, Hafoca," Murid said.

Hafoca approached her and warmly embraced her. She returned the hug and accepted a soft kiss on her cheek.

"She performed well enough . . . for a shield maiden," Egill said.

AUGURY ANSWERED

Murid clenched her jaw. Egill was an amazing teacher and a fierce warrior. Murid had felt immense pride when Egill had taken over her training from Olha, but over the years he had frequently reminded her she was *only* a woman. Murid often ignored the barbs, but with Hafoca listening, it meant he would try again to set a date for their wedding.

"That's all the future queen of Vikisoteland needs to be," Hafoca said. "Princess Murid is more than capable of defending herself and my future children. Now that she's come of age, we may establish the ceremony."

Twenty-two, that's how many years it took to reach adulthood in Vikisoteland. Her birthday had been two weeks earlier. Hafoca had celebrated it each day since. Murid had long accepted that Hafoca would be her husband. It was an acceptable match, but she knew in her heart she could never marry until Vikisoteland avenged her parents' murder. Fifteen years wasn't enough time to make her forget her fury, but it was far more than enough for Vikisoteland to have retaliated in her honor. The few disagreements that Murid and Hafoca had often begun with her pointing out this lack of justice.

"My love, you know the gift I desire before I'll feel comfortable settling down and providing Vikisoteland with strong heirs. Corla mocks us and the rest of the world. They rape, steal, and murder their way across Glostaimia, yet we do nothing," Murid said.

Egill cleared his voice. "Princess Murid speaks the truth of Corlain aggression. There are already Corlain outposts on our land. I could send a war party to wipe them out. It would send a strong message to Corla that we won't be as easily intimidated as other nations."

Hafoca sighed forcefully. "Do you believe I don't know your opinions? I was there when the Corlains killed King Haymel and Queen Colchi."

"With all due respect, Prince Hafoca, that's more reason why we must attack the Corlains in Vikisoteland. They killed our allies. They killed our queen, your mother, and felt no repercussions," Egill said.

"Untrue! We broke ties with their government," Hafoca said.

"Which they laugh about behind our backs!" Murid shouted.

"Perhaps, but that's no reason to overreact. War is easily entered but not so easily ended. How many more daughters must lose their parents simply because of our pride and arrogance?"

Murid clenched her fists by her sides. For all his qualities, courage was in short supply with Hafoca. It was likely the obstacle that kept her from loving this man.

"Be that as it may," Murid said, "I need a victory over Corla before I can wed. You may force me to abandon this position, but you *will* lose my heart in the process."

Hafoca gazed at his own feet. Murid knew he wanted her to care for him as much as he loved her. It was the only reason they weren't married the morning she turned twenty-two.

"I don't want you to fall in battle. I want you to

raise my sons," Hafoca said.

"I won't fall. I've survived one massacre already. The gods want me to defeat Corla!"

Murid referred to the prophecy that Faida had groomed her to believe. Too many of the passages seemed to speak exactly of her life. Corla would be conquered, and she would be the one to do it.

"Marry me. Tonight. I'll help you turn Father to your side. You know he's unwell. Don't deny him the chance to see his only son married before he joins the gods in the halls of Mount Heilagt," Hafoca said.

Murid felt a pang of sympathy for Hafoca's plight. His mother had died with her own parents. King Viktor had been wounded. His arm was amputated after they escaped the massacre at her home. King Viktor had always loved her like his own child. She wanted to give this gift to her new king, but she knew the second she officially became Hafoca's wife was the moment he would only see her as the mother of his children. If she wanted to gain her vengeance, she had to gamble that King Viktor would linger just long enough to let her.

"I need justice."

"I need an heir first."

"A male heir," Egill added.

Hafoca smiled at what the two men likely assumed was *obvious*. Murid forced a fake smile of her own. Her mother told her that most men thought less of women, but the Vikisotes took it further than the majority.

"If you'll excuse me, my lord," Murid said with a curtsey.

"Please don't go," Hafoca begged.

Murid turned and walked away. She left her sword and shield laying in the mud.

Murid strolled through the mountain kingdom that had become her home. It was a sprawling ring fortress that stretched across more than a kilometer. The ground was rocky, but occasionally cobbled-stoned streets, long unkempt, impacted her feet. Longhouses stretched thirty meters. They looked half buried from the street with triangular thatched roofs and stone walls. The smell of peat invaded her nostrils when she passed too closely. Murid closed her eyes and accepted it. That odor was one of the few things that reminded her of her parents' home. Everything else in this country was hard and gray, not the vibrant green of the swamplands she grew up in.

"Princess Murid!" a child shouted in passing.

Murid nodded and waved. Several more children chased the girl in a game of tag. Murid quickly stepped to the side to avoid a collision with the young Vikisotes.

"Princess Murid, will you be watching the children's performance tonight?" a middle-aged mother asked.

"I never miss a chance to hear them sing," Murid responded.

The woman nodded and continued tending to her personal spice garden.

"Princess Murid! Catch!" a teen shouted.

Murid turned to face the voice. She couldn't identify the speaker because she had to catch a hundred-centimeter snake thrown at her face. Murid stepped to the side and plucked the innocuous creature from the air.

"Isak, by the gods, what have you done?" a man shouted.

Isak looked shocked that he was so quickly caught by his father. The older man smacked Isak twice on the head; the second blow knocked him to the ground. Isak's father looked ashamed as Murid placed the snake among a small patch of grass.

"I apologize, Princess Murid. The boy will learn his place, and my belt will be his teacher," the father said.

Murid held up a hand as she smiled. "No offense taken. I understand that boys will push against their boundaries. I hunted far more dangerous animals when I was a child. It was all in good fun."

The father looked relieved. Isak cracked a smile.

"Thank you, Princess Murid," the father said. "The boy will still learn his lesson, but perhaps his studies won't have to be as long."

Isak cast his eyes downward. Murid offered a second smile and continued walking. It was a good prank, but a sore bottom sped the process of gaining wisdom.

After several minutes of meandering, Murid found herself at her destination. Three runes were carved into the stone pillar before the building, a hammer, a hoe, and a water can. They were the proud symbols of the Vikisotes' religion. The hammer symbolized the pounding and shaping necessary to become a productive citizen. The hoe represented the need for society to tend to the environment necessary to thrive. The water can indicated the need to provide sustenance to foster growth. Murid now claimed these principles as her own. The gods had placed many obstacles in her life, but they had also guided her around them.

Murid rested a hand on the pillar with the runes and closed her eyes. Moments later, she opened them and went inside to speak with her best friend.

Incense burned throughout the room. The burnt honey aroma reminded Murid of molasses cookies. The interior of the stone building was cool. A dirt floor was beneath Murid's feet. A stone table sat in the middle of the single room. On it were many totems of the more important gods. Arranging the totems was Faida.

Faida placed a small pool of honey on a stone dish before the most prominent god, Jorosolman. It was dark after being poked by the red-hot rod Faida used to burn it. Her eyes lit up as she recognized Murid.

"Princess Murid, how nice to see you again."

"I hope I'm not disturbing you or the gods?"

"Nonsense, royalty is always welcomed among the gods. Come in, come in, sit with me."

Faida brushed away some dirt from the single bench that functioned as the only furniture the two could sit on. Faida smiled as Murid got comfortable.

"What brings you here today?" Faida asked.

"I just wanted to escape Hafoca's constant badgering," Murid answered.

"You're a woman now. You had to know he would press the issue of marriage."

"I did, but I thought his mistresses would keep him satisfied for at least a few months."

"It's different for a man when it's the woman who

will have his children. He's older than you. He's waited for this day longer than you have."

"I suppose. I never thought of it like that before."

"I know you think marriage will make it impossible for you to destroy Corla's evil reign over this planet, but I believe the opposite is true."

Murid arched an eyebrow.

"The prophecy clearly states that the survivor of a massacre will defeat an army from foreign lands. It implies that survivor will be a foreigner himself."

"Exactly, *himself*; it's always a man in the stories," Murid said.

"That's because it's always men who tell the story. However, the gods have spoken to me. I know that the gender of the hero isn't important. You survived the decimation of your people. Only you. You *are* the chosen one the prophecy foretold. Vikisote customs can't change the will of the gods. Marry Prince Hafoca. Then, as his wife, you'll convince him you're the person the gods sent to free us from Corlain tyranny."

"The moment I'm his wife, he'll be so busy pumping babies into me I won't have a second to get a word in."

Faida and Murid shared a laugh. Faida wiped a tear from her eye as she spoke again.

"Princess, that's the easiest way to get a man to see your point of view."

The two women broke into another round of laughter.

"Perhaps you're right."

"You don't want King Viktor to die before he can

officially welcome you into the family, do you?" Faida asked.

Murid stared Faida in the eyes. "No. He and you have been the best part of having to live in this country."

"Don't sound so excited."

"You know what I mean."

"I do. I'd like to think Prince Hafoca could be added to that list too."

"Some days he is, but then there are days like today, and I just want to strangle him."

"As I hear it, that's a sign of a strong marriage too."

The women shared another laugh.

"Have you been getting into the holy ferm supply?" Murid asked.

Faida presented a jug hidden along the side of the bench.

"I was waiting for you to ask, Princess."

Murid smiled as Faida poured two cups of honey ferm. Murid and Faida clinked their mugs and drank. The sweet liquid caressed her throat. Murid smiled as she swallowed.

"Would you care for more?" Faida asked as she jiggled the jug of ferm.

Murid covered the top of her cup. "No, thank you. I want to stay annoyed with Hafoca a while longer. This stuff always speeds the process of me forgiving him."

"That's what the gods want. That's why they gave us this gift."

Someone pounded on the door from outside.

"Princess Murid, are you in there?"

"Yes, you may enter," Murid replied.

Two warriors entered the small temple. Each carried a long sword and a round shield. Murid became instantly concerned.

"What is it? What's happened?" she asked.

"The king needs to see you immediately," the first guard answered.

"Why? What's wrong?" Murid asked.

"His father has died," the second guard answered.

CHAPTER 4

Two Dogs rested on his knees and moaned. Dawn had fully arrived, but the warm sun could do nothing to remove the cold despair he held in his soul. The old hag in the Corlains' prison wagon continued to scream at him, but he wasn't listening. His grief consumed him. Stretched between him and the old woman were the ruins of his village and the bodies of his community. Many mangled by the advanced weaponry the Corlains brought.

"Are you listening to me?" the hag shouted.

Two Dogs slowly raised his eyes and fixed them on the woman. Her cage was at least a hundred yards away, but her white hair was distinct in the morning light.

"Now is not the time to mourn! There are more coming! We must make haste!" the woman screamed.

Her words sounded off. She was a child of Mother Turklyo but not from a tribe near his lands. That meant he couldn't trust her. Perhaps it would be best to leave her.

"We must leave now! Let me out of this thing! Please! Do not forsake one of Mother Turklyo's children because you're too busy weeping like a child!"

She was right. Two Dogs hated to admit it, but he couldn't change the past. He needed to prepare the bodies for Mother Turklyo; it would take time ensuring each person had his or her appropriate igsidian.

Two Dogs slowly rose.

"Finally, now get me out of this infernal cage! More Corlains could be here any moment!"

The hag was in shock. Bright Stone ensured all the Corlains had died. Two Dogs turned to face away from the Corlain prisoner. His loyalties were with his friends and family. He already knew the fates of Owl Talon, Bird Song, Proud Wall, and Bright Stone. Each had perished before his eyes. He needed the answer to how Swift Shot had fallen. She would be the first he would prepare to meet Mother Turklyo.

"Where are you going? I'm over here! I can help you fulfill Mother Turklyo's augury! Clearly you're the one who survived a great massacre! You *are* the one who will lead our people to victory over the greedy Corlains!"

Two Dogs scoffed. *Auguries* were tales meant only to inspire the children. He searched for the spot he last saw Swift Shot. Two Dogs stepped over the remains of the Corlains he'd slaughtered. He beamed at his skill. It was a shame he hadn't left a survivor. The psychological horror of what a few Lacreechee warriors could do would give more than one Corlain reason to halt their advances through Mother Turklyo's land.

As Two Dogs snickered at his comforting thought, a pained murmur drew his attention. Lying in the grass was a young Corlain. He was a boy, perhaps no older than fifteen, with a Corlain drum lying on his legs. A long arrow stood erect from the boy's stomach. The youth squirmed as he tried to remove it.

Two Dogs' gripped his knife firmly as he slowly approached the child. The arrow in his stomach had stripes along the shaft. It wasn't one of Swift Shot's projectiles. Perhaps Keen Gaze? If it was his arrow, the boy was in for a cruel morning. Keen Gaze used toxic magic. There would be no cure. The boy would suffer for days before ultimately dying. A cruel smile spread across Two Dogs' face, but the boy's bawling fought to erase it.

The boy must have spotted Two Dogs.

"Please . . . help me."

Two Dogs walked closer to the boy and kneeled by his head.

"Why?" Two Dogs asked.

The boy coughed blood that dribbled down the sides of his cheeks.

"Please . . . wa . . . water."

The boy's youth tormented Two Dogs. His suffering seemed unfair, but his people caused the events that led to his pain. Still, he was a child. Two Dogs nearly ran to grab a cup, but his eyes passed over the remains of Proud Wall and the children. Their mangled bodies reignited the fire of pure hatred in his soul.

"No," Two Dogs said through clenched teeth.

The boy looked confused. He cried and moaned

even louder.

"Please! End . . . end my misery."

Two Dogs stood and took his first steps away from the doomed child.

"Honorable Namerian, I beg you."

The boy's choice of words instantly halted Two Dogs' departure. Corlains relished disparaging Mother Turklyo's children with that word. He turned and presented his knife so his enemy could see it.

"What did you just call me?" Two Dogs asked.

The boy stopped his moaning with his mouth agape. He seemed confused. Why should he be? He knew better than to use that word.

"I'm sorry—" the soldier started.

He didn't get any further. Two Dogs slit his throat and gave him the mercy he'd begged for.

Two Dogs wiped his blade in the grass and used his sleeve to wipe his eyes. That boy was too young for this business. Like so many of his tribe's children. With the distraction dealt with, Two Dogs continued his search for Swift Shot.

Two Dogs searched for his friend. A green legging drew his attention. The fringe on the side resembled arrowheads. Two Dogs' heart sank as he cautiously approached his friend's body. He grimly smiled as he counted the four Corlain bodies keeping Swift Shot company. They ambushed her like cowards while she supported Bright Stone.

A moan broke Two Dogs from his self-pity. He focused on Swift Shot. She uttered a second moan. Two Dogs rushed to her, falling to his knees to better cradle her head.

"Swift Shot, are you okay? Speak to me," Two Dogs said.

Two Dogs laid her head on his thighs and brushed her blood-matted, dark hair from her eyes. She didn't reply at first, but each moan gave Two Dogs more hope that at least one other Lacreechee warrior survived.

"Swift Shot, can you hear me?" Two Dogs asked.

She still didn't reply. Two Dogs looked her body over to discover the source of her wound. The answer wasn't good, but it didn't look mortal either. Swift Shot was the owner of both an entry and exit wound, likely from a single musket ball. Her wound was exactly where her torso met her right hip. Two Dogs placed his hands on both injuries and pressed.

"It's okay, Swift Shot. I've got you. I'll take care of you."

"Mmm . . . mmm," Swift Shot murmured.

Two Dogs held his ear close to her mouth. "What was that?"

"Wa . . . water," Swift Shot said.

Her voice was tired and raspy. Two Dogs raced to the jugs from the celebration earlier. Nearly all were shattered or empty of their contents. Two Dogs had to settle for something more substantial than plain water.

Two Dogs raced back to his friend and poured the corn ferm gently into her mouth. Swift Shot swallowed a little, but most spilled trails from the corners of her mouth.

Swift Shot's eyes fluttered. "You think . . . I'm that much . . . of a drunk?"

Swift Shot began a fit of coughing at her own joke. Two Dogs felt immense relief. He held her close to his body.

"How are you feeling?" Two Dogs asked.

Swift Shot forced her eyes open. She blinked rapidly as they adjusted to the bright light of the morning sun. Two Dogs felt her misery as she took in the sights of the battle. She buried her head into his chest and sobbed. Her reaction was the catalyst to Two Dogs sharing in her cry. The two bawled for several minutes and held each other. The pity only ended when Swift Shot shouted in pain from her wounds. Two Dogs instantly focused on saving his first, best, and last friend.

"Tell me what to do. I'm not a healer," Two Dogs said.

"Neither am I," Swift Shot replied.

Two Dogs challenged his mind to remember anything beyond simply putting pressure on a wound. Strong Cure or one of the other healers would have had no problem aiding Swift Shot. Perhaps one of them survived as well! Though it broke his heart, Two Dogs knew he had to leave his friend to find a healer. Even a body could provide a vial of medicine.

"Swift Shot, swear to me you won't die while I go to find something to help you."

"Only if you make the same promise." Swift Shot barely finished her sentence before more coughing and moaning overtook her.

"I swear it," Two Dogs said.

"Me too," Swift Shot responded.

Two Dogs gently laid Swift Shot's head to the

ground. He jumped to his feet and sprinted back to the bodies decimated by the Corlains' ultimate weapon. Each step made him nauseous. Blood saturated the ground. His moccasins were more red than green. Viscera clung to him as he waded through the body parts.

Two Dogs didn't see Strong Cure or any other healers. Nor did he find any survivors. His next instinct was to check by Bright Stone's body. Two Dogs charged up the sloping hill to find more death. Though this time the bodies gave him joy. The shiny Corlain armor had completely transitioned from the black used to camouflage them at night. The glare slowed Two Dogs' pace as he attempted to protect his eyes. Two Dogs didn't want to think about the implications that would let people who weren't Mother Turklyo's children enchant their equipment. However, not all the tribes were as devout as the Lacreechee. Two Dogs brushed the unsettling thought aside.

"What are you looking for?" the hag asked.

Two Dogs had forgotten about the prisoner. The Corlain prisoner. The Corlain prisoner who was a daughter of Mother Turklyo. The Corlain prisoner who apparently knew the Lacreechee language. The answer to his doubts seemed obvious.

"You."

Two Dogs practically spat the word at the woman. Now that he was close to her, he truly considered her haggard features. She was extremely thin, with leathery skin stretched across her body. Her hair was white, long, and unkempt, but the Corlains weren't known for their hospitality. She no longer had stones embedded in her *clothing*, yet she held an igsidian knife before her. It was a knife Two Dogs recognized. It was Bright Stone's knife!

The hag tucked the knife into her robe's belt that served as her only clothing. Tattered fragments hung from it, but it held closed the dirty sack wrapped around her.

"I don't know what you're accusing me of, but we're on the same side," the hag said.

Two Dogs ignored her. As much as he wanted to choke the life from her body for betraying Mother Turklyo, Swift Shot was more important. He removed her from his thoughts as he searched the Lacreechee bodies that were the last to fall.

"Your chief was magnificent in battle," the hag said.

Two Dogs moved to the next battered body; it was Unstoppable Force. It didn't surprise Two Dogs that the mightiest Lacreechee warrior after Bright Stone would be next to her.

"Your chief almost had them, but she knew there weren't enough of you left. She threw her knife to me," the hag continued.

The next body Two Dogs found forced him to hurry. It was Quick Nectar. She was one of Strong Cure's apprentices. Two Dogs rolled her body over to search her belt. The sudden movement revealed that Quick Nectar had an upper and lower half that moved independently of each other. Two Dogs looked away.

"She surprised me in battle. Your young healer stayed close to the hip of your strong warriors. As they were wounded, she quickly applied magic to heal the superficial cuts. It did little more than inspire."

Two Dogs was sick of the woman's yammering. "Listen, old woman, I don't know you or your tribe, but I smell a traitor. Distract me again and I'll gladly let you explain yourself to Mother Turklyo in person."

"I'm standing inside a cage, and I'm the traitor? Who do you think summoned the spirits of your fallen to capture victory from certain defeat? It was me, Ancestors' Hand. I'm of the Intakee people. We spit on the Corlains. I was brought here to see what would happen to my own people if I continued to defy them."

Two Dogs emptied the various vials from Quick Nectar's belt. Most of the pouches were empty. Two small bottles were all that remained. One had a pale green liquid, the other had a fine gray powder. Neither meant anything to Two Dogs.

"Do you know what those are for?" Ancestors' Hand asked.

Two Dogs grasped them firmly and stood. He turned back toward Swift Shot and ran.

"Because I do!" Ancestors' Hand shouted.

Her admission stopped Two Dogs in his tracks. He turned and slowly walked back to the Corlain prisoner.

"You're a summoner, not a healer," Two Dogs said.

"Oh ho, and you know everything about me? I'm a summoner, this is true, but you don't get as old as me without picking up a few healing spells. Did you find a survivor?"

"That's none of your concern." Two Dogs held up

a vial in each hand for Ancestors' Hand to see. "What do these do?"

Ancestors' Hand smirked. "The gray one will help with baldness. The green one makes it easier to relieve yourself when you're tired of squatting and pushing."

Ancestors' Hand laughed at Two Dogs' reaction. He threw both vials onto the ground and screamed at the white clouds slowly moving above him.

"Don't waste them. You never know when those long locks will abandon you with age." Ancestors' Hand cackled again.

Two Dogs marched toward Ancestors' Hand. She hesitantly stepped to the far end of her cage. Two Dogs wrapped his fingers around the bars that separated the two.

"You will help my friend," he demanded.

A piercing scream of pain came from Swift Shot's direction. Two Dogs turned to run toward her when she added, "I'm good! Hurry up with that medicine!"

Ancestors' Hand looked confused. "But you should be the only survivor. The augury doesn't mention a second."

"I don't care about any augury. *I'm* the master of my own fate. Right now, I'm the master of yours as well. You *will* save my friend's life, or I'll leave you here to starve. Something tells me that if you could leave this cage, you would have by now."

"That's true. I can get the spirits to fight for me but not to be polite and get the door for an old woman. I can help your friend if the wound isn't too serious."

"Good."

"But we leave immediately after. There are more Corlains than just this one battalion. The rest of the Black Cloud division is close behind. I'm sure many are coming here to discover what happened to their soldiers as we speak."

"Leave Bright Stone's knife with her," Two Dogs commanded.

"What? No, I need something to focus my magic with."

"You may borrow from Swift Shot's igsidian. You will *not* claim any Lacreechee stones."

"This is foolish."

Two Dogs pressed his chest against Ancestors' Hand's prison.

"Fine. Fine. Make this harder than it has to be," Ancestors' Hand said in protest.

Two Dogs stopped listening again. The stones in his necklace and clothes glowed as he adjusted his grip on the metal bars. He didn't even have to strain. The bars bent, then snapped off with minimal effort. Two Dogs tossed the useless metal to the ground and stepped aside for Ancestors' Hand to leave.

"You must be a powerful protector to free me so easily. Mother Turklyo chose wisely when she selected you to personify her augury."

"No more talk of auguries. Come with me."

Before Ancestors' Hand could answer, Two Dogs scooped her up and cradled her in his arms. The woman was light enough that he only had to enhance his speed. She yelped as Two Dogs took off for Swift Shot.

Two Dogs found Swift Shot leaning against a

boulder. She was in a seated position, but the fact that she looked alert and aware forced Two Dogs to relax.

"It took you long enough. I'm out of corn ferm and would like a second cup." Swift Shot held her mug upside-down to prove her point.

"You Lacreechee have a strange sense of humor," Ancestors' Hand said.

"Who's she?" Swift Shot asked.

"Either my new friend or the last person I'll kill in this battle," Two Dogs answered.

"There's that odd humor again," Ancestors' Hand said.

Ancestors' Hand approached Swift Shot. The young warrior slowly stood against the boulder despite obviously putting herself into some discomfort as she did.

"I'm one of Mother Turklyo's summoners, but I do know a few healing spells." Ancestors' Hand inspected Swift Shot's wounds. While Two Dogs had been gone, she'd taken it upon herself to use her fire magic to cauterize each wound to stop the bleeding. It was clearly what caused the scream from earlier. "Fortunately, the ball went through your body. You did a respectable job sealing the wounds. Since he took my knife away, I'll have to focus using the igsidian in your shirt. I apologize for the intrusion. I can cast a simple spell to ensure infection doesn't take you as we continue on our journey. It'll also help dull the pain."

"What journey?" Swift Shot asked.

Ancestors' Hand summoned magical energy to Swift Shot's body. The old woman's hands glowed with yellow vapor as she held them on Swift Shot. The young woman's scars remained the same when Ancestors' Hand finally ended her spell.

"She should be fine now. Perhaps a bit sore, but she can travel with us to Intakee lands," Ancestors' Hand said.

"Why are we going to Intakee lands?" Swift Shot asked as she rubbed her burns.

Ancestors' Hand turned toward the closest tipi marked with the symbol of a healer. The flap was open, and Ancestors' Hand stepped inside. Two Dogs and Swift Shot followed. Inside, Two Dogs identified this home as belonging to Strong Cure.

"We shouldn't be in here," Swift Shot said.

"It won't take but a moment. You need plenty of clean bandages to keep yourself from picking at your wounds," Ancestors' Hand said.

Swift Shot immediately dropped her hands to her side. Two Dogs suppressed a giggle as he watched her flick dry specks of blood from her fingernails.

Ancestors' Hand flipped through some containers until she found clean bandages. She wrapped the green fabric around Swift Shot's waist and tied it with an intricate knot.

"That should do . . . for now. Follow," Ancestors' Hand commanded.

Two Dogs and Swift Shot obeyed as they left Strong Cure's tipi.

"Thank you for your help, but you aren't in charge here," Two Dogs said.

Ancestors' Hand stopped and turned to face the

Lacreechee. "What do you propose we do?"

"We need to gather the igsidian of the fallen," Swift Shot said.

"Exactly," Two Dogs agreed.

"We should grab some, but there isn't enough time to gather it all. Just take the best pieces," Ancestors' Hand said.

"We won't be stealing igsidian from our neighbors!" Two Dogs shouted.

"Your neighbors? Your neighbors are dead. Just as Mother Turklyo has willed it."

Two Dogs grabbed the shabby sack protecting Ancestors' Hand's modesty and shook her.

"Don't speak ill of the Lacreechee!"

"I'm not!" Ancestors' Hand shouted back. "However, I guarantee another Corlain battalion is coming, perhaps a whole brigade. We have thirty minutes at best to gather some supplies and leave."

"We must defend their bodies. Mother Turklyo will want them burned with their igsidian since there aren't any children to receive them," Swift Shot said.

"What? Why would Mother Turklyo want you to burn igsidian? It's her gift to her children. It doesn't follow bloodlines."

"You Intakee have perverted Mother Turklyo's teachings," Swift Shot said.

"No, apparently it's the Lacreechee who don't know their history. Starting with the augury of defeating a foreign oppressor."

"Not this again!" Two Dogs shouted.

He was about to say something else when the faint

beating of drums punctuated the silence between them.

"What's that?" Swift Shot asked.

"Shh," Ancestors' Hand said. "It sounds like war drums."

"Good," Two Dogs stated. "More Corlains to kill. My blades will free their bodies of the burden of their blood."

"As will I," Swift Shot said while nocking an arrow.

"You imbeciles are determined to kill yourselves," Ancestors' Hand said.

"I thought we were the *chosen* ones? How can the Corlains defeat us?" Two Dogs mocked.

"You need to learn Mother Turklyo's lessons. Her augury proclaims that the survivor of a massacre will be our champion against a foreign army. It doesn't say anything about that champion being able to do it without an army at his back," Ancestors' Hand said.

Ancestors' Hand removed her scraggly garments and tossed them onto the ground. Two Dogs and Swift Shot averted their eyes in disgust.

"I need new clothes with igsidian," Ancestors' Hand matter-of-factly stated.

"You aren't Lacreechee and may not take any of our stones," Two Dogs declared.

The drumbeat grew louder.

"Do you hear that?" Ancestors' Hand asked. "The Corlains are about to take all the igsidian for their own evil purposes. You'd rather they get it?"

"They'll face Mother Turklyo's judgment for stealing from her children," Two Dogs answered.

Ancestors' Hand threw her arms up in disgust.

"Fine. A plain robe will do. We must leave now. We can take a canoe up the Fraz River to Intakee lands."

Swift Shot handed Ancestors' Hand a plain turklyo-skin dress. Igsidian wasn't embedded in it.

"I hope you two know what you're doing, because I won't be able to fight," Ancestors' Hand said as she pulled the dress over her head.

"What about the igsidian from the bull?" Swift Shot asked.

"I suppose some wasn't gifted yet," Two Dogs said. "Let's grab the rest of that. We can sort it out on the river."

The drumbeat grew even louder. Across the plains, Two Dogs could see banners flapping as the sun reflected off an endless mirror of bodies. Two Dogs had to look away. He searched the ground for a discarded Corlain helmet and used his knife to break out the red lens. It fractured with his blows, but Two Dogs grabbed a large enough piece to use as a monocle. He looked again at the approaching army.

Now that the lens filtered the obnoxious light, Two Dogs could take a count on what was approaching. The army was at least three times larger than the one they barely defeated an hour earlier. They also had more of the tubes on wheels that created so much carnage. Despite his eagerness to die in his homeland, he knew his tribe and Mother Turklyo wouldn't forgive him for giving up without getting justice first.

"Five minutes, then we're on the water," Two Dogs said to the women. "I'll get the igsidian my father hadn't crafted yet. Swift Shot, you get food and water.

Ancestors' Hand, go back inside Strong Cure's tipi and grab whatever medical supplies will best suit us. Five minutes and we meet at the river."

"Got it," Swift Shot said.

Ancestors' Hand left without another word. Two Dogs rushed to his home. Inside, he found the bag with the remaining igsidian and his father's tools. He must have worked quickly to make Swift Shot's arrows and quiver before the celebration. It surprised Two Dogs that he had enough time left to make his necklace. They were simple enough jobs, but that meant his father forfeited the chance to boast about his son to the tribe when they had first returned. The thought made Two Dogs sniff.

Inside the bag were the last three pieces of igsidian. The first two were of equal length, approximately four inches long and two inches thick, likely meant for a pair of spears. The remaining piece was a disc about three inches across. Two Dogs secured the pieces and Owl Talon's tools inside a turklyo-skin backpack.

He turned to leave, then stopped. On the floor was his newest eagle feather. Two Dogs' hands trembled as he picked up his recent trophy. His heart pounded and his eyes burned. He let out a slow, calming breath as he took one last look at his home of the last thirty-two years. Two Dogs blinked away his tears and left.

Swift Shot and Ancestors' Hand waited for him by the river. Three canoes drifted away with the current to the south. Swift Shot already sat in a fourth canoe. She also wore her new eagle feather.

"Take this," Two Dogs told Ancestors' Hand as he

handed her a pouch containing the disc-shaped igsidian.

Ancestors' Hand graciously accepted it. "Thank you. I accept the gift."

She hung the pouch around her neck.

"Say nothing more of it," Two Dogs said. "How do we get to your people?"

"We'll have to fight the current to get to Intakee lands, but the Corlains will hopefully expect us to go south to our Azca allies," Swift Shot said.

"Good idea," Two Dogs agreed.

"Yes, yes, genius. May we please go?" Ancestors' Hand asked.

Two Dogs nodded. He and Ancestors' Hand joined Swift Shot in the canoe. The young warriors grabbed an oar each and paddled at full strength. Swift Shot steered the canoe from the stern while Two Dogs used his enhanced strength to paddle from the bow.

"Don't forget to add protection to our canoe," Ancestors' Hand said. "The Fraz River is known for its aggressive dakydile population."

CHAPTER 5

Murid crouched behind Egill, Hafoca, and several burly Vikisotes. Behind her were another dozen warriors, King Hafoca's royal guard. The minty urine smell of crick oil surrounded her, if the aggressive grunts from warriors wasn't enough of a sign. King Viktor's death brought sadness throughout the kingdom. Although Murid felt terrible about losing the kind man who saved her when her parents were murdered, it relieved her knowing the month-long mourning period prohibited any further talk of marriage. Although, this meant that twenty-seven days from now, she'd likely be forced to marry. A king would always need his queen.

The Vikisotes had specific events required in a certain order following the death of royalty. When the queen had died fifteen years earlier, Murid had been too young to partake in most. Now, as the queen apparent, she found herself hiding behind one of many white spruce trees in the dense mountain forest. To prove the new king's courage, he must track and kill a wild crick. Murid had never seen a living crick, but she slept under the warm pelt of one each night.

The rules stated Hafoca could bring up to thirty people with him, but for each reduction, he would earn more favor from the gods. It didn't surprise Murid that he still brought twenty with him. That was eight more than King Viktor had deemed necessary. Many throughout the kingdom had murmured as much.

The guards ahead of Murid halted. Those following also ceased to move. Murid gripped the spear in her hand tightly. Stopping could only mean the trackers had found a clue to where there may be a crick den.

"What have you found?" Hafoca whispered loudly.

One of the trackers scrambled over to Hafoca. He quickly caught his breath before speaking.

"King Hafoca, we have a den about forty meters north of here," he answered.

"What's the problem then?" Egill asked.

"A juvenile went in moments after we spotted the den. We're upwind of the den, so we must sneak back and circle around," the tracker said.

Hafoca was incredulous. "What? Why would we sneak away like cowards? We only need to fell a crick. It doesn't matter the age."

"King Hafoca, a juvenile and a den mean a mother is close by. She'll fiercely defend her young, which could be as many as six cubs," Egill said.

"Plus, the juvenile crick was very close to maturing. We don't have enough men here to guarantee no casualties. It'll be safer to leave," the tracker said.

He looked increasingly nervous as the group stayed so close to the den. Murid didn't fully understand the fight, but she knew enough to listen to experience when it spoke.

"Hafoca, we should turn back," Murid said.

Hafoca smirked like she was still a child and he knew better. "Relax, my love, the mother is likely away hunting for food. We can claim one of the young and leave before she returns."

Murid glanced between Egill and the tracker. Neither looked pleased with Hafoca's false confidence. However, if the past fifteen years had taught her anything, it was that Hafoca was prideful. He was likely more terrified, but he would never admit that to his warriors. Despite the taste of bile that always accompanied this particular thought, Murid knew what she had to do.

"Hafoca, please." Murid tugged on his arm and added false fear to her voice. "I don't want to be here. I'm sorry for coming in the first place, but I know I'm not strong enough to face a crick, regardless of its size."

Egill nodded. He likely knew she was manipulating Hafoca, but Murid also knew he believed women should never be on these hunts. Hafoca seemed to fall for her ruse once again.

"My sweet Murid, somehow I knew your courage would wane. Do you see why I think it's foolish to want to go to war with Corla?" Hafoca said. "On our wedding night, I'll bathe you in your first crick oil. It will give you the courage you desire."

Murid clenched her jaw. Was Hafoca manipulating

her? Murid shook the thought away.

"Hafoca, when we attack Corla, we'll bring our full might at their weakest outposts. Here we are weak and the prey has all the advantages," Murid said.

Egill suppressed a smile, but Hafoca seemed to notice it. His eyes grew hard as he squeezed his right hand into a fist.

"Flush them out," Hafoca commanded.

"Yes, King Hafoca," the tracker said.

Hafoca nocked an arrow as the tracker grabbed three warriors with halberds. The four men moved to the mouth of the cave the juvenile crick used for a home. Two stood on each side with their weapons at the ready. Hafoca moved to the clearing directly in front of the cave. He signaled with his head for the tracker to begin.

The tracker pulled a small pouch off his belt. He loosened the cord that held it closed, then placed a pinch of magnesium flakes into the pouch. The chemical mixture produced a dense cloud of white smoke. The tracker tossed the binary reaction into the mouth of the dark cave and immediately moved away from the entrance, his own halberd now firmly in his hand.

Murid listened as howls roared from the den. Those closest to Murid, even Egill, shifted uncomfortably. Mother was apparently home.

"Be ready," Egill said.

"For what?" Murid asked.

"You'll see."

The first crick that raced out of the den was a juvenile, likely the one the tracker initially identified. It howled in pain as it ran in frantic circles. Hafoca sent three arrows into its face and cut its misery short. The young brown animal rolled over and could easily have been mistaken for a harmless grizzly cub.

"You see? Simple!" Hafoca shouted to his citizens.

The mother crick roared again and emerged. It stood on its hind legs and screamed a challenge at the humans before it. Murid wet herself when she saw what was before her. The crick was nearly two hundred kilograms and stood over two meters. The thick shaggy hair still smoked from the tracker's grenade. It had black claws that were twelve centimeters long and dripped with a venom that could kill a man inside three minutes. The most terrifying aspect of the beast was its head. The body may have resembled a bear, but the face reminded Murid of a serpent. It was scaly with a forked tongue. Its hood flared as it roared another challenge at Hafoca and the rest of the Vikisotes.

Hafoca fired an arrow at the crick. It dug into the chest of the animal and made it furious. It dropped to all fours and charged Hafoca. Hafoca panicked and tripped backward. His arrows spilled from his quiver as he scampered away on his hindquarters. The tracker swung his halberd and cut deeply into the crick's rear leg. The animal roared again and changed its direction.

The tracker had just enough time to scream before the crick unhinged its jaw and bit the man's head. The animal lifted the tracker off the ground and flung him into the rock wall of the cave's entrance. The crick flailed its front paws and left furrows in the throat and chest of a guard standing by the cave.

"Stay here," Egill commanded Murid. He gripped his axe and charged toward the crick.

The remaining warriors followed Egill except two who stayed with Murid. They formed a circle around the crick. It spat venom at one warrior but only splashed on his leather armor. The man frantically removed his bracer before the venom could burn through. Egill swung with his axe and pushed the crick farther back. A warrior stabbed it in the back with his spear while its attention was divided.

Hafoca stood again and fired an arrow. His aim was off due to the shaking in his arms. The arrow flew wide and passed through the hood on the crick's head. The animal roared again. All the warriors stepped back, widening the circle. They poked at the enraged crick, but none of the attacks, save those by Egill, seemed legitimate.

Another guard, careless with his distance, shrieked after being scratched on his hand. He screamed as he fell to his knees. Murid watched as the man convulsed. White spittle frothed around his lips. Nobody seemed inclined to help the man as they continued to bait the crick with ineffective thrusts.

Hafoca appeared to lose any will to fight. He stood there with his bow in hand, but all arrows remained scattered at his feet.

"Hafoca! You have the only bow! Shoot her!" Murid shouted.

"We have her, King Hafoca," Egill said. "The shot is yours to take."

Hafoca grabbed an arrow, but his trembling fingers

couldn't secure it. It, along with the next two, fell back to the leaf-covered forest dirt.

"This is ridiculous," Murid said, more to herself than anyone else.

She sprinted past her two bodyguards and raced into the clearing where Hafoca shook with fear. Without a word, she snatched the bow from his hand. Then, she retrieved the arrows that Hafoca dropped. She ensured the guards still had the crick at bay. It looked like the same stalemate. She stabbed two arrows into the dirt and aimed with the third. Thankfully, the animal was taller than the warriors. She was clear to aim at its face.

Hafoca collapsed to his knees and covered his eyes. More than one warrior spared a glance in his direction as he detached himself from the moment. Murid calmed her breathing and focused on the space between the crick's eyes. She let the first arrow fly. Before she registered the roar of the animal, she fired again. Then, again. Murid moved to the next closest arrow behind her and grabbed it. When she turned back to her target, she heard cheers.

She watched as a dozen guards repeatedly stabbed the prone crick.

"Stop!" Egill shouted. "It's dead. Don't ruin the pelt and meat."

The warriors obeyed but kept their weapons raised, lest the crick proved more resilient than was physically possible. Hafoca stood and patted his leather armor.

"Well done. Our combined might felled the beast!" Hafoca boasted.

Murid clenched her teeth to keep from speaking.

Clearly the three arrows lodged inside the crick's brain were the reason it died, not the one absorbed by its ample blubber or the superficial wound to its hood. The faces of the surviving Vikisotes indicated everyone realized this. Hafoca's boasts were embarrassing to hear.

Hafoca grabbed his bow away from Murid.

"Thank you, my love. I believe this belongs in a man's hand," Hafoca said.

Egill cleared his throat. "King Hafoca, your hunt was successful. Your steady hand and keen eyesight killed the juvenile crick. Would you care to field dress it?"

Hafoca scowled before answering. When he spoke, his voice was pleasant, but Murid sensed his internal embarrassment.

"Yes, I *will* clean the young, as well as the mother. We all contributed to its death, but don't forget that I inflicted first blood. Its wound sapped its energy while my bride-to-be shared in this moment with me," Hafoca said.

Murid was impressed when nobody offered even the slightest snicker at a pathetic lie. She knew this man would never agree with fighting the Corlains. He was the epitome of a coward. She couldn't understand how she had ever respected him. It hurt her to know this man would be the father of her children. However, a coward was easily controlled. None of them may speak about it openly, but there would be whispers of what really happened. Because Hafoca would want them silenced, she'd have power over him. Since courage inspired the Vikisotes, she now had more sway over *them* as well. She only had to walk the narrow bridge between both camps.

Murid took Hafoca's head in her hands and kissed him passionately. Hafoca looked shocked at first but soon closed his eyes and enjoyed the tenderness of her lips. When they broke away, Murid faced the curious expressions of the Vikisotes.

"Thank you, King Hafoca, for giving me the greatest gift of overcoming my own fear. I was paralyzed in my terror when only you stood up to that monster. Seeing you put yourself in danger summoned my own courage. I understand now the respect you hold for life, as I know you will do everything in your power to save me."

Murid filled her voice with sweetness and affection. Some Vikisotes even looked like they believed her. Hafoca stared at her face. Murid wouldn't have thought it possible for him to love her more, but in that moment she knew he was securely wrapped around her finger.

"Please, my lord, show us how to remove the venom sac?" Murid asked.

Hafoca smiled. He stepped forward with the bravado he usually displayed. "Certainly, my love. The key to removing the venom we use in our poisons and medicine is to cut far away from the gland, like this."

Hafoca stabbed into the mother crick and flayed open her torso. He removed many organs and placed them inside separate pouches for that evening's dinner. He eventually removed a milky white organ and held it up for Murid to inspect.

"This is the poison?" Murid asked.

"Yes, like this it can kill within minutes," Hafoca answered.

Murid spared a glance at the two guards who had already succumbed to the poison. The time estimate was precise.

"However," Hafoca said, "we dilute it with water to multiply its uses. Many diseases can be cured if you drink a heavily diluted mixture. Assassins revel in a fifty percent mix. That gives them enough time to quickly escape before their target feels the first pangs of the end."

"Very interesting," Murid said.

"Yes, it is. We may not have the recipe for making the Corlains' black powder, but they must respect our crick venom. Too bad the animals don't live south of our border," Hafoca said.

"If we mixed the venom with fruit ferm, grape for example, could we kill many?" Murid asked.

Egill smiled as he apparently understood where she was going with this.

"Yes. Why, my love?" Hafoca asked.

"I'm just thinking aloud. It is wedding season, after all," Murid answered.

"The Mayor of Samburg will wed soon. Perhaps we should help the city celebrate," Egill said.

Hafoca ended his demonstration. "Samburg is in Tomeron."

"I believe it is," Murid answered with a smile.

"Tomeron is an ally of Corla," Hafoca said.

"Yes, my love, I believe you're right," Murid said.

Hafoca threw his hands up and shouted, "We are

not going to war! Guards, continue harvesting these animals. I suddenly feel the need to go home."

Murid frowned. She pushed Hafoca too far, too fast. It was best to let him calm down before trying again. Hafoca marched back to his horse like a petulant child. His ego was likely still bruised, but any repair she had provided was thrown away by yet another display of cowardice.

Egill grabbed Murid's arm. "May I speak with you for a moment, Princess Murid?"

Murid nodded. She allowed the Vikisote captain to lead her away from eavesdroppers.

"I know what you're trying to do," Egill said.

"I haven't hidden my intentions. Corla must pay. I'll get Hafoca to see that, I swear it," Murid said.

Egill held up his hands in defense. "I'm on your side. The Corlains are evil. They continue to claim more land, usually while stepping over the bodies of the men, women, and children who have the audacity to choose freedom over oppression."

"That's why good people need to stop them. Help me convince Hafoca that if we attack Samburg, others will rally behind us."

"Do you think you're Faida's hero? Are you buying into the prophecy?"

"What if I am? I survived a massacre. I even come from a foreign land. I should have died, but I'm still here. The gods have a plan for me. I *will* save this planet from tyranny."

"The gods' prophecy clearly states *he* will defeat a foreign army."

"So? I think we can agree, *King* Hafoca won't do anything."

Egill rubbed his temples. Murid had known for some time that the Vikisote champion rarely agreed with Hafoca and had even less faith in him as the new king.

"May I speak freely?" Egill asked.

"Of course, I respect candor."

"King Hafoca is a coward. He always has been. Even King Viktor knew this. It doesn't matter. He's king now. The gods chose his bloodline to rule, and we must respect that decision. I was hoping King Viktor would last long enough to pass on his courage to a grandson. Now, there aren't any strong leaders left."

"I'm here."

"You are," Egill agreed. "I know you have the courage King Hafoca lacks. The men do too. I wish the gods had put your soul into a man's body."

"Why do I have to be a man? You just said the men respected me."

"Wrong. I said they knew you were courageous. Courage can inspire. You can easily be the symbol we rally around and die for, but you will never lead the charge. Few warriors will accept the stigma of kneeling before a woman without a man."

"So, you'd rather be kept in Corlain chains with a king shackled to you than take their power away with me?"

Egill laughed. "Oh ho, so you're going to crush them now? Even if every Vikisote fought wholeheartedly for you, our numbers are nothing compared to Corla."

"The prophecy says I will. Faida believes in me, and she knows more about the gods than any other I've met."

"She does know a lot. I pray she's right about you, but we must be pragmatic. You'll be our queen. Perhaps, you can get King Hafoca to support our desires. If not, make sure he has an heir before he passes. If you're the mother of his child, you'll maintain the throne."

"Are you saying what I think you're saying?" Murid asked.

"I'm simply laying out the succession of the throne. You may not want to marry him, but you must. You must bed him. You must have his *sons*. That's how you'll contribute to the prophecy." Egill looked over his shoulder. The cricks were completely stripped clean and packed up. "We should go. The king is in a foul mood. I'm eager to get this silent trip over with."

Murid nodded and followed Egill back to her horse. His prediction of the quiet ride home was exact. Hafoca didn't utter a single word. Once they arrived back at their ring fortress, he immediately "escorted" her to her chambers. He jerked her arm as he practically threw her into the room.

"Why are you upset?" Murid asked.

She assumed a subservient persona. Hafoca would need his ego stroked if she was to keep her plan of attacking Samburg as an option.

"They all laugh at me because of your actions," Hafoca accused.

Murid walked toward Hafoca. He turned his head to avoid her eyes.

"No," Hafoca said.

"My love, look at me," Murid said.

She turned his head to face her, then she rested her hands on his shoulders.

"They're ashamed of me," Hafoca said.

"No, my love, they aren't. They were confused. We all were. In the heat of battle, it's hard to remain aware of all imperative information."

"They love you more than me," Hafoca said.

"That's not so. Even if it were, my love is for you alone. They'll prove their love for me by following your instructions."

"Sweet Murid, I love you, but you can be so naïve."

That makes two of us, Murid thought. "Why do you say that?"

"I already had too many warriors with me. I demanded we ambush a crick barely out of the womb. I cowered when the mother attacked. Three men lost their lives because of my actions. They all saw it. Word will spread. I'll sleep tonight a king and wake as a buffoon."

"Then change their minds before that impression takes root in their hearts and minds."

"How?"

Murid gave Hafoca a kiss. She allowed her mouth to linger on his, then whispered into his ear, "Give them a reason to believe you'll fight."

"We can't defeat Corla," Hafoca protested.

"No, we can't. Not yet, but the gods have decreed that eventually we will. We may not be able to defeat Corla, but we can easily take Samburg. Especially if we do it covertly. We have ample crick venom. I say we gift it to the mayor and his guests. Those in power wouldn't have it if they weren't Corlain sycophants. They serve their evil masters, so they deserve death."

"Assassinations are a tricky business. A wedding will make it easy to have collateral damage. We can't afford to turn the people against us by killing children."

"Of course not!" Murid shouted. "We aren't monsters. We poison the goblets on the head table. Perhaps the closest ones to it too. The greedy will die; the meek will just be witnesses."

"You ask too much of me. The wedding is a month away. We can't plan an attack in so little time."

"We can. I've been thinking about it for weeks already. We can make this happen."

Hafoca stared into Murid's eyes. She saw the fear that resided just beneath the surface. He was going to say *no*. She had one last gamble she could make.

"Consider it a wedding present."

Hafoca's gaze changed from fear and reluctance to immense joy.

"Do you mean that?"

"Yes. We'll have our wedding three nights before the mayor. That's plenty of time to begin our family. We wed, then we eliminate this one small target. It'll inspire those suffering near our borders. Then, I'll have some small justice. It'll keep me content while your son grows inside my womb."

Murid felt pity for Hafoca. His entire demeanor had changed as she fed him as much false hope as she dared. She would get this single ambush from him.

After that, she'd find a new way to entice him to give her a second attack. She may have been young, but she knew men were easily controlled by their carnal desires.

Hafoca kissed Murid passionately. She returned the kiss. Her worries surfaced as Hafoca began tearing her clothing. He clawed at the ties on the back of her dress. Murid allowed him this moment. To deny him now would ruin her plans. Just as quickly as it started, it ended. Hafoca pushed Murid away. She lost her balance and fell.

"What? What did I do?" Murid asked with genuine interest.

Hafoca rubbed his face in frustration. "I'm sorry. It wasn't you. It was me. I'm still in mourning, and we aren't wed. I've waited this long to be with you. I won't dishonor you or the gods by giving up weeks before we're joined. Enjoy your evening. We'll discuss your plan with Egill in the morning."

With that, Hafoca quickly left the room. Murid suspected his next stop would be to see one of his whores. She didn't care. She had her promise now. That promise would lead to an ambush; the first step in getting the justice denied her for the past fifteen years. Murid allowed herself a moment to fantasize about the fall of Corla.

CHAPTER 6

Two Dogs panted as he paddled deep into the Fraz River with his oar. For a week he'd been at it. They'd camp at night and dine on the tasty fish Mother Turklyo provided, but even magically enhanced strength had its limits. With the afternoon sun beating down on him, he would soon reach his.

"Do you need another break?" Swift Shot asked.

Two Dogs looked back at her. She showed concern. That was a bad sign. Her default state should have been to mock him on his "weakness." If she was offering the suggestion, he needed to double his efforts.

"I'm fine. It wouldn't be a problem at all if I didn't have to keep a barrier around the canoe. Every time I've dropped it, the dakydiles have reminded me why it was up in the first place."

"Mother Turklyo must have had an off day when she created those vile river monsters," Swift Shot joked before chuckling.

"Don't blaspheme," Ancestors' Hand said.

"Take it easy, Intakee, it was simply a joke," Two Dogs said.

Two Dog watched the dakydiles beneath the surface of the river. There were always a few following the canoe. They would strike occasionally, but Two Dogs' magic kept them from damaging the turklyo-skin keeping them afloat. At the moment, Two Dogs thought he saw at least three stalking his canoe.

Dakydiles were one of the world's ugliest creatures. That meant they had to be especially vicious. They usually stopped growing when they reached four feet, but at three hundred pounds, hunting them was difficult. Thick, reptilian scales served as effective armor. Even igsidian blades had difficulty piercing the vital organs beneath the hide. The head of a dakydile was unusual. It had a long beak that resembled a stork or a crane, but inside were hundreds of tiny teeth, serrated on both sides. Two Dogs remembered seeing a dakydile spear a large fish as a child. After it punctured the fish, two younger dakydiles swam to the first and quickly eviscerated the flesh. He wasn't sure if it was a mother feeding her young or just opportunistic poachers, but the vision of their lethality stayed with him. It was weeks before Owl Talon and Proud Wall could get him back on the river.

Two Dogs slowed his pace again. The current had picked up. Two Dogs had to reduce his magical speed to increase his strength. He was vocal with his breathing. Both Swift Shot and Ancestors' Hand shared a look of worry.

"I can handle it," Two Dogs lied.

"Remove your protective barrier," Ancestors' Hand said.

Two Dogs scoffed. "Intakee may not be aware of this, but dakydiles are rather aggressive. They'll swim below and pierce our canoe. We'll sink, and you'll be eaten. If I'm lucky, I'll get a barrier up around myself and float to the shore, where *I'll* be eaten. So, no, I won't be putting down my barrier."

"Trust me," Ancestors' Hand said. "We're closer to Intakee land than we are to Lacreechee. We have our own way of dealing with the dakydiles that doesn't require us to make our men beasts of burden. Observe."

Two Dogs and Swift Shot followed Ancestors' Hand's pointed finger. The murky brown water seemed lighter. Two Dogs focused harder and could see a large yellow glow. The water was too muddy to determine what monstrosity Ancestors' Hand had summoned, but clearly whatever it was, it had scared the dakydiles away.

"Perhaps there are *some* benefits to summoning magic," Swift Shot said.

Ancestors' Hand snorted and smirked. "You mean beyond raising an army to save your lives?"

"We were taught that summoning magic was easily corrupted. Nobody wanted to learn it and become a pariah," Swift Shot said.

"Who said I *wasn't* a pariah?" Ancestors' Hand asked.

She cackled to herself as she confirmed to Two Dogs that few people must care for this crazy Intakee woman.

"What exactly did you summon?" Two Dogs asked.

"Something bigger. I considered just making more dakydiles, but that likely would have led to the real dakydiles fighting with them. Now, they're a safe distance behind us," Ancestors' Hand answered.

"But they're still following us?" Swift Shot asked.

"Of course; this is *their* river. We just fish in it," Ancestors' Hand said.

"Two Dogs, take a break. The current is weak here. I can keep us heading north while you rest. Then, you can paddle again, but you'll only have to increase your strength. Ancestors' Hand will keep the dakydiles at bay," Swift Shot said.

Two Dogs nodded. He laid his oar inside the canoe and wiped sweat from his brow. Ancestors' Hand handed him a pouch of water. Two Dogs drank greedily from it.

"Because you aren't tired," Swift Shot joked.

Even Ancestors' Hand laughed at Two Dogs. He smiled and finished the half gallon of water she gave him.

"Ahhh," Two Dogs said. "I kind of like having women do the work for me while I just lie back and relax."

Two Dogs closed his eyes and smiled. Soon, he sat upright after a handful of river weed plopped onto his face. Two Dogs hacked as he frantically ripped the plants off his body. The two women laughed hysterically. In fact, the canoe drifted backward because Swift Shot stopped paddling.

"Very funny," Two Dogs said as he shared in the end of the laugh.

"We're almost there," Ancestors' Hand said. "I'm beginning to recognize the trees."

"Good. I don't enjoy being on the water this long. Lacreechee are meant for the plains and the forest," Two Dogs said.

"I'm afraid we're heading in the wrong direction for your plains, but you'll get plenty of forest. Perhaps even some mountains," Ancestors' Hand said.

"Unless it's a mountain of igsidian, I have no use for it. Whew!" Swift Shot said.

"Well spoken," Two Dogs agreed.

"The mountains are where brigands go to hide. They're the type of people we need to ally ourselves with if we desire a willing army to defeat the Corlains," Ancestors' Hand said.

"Why? Shouldn't the Intakee be able to summon their fallen warriors and build our army that way?" Two Dogs mocked.

"Don't assume your power rivals that of my tribe," Ancestors' Hand said. "We'll get my people to help, but we'll need cannon fodder too."

"*Cannon fodder*?" Two Dogs asked.

"You must have noticed the Corlains brought their cannons. They're too loud to miss," Ancestors' Hand said.

"That's the name of those long tubes? The ones with wheels?" Two Dogs asked.

"You Lacreechee are far too isolated. If you want to defeat your enemy, you must know him. Their black powder is their advantage. Muskets are the common tool they use, but their cannons can level villages, as you saw. Their enchanted armor protects, even from some of the gifts Mother Turklyo gave us."

"Can you teach us?" Swift Shot asked as she grimaced.

Two Dogs would soon have to take over again.

"Of course, I will. So will the rest of the Intakee. You'll need to bring a gift of igsidian," Ancestors' Hand said.

"We have two stones remaining," Two Dogs said. "They'll make fine spears for your warriors."

Ancestors' Hand nodded. "That'll be a fine gift."

"What can you tell us about the Corlains that we don't already know?" Two Dogs asked.

"For starters, don't fear their muskets. They're loud. They're deadly, but they're far from accurate. Unless a dozen of them line up shoulder to shoulder, you're of minor risk of any ball hitting you," Ancestors' Hand said.

"Muskets don't concern me," Two Dogs boasted.

"How much do you know of their armor then?" Ancestors' Hand asked.

"It's black as night, yet they can still see us," Swift Shot answered.

"It's only black when the stars shine. I told you, it's enchanted. As you probably saw the morning after the attack, it transitions into a reflective silver when Mother Turklyo's sun rises."

"I know this already, old woman. The red in their helmets allows them to see," Two Dogs said.

He pulled out the fragment of glass he took from the helmet and held it up for the women to see.

"Too bad it easily shatters when you try to remove it, huh?" Ancestors' Hand asked.

She cackled again as Two Dogs grabbed his oar.

"I need to paddle again. Listening to this hag babble is more tiresome than fighting the Fraz River."

Swift Shot sighed with relief as Two Dogs dipped his oar back into the river. He increased his strength and made two pulls before the serenity surrounding the boat vanished. The crack of muskets forced all three to search the eastern bank.

"There!" Swift Shot screamed.

She pointed at a plume of gunsmoke. Standing directly behind it were seven Corlains. They reloaded quickly and aimed a second time. Thankfully, their numbers were too few to blind them with a never-ending armor glare.

"Look out!" Ancestors' Hand screamed moments before they fired.

The glow beneath the water vanished. Two Dogs watched as Ancestors' Hand directed the spirits of small mammals and lizards killed along the river bank. Two Dogs thought he heard the Corlains laughing while they stomped on the apparitions or smashed them with the stocks of their muskets.

"I said *help*!" Swift Shot screamed.

The worry in her voice redirected Two Dogs' attention. Apparently, the two volleys were more accurate than he'd suspected. The canoe was taking on water. Ancestors' Hand and Swift Shot frantically bailed it.

"We'll be fine," Two Dogs said. "I'll get us out of here. Those holes won't sink us."

There was an old saying among the Lacreechee, "Never give Mother Turklyo a challenge." Two Dogs remembered this wisdom as the first beak of three dakydiles poked through the skin of their canoe. Thankfully, none of the passengers were wounded, but as the animals screamed, their mouths widened and tore large gashes into the canoe. The musket balls may have been manageable, but the dakydiles were about to turn inconvenience into a nightmare.

"Shit," Two Dogs muttered as he summoned a barrier around himself.

Swift Shot charged an arrow with ice magic. She shot at the water on the east side of the canoe. A small ice raft formed. The Lacreechee warrior quickly jumped onto it. It shifted under her weight and drifted to the east bank. Swift Shot briefly held her right hip. Ancestors' Hand halted her own jump as a dakydile passed between the ice raft and the canoe.

"I hope you can heal your own broken bones," Two Dogs said.

Before Ancestors' Hand could respond, he wrapped his strength-enhanced arms around her and chucked her to the waiting hands of Swift Shot. Ancestors' Hand landed harder than she probably wanted, but her grunt brought a quick smile to Two Dogs.

"Catch!" Two Dogs shouted.

He tossed the packs to Swift Shot. She caught them while Ancestors' Hand mended a sore ankle. A dakydile stabbed at Two Dogs' foot. His magic protected him. The dakydile swam away, but two more continued to thrash at the last remnants of the canoe. Two Dogs fell into the river.

He instinctively grabbed his tomahawk and knife. Both were still tucked inside his belt. His necklace was also present. Losing igsidian wasn't a problem he wanted to add to his list of issues.

The current swept Two Dogs past the ice raft. They were floating back toward the waiting Corlains. Ancestors' Hand must have been too distracted by her injury to summon more spirit animals. Swift Shot was distracted by the dakydiles smashing holes into the ice. She had to concentrate to fill them with new ice the moment they appeared. She left her back exposed to the real enemy. The Corlains had ample time to aim at both women on the ice raft.

Two Dogs increased his strength. He felt a dakydile clawing at his magical barrier. The animal's persistence gave him an idea. Two Dogs grabbed the scaly tail of the dakydile and flung it out of the water toward the waiting Corlains.

The soldiers were caught unaware. There was no reason for them to anticipate an attack like this. The men screamed like young children as the dakydile proved it was an efficient hunter on land as well as in the water. Six of the Corlains fired their muskets into the back of the dakydile. The seventh was too busy screaming as the animal tore chunks of his leg free.

Two Dogs increased his strength and speed as he swam to the bank behind the distracted Corlains. Two were dead by the time Two Dogs reached them. The other five were using their muskets as clubs to beat the frenzied dakydile. Two Dogs' tomahawk and knife glowed orange as he attacked the nearest two Corlains. One took a knife deep into his spine. The other convulsed as Two Dogs put a foot onto his back to help remove the tomahawk from his skull.

The remaining Corlains turned toward Two Dogs. One struggled with an attack from behind by the still angry dakydile. The other two fell when an arrow briefly poked through each's neck before vanishing. The return arrows appeared in Swift Shot's quiver as she and Ancestors' Hand set foot on the bank.

The Corlains were dead, but Two Dogs still had an enraged and wounded dakydile to deal with. The animal appeared to sense the massive threat that three of Mother Turklyo's children represented. It hissed at Two Dogs and his companions.

"This is your chance to leave," Two Dogs said to the dakydile. "Consider it a professional courtesy among Corlain killers."

The dakydile hissed again. Its muscles tensed as it gave the sign it intended to spring at someone. Swift Shot fired an arrow that sparked when it hit the dirt in front of the dakydile. She continued to do this until the dakydile was corralled back toward the river. It entered the water and allowed the current to take it away. All three combatants let out a sigh of relief as the serenity of the forest overtook them once more.

"Is everyone alright?" Two Dogs asked.

"Yes," Swift Shot answered.

"Now that I have a moment to heal my ankle, I should be fine," Ancestors' Hand said.

Two Dogs kicked the body of a dead Corlain over. The left shoulder of the plate armor had a black cloud painted on it with yellow bolts of lightning sticking out.

"The Black Cloud Division," Ancestors' Hand said.

She spat on the ground to show her distaste for the infamous unit.

"None are as evil or barbaric as these bastards," Ancestors' Hand said.

"Why are they here?" Swift Shot asked.

"Chasing after us?" Two Dogs suggested.

"No." Ancestors' Hand shook her head. "If they were tracking us, they would have engaged before now. They'd have come with more too. This is something else."

Two Dogs unfastened the leather belt around one of the bodies. He rifled through the pouches and dumped their contents. Musket balls, black powder, bandages, then some igsidian fell out. All three looked at the small stones and their implication. These weren't the rough stones found on the head of a turklyo. These stones were expertly cut and polished.

"No!" Ancestors' Hand screamed.

She sprinted, as much as a woman in her sixties could, northeast of their position. Two Dogs and Swift Shot shared a look of concern before following the Intakee woman. She had already said she recognized the trees. Two Dogs realized the only possible conclusion. Minutes after leaving the bank, Ancestors' Hand wailed and confirmed what the Lacreechee already knew.

Two Dogs and Swift Shot emerged from the forest into a clearing. What should have been a vibrant sign of Intakee village life was instead misery for Ancestors' Hand. Smoke still spiraled off the remains of tipis, canoes, and people. Charred skeletons smoldered in the center of the clearing. Piles of igsidian-free clothing accumulated everywhere.

Ancestors' Hand fell to her knees and bawled. The Lacreechee gave her the space to mourn. Two Dogs' heart was too raw to allow her sorrow to affect him. He realized he left the bodies of his community where they fell a week earlier. There was no doubt in his mind that his own village now looked exactly like this one. Swift Shot pulled him in for a hug as she sniffed.

"Ancestors' Hand?" a weak voice asked.

Two Dogs searched for the source of the question. Tied to a tree was a young woman. Her tattered clothes hung from her body. Frantic hands must have yanked her igsidian free. Tear tracks stained the woman's face. Her eyes were puffy, her voice hoarse.

"Scarlet Turtle!" Ancestors' Hand shouted.

She rushed to the woman. Two Dogs and Swift Shot followed. Two Dogs drew his knife and cut the Intakee woman free. She collapsed into Ancestors' Hand's waiting arms. She gripped the elderly Intakee woman firmly and cried into her chest. Ancestors' Hand stroked her back.

"Scarlet Turtle, I'm going to make you better," Ancestors' Hand said.

Scarlet Turtle shook her head. "They made me drink something. I don't know what it was, but I hear

Mother Turklyo calling for me. I miss my husband. I miss my children. I don't want you to reverse what those bastards did."

Ancestors' Hand swallowed. She blinked repeatedly and stared at the sky.

"If that's what you wish," Ancestors' Hand quietly said.

"It is," Scarlet Turtle confirmed.

"Before Mother Turklyo greets you, can you tell us if there are any more Corlains?" Two Dogs asked.

Ancestors' Hand shot a nasty look at him. It may have been a callous question, but the information may save their lives.

"No," Scarlet Turtle barely whispered. "They left earlier today. Only a few remained."

"How did they defeat an entire tribe of Mother Turklyo's children?" Two Dogs asked.

He already knew the answer. His tribe experienced the same gruesome fate. He'd convinced himself that he'd destroyed the only cannons the Corlains had. Ancestors' Hand's words and a second burning village contradicted his belief.

Scarlet Turtle ignored the question. Her fragile body shook as her voice became weaker. "They have spies every..."

Scarlet Turtle couldn't finish her sentence. Her body went limp as her voice trailed off. Ancestors' Hand held the young woman to her bosom and wailed again. Swift Shot grabbed Two Dogs' shoulder and led him away.

"Give her a moment," Swift Shot said.

Two Dogs nodded. "So much for our army."

Swift Shot dug into the backpack that Two Dogs wore. She pulled out the igsidian stones shaped for a pair of spears.

"What do you plan to do with those?" Two Dogs asked.

"You'll see," Swift Shot coyly said. "I was given an expensive gift. You deserve one as well."

Two Dogs raised an eyebrow as he canted his head toward her. He watched as Swift Shot placed both hands on the grassy soil beneath her. She scooped a handful of dirt in each hand and slapped her palms together. Dirt spilled back to the ground. Swift Shot pressed her hands firmly together and pulled them apart as wide as she could stretch. As her palms separated, a long shaft of wood formed. It looked like Glostaimian Fir, a wood as light as it was strong. Swift Shot fell to her ass and gasped.

"Impressive," Two Dogs admitted.

Swift Shot gasped again. "I'm . . . not done . . . yet."

Swift Shot held one of the igsidian stones to an end of the smooth shaft she created. Her igsidian burned so brightly that Two Dogs had to look away. She must have repeated this step with the second stone, because when Two Dogs looked back at her, she offered him a weapon.

The two igsidian stones stretched several inches from each end of the four-foot long shaft. Two Dogs admired how smooth the gift was. He spun it around his body as he practiced a few simple slashes and thrusts.

Two Dogs stabbed his doubled-tipped spear into the ground as Swift Shot fell again in complete exhaustion.

"Are you okay?" Two Dogs asked.

Swift Shot nodded. "Now I know why they say not to craft materials from magic. I feel like you must have when you had to swim against the current of the Fraz. Maybe even after you earned your second eagle feather?"

Two Dogs smiled briefly. "This makes us even. Don't overexert yourself, especially when we're sitting on the remains of a recent battle with the Corlains."

Swift Shot nodded again. She closed her eyes and soon fell asleep. Two Dogs watched his friend as she snored louder than any man he'd ever known.

Ancestors' Hand approached him. She no longer looked sorrowful. Instead, pure hatred flared in her eyes. She stared at the spear next to Two Dogs.

"That's a warrior's weapon," she said with a nod. "Only the ultimate man should have something like that. Do you still believe Mother Turklyo hasn't chosen you? Why else would she spare your friend to gift this weapon?"

Two Dogs ignored the talk of the alleged augury. "What do we do now?"

"We get answers," Ancestors' Hand responded. "Samburg is northeast of here, just below the mountains that border Vikisoteland. Loyalties to Corla are strong among the city's elite, but the commoners have much to complain about. We'll go there and find allies."

Two Dogs tugged at his igsidian-encrusted shirt. "Dressed like this? You know the Corlains will strip us of our igsidian the moment they see us. They'll steal the gifts that belong to Mother Turklyo's chosen people."

"That's why we'll cover ourselves. Once your friend is rested, we'll go hunting. There are some of Mother Turklyo's other blessings that will sacrifice their coats to us. We'll make cloaks out of these gifts. Inside Samburg, we'll stick to the shadows and listen. Anyone who can help us won't want to inform the Corlains of our igsidian. We'll find the right friends there, then we'll kill our enemies."

"I like the part about killing Corlains."

"I figured you would. We'll kill the mayor and his cronies. Corla is an arrogant country. They'll send soldiers to determine why communication is lost. With each new unit that arrives, your legend will grow. Many will want to bask in the glory that Mother Turklyo provides you."

Two Dogs waved her off. She talked too much about things he didn't believe in, but he hadn't lied. He liked the part about killing Corlains.

CHAPTER 7

A **Corlain skirmisher** plunged his spear into the dead body of a fallen rebel. As the smoke cleared from the burnt gunpowder, Githinji could watch as the melee soldiers who defended the flanks of his riflemen moved forward and sent the wounded either to a prisoner collection point or on to a personal meeting with the deity of their choosing.

Githinji sat upon his horse. His armor shone brightly, but this nuisance didn't bother the other Corlains. Githinji smiled as more than one rebel prisoner closed his eyes to avert himself from the annoyance of the shine. Those brave enough to face the glare showed their distaste as they passed Githinji. The blue hackle on his helmet identified him as the general who crushed their pitiful attack. These people would be forced to recognize the will of Corla. Githinji would see to it personally.

"Sir, we have the leaders assembled," a colonel

said.

Githinji looked at the man. Like all Corlains, he had a full helmet, but the red hackle identified him as a commander of troops. The black cloud emblem on his shoulder had two lightning bolts, indicating he was from second brigade. If this was the second brigade commander, that meant *her* name was Zoya.

"Thank you, Colonel. Take me to them," Githinji answered.

Githinji dismounted and adjusted the sword and pistol secured to his belt. Zoya led Githinji to a collection of men and women kneeling together, their hands secured behind them. Many wept, some hurled curses; most were simply quiet. Githinji smiled beneath his helmet. Cowards always tried to remain silent, as if his eyes no longer worked.

"I am Githinji, general of the Black Cloud Division. I'm here to pass judgment on you for your crimes against Corla."

The prisoner closest to Githinji spat on him. It was a mucus-filled glob that landed on Githinji's knee. Githinji ignored the snot. He casually drew his sword and stabbed it through the man's throat until his chin bumped into the cross-guard. The man gurgled momentarily and died. Some prisoners shrieked. Nearly all wept after they saw what happened to their comrade.

"As I was saying, I'm Githinji. You've committed crimes against Corla on its frontier lands. I'm here to bring order to the chaos you revel in."

The rebel leaders wept and wailed. They begged for forgiveness. They showed how weak they really were. It insulted Githinji that men like this were his enemy. Corla wasted his military genius on dogs. As he continued to speak, he motioned for his executioners to line up behind the six remaining leaders. The begging increased in hysteria.

"Die like soldiers!" Githinji shouted.

It had the opposite effect. The rebel leaders proved they were inferior in every way to Corlains.

"You disgust me. I was going to inform you that your deaths were honorable because we recognized the charisma each of you had to lead this rabble. Now, I'm just killing you because you've embarrassed yourselves."

Githinji motioned with his finger. The executioners immediately stabbed each leader between their shoulder blades. The rebel leaders uttered their last pitiful cries and fell to the ground. Their blood soaked into the dirt, but Githinji was already moving to a new group of rebels. These were the subordinate soldiers. Githinji knew that after seeing their leaders die like animals, many of the common people would gladly share the secrets they knew. Collectively, this data would combine to give Githinji the answer to where to strike next.

A folding table was brought before the rebels. A map of this part of the continent was placed on the table. Githinji stood to one side of it and gestured for the rebels to move in closer. None seemed willing to move, but Githinji's soldiers yanked them to their feet and pushed them toward the table. The rebels fell and cried but quickly scampered to stand and approach the table.

"This, as you know, is a map of our world. As you

can see, Corla takes up most of it. People like you want to stop this progress for mankind. I've been tasked to end this rebellion. It will be much easier for all parties involved if you just pointed out who I should kill next," Githinji said.

"How about your mother's ugliest bastard?" one rebel mocked.

The man's head left his shoulders before he could ever hear any support from his companions. Zoya wiped her sword clean before returning her blade to her scabbard. That was what Githinji loved about his soldiers. They not only knew their place, but they could anticipate his orders. The same couldn't be said for other Corlain commanders. Perhaps if those in power recognized Githinji's value to Corlain society, that would change. At least he had duty in the frontier. The land smelled, and the people lived like animals, but he never ran out of military "challenges."

"I should probably have started by saying that your lives mean nothing to me. I'll kill each of you and sleep soundly tonight because I won't have to listen to you bawl like children denied a favorite toy. However, I'll sleep just as soundly if you're in my prison. The choice is yours. Give me the information I want, or I'll let you tell it to my interrogators instead. I'll let you guess which method involves more pain."

Githinji tapped the handle of the pistol on his right hip. He laughed internally as more than one rebel focused on it. He almost wanted to toss it to them and see what they would do if given a weapon. Likely, they would disappoint him.

"Milord?" a man said as he timidly raised a hand.

"Don't do it, Aron," another said.

With a nod, Githinji instructed Zoya to execute the second speaker. After another round of shock and misery, Githinji addressed the first man.

"You were saying?"

The man hobbled around the table and pointed to a section of the map deep within Vikisoteland.

"King Hafoca married his fiancée just last night. She very much wants to kill Corlains. Warriors are flocking to his banner," the rebel said.

"How many warriors does he have?" Githinji asked.

"I don't have my numbers, milord, but when I was last there, the warriors filled the barracks inside their ring fortress."

Idiot. Another reason these people needed stern education. The Corlain way was the only way. Githinji looked at Zoya and hoped she had an estimate based on this moron's description.

"Hafoca has one of the larger fortresses. If his barracks are full, he likely has over four thousand warriors," Zoya answered his unspoken question.

Githinji sighed. These people couldn't even pull together an army to meet his division on equal ground. How could they ever hope to defeat the entire Corlain military when they had zero chance of facing the Black Cloud?

"You should all thank your friend. Between his statement and your combined stench, I've decided to spare the rest of you."

A collective sigh sprang from the group of rebels. Some even blessed Githinji in the names of their heathen gods.

"Take these *people* away." Githinji dismissed the prisoners with the flick of his wrist. "Zoya, a moment."

Zoya approached her general. "Yes, sir?"

"How long until we can reach Hafoca's ring fortress?"

"Vikisoteland will take about two weeks to travel to. That, of course, is if we push the soldiers hard."

"Are you saying we shouldn't?"

"I am, sir. We've fought many skirmishes over the past two months. The soldiers are getting restless. They need a break and we need supplies."

"I hope you've come with solutions to our problems?"

"Of course, sir. We should head to Samburg. The mayor there will marry in a few nights. We could make it there in time to partake in the celebration. A little ferm and some warm bodies will go a long way with morale."

Githinji considered Zoya's suggestion. "How many days do you propose we rest?"

"No more than a week, sir. That'll be plenty. By that point the troops will be anxious to kill more rebels."

"Make it happen, and let the soldiers know it was your idea."

"Yes, sir," Zoya said.

Githinji spun on his heels and headed for his tent. He undressed from his armor. He soothed his brawn by rubbing oil into his skin to smooth the calluses that had formed. His body was muscular. He allowed a moment to admire his muscles in the full-length mirror. Despite his decades of service, he was *still* the best the Corlains had to offer. He would gain victory by crushing all rebels. This would ensure his ascendancy through the ranks.

Githinji laid his head down on the plush pillow laying on his soft mattress. He allowed himself to fall asleep.

Hours later, Githinji woke in the middle of the night. His armor was cold and black, but Githinji threw it back on. He exited his tent and searched for the prisoners he had spared earlier.

They huddled inside a few prison wagons. Their snoring surprised Githinji. How easily they'd forgotten the plight they were in hours earlier. Four guards approached Githinji.

"Something I can do for you, sir?" the sergeant asked.

"Yes," Githinji said. "You can keep these prisoners from escaping."

"Sir?"

"One of them must have been a sneaky Namerian, because all four wagons just burned down," Githinji said.

The sergeant nodded. He pointed at his soldiers. They grabbed jugs of oil and poured it through the metal bars.

"It's a shame. I wanted them to stand trial,"

Githinji said.

The sergeant threw a torch onto the nearest prison wagon. They were close enough to each other that soon they all burned. Githinji barely recognized the screams as he marched back to his inviting bed. True to his word, he slept great.

CHAPTER 8

"**On your left!**" Swift Shot shouted, rolling to avoid an attack.

Two Dogs dove to the right as a yellow ethereal wolf snapped at his ankle. Two arrows flew through the wispy adversary. Both the wolf and the arrows disappeared. The arrows returned to Swift Shot's quiver; the wolf rested again in the afterlife.

"Excellent shot," Ancestors' Hand praised.

Two Dogs and Swift Shot had vanquished another wave of Ancestors' Hand's apparitions. Their skills were already acute, but this level of realism ensured their combat prowess remained as sharp as the igsidian that made their blades.

"You don't have anything bigger than that, old woman?" Two Dogs challenged.

"Summoning spirits isn't as simple as making your body more resilient. I must search for the souls, identify that they would have been an ally in life, and give them a purpose to act on our behalf. You try doing that in the span of three seconds," Ancestors' Hand said.

"I just heard a lot of excuses," Two Dogs said.

Swift Shot stifled a giggle.

It's good to know she's still on my side, Two Dogs thought.

Swift Shot and Ancestors' Hand were becoming strong friends. Each having saved the other's life created a bond that only warriors understood. Two Dogs had the same bond with Swift Shot, but sometimes he wondered if the Intakee woman was trying to steal his last remaining friend.

"You do realize I can only summon a spirit if it died in the immediate area?" Ancestors' Hand asked.

"So?" Two Dogs said.

Swift Shot laid a calming hand on Two Dogs' shoulder. "We're in the middle of nowhere. How many wild animals do you suppose died in this exact field?"

"Over the millennia? I'd assume . . . a lot," Two Dogs answered.

"And if my power worked across that length of time, you'd be right to criticize me. Anything longer than a month or two will be too corrupted to use as an ally," Ancestors' Hand said.

"Well, thank you then, for proving that being a protector is the best magical school for Mother Turklyo's children," Two Dogs said.

A snowball hit him in the back of the head. He tensed as the slush slipped beneath his shirt. He patted frantically to try to help it along its path. Swift Shot and Ancestors' Hand shared a laugh at his expense while he executed his dance.

"That was a dirty trick," Two Dogs said while pointing an accusing finger at Swift Shot.

The Lacreechee woman held up her hands and feigned innocence. "What? That was a freak whim of Mother Turklyo. One of her rogue snowballs."

Ancestors' Hand laughed again. Two Dogs redirected his gaze on the old Intakee woman. The moment he turned from facing Swift Shot a second "rogue" snowball hit him in the same spot. He twirled and charged Swift Shot.

"Devil woman!"

Swift Shot defended herself by sending an endless supply of snowballs at Two Dogs. He increased his speed and reflexes. He easily dodged the icy spheres. Occasionally, he plucked a snowball out of the air and hurled it back at Swift Shot. When the first one connected with her face, she showed outrage, but soon the two Lacreechee warriors were laughing as they had an impromptu snowball fight in the middle of summer.

"Children, behave," Ancestors' Hand eventually said.

It was the wrong choice of words. The Lacreechee called a momentary truce as they stared at the third member of their party. Ancestors' Hand held her palms toward the Lacreechee. She backed away as she protested.

"Don't even think of it. I'm too old for these types of games."

Two Dogs and Swift Shot slowly advanced on Ancestors' Hand. Each held a pair of snowballs that were rapidly becoming liquid.

"I'm warning you. I have bigger animals I can sic on you."

Two Dogs and Swift Shot continued to walk toward her.

"Just . . . not the face," Ancestors' Hand said.

Two Dogs agreed to the terms. He chucked both snowballs. They were mostly water and spread as they left his fingers. Ancestors' Hand yelped as the icy water hit her chest. Swift Shot's snowballs had been re-frozen before she threw them. They exploded in powder as they collided with Ancestors' Hand's arms.

"Do you feel better now?" Ancestors' Hand asked as she wiped the residual snow from her body.

"I kind of do," Two Dogs admitted.

A snowball exploded after colliding with the back of his head.

"Okay, now I've got it out of my system," Swift Shot said.

"Good, because we're close to arriving at Samburg," Ancestors' Hand said.

Two Dogs instantly became serious. "How much farther?"

"Only a few more hours. Three or four at most," Ancestors' Hand answered. "We should wear our new cloaks from here on out. We're avoiding the roads, but you never know when a shepherd will decide to take his flock the long way home."

"Maybe I should scout ahead. I'll make sure the way's clear," Two Dogs suggested.

"I know you want to be the hero in your own story,

but I think it's better if we all stay together," Swift Shot said.

"I agree with her. The chosen one of the augury shouldn't be alone," Ancestors' Hand said.

Two Dogs rolled his eyes but kept his comments to himself. "Lead the way, then."

Two Dogs followed Ancestors' Hand and Swift Shot, continuing their journey to Samburg. Ancestors' Hand was correct in her estimate. Barely two hours later, the three entered the west gate. They each wore long brown cloaks that fully covered their ethnic clothing. Each kept their hood up and their eyes down as they passed Corlain soldiers guarding the entrance. Squads of Corlains marched throughout the city. Two Dogs gripped his weapons more than once as they passed the patrols. Fortunately, he could barely conceal his new spear within the lengths of his cloak.

"I feel exposed," Two Dogs whispered.

"That's because we are," Swift Shot responded.

The city was bustling with energy. Nobody seemed to care about the three strangers in foreboding clothing as they rushed about their tasks. Everywhere Two Dogs looked he saw banners and flowers. He couldn't read the strange Corlain language, but his instincts told him the Corlains were celebrating. It sickened him that these people were so happy while his people were likely ash by this point. His disgust multiplied tenfold when he noticed not everyone in the city was Corlain.

"They're actually helping the Corlains?" Swift Shot whispered.

Two Dogs faced Ancestors' Hand to consider her

eyes before she answered. The woman looked equally disgusted.

"Many of them look like Azca. I'd like to believe they're refugees, but smiles rarely accompany the downtrodden forced out of their homes," Ancestors' Hand said.

"Didn't any of these people learn about what happened to the Belloots?" Two Dogs asked.

The Belloots were a shunned people among the true children of Mother Turklyo. Before the Corlains controlled most of Glostaimia, the Belloots lived on the land southeast of the Lacreechee, even farther away than the Azca. The Belloots met the Corlains first when they claimed to come in peace. The Belloots were too trusting. They took pity on the weary travelers. The Corlains repaid that generosity by taking everything they had. The Belloots made the fatal error of showing the Corlains their igsidian. Months later, the Belloots no longer existed, and the Corlains were spreading across the continent. Two Dogs sneered at the foolish Azcas making the same mistake now. No wonder they lost their lands. At least the Lacreechee fought the Corlains to a victory when the invaders came.

Swift Shot spat on the ground at the mention of the Belloots. "The traitors turned on Mother Turklyo. They deserve their misery."

"It's not just Azcas here. I see at least three other tribes. Wait . . . that group there looks like they're Shahonist," Ancestors' Hand said.

"Not a single stone among them. Where is their honor? You couldn't force me to live without my magic," Two Dogs claimed.

"It looks like the mayor's wedding will soon begin. The Corlains will move to their chapel. Any servants milling around will be our best chance at finding allies here," Ancestors' Hand said. "It would probably be best to take a seat in the mud with our hands cupped and our eyes down."

"Why?" Two Dogs asked.

"The Corlains require something called *coins* to get goods. They don't work as one people for the betterment of the tribe. Corlain victims sit like that to ask for some of these coins. It's the easiest way to become invisible," Ancestors' Hand answered.

Ancestors' Hand led them to a small stable. It overlooked the tables being arranged for a reception after the marriage ceremony. Two Dogs sniffed as the manure of various animals assaulted his sense of smell. The answer to why the air was so pungent revealed itself as Two Dogs sat in piles of droppings.

"The many things we do for Mother Turklyo," Ancestors' Hand joked.

Two Dogs and his companions waited in relative silence. At least he could finally set his spear behind him instead of walking stiffly with it tucked under his cloak. The sun slowly set as they sat in filth. It was a dehumanizing experience. Two Dogs' hatred for the Corlains grew. Despite not needing these *coins* that Ancestors' Hand spoke of, Two Dogs couldn't stomach the fact they hadn't received any. Not even the old woman of the group. Two Dogs made it a point to stare into the eyes of the Corlains as they passed on their way to the ceremony. Most were blatant in their desire to pretend not to see them. The few who mistakenly afforded a glance quickly looked away when Two Dogs' deep brown eyes fixed them with a fierce stare. Some offered an apology or excuse in their vile trade language that Two Dogs hated. Visitors had been rare to his tribe, but Owl Talon and Bright Stone were adamant that the younger generations learn to communicate with their enemy.

Faint chanting eventually drifted from the *chapel*, another unfamiliar word that Ancestors' Hand taught him. The incantation bothered Two Dogs, but he had to admit the music was lovely. The sweet sounds of unfamiliar instruments surrounded him until Swift Shot nudged his arm.

"Look at that," she said.

Two Dogs focused his gaze. In the center of the town, rows of elaborate tables and chairs were arranged. Plates and goblets were placed with distinct planning. Two Dogs was about to ask Swift Shot for clarity when he recognized her intent.

Servants who hadn't been there all day poured liquid into the goblets at the most prestigious tables. At first, Two Dogs believed they were simply bringing out the ferm early, then he paid more attention. The men and one woman were pouring a small amount of a liquid into the goblets, then swirling the cups. They wiped the insides with the cloth napkins provided. Their behavior plainly indicated they were trying to be nonchalant. They probably shouldn't have brought a woman with bright red hair, a feature Two Dogs had never seen before.

Two Dogs allowed himself additional time to consider this woman with the unusual hair. She was young, likely barely into her twenties. She had a small body that many men would appreciate. Despite the men who clearly came with her, she looked to be the one in charge. Something about this woman commanded Two Dogs' attention.

"They're Vikisotes," Ancestors' Hand whispered. "At least the men are. I don't know where that woman calls home."

"Do the Vikisotes have any alliance with the Corlains?" Swift Shot asked.

"No," Ancestors' Hand answered. "The Vikisotes have suffered at the hands of the Corlains. They used to have many apothecaries across Glostaimia, but the Corlains have killed the healers and destroyed the medicine."

"Why are the Corlains so cruel?" Two Dogs asked.

He needed this answer.

"Sick people are easily controlled. When a leader can heal a young child, the parents will do anything to ensure precious medicine is received," Ancestors' Hand answered.

Two Dogs adjusted his cloak. His igsidian glowed as he firmly gripped his weapons. He wanted to kill the mayor and all the Corlains celebrating with him. These people had no right to their happiness when it was built on the suffering of so many.

"We should speak with the Vikisotes," Swift Shot said.

"I agree. They'll leave once their trap is set," Two Dogs said.

Two Dogs stood, but Ancestors' Hand grabbed him and pulled him back down.

"Stay seated. The mayor is returning," she said.

Two Dogs remained silent as he watched the Samburg elite walk in two files to their seats. The mayor and his bride were each dressed in purple. The remaining guests were in fancy outfits that looked far too uncomfortable to be practical. It took all of Two Dogs' discipline not to rush his enemy. They wouldn't be a match for him, not in those clothes with ceremonial weapons.

Two Dogs searched for the redheaded woman. He expected to find her and her people to be quietly moving toward the nearest exit. Instead, they were positioning themselves around the tables. Their backs were always close to a location that looked prime for hiding a weapon. The men poured something into their hands and rubbed the liquid into their skin. Surprisingly, the woman didn't, even when offered a little.

"Are they seriously going to attack too?" Swift Shot asked.

"It looks like it," Two Dogs said.

"How can you tell?" Ancestors' Hand asked.

"Trust us. A warrior can sense an approaching battle. The fact that those lazy Corlain bastards can't tells me everything I need to know about them."

The mayor stood from his seat. He looked at his beautiful bride and raised his glass.

"I'd like to thank you all for attending my wedding.

I've searched many years for the perfect spouse, the woman who is my better in every aspect of the word. We're dressed in purple to represent the royal status our relationship has, but I think we all know this kingdom only has a queen."

The guests laughed as if it was a hilarious joke. Two Dogs was still trying to decipher if the people were already drunk on ferm or simply being polite when the mayor spoke again.

"I would be remiss if I didn't offer special thanks to our guests, the Black Cloud and their astounding commander, Githinji."

Several men and women stood as the guests applauded once more. The leader was a fearsome-looking man, but without his armor, he wouldn't be a threat. Once again, Two Dogs had to force himself to relax the hold he had on his weapons.

"To my lovely bride," the mayor said as he lifted his goblet higher.

The other guests repeated the toast and swallowed a sip from their goblets. The Vikisotes pulled weapons from the barrels and haystacks surrounding the tables. They quickly threw on leather armor and strapped swords and daggers to their waists. Several grabbed bows and nocked arrows. They executed their tasks with efficient precision. Clearly, they'd spent days practicing the proper order of their attack. The Corlains may have noticed, but many were frightened by why the mayor, his bride, and those at the nearest tables to them were foaming at the mouth and convulsing. Two Dogs was unsure whether he was upset that the Black Cloud soldiers weren't consuming alcohol or relieved. After all, poisoned men couldn't fight him on the battlefield.

"Sound the alarm!" Githinji shouted.

Bells clamored as the Black Cloud formed a circle around Githinji. He allowed them to escort him away. Swift Shot aimed an arrow at the Black Cloud commander, but Ancestors' Hand pulled her arms down.

"No, you fool. We need to get out of here while we can," she said.

"We should help them," Two Dogs argued.

"We will. We'll help the survivors, but these fools are sending a message, not trying to win a battle," Ancestors' Hand said.

"She's right," Swift Shot said.

Two Dogs nodded. "She is."

Two Dogs, Swift Shot, and Ancestors' Hand rose from their disgusting positions. They each grabbed their weapons and stepped toward the east gate. Two Dogs' conscience protested with each footstep. He continued to observe the battle and offered emotional support to the Vikisotes.

The woman seemed to know her way around a sword. The Black Cloud soldiers may have retreated, but Samburg had its own force. Their armor was just as black and enchanted, but the soldier facing the redhead quickly discovered that sometimes plate armor was a burden that a nimble opponent could exploit. She ducked the swing of a halberd and shifted to the soldier's right side and thrust with her sword. Her blow stabbed into the man's armpit. She pressed the front of her shield against her pommel and pushed. Several inches of her blade burrowed into the man. She kicked his ribs once and forced his dead body into the table behind him.

A Corlain soldier with a sword charged the woman from behind. She seemed distracted by another two soldiers coming from her front. Two Dogs winced as he prepared himself to watch this fascinating woman die. Swift Shot must have been just as enamored, because the man briefly had an arrow sticking out of his neck before it disappeared.

"I saw her first," Two Dogs joked.

Swift Shot smiled and nodded.

The woman was unaware she was just saved from death, but an older Vikisote seemed to offer the slightest of nods toward the Lacreechee. His attention soon went back to battling the three Corlains opposing him. His axe was swift as it battered the lesser men.

The walls surrounding the city were high. Two Dogs looked up as Corlain soldiers with muskets lined the building. They aimed at the remaining Vikisotes and fired. Most of them missed, but some found their mark. At least four Vikisotes died, others had wounds, but one man apparently claimed priority.

"Save the King!" the grizzled axe-wielding Vikisote shouted.

He and the redhead grabbed a man writhing in pain. The soldiers on the walls reloaded. The Vikisotes had no chance of surviving this. Two Dogs decided to change that fate.

"Swift Shot, I need you to blow the guards off the walls," Two Dogs commanded.

"What happened to meeting them later?" she asked.

"There won't be a later if we don't do something. Now shoot!" Two Dogs shouted.

Swift Shot obeyed. She enhanced her arrows with tornado blasts of wind. Many guards on the north wall launched over the far side. Their screams perished beneath the next volley of musket shots. Thankfully, Two Dogs had erected a magical barrier over the woman and the wounded man who meant so much to her. The Vikisotes closest to her were spared a similar fate.

"We're making ourselves into targets," Ancestors' Hand warned.

"Let them come," Two Dogs responded. "Swift Shot, keep them down."

Swift Shot continued to fire her arrows. She alternated among the walls. The soldiers on top were no longer inclined to fight. They were obviously inexperienced with a magical battle.

"The Vikisotes are heading for the north gate. If we don't leave now, we'll lose them in the wilderness," Swift Shot said.

"Give the Corlains something to worry about here," Two Dogs said.

Swift Shot nodded and fired arrows of fire into the hay set aside for the livestock. It didn't take long for the fear of a burning city to trump all other concerns.

"Let's go," Ancestors' Hand said.

Two Dogs grabbed his spear and ran toward the east gate. He allowed one last look. The city was burning, a statement was made, but Two Dogs swallowed as he saw the frightened eyes on the bodies of dead children. Two Dogs wasn't sure how they died, but it reminded him of seeing the Corlain cannons decimate Proud Wall and the children he was protecting. It even reminded him of the Corlain drummer boy. Some guests killed by the Vikisote poison looked more like victims than warriors. Two Dogs knew in his heart that these people stole from Mother Turklyo. He also knew the only reason they looked peaceful was because they hadn't had time to get their weapons and armor. Still, the Corlains started a war that led to children suffering. Two Dogs resolved himself to end the violence quickly.

As Two Dogs led his companions to the east gate, he saw the portcullis close. Several soldiers blocked the exit with muskets and broadswords drawn.

"Do you want this one or should I take it?" Swift Shot asked.

Two Dogs lit up the night sky with his numerous stones. These soldiers would get the honor of being the first of many to die by his new spear. Two Dogs used his magic to increase his speed, strength, and resilience. He wouldn't be able to fight for long at these levels, but the dozen soldiers in front of him wouldn't require much time to kill.

Two Dogs threw his spear a hundred yards. It hit the leader of the group squarely in his chest with enough force to launch him into the man behind him. Both were skewered. Two Dogs' tomahawk followed. It split the helmet of the guard it hit and lodged itself in his head. Before the man fell to the ground, Two Dogs had closed the distance. He plucked his tomahawk from the dead soldier's head and twirled as he intercepted the returning attacks by the Corlains. These men clearly lacked experience fighting Mother Turklyo's children. After Two Dogs slaughtered two more soldiers, the rest attempted to flee. Two Dogs was unwilling to allow them this mercy.

He grasped his spear from the two bodies it had joined. He twirled the weapon behind him and tripped one of the fleeing men. The young soldier begged for his life. His cowardice led to a more painful death. Two Dogs stabbed the man three times in his stomach. The man screamed with each wound. Two Dogs gave a war cry as he threw his spear again. Once more, it found itself between the shoulder blades of a fleeing Corlain.

"We must leave now!" Ancestors' Hand screamed.

Despite watching a few soldiers scamper away, Two Dogs calmed himself enough to let them go. He grabbed his spear. Next, he put all his remaining reserves into augmenting his strength.

"Allow me to get the door," Two Dogs joked.

He grasped the bars in the portcullis and strained, then ripped the gate and some stone it was secured to off the wall.

"We've got Black Cloud coming toward us," Swift Shot said as she fired lightning arrows at the approaching soldiers.

They took up positions to return fire. Two Dogs had a better idea. He threw the portcullis at them. Combined with the fireball arrows that Swift Shot fired, Two Dogs and his allies had enough time to escape out the new east gate and into the safety of the wilderness.

CHAPTER 9

"**More bandages, now!**" Faida shouted. "I need more hot water!"

Her sleeves were soaked with Hafoca's blood. She had the new king lying on the table in her small temple. Many of her figurines had been knocked away when the Vikisotes brought in their leader. Murid knew Faida was furious about the indiscretion, but few Vikisotes feared the gods for slight offenses. They were terrified of what would happen if a chosen king died on their watch, especially so soon after the last.

"Bring me more ferm too!" Faida screamed.

Murid stood against the wall as men and women obeyed her commands. Hafoca screamed as he was poked and prodded by Faida. She had two musket balls already sitting in a tray meant to receive offerings for the poor.

"How many more are in him?" Murid asked.

Faida didn't look up as she dug once more into

Hafoca's flesh. Hafoca screamed throughout as Faida fiddled with the third musket ball lodged in his left thigh. She grimaced as she tried to clamp down on the elusive projectile. Hafoca shrieked again. Murid could sense many Vikisotes were uncomfortable with how effeminate his cries were.

"Give him more ferm!" Murid screamed.

Egill held a flask to Hafoca's lips. The man drank greedily. He managed to swallow three gulps before something Faida did made him scream again. Ferm and saliva sprayed those surrounding the Vikisote king. Even Murid felt a little mist hit her arm, though she stood a meter away.

"Hold him steady!" Faida demanded.

Egill and a few others applied additional weight on Hafoca. The king voiced his disagreement. He kicked his leg while Faida operated. She lost hold of the medical tools. Both fell onto the dirty, blood-stained floor. The survivors of the Samburg ambush brought in most of the filth. Faida let out a frustrated sigh before reaching down and grabbing the tools. She briefly dipped them into a bowl of cloudy crimson water. She shook the instruments a few times, then proceeded to operate on Hafoca's leg.

Murid heard a sucking sound as Faida removed the musket ball from Hafoca's leg. He screamed an extra octave as she finally retrieved the metal sphere from his thigh.

"Was that it, Faida?" Murid asked.

Faida shook her head solemnly. "I have no way of knowing. He had two wounds in his chest, one in his leg, and two more in his back. Some of them could be exit wounds, but he could also have two more in him."

"What do we need to do?" Murid asked.

"He's losing a lot of blood. We need to sear his flesh closed. He'll bleed out before I finish searching for more musket balls. He lost a lot of blood just getting here," Faida answered.

"Will he survive?" Egill asked.

A hush, except for the semi-lucid Hafoca, fell upon the room. Murid had asked herself the same question likely everyone in the room had. Still, to hear the question asked aloud was unsettling. Especially for her. She loved Hafoca but only as a pesky older brother. She enjoyed the privileges afforded her as the Queen of Vikisoteland, but she hadn't given the country a male heir. She may not have been a virgin any longer, but something told her she wasn't with child. That meant Hafoca's death may have more impact on her immediate future than simply having to grieve as a widow.

"Our king was blessed by the gods," Faida said. "If they require his presence in Mount Heilagt, who are we to question that? He selected a queen who survived a massacre. I believe the gods may be making their will known."

Egill scoffed. "Perhaps if she had a son already, I could believe that, but if King Hafoca perishes tonight, that will hardly be proof the gods have chosen Queen Murid to lead our country."

"Don't speak of my husband's death!" Murid yelled, more for appearances than anything else. "And definitely do *not* speak of me as if I'm not in the room."

Egill offered a slight nod of apology. Faida beamed at Murid. Hafoca continued to scream.

"Can we give him anything?" Murid asked. "Faida, what was that potion you had me drink to fall asleep when I escaped the Corlains as a child?"

"That was popistra oil, and it was watered down," Faida answered.

"Can't we give my husband any?"

"That would be unwise. In his state, it's just as likely to kill him as it is to help him," Egill said.

"But would it give him peace?" Murid asked. "He's in so much pain right now."

"He's in the pain the gods have willed. We must respect their decision. In a few hours, if he's stable, I'll be able to give him something to help with the pain," Faida said.

Hafoca screamed again. Egill and the Vikisote warriors nearby had to place additional weight to keep the man from thrashing. Tears streamed down Hafoca's face. Murid pitied him. She needed him alive, but a large part of her soul begged her to help him die. It didn't matter what it would mean to her future. She didn't think queens still burned when their kings died. Faida had assured her *that* practice had gone out of fashion centuries ago.

"I need a moment," Murid said.

She wiped genuine tears away as she pushed past the bodyguards to leave Faida's chapel with haste. As Murid cleared the doorway, she felt a hand grab her. She turned to see Egill standing there.

"May I have a moment to speak with you, Queen

Murid?" Egill asked.

Murid nodded. Egill led her away from the hut toward an isolated tree along the road heading toward the western gate of the ring fortress.

"I'm sorry if my *feminine* emotions embarrassed you," Murid said.

"My queen, if I may be so bold, I believe your husband is far more feminine than you've ever been."

Murid clenched her teeth to keep from smiling. Egill was a good man who understood competence. If he wasn't so stubborn concerning gender norms, he would be exactly the type of person who should lead a country.

"What do you wish to discuss?" Murid asked.

"Strategy."

"Concerning what?"

Egill rubbed his face. "King Hafoca isn't long for this world. We all know this. By the time Faida is through with him, he'll be lucky to still have all his limbs. If he survives the night, I'll be impressed. If he survives the week, I'll try to make Faida my wife."

Murid chuckled. It felt good to let herself embrace the joke.

"What happens if Hafoca dies?" Murid asked.

"We'll mourn him, but I suspect you're asking what will happen to *you*."

Murid nodded. "I won't be burned, will I?"

Egill roared with laughter. A few Vikisotes passing by on the road stopped and stared. Upon seeing who was having the conversation, they quickened their pace to get out of listening range.

"Thank you, Queen Murid, I needed that," Egill said. "If this had been two weeks ago, you'd be a nobody. A fiancée has no rights to the throne. Since you were wed, we'll be in a state of limbo."

"Until you determine if I'm pregnant or not?"

Egill nodded. "You've always been the smartest person I've met. If you have a child, you'll remain queen until birth. If that child is a son, then you'll remain queen until his twenty-second birthday. At which point your son will become the new King of Vikisoteland."

"If I have a daughter?"

"You'll still have power and luxury here, but you won't be queen. Your chances of enacting the revenge both of us know is necessary requires you to have a son growing in your belly. I hate to be so forward, but how likely is it that you're pregnant?"

"We were together each night since our wedding until this one. I don't feel any different, but it's so early that I don't think I would."

Egill nodded as he rubbed his chin. He briefly turned away from Murid as he thought.

"The gods will know if a pregnancy is not from the chosen king. Hopefully, your belly will swell over the next four months. We could find out earlier if you bleed, but Faida and I will protect you from having to confirm or deny your flow. Do you understand what I'm saying?"

"It means I have four months to prove myself to my people. If more believe in me, like you and Faida, then I'll stay queen."

"That's partially true. You'll need a new husband,

and quickly. I know your character. You can lead us but only temporarily. The gods demand we have a king. I suggest you start looking for candidates. A strong warrior we can rally behind. Six months from now you'll either still be married to King Hafoca, or you'll be married to another."

"Unless I announce I'm with child."

"There's always that, but—"

Clanging bells and shouts of alarm interrupted Egill. Murid and Egill stared in the commotion's direction. Many laborers, women, and children raced along the western gate road to find safety in the center of the ring fortress. Egill smiled at Murid as he raised his axe. Murid drew her sword and followed him; they sprinted toward the western gate.

Murid quickened her pace as she approached the gate. Several warriors had weapons drawn and were screaming at something that Murid couldn't quite make out. All she could see were several bright orange lights filling the night sky. Murid felt like she'd seen lights like these before when she was in Samburg. That fight was so chaotic that she hadn't focused on them too much. The orange circles moved erratically. Murid realized why as she arrived with Egill at the western gate.

The orange glow was from the igsidian stones that three Namerians wore. One was an old woman holding a spear who stood with a younger woman. The younger woman had a bow aimed at several Vikisotes, but the arrowhead burned with fire. Not the fire from rags soaked in oil and lit; this fire didn't harm the arrow. Murid now understood why the Corlain riflemen suddenly stopped firing at them when the wind became strange in Samburg. The two women stood defiantly, but they weren't engaging the Vikisotes. Their posture was defensive. The same couldn't be said about the attractive man standing in front of them.

He had stones glowing orange sewn into his green shirt. He also had a necklace that alternated between stones and claws. He had a knife and a hand axe on his belt but seemed to refuse to use either. Perhaps it was because it didn't seem necessary. The man moved at alarming speeds. Six warriors engaged him. They *did* use their swords and axes. It didn't seem to matter. The man dodged all strikes meant for his body. He actually *laughed* as he did this. All the warriors were enraged by how he mocked them. Many rubbed in a fresh dose of crick oil. They clenched in rage as they prepared to attack.

One swung his sword at the Namerian. The man hopped over the blade. The jump was impressive. It must have been over a meter and a half he cleared, but what was truly stunning was the fact that the Namerian "playfully" slapped the warrior. The smack of palm to cheek was audible for many meters. Murid held a hand to her lip as she sucked in air. The Namerian landed gracefully and tripped the man to the ground. Soon after, another pair of Vikisote warriors were rubbing their own red faces. Despite how humorous it was, these three were still intruders. Murid advanced on them, but stopped when Egill shouted.

"Stop! Put away your arms. These Namerians were the ones who saved us in Samburg."

AUGURY ANSWERED

Murid jerked her head toward Egill. She searched his face and her memory for something she'd missed. She didn't recall seeing Namerians, but apparently Egill had. Murid couldn't argue that the magic she just witnessed didn't coincide with what she thought she remembered about the ambush that cost so many lives.

Egill had spoken to his people in the Vikisote's language. The Namerian man continued to slap the distracted warriors. Murid repeated Egill's command in the common tongue.

"Stop. These Namerians are our friends. I think?" Murid said.

This time the man ended his attack. The young woman lowered her bow. The older woman handed the spear to the man.

"We aren't your friends . . . yet, but we aren't your enemies either. We definitely aren't *Namerians*," the man said.

The man spoke that last word with utter contempt. It was odd to Murid. It was just a word for their people. How could it possibly be offensive?

"Who are you?" Egill asked. "Why are you here?"

"I'm Two Dogs, and this is Swift Shot. We're from the Lacreechee tribe. The hag is Ancestors' Hand; she comes from the Intakee people," the man answered.

Their names were peculiar. Murid assumed they received names that appealed to their character, but then what did they call their children? It was a silly thought, but the first one to pop into Murid's head.

"I'm Egill, the commander of the Vikisote army. This is Queen Murid. You will show her respect."

Two Dogs and Swift Shot seemed to stare at Murid. She became embarrassed. She had to restrain herself from hiding the freckles that covered her face. She'd gotten used to the Vikisotes' jokes and whispers, but something about these Namerians, or whatever term they preferred, brought fresh waves of discomfort.

"We came here to speak with you," Two Dogs said. "We believe we can help each other with our Corlain problem."

"If I command my men to stand down, you'll behave yourselves, right?" Egill asked.

Two Dogs laughed. His outburst encouraged the Vikisotes to raise their weapons again. Swift Shot joined her friend in laughter.

"What's so funny?" Egill asked.

"If we wanted to cause problems, I wouldn't have been slapping your guards," Two Dogs answered.

Egill squeezed his fists by his side as he swallowed behind his clenched jaw.

"True. My men embarrassed themselves," Egill said.

The Vikisote warriors looked thoroughly chastised. A few grumbled to their neighbors. Murid sensed that some would have gladly liked another chance to fight the visitors.

"Egill, they're clearly friends. Worry about your egos later, for now we have matters to discuss," Murid said.

"Thank you, Queen Murid. May we speak with you in private?" Two Dogs asked.

Murid tensed when she heard a few Vikisotes

chuckle mildly. "Unfortunately, you need to speak with my husband, King Hafoca, but he's . . . unavailable."

Ancestors' Hand stepped forward. "It's vital we speak with him now. The Black Cloud will follow your trail just as easily as we did. Eventually, they'll come for this place. We must speak with the king."

"I wish you could, but my husband was wounded in the battle at Samburg. If not for your help, I fear we all would have perished, but he isn't able to speak with anyone," Murid said.

"The king is wounded, and you've wasted our time with prattle?" Ancestors' Hand exclaimed. "You must take me to him immediately. I may be able to help."

"Our healer is already seeing to our king," Egill said.

Ancestors' Hand scoffed. "Does your healer speak with the spirits? Does your healer have the gifts of Mother Turklyo?"

"What?" Egill asked.

"Your magic can help?" Murid asked.

"Possibly, but we won't know unless you take me to him now."

"Follow me," Murid said.

Her thoughts raced through her head as she briskly guided the visitors to Hafoca. Soon Faida blocked the entrance to her chapel. Hafoca's hoarse screams spilled from inside.

"You aren't bringing heathens into this holy place," Faida shouted in the Vikisote language.

Murid tried to keep her temper under control. Faida was a dear friend, but she was allowing emotion to keep her from possibly saving her king.

"Let them in, now!" Murid responded in the same language.

"No. The gods won't forgive it. Not even the chosen one of the prophecy can defy them with this level of blasphemy," Faida said.

"They have magic!" Murid shouted.

"They only have it because they deal with demons. Their souls are cursed. They want nothing to do with us but to corrupt us. Their magic will likely kill the king before saving him. The only people who can save King Hafoca now are the gods. It's in their hands."

"Egill, help me," Murid said.

Egill held up his hands in surrender. "I'm not going to step into a theological debate. If Faida says it's against the rules, I don't want to go against her."

Murid rubbed her face in aggravation. Next, she held her hands on her red hair as she screamed, "Can you at least let her stand in the doorway?"

"No. They're heathens," Faida said.

Murid transitioned to the common tongue. "Ancestors' Hand, if you stood in the doorway, could you heal my husband? You don't have to touch him or anything, do you?"

Ancestors' Hand laughed despite the seriousness of the situation. "That heathen won't let us use magic to save him, will she?"

"*Heathen?*" Faida shouted in the common tongue. "You're the heathen. You and all the Namerians."

Two Dogs and Swift Shot reached for their weapons. The speed, especially from Two Dogs, caught most of the Vikisotes unaware.

"We aren't *Namerians*!" Two Dogs shouted. "Your kind invented that word. We're Mother Turklyo's children. We're Lacreechee and Intakee. Call me *Namerian* one more time and see what happens."

Murid was afraid. There was fire in all three sets of eyes. Perhaps the small number of Mother Turklyo Children couldn't take out the entire Vikisote army, but Murid knew those closest to them would die long before they ever achieved *victory*.

"Faida, you *will* listen to your queen. You'll step aside and allow Ancestors' Hand to do what she must to save my husband."

"Queen Murid, you're the chosen one. We don't need these people," Faida protested.

"Egill," Murid said.

Egill sighed, but he obeyed his queen. He grabbed Faida by the wrist and forced her out of her chapel. He released his firm hold after the three visitors entered the Vikisotes' holiest building.

Hafoca must have passed out again from the pain. He did that several times while the Vikisotes were racing him back to the ring fortress. Murid wiped a tear. Her fate had been tied to this man for so long that she feared what would happen if Ancestors' Hand couldn't heal him. The elderly Intakee woman's face showed distress.

"He's hurt far beyond my power," Ancestors' Hand admitted.

"I told you so," Faida screamed from outside. "The gods will punish us for this."

"Get her out of here," Egill commanded.

Faida struggled as Vikisotes pulled her far away from the doorway.

"Is there anything you can do?" Murid asked.

"I'm sorry, I don't think so," Ancestors' Hand said.

"There must be something," Swift Shot said.

Her confident voice took Murid by surprise. The woman hadn't spoken until now. Murid had wondered if she was a mute. She assumed she had to at least be shy or unable to understand the common tongue. Clearly, she was just one of those rare people who made sure her words kept power by only using them when necessary.

"His wounds are too severe. He's lost a lot of blood," Ancestors' Hand said.

Murid wiped away more tears. "I understand. He's just in so much pain. It hurts to see him like this."

"There may be something I can do," Ancestors' Hand said after a moment of thought. "His wounds are likely fatal, but I can keep him from feeling them."

"How?" Murid asked.

"I'll alter his reality. I pull spirits into our world; I can temporarily send his spirit to theirs. His body will still be here, but his mind can be spared the suffering."

"That will kill him," Egill said.

"No, he'll be in a sleeplike state. I can bring him back, if his body survives. If his body recovers, you'll still have your king," Ancestors' Hand said.

Murid shared a look with Egill. They had a silent conversation through their eyes. Murid wanted him to tell her it was okay.

"You have to make this decision yourself, my queen," Egill eventually said.

Murid closed her eyes and sighed. She suspected he would defer to her. Her revenge required Hafoca to survive as long as possible.

Murid opened her eyes and stared at Ancestors' Hand. "Do it."

CHAPTER 10

"**Sir, we've reached** the southern border to Vikisoteland," Zoya said to Githinji. "It may have been out of the way, but the roads here will better accommodate our formations and equipment."

Githinji sat upon his horse and nodded. Before him was a small village. The Northmen living there had shut themselves inside their homes as quickly as they recognized the Corlain banners flapping in the morning breeze. Most had left their livestock to graze rather than spare the time necessary to bring them back into proper enclosures. Githinji relished their apprehension. They should know to fear the Black Cloud. They should know that defying Corla will never work. They definitely should know that Githinji couldn't allow any forgiveness after the cowardly attack on Samburg.

"Tell the soldiers that no village, hamlet, or single farm will be spared. They attacked civilians. Their *king* chose to openly attack Corlain citizens. Burn this village," Githinji said.

"Sir?" Zoya asked. "Hafoca doesn't live in this region. These people likely had no idea what he planned or even did."

"That may be true, but *Vikisoteland* allows their leaders to behave this way. That means they condone his actions. None are innocent. We'll slowly move through Hafoca's territory so all the Vikisote citizens equally pay the price for what they allow their leaders to do. If they want a rebellion so bad, they should look inside their own community," Githinji said.

"I understand, sir, but shouldn't we heed the reports from our spies?" Zoya asked.

Githinji turned toward her and canted his head. "Which report specifically?"

"The one that claimed Namerians arrived at Hafoca's ring fortress. Apparently, they followed them after distracting our forces last week."

"What's your point, Zoya?"

"The Vikisotes and Namerians have formed an alliance. That can't be easily set aside. Namerians have dwindling numbers, but their magic makes them formidable."

"So do our cannons."

"Sir, if we waste our time with each village, we may miss our true targets. The Vikisotes aren't fools. The Namerians require additional strategy. We should move on Hafoca's ring fortress before he decides to hide his forces within their mountains. It'll take at least a week to march straight to the Vikisote capital. If we stop along the way to punish civilians, you can triple that timeline."

"Are you finished?"

"Yes, sir."

"Good. I understand what you're trying to say, but it's unnecessary. That same report you quoted indicated Hafoca was near death. They won't move him. True warriors will allow themselves to die before they abandon their king. We may take our time, because Hafoca is going nowhere. These barbarians are indecisive. They'll be there months from now trying to decide whose dick is longest. That man will be their leader. We'll kill them long before he earns the title."

"Understood, sir."

"Zoya."

"Yes, sir?"

"Take the village. Separate the children and adults. Then get me answers to the questions our report didn't have."

"Yes, sir."

Githinji nodded. Zoya rallied her troops and led them into the village. The battle, if you could even call it that, was decidedly one-sided. A few men and women tried to fight back. Their blunted blades and rusted tools were still clutched in their hands unused when the Corlains opened up with their muskets. Children whimpered, as they often did in battle. It was over in minutes. Not a single Black Cloud soldier was even injured. Githinji realized he should have expected that, but it was always nice to get confirmation of an opinion.

After Zoya segregated the adults, Githinji dismounted his horse and strode forward. As expected, most were crying and begging for their lives. Githinji searched the eyes of his prisoners. He knew he'd find the warriors hidden among the farmers. This particular village seemed to lack the former. One woman at least had enough spirit to gaze back at Githinji. He sighed and pointed at her.

"That one."

Two Corlain skirmishers grabbed the woman and dragged her toward the nearest home. She screamed and kicked but didn't cry. She would have to do.

A Corlain scout on horseback galloped to Githinji. "Sir, orders have come from Zonwalgoo!"

Githinji halted. He gestured for his skirmishers to take the woman into the home and wait. It wasn't wise to ignore orders from the Corlain capital. That didn't mean they were ever good news. Corla was an empire like none other, but decisions were slow and often wrong. Githinji suspected this new communique would inconvenience his mission to tame the frontier. He couldn't be distracted from his mission in Vikisoteland.

The rider halted his horse and jumped from his saddle. He was out of breath as he handed the message to Zoya. She unsealed it and read the contents. The square paper had few words. Zoya hesitantly handed the message to Githinji.

"Just tell me what it said," Githinji said.

"Sir, Zonwalgoo wants you to return. They require a full after-action review."

"The action isn't complete. We can't give them a report on something that isn't finished. They must know this."

"Sir, would you like me to send a message saying as

much?"

"This reeks of deception. A competing commander is trying to distract me from my mission so he can claim more of his own glory."

"Perhaps, sir, but if it's genuine—"

"If it's genuine, they'll send another. I'll obey as commanded, but we need verification."

"Shall I have the soldiers prepare our camp, sir?"

"No. We won't halt our advance through Vikisoteland. Even a short delay can help the other commanders convince our leaders that my accomplishments are theirs. Tell the men to burn this village. Have them shackle the prisoners and move them back to the rear lines south of the frontier limit. We'll continue north. How many more Vikisoteland villages are there between here and Hafoca's ring fortress?"

"Two more villages and several isolated farms," Zoya answered.

"Good. We'll see to them as we have this village. That will be all, Zoya, I need to speak with our host."

"Yes, sir."

Zoya saluted Githinji. He returned the salute and stepped inside the longhouse. It was empty except for the prisoner and the pair of Corlain skirmishers that guarded her.

"Thank you. You may wait outside while I interrogate our guest," Githinji said.

The two skirmishers nodded. They both left the room without a word spoken. The woman looked hesitantly at the skirmishers until they left. Once gone, the fear she displayed vanished.

"Would you care to take a seat?" Githinji asked as he pointed toward the bench on her side of the sole table.

"Thank you, sir."

The woman sat on her side. Githinji removed his helmet and sat across from her.

"Give me your report," Githinji said.

"Yes, sir. The Vikisotes constantly complain about taxes and regulations. There are secret meetings at night among the most vocal. They won't allow women to listen in. I'm sorry, sir."

Githinji held up a hand. "It's not your fault. I understand. Did anyone from outside the village come or go on the nights of these secret meetings?"

"Most of the time strangers came earlier in the day."

"Were any of them Namerians, or were they always Vikisotes?"

"Always Vikisotes, sir. Why?"

"Don't worry about it. We've had some reports of alliances forming, but they sound new. Be on the lookout for any savages, though. They may have powers that will discover you."

"The savages don't frighten me, sir."

Githinji chuckled. "Good. You wouldn't be the woman for this job if every opponent caused you concern. Have your spies relayed information from the surrounding towns to you?"

"Not in the past two weeks. I'm due another report within the next seventy-two hours," the spy answered.

"Understood. I'll receive their reports in person as

I move on to Hafoca's fortress."

"Will that be all, sir?"

Githinji steepled his fingers on the table. He considered how best to use his agent.

"That will be all. I believe you're close to being able to get more information of the leaders between you and Hafoca. I'll have to resort to unpleasant actions to ensure your ascendancy."

"I understand, sir."

"I'm going to strike you in the face to force you to bleed. I'll also tear your dress and undergarments. Whichever man is most likely to take pity on you *and* have contacts is the man you will immediately seek comfort with. Cry and tell him how terrified you are of having a Corlain's child. These men will want to protect you. They'll whisper secrets. Your job will be easier."

"I understand, sir. Thank you for having so much trust in me."

"Thank you for deserving it. I apologize."

Githinji reached across the table and struck his spy in the face. His heavy gauntlet easily opened a gash on her forehead. Githinji smiled. His spy didn't even reach up to touch the blood. She stood and placed her hands on the table. She screamed. It was a magnificent performance. She seemed to enjoy it as she ripped her own dress while crying pitifully. Githinji allowed her to act her role for a handful of minutes before clapping his hands once. The spy instantly stopped grunting and screaming. She changed her role to one of a recently violated woman, then whimpered and moaned on the table as Githinji left her to her "misery."

CHAPTER 11

Two Dogs sat on the posts of the fence surrounding the Vikisote training pit. Clouds covered the midday sun, making the temperate day slightly cool. Swift Shot rested her forearms on the topmost post and leaned in. Both Lacreechee watched as Murid engaged a Vikisote man with her sword and shield.

The man also had a sword and round shield. He parried Murid's thrust with his shield. The man looked slightly younger than Murid. He wasn't much larger either, but Murid had overextended herself. A more experienced warrior may have exploited her slip up, but the young man didn't press the advantage. The two warriors each took a step away from each other and heaved with exhaustion.

"This is embarrassing to watch," Swift Shot said to Two Dogs in Lacreechee.

He shrugged. "She's giving up a lot of weight. She'll still win the day. The boy doesn't know what he's doing, so his strength is barely an advantage."

Two Dogs leaned in with interest as now it was the young man's turn to overextend his thrust. Murid pushed his blade away with her shield and continued to roll around the weapon. She swung her sword in a wide arc as she spun against the man's body. Her blade stopped moving when it rested on the man's left shoulder. If it had been a battle, the man would've been a head shorter.

"I told you so," Two Dogs said.

He stood and gave off a war cry while the Vikisotes applauded Murid's win. Many Vikisotes turned and stared at Two Dogs. He didn't give it much consideration. Their guttural screams and shouts were just as odd to him.

Murid locked eyes with Two Dogs. He smiled at her. She removed her helmet and wiped sweat from her matted red hair. Those strange-colored locks still enchanted Two Dogs. She returned his awkward smile and approached.

"Congratulations," Two Dogs said as she arrived.

"Thank you," Murid responded.

"You don't seem too tired," Swift Shot said.

Murid shrugged. "I have to show these men I'm capable in combat. Weakness is easily replaced around here."

"Who thinks you're weak?" Two Dogs asked. "What I saw was a proud warrior showing her worth."

Murid seemed skeptical. Two Dogs understood. In the few days he'd spent with the Vikisotes, he saw a clear hierarchy of men over women. Many cultures outside of Mother Turklyo's children had the same issues. Two Dogs respected competence and loyalty far more than gender and facial hair.

"I'm not Vikisote by birth. I married into this culture. That and my husband's condition means I'm not a favorite to remain queen. That's why I'm working so hard to change perception."

"In our tribe, the person with the best magic leads. Bright Stone was our most recent chief. She easily held off dozens of Corlains at one time. If another had been chief, we likely wouldn't be standing here," Swift Shot said.

"That would have been a sight to see," Egill said.

His sudden appearance made Swift Shot and Murid stiffen. Two Dogs smiled at his Lacreechee friend for being so easily startled. He turned to face the Vikisote commander.

"Grab a good mug of ferm, and I'll tell you about it sometime," Two Dogs said.

"That will definitely happen in our future," Egill said. "Vikisotes respect brave men. You saved us in Samburg. I'm your man, always. Sharing ferm with you would be a magnificent honor."

Murid tensed at Egill's words. She appeared to laugh it off, but Two Dogs sensed her betrayal at how quickly a stranger would gain his loyalty.

"You may not want to commit to that. This one can tell stories for a long time. Often, they end up being about himself," Swift Shot teased.

Her comments seemed to erode any lingering tension coming from Murid. Either that, or she quickly recovered. She was an impressive person.

Two Dogs held out his hands and smirked. "I do have this exceptional story about hunting a massive bull turklyo."

Now it was Swift Shot's turn to smirk. She must have noticed how he neglected to mention her name regarding their recent history.

"You were quite impressive the other day when you arrived," Egill said. "I wish the gods would bless us with the same magic your gods have blessed you."

"Wise Mother Turklyo only blesses *her* children," Ancestors' Hand said.

The old woman must have tired of arguing with Faida about religion. The two women had quickly become bitter rivals. The only way Murid seemed capable of appeasing Faida was to finally agree to stop using magic to heal Hafoca. Regardless, the women had found new ways to bicker. The current contest apparently was about which was more devout to her chosen religion.

"That's why the gods are more generous," Faida quickly added.

Ancestors' Hand turned to apparently confront the Vikisote healer, but Two Dogs clicked his tongue. Ancestors' Hand surprisingly obeyed his command. She rested her hands on the posts of the pit. Two Dogs smiled as he saw her knuckles whiten from pressure.

"Faida, please respect our guests and their religion," Murid said.

Faida grunted. "Some religion."

Two Dogs clenched his teeth as Ancestors' Hand

dug her nails into the soft wood post. Two Dogs understood when she couldn't hold her tongue after the barb against Mother Turklyo.

"Any one of us could take any ten of you without even trying," Ancestors' Hand boasted.

"I accept," Egill quickly said.

"What?" Murid and Two Dogs asked together.

"I didn't get my chance against this one at the western gate. My pride won't let me sleep until I get a chance to prove myself against you in the pit."

"Perhaps another time," Two Dogs said.

He didn't want to embarrass the Vikisote commander. He was close to cementing an alliance. Showing them up could jeopardize the relationship.

"You're being polite. I can smell the warrior inside you. You want to test yourself against me just as much," Egill said.

"Eventually," Two Dogs admitted.

"Why wait?" Egill asked. "I'll wager a full sack of Vikisote silver I can defeat you."

"I don't have coins, but since it means so much to you, I'll fight you for honor," Two Dogs said.

"Ha! You don't have any of that either," Swift Shot said.

Two Dogs glared at his friend. Somehow, she'd found a mug of ferm while the Vikisotes gathered around the two fighters. How she could put so much ferm away and still be such a formidable warrior, he'd never know.

"Have you forgotten what side you're on?" Two Dogs asked Swift Shot.

She held up her mug for him to see. "This is a convincing argument for me to trade teams. It's so sweet; you should try some."

"So, what say you, Two Dogs?" Egill asked.

Two Dogs lifted his hands and slapped them onto his lap. He jumped from the fence post.

"I might as well show you now," Two Dogs said. "What are the rules?"

The Vikisotes assembled cheered, except for Murid. She scrunched her face with apparent displeasure. Two Dogs considered changing his mind, then realized Egill was already explaining the rules.

"Pick your weapon. I don't want unfamiliarity to be the reason you deny my victory. We fight to knock down, first blood, or until one of us yields. As long as you don't try to kill me or seriously injure me, anything goes. However, you must stay inside the pit."

"Understood," Two Dogs said.

He grabbed his spear resting along the fence. He twirled it in front of him and descended the dirt slopes into the central arena inside the pit. The ground was rocky. It wouldn't do to allow the powerful Vikisote to slam him into it.

Egill swung his axe before him. Two Dogs took a moment to ensure his tomahawk and knife were still in his belt. He almost felt bad for the Vikisote. There was no scenario where Two Dogs would lose to a single opponent not belonging to Mother Turklyo's family. Two Dogs briefly considered fighting the man on equal footing and withholding his gifts, but he believed Egill would take more offense to that. He would demonstrate his strength to this man and further cement the man's claim of loyalty to him.

"Are you ready?" Egill asked.

"Yes," Two Dogs responded.

Egill raised his axe and roared. The Vikisotes watching roared as well. Two Dogs bit his tongue to keep from laughing. He gave his own war cry. He was honored when Swift Shot added a war cry of support. He knew she knew it was unnecessary, but apparently good ferm *didn't* trump good friends.

Egill took two practice swings with his axe and charged. Two Dogs didn't even raise his weapon. He simply placed all his magic into building a barrier between them. Egill quickly closed the distance and swung at Two Dogs. The moment his axe hit the barrier, a bright flash announced his ascendancy into the sky. Egill soared ten feet backward and landed hard. Two Dogs felt brief concern until he heard Egill laughing. Egill was slow to stand. Two Dogs walked over to him and placed his spear against Egill's neck.

Egill waved his hand in surrender. "You'd already won by knocking me on my ass like that."

Egill rubbed his backside as he hobbled toward the fence.

"Demon magic!" Faida accused. "They allow their souls to be corrupted."

Two Dogs forced his mouth shut. That woman was trying his patience, but Murid cared about her. It would do no good to antagonize the queen's confidante.

"That's what all heathens say when they're soundly beaten by Mother Turklyo's magic. Much less when it's the chosen one from Mother Turklyo's augury," Ancestors' Hand said.

Damn it. She had to bring up the augury. That would set the Vikisote healer off. Two Dogs wasn't prepared for how Faida responded.

"The *chosen one*? The *prophecy* was written by *our* gods. You will *not* appropriate Queen Murid's legacy!" Faida screamed.

Interesting. Apparently, the Vikisotes had a similar belief in a renowned warrior fighting for his people. Faida's willingness to admit she believed a woman was the chosen one shocked Two Dogs. He doubted many of the Vikisote men agreed with her. Two Dogs looked at Murid for a response.

Murid looked conflicted. Ancestors' Hand and Faida continued to bicker, but Two Dogs watched the queen. Two Dogs didn't put much stock in hokey stories, but he sensed Murid's displeasure. Did she believe? He needed to move the conversation away from one as volatile as religion.

"If your queen is the *chosen one*, shouldn't she be able to defeat one of Mother Turklyo's children?" Ancestors' Hand asked.

"Enough, old woman. Behave yourself," Two Dogs said.

Ancestors' Hand looked embarrassed, shocked, and annoyed all at once. She opened her mouth to speak again but snapped it shut when Two Dogs glared at her.

"I can defeat him, if the gods will it," Murid said.

All present turned to look at the young queen. Two Dogs expected her to burst into laughter, but her eyes were determined. She actually believed her boast!

"Will you face me?" Murid asked.

"Murid—" Two Dogs started.

"*Queen* Murid," Egill interrupted.

"I apologize. Queen Murid, I think we should move on to speaking of strategy and alliances. You have your gods, we have Mother Turklyo. Let's set the deities aside for a moment," Two Dogs said.

"Are you afraid of a little girl?" Murid asked.

This time Two Dogs heard the humor in her voice. His thoughts wandered to their discussion from earlier. She had to know she'd lose, but perhaps that was the point. Egill lost in ten seconds. If the Vikisotes saw the queen fight the man who had so easily defeated their commander, more would respect her.

"I don't want to be the reason so many of your warriors want to face me," Two Dogs said.

"I'll be the last challenge. Face me. I too would like to see what a Lacreechee warrior can do," Murid said.

Two Dogs sighed. He was in a dangerous position, but she was right. If he didn't accept the exhibition, he'd face a never-ending line of challengers. He'd look like a coward or an opportunist. Two Dogs was neither.

"What are the rules?" Two Dogs asked.

"The same as before." Murid answered so quickly that it even shocked Two Dogs.

"Don't do it, my queen. He'll cheat again with his demon magic," Faida warned.

The grumblings by many Vikisotes convinced Two Dogs that they believed he was only the gifts Mother Turklyo had given him. Perhaps this solved his problem.

"If it will make you feel better, I'm curious to test myself against the greatest of the Vikisotes. I've heard of the strength of mighty shield maidens, like your queen. I'd like to fight her without Mother Turklyo's gift. It will satisfy my own curiosity. Just make sure someone actually yields. I don't care if it takes third blood, I want you to admit you can't take anymore," Two Dogs said.

Two Dogs thought he saw the slightest curl of Murid's lips. Had he been out-maneuvered? This woman was extraordinary!

"He'll still cheat. Don't do it, my queen. We can't verify his honesty," Faida said.

"You're a bigger fool than I thought," Ancestors' Hand said. "Our igsidian stones glow orange when we use our magic. His are currently black. If Two Dogs cheated, you'd know immediately."

The Vikisotes grumbled again. They seemed convinced dishonesty couldn't be hidden.

"I agree to your terms," Murid said.

She grabbed her sword and shield. The weapons looked large in her hands, but Two Dogs knew she wielded them well. The two opponents squared off. More people lined the fence surrounding the pit. Many elbowed their way past each other for the best view. Two Dogs wondered if the entire ring fortress was present for this exhibition.

"Don't go easy on me, because I won't go easy on you," Murid said.

Her voice was hard. The Vikisotes may not appreciate a woman warrior, but Two Dogs did. He stabbed his spear into the ground, then pulled his tomahawk and knife loose.

"I don't expect—"

Murid's unexpected charge interrupted Two Dogs. She swung low, three times. Two Dogs nearly enhanced his speed and strength but remembered in time to resist. This battle would be harder if years of instinct must be constantly ignored. He stepped high with alternating legs as he retreated. The third swing nearly grazed the bottom of his turklyo-skin moccasins. Soon, Two Dogs found his back against the inner limits of the arena. Two Dogs spun away as Murid thrust again. Two Dogs kicked her in the back. Her sword got caught between the gaps of the arena fence.

Murid brought her shield up just in time to block the rapid hacks of Two Dogs' tomahawk. He swung high, low, and to both sides, but Murid calmly intercepted both his tomahawk and the occasional knife stab. Through it all, Murid seemed in control as she calmly removed her sword while simultaneously defending herself. Once freed, she leaned into her shield as she pushed against Two Dogs.

Two Dogs tottered on his heels. He hadn't expected her to plant so firmly. He fell backward and turned his fall into a roll. It was a good thing too, because Murid's sword came down just as quickly as he moved away.

"That's it, my queen! The gods want this victory!" Faida shouted.

Not to be outdone, Ancestors' Hand added, "Two Dogs, not all of Mother Turklyo's gifts were magical. Show your opponent your strength and speed. Show her what it means to be a child of Mother Turklyo! What it means to be Lacreechee!"

Two Dogs rolled to avoid another sword swing. However, this time Two Dogs rolled closer to Murid. He snaked one leg between hers and used the other to apply pressure to her knee. Murid yelped as Two Dogs forced her to the ground. The moment her back hit the dirt, Two Dogs pounced. Murid got her shield up to defend against his attacks. She jerked, and he lost both weapons. Rather than reach for them, Two Dogs pressed against the shield. The top of it smashed into Murid's lip.

Two Dogs got a firm grasp on the end of the round shield and jerked it sideways to hit Murid in the wrist. She gasped and released her grip on her sword, just as Two Dogs hoped she would. He grabbed the Vikisote sword. Murid still proved elusive. She blocked his first attack, then kicked. Two Dogs screamed as the fact that he was straddling her legs became quite apparent.

Two Dogs stumbled away and tried to catch his breath. Murid stood but didn't charge. She seemed just as willing to take a moment and steady her breathing. She stood between Two Dogs and his lost weapons and calmly retrieved her sword he'd dropped. Two Dogs, somewhat recovered, glanced to his left. His tomahawk and knife were behind Murid, but his dual-tipped spear stood erect to his left. Murid saw his glance and charged.

Two Dogs sprinted for his weapon. He dove through the air as Murid's swing went wide. He turned his dive into another acrobatic roll that conveniently ended near his spear. He clutched it and ripped it from the dirt, then sent two quick jabs at Murid to force her to abort her next volley of sword swings.

"You're amazing!" Two Dogs shouted, more for the audience than for Murid.

The two warriors were in a standoff. Two Dogs knew she was wary of his new range, but her defensive weapon concerned him. His new goal was to strip her of that shield. Without it, he was certain he could force her to surrender. As much as losing might help his alliance, it would hurt his ego. He refused to give Swift Shot such a gift.

Two Dogs considered Murid's shield. It was round and made of wood with a metal boss in the center. A thin circle of metal surrounded the perimeter. The shield was large in Murid's hands. The outermost part of it would be the best point for him to strike. The leverage of the attack would force her to maneuver. That would take away her concentration and lead to fewer attacks. Two Dogs didn't have time to think any more on the subject. The shifting of Murid's feet suggested she planned to strike soon. He lunged first.

His spear hit the edge of Murid's shield. Just as he'd hoped, it knocked her slightly off balance and forced her to take a step to regain it. Two Dogs continued to thrust with his spear. The result was the same. His strikes landed in nearly the same spot. On his sixth jab, he felt the tip of his spear catch against the metal. Now he had leverage. Two Dogs used all his might to hit the same spot again. Once he felt it slam into the groove, Two Dogs jerked downward.

Murid was tugged by her left arm and sprawled onto her stomach. With the same motion, Two Dogs flung the shield behind him and brought the point from the opposite end of his spear to rest on Murid's back. She pounded her fists into the dirt. The Vikisotes were quiet. Swift Shot, and especially Ancestors' Hand, roared with approval at Two Dogs' victory.

Two Dogs panted as he wiped his brow. He stabbed his spear into the dirt. This freed his hands, which he now offered to Murid. He was thankful she accepted them. Some opponents got salty after a defeat.

"Great match," Two Dogs said.

"It usually is when you're the victor," Murid said.

She dusted the dirt from her chest and legs. Then, she held Two Dogs' arm above their heads.

"The winner!"

The Vikisotes offered polite cheers. Swift Shot and Ancestors' Hand screamed war cries. Murid and Two Dogs retrieved their weapons and climbed the hill back toward the spectators.

"You got further than I did," Egill admitted.

Murid smiled. Two Dogs nodded.

"I told you Two Dogs was the chosen one of Mother Turklyo's augury," Ancestors' Hand said.

Egill smiled with Swift Shot.

Faida grunted. "Queen Murid has plenty on her mind at the moment. She could very well be with child. Things will go differently next time."

Faida grunted and stormed off. Two Dogs felt a pang of guilt. Murid landed on her stomach; he hoped she wasn't pregnant. Sparring like that couldn't be good for a baby.

"Don't worry," Murid said. "I'm not with child."

"That we know of," Egill said.

"Will any other of Mother Turklyo's tribes join our cause?" Murid asked. "You fought like the possessed. I mean that as a compliment. We can use your magic."

"And we can use your numbers. I'm not sure how many of Mother Turklyo's people still live. The Corlains have constantly attacked, stolen, and raped us. The only people I've seen since our village was destroyed were in Samburg. They were stripped of their stones," Two Dogs said.

"Samburg was a victory, but it came with a cost beyond our king being wounded," Egill said.

"What cost?" Murid asked.

Egill stared at the ground. He seemed hesitant to speak.

"What cost?" Murid repeated.

"Queen Murid, I apologize. I came here to speak with you on the matter, but I was distracted by my own desire to prove myself," Egill said.

"What cost?" Murid shouted.

Egill flinched. "Our southernmost village was burned by the Black Cloud. They're moving north to our position, but they're stopping at every Vikisote community. They're making our people suffer."

Murid rubbed her face. Two Dogs watched as her shoulders shook with her rage.

"My queen, we must strike again," Egill said.

"I agree," Two Dogs said. "If we don't answer

their violence, those who would join us will assume we were only good for a single victory."

"There's a Corlain outpost near the western border," Swift Shot said. "We could easily eliminate it."

"The Black Cloud must be our focus," Two Dogs said.

"It will be, but why give up the advantage of this fortress to meet a much larger force? If we attack their small outposts, word will reach them. It'll make them choose between sacrificing their troops or separating their main force. Both outcomes give us an advantage," Swift Shot said.

"I agree with her," Murid said.

"As do I," Egill said.

Two Dogs slapped Swift Shot on the shoulder. "So that head is for something more than swallowing ferm."

"Speaking of, I'm empty. Be a friend and get me some more," Swift Shot said.

Two Dogs and his new allies laughed at Swift Shot's joke. Faida rushed back, ran straight for Murid, and interrupted their laughter. The middle-aged woman planted both hands on her knees and gasped when she arrived. Her information must be important; she neglected to insult Ancestors' Hand.

"Faida, what is it?" Murid asked.

"I'm sorry . . . my queen." Faida tried again to compose herself. "I'm sorry. It's your husband."

Ancestors' Hand smirked. "I suppose you need my magic again. You shouldn't have made me remove my spell. His screams kept us all up last night."

"Please go and help King Hafoca," Murid said.

She sighed as she seemed to reconsider her decision to remove the magic. Ancestors' Hand nodded and moved. Before she could take the road to Hafoca's bedside, Faida grabbed her arm.

"Let me go!" Ancestors' Hand shouted.

"What is it?" Murid asked. Fear crept into Murid's voice. "Faida, what happened to my husband?"

Fat tears spilled from Faida's face to soak into the dirt beneath her. "I'm sorry, my queen. King Hafoca is dead."

CHAPTER 12

"**I told you** this would happen!" Egill shouted at Murid.

They were behind closed doors inside Murid's chambers. Egill was free to express his true opinions. The death of Hafoca had clearly set him on edge. She knew he wanted her to remain queen, but he was positioning people to take over the true leadership position of king. Hafoca's untimely death, partly due to her decision to end the magical coma, had considerably pushed up the timeline.

"Faida is important to me. She's important to many of us. If she had been ignored much longer, she may have left us. I can't allow that to happen. Ancestors' Hand has provoked Faida. If we allowed the Intakee woman to claim saving Hafoca, Faida would have lost all self-worth."

"What do you suppose Hafoca's death has done to her? Ancestors' Hand is a boorish old hag, but she's competent. All the Namerians are," Egill said.

"Don't call them that! They don't like it. Now more than ever we should keep them happy. Some of our people blame them for killing Hafoca."

"Faida may have had a hand in convincing them of that. She doesn't like having to admit weakness or ignorance. If it isn't the gods' will, then it must have been sabotage by savages."

Murid nodded. She turned and ran her fingers along the trim of the dresser she begged Hafoca to make for them. Her wealth and position afforded her the luxury of her own longhouse. The tables and benches were nice for hosting visitors, but she couldn't ignore the need to keep a little of her true heritage alive. It may have seemed like an indulgence to most Vikisotes; Egill had had his say on the matter, but it brought her comfort. In trying moments like this, Murid enjoyed looking in the mirror and pretending the reflection was her mother.

"It's all my fault. I should have listened to the Lacreechee. I should have trusted Ancestors' Hand."

Egill sighed. He rested his hands on Murid's shoulders while she faced away from him.

"I wish you hadn't made the decision you had, but it wasn't your fault. King Hafoca likely would have died of his wounds no matter what happened."

Murid turned around and faced Egill. He let his hands rest at his sides and took a step back. Murid smirked. Egill had never been one to give even the slightest impression he had romantic feelings for her.

"It doesn't matter. My people, if I can even call

them that now, won't support me. They'll wait another month or two to prove I'm not pregnant, then they'll demand a competition to select a new king. With Celestial between now and then, all I'll have time to do is preside over a party. The fact that I wasn't born in Vikisoteland may even take Celestial away from me."

"Never. Celestial is too important. Besides, you have more support than you believe. At least two-thirds of our warriors will back you. Between your charisma and my influence, we can keep the others in line," Egill said.

"Thank you, Egill. I can always rely on you."

"Always, my queen. Just make sure you make the most of the next few months. I expect to see you on that throne this winter with a new husband by your side."

A knock on the door echoed throughout the longhouse.

"Queen Murid, may we have words?" Two Dogs asked from outside.

Egill smirked. "It's almost as if his ears were burning."

Murid swatted playfully at Egill. His innuendo surprised her. Two Dogs was a remarkable man, true, but he wasn't a Vikisote, and neither was she. The pairing would lead to more turmoil, not less.

"Come in, Two Dogs," Egill said.

Two Dogs opened the door and entered.

"Am I interrupting something?" Two Dogs asked.

"Not at all," Egill said. "I was just leaving, anyway. I received reports this morning that Black Cloud scouts were spotted south of here."

Egill winked at Murid, slapped Two Dogs on the shoulder, and left the longhouse. Two Dogs followed him with his eyes until he left.

"What is it?" Murid asked.

Two Dogs faced Murid once more. "I wanted to apologize."

"Apologize? For what? If anything, I owe you an apology. Some of my people will be untrusting of you and yours because of my husband's death."

"I don't believe your king would have survived with or without magic. Ancestors' Hand may have implied otherwise, but that was more as a way to antagonize Faida."

"That's probably true, but truth and perception don't always align."

"No, they don't." Two Dogs sighed.

"It sounds like you have more on your mind than a simple apology. Would you care to have a seat?"

"Thank you." Two Dogs walked to one of the benches opposite the highly polished table in the center. It was close to the fire and offered warmth, though at this point in the summer, Murid understood why Two Dogs slid farther away on the bench. "I do have more to say."

Murid took a seat across from Two Dogs. She took a moment to admire his features. He was like no man she'd seen before. Egill's veiled suggestion was still on her mind. She allowed herself a minute to imagine if she could make this work. The power he'd bring would be quite useful.

"Would you care for some ferm?" Murid asked.

"The sun is fully over our heads. I suppose it's late enough for a cup."

Murid smiled. She stood, grabbed a pair of mugs, and poured from the pitcher on her dresser. She walked back to Two Dogs and offered him one of the mugs. He sniffed the drink and scrunched his face.

"What's this?"

"Ferm."

"It doesn't smell like any ferm I've had before."

"Not all ferms are made from the same ingredients. Try it before you criticize it. Skal!"

Murid held out her mug. Two Dogs sniffed again. His face indicated he wasn't looking forward to a deviation from the taste he'd already envisioned. Murid continued to hold out her cup. Two Dogs shrugged and clinked his own mug against hers. Both drank from their cup. Murid savored the sweet flavor and swirled it over her tongue. Two Dogs swallowed, then smacked his lips and clicked his tongue on the roof of his mouth.

"What kind of ferm is this?" He smacked again. "It tastes like a dessert for a child's birthday."

Murid laughed at the absurd comparison. "This is honey ferm. What kind of ferm do you drink? It isn't much sweeter than the pear or plum ferm served at weddings."

"Pear ferm? Why? Ferm isn't meant to be sweet. It should burn and remind you that you're a warrior."

Now it was Murid's turn to furrow her brow. "Burn? Why? Ferm is a reward, not a punishment. What kind of ferm do you normally drink?"

Two Dogs sat a little straighter as he answered, "Corn ferm. That's a warrior's drink."

"Corn ferm? That doesn't sound good. My father drank wheat ferm when I was a child. I tried a sip once and immediately regretted it. It tasted horrible," Murid said.

"Wheat ferm? It sounds interesting, but I don't know. It can't be worse than this stuff." Two Dogs gestured toward his mug.

"Then make your own ferm. I won't have you wasting mine!"

Two Dogs looked shocked by Murid's outburst. She tried to hold a stern gaze, but the absurdity of the situation hit her. They were fighting over ferm preferences. Two Dogs must have come to the same conclusion. They both laughed hysterically. Two Dogs even took a moment to finish the ferm in his cup. He didn't look any happier to drink it, but Murid appreciated the gesture.

"You're trying corn ferm in the future," Two Dogs said.

"Fair enough. Shall we get back to business?" Murid asked.

"Yes. In addition to my apology, I came to clearly state why we're here. My tribe and Ancestors' Hand's tribe were destroyed by the Corlains. Many other tribes have also been eradicated, moved, or forced to assimilate. A fire burns in me to change this reality. I've spoken to many of your people. They've told me you feel the same."

"I do, for different reasons, obviously."

"Obviously. You have the numbers to help us survive more than one or two attacks. We have the power to make the Corlains hesitate. Vikisotes shouldn't be casting magical spells. Our presence will confuse them, allowing us to kill more. Any delay on their part will lead to more success for us."

"I agree. I'll help you as long as I'm in power."

"Which brings me to the *real* reason I'm here. Did you hear what Egill said before leaving?"

"About the Corlain scouts?"

"Exactly. I think we should ambush them."

Murid stood and poured herself a second mug of ferm. She sipped slowly. Her eyes fell on Hafoca's bow, displayed on the wall across from her.

"There's one minor problem. I'm in mourning."

"What exactly does that mean?"

"It means I should hunt a crick. Hafoca's hunt didn't go well. He had many warriors with him. I feel that my best way of cementing my power is to hunt by myself."

"Are cricks large animals?"

"Yes. They're deadly and swift as well. One mistake will lead to an immediate death."

"Sounds like my kind of hunt, but wouldn't hunting men make a stronger statement?"

"Perhaps, but the Vikisotes love their traditions. They'll stubbornly face death before breaking with certain ones. I can't blame them; I feel the same. You've already heard Faida scream about prophecy. I need to hunt this animal."

"Then I'll help you."

Murid considered this. Hunting a crick with one person would give her much prestige, but would that change if the other person had magic? Does one mage equal the dozens of warriors Hafoca had? Those present saw her kill a crick. Perhaps that original hunt already gave her the clout she needed.

"Where can we find a crick?" Two Dogs asked.

"They roam all over these lands. That's part of the problem. Several of them could find us if we aren't cautious."

"So, if we head south, we'll find some?"

Murid pushed her bottom lip out with her tongue as she considered his implication. She could find cricks to the south, and she may find Corlain scouts too. Two Dogs likely wanted to find both. Then again, Vikisotes valued strength, and they all had egos. If she and Two Dogs came back from a secret hunt with a crick carcass and dead scouts, nobody could challenge her easily. Several warriors would be interested in attacking Corlains to prove their own abilities. This would buy her time.

"You're a clever man," Murid said.

Two Dogs acted shocked. "Me? I just want to go on a hunt."

"I think we'll go on two."

Two Dogs grinned from ear-to-ear. "Somehow I knew you'd see the merit. We think a lot alike. I would have been proud to have a chief like you."

Murid had to turn to hide her blushing. Compliments from a man for anything other than beauty wasn't something she was used to.

"Please don't turn away," Two Dogs said. "How else can I admire you?"

"You're a flatterer. I'm sure many Vikisote women would love the attention."

Two Dogs moved closer. Murid felt her body heat increase as his breath rested on her neck.

"The Vikisote women don't stand out like you do. Your hair is a beacon. Your eyes are so deep I feel you can see my soul."

Eyes and hair. He mentioned the same two points that every other man spoke of. Perhaps he wasn't too different.

"What do you call these?" Two Dogs asked.

He had turned Murid's head to face him and pointed at the freckles that covered her face. Murid felt immense shame. She refused to cry in front of this man who would so openly mock her.

"I've never seen such beauty before. These marks remind me of war paint. It's like Mother Turklyo knew your warrior spirit could never be washed away."

Murid's embarrassment immediately vanished. Two Dogs was clearly being honest. What she considered ugly was the very thing he felt made her the most beautiful. Murid had to double her efforts to keep from crying in front of him. Why couldn't Hafoca have been like him? She would have given him a dozen sons if he had.

"They're called *freckles*," Murid said.

And the embarrassment came flooding back. He was courting her, at least she thought he was, and all she could think to say was to directly answer his question.

"Freckles." Two Dogs struggled with pronouncing the word. "They burn like igsidian."

Two Dogs stared into Murid's eyes. Her heart pounded. Hafoca had his whores. Even though she was mourning, she would gladly pounce this man if given the chance. Murid's feelings sank when he spoke again.

"I'm sorry, I'm rambling. Grab your bow, and we'll leave."

Murid offered a weak smile as a response.

"It's a beautiful weapon," Two Dogs said as he stroked Hafoca's bow.

"Thank you. It was a gift I gave my husband four years ago."

Murid winced. Why did she remind Two Dogs that she was a recent widow?

"I'll see you at the southern gate?" Two Dogs asked.

Murid slowly nodded. Without a word, Two Dogs left her longhouse. Despite being alone, she covered her face. Some queen. It wouldn't surprise her if Swift Shot suddenly showed up on their hunt. Oh well, two Lacreechee would make her feel more secure. The Vikisotes' opinion likely wouldn't change any more with a second Lacreechee.

Murid let out a slow sigh and grabbed Hafoca's bow. It may be a reminder of her marital status, but that didn't make it any less of an exceptional weapon. She took a moment to wrap her belt around her waist. She sheathed her sword and slung a quiver across her back, then finished her transition from queen to warrior by adding her leather helmet. With her round shield in her left hand and Hafoca's bow in her right, she left to meet up with Two Dogs.

Murid saddled her horse and walked it to the southern gate. The horse followed without issue. Murid missed Willow. She'd had many horses since, but her first one still held a special place in her heart.

Murid followed the road leading to the southern gate. She greeted her citizens as she passed and tried to judge their loyalties by how quickly and enthusiastically they responded. It looked like Egill's proclamation of two-thirds support was accurate.

Egill approached her as she walked. "Queen Murid, where are you going?"

"Best you not know," Murid responded.

Egill blocked her path as her horse whinnied. "You're my queen. I must know."

Murid glared at him. He held up his hands and stepped out of her path.

"I'm sorry, my queen. It's just, I just spoke of Corlain scouts, and you seem to be heading toward the southern gate dressed for battle."

"Am I? I hadn't noticed."

Murid started walking again. Egill paced her on her left side.

"Please wait. Let me at least get an honor guard assembled."

"They won't be necessary. Two Dogs is coming with me."

"Oh?" Egill slowed his pace. "This still feels like a situation that requires more guards."

Murid stopped with a stomp. She whirled on Egill

and marched the two steps back to him.

"I'm *queen*. *I* choose who travels with me and when. If you're so *loyal* to him, you should trust he can protect a *simple woman*."

Murid suddenly realized her finger was firmly pressed against Egill's massive chest. The burly man looked down at her digit, then back at her. Hurt shone in his eyes. He swallowed. Murid withdrew her hand.

"I'm sorry," Egill said. "I'm loyal to you as well. It's just—"

"It's just *he saved our lives*, right? You owe him allegiance over a woman pretending to be queen?"

"I didn't mean to upset you. A warrior's bond in battle is a righteous thing. Two Dogs saved our lives. That doesn't mean you aren't my queen. I trust and respect your wisdom *and* Two Dogs' capabilities."

Murid sighed. Egill was a good man. She had no reason to treat him like this. Perhaps she felt guilty about looking forward to time alone with Two Dogs while her *husband's* body was still cooling off.

"No. I'm sorry, Egill. That was rude of me."

"But you still need to do whatever this is?"

Murid nodded.

Egill nodded too, then smiled. "Then I'll ensure nobody else hassles you about it. Not even Faida."

Murid snorted out a chuckle. "Good luck."

Egill spread his arms. "I still have two Nam—er, Swift Shot and Ancestors' Hand. I'll bring both to defend me against Faida's wrath."

Murid laughed again. Egill joined.

"Good luck," she said.

"To you as well," Egill responded.

They each waved at the other before heading in opposite directions along the ring fortress road.

When Murid reached the gate, she almost gasped. Standing there was Two Dogs, without Swift Shot, but with a wagon and no horse. He looked just as perplexed to see her leading her mount.

"I'm sorry. I guess I assumed we'd walk," Two Dogs sheepishly said.

"It never occurred to me you would think that," Murid admitted. "Do you plan on dragging that wagon the whole way?"

Two Dogs stared at the ground. "Yes."

"Really? Won't you get tired?"

"A little, but this isn't the pit. I planned to increase my strength and stamina. Constantly using my magic has built my stamina and connection to Mother Turklyo. Many of her children can only cast a few spells before becoming exhausted and incapable. My spells last much longer than most. It's the reason this is how Swift Shot and I normally hunt."

"Impressive, but you don't have horses?"

"*I* don't have horses," Two Dogs said. "They're loud and can give you away. Protectors like me shun them. Swift Shot's just a good friend who didn't mind long walks."

"What exactly is a *protector*?" Murid asked.

"The school of magic I focused on. I'm a protector, Swift Shot's an elementalist, Ancestors' Hand is a summoner."

"I see. What other schools are there?"

"I can't list them all. There are also healers, creators, and beast tamers. The list goes on."

"That's fascinating."

"Shall we?"

Two Dogs stepped to the side to let Murid lead the way. She mounted her horse and nodded, keeping her pace at a walk at first, but Two Dogs teased her for this. She couldn't believe it when he could keep up with the wagon at a trot. He even held a conversation with her.

"Your people accept you leaving by yourself?"

"I'm not alone. I have you. They know the power of your magic."

Two Dogs smirked.

"Are we heading toward soldiers or cricks?" he asked.

"We're heading toward a known crick den, but we'll take the roads to get there. The Corlains are likely watching the roads. It should entice them to ambush us and perhaps try to ransom me."

"The Corlains don't ransom; they just kill. Regardless, I love this plan. You can't corner *this* attack dog."

"Do you mind if I ask you a personal question?" Murid asked.

Two Dogs shook his head as he jogged alongside Murid. He seemed to be showing off, but his heavy breathing apparently kept him from speaking.

"How do your people get their names?"

Two Dogs laughed. "Always with the names. Let me guess. You've heard the joke about two dogs humping, or shitting, or sleeping?"

Murid had heard those jokes. Her version was the

humping one, but she pretended she hadn't. "Nope."

Two Dogs nodded knowingly. "Well, each tribe is different. Many of us have two-word names. It's a way to honor Mother Turklyo by not assuming to be important enough to require a third word."

"I see. Do you get these names at birth or after a deed?"

"Both. I was born *Slow Grunt*. Apparently I took long shits when I was a baby."

Murid snorted out laughter. Two Dogs laughed with her.

"As you can see," he said, "I quickly found a way to change it. As we age, we can earn new names to reflect our contributions to the tribe or strong personality characteristics."

"How did you become *Two Dogs*?"

"I was about nine years old, and I broke my arm."

"Breaking your arm counts as a deed?"

"It does when you're fighting a group of much older boys. I don't even remember why we were fighting, but I was punching teenagers. They were going easy on me at first, but a few bloody noses later and they decided I needed to feel a little of the pain they were experiencing. Some mentioned that I fought like a dog. Then another adult pointed out I had the fight of two dogs. I hated the name at first."

"Why?"

"Because it reminded me that I lost. Eventually, it grew on me. It's a much better story than Swift Shot's. Let me summarize it for you. She can shoot arrows really fast."

Murid laughed again. Two Dogs would have too, but he began panting again. Murid spared his ego and slowed her horse back to a walk.

"Thank you." Two Dogs wheezed. "Let me know when you want to pick it up again. May I ask you a question now?"

"Absolutely," Murid responded.

"Where are you from? Ancestors' Hand had mentioned you weren't from Vikisoteland."

Murid glanced away from Two Dogs and blinked rapidly. She slid her right hand and nonchalantly wiped away a tear. Two Dogs seemed to notice her demeanor.

"You don't have to talk about it," he said.

"Thank you. It's a hard topic. The Corlains slaughtered my family when I was only seven. They enslaved the people of my kingdom."

Two Dogs nodded slowly. "I understand. The Corlains constantly steal our stones. What did your people have?"

Murid scoffed. "The *audacity* to want to live free. For wanting to determine what we did with our lives, with our property."

Murid looked down and noticed her fist was clenched. She relaxed her fingers.

"*That*, I completely understand," Two Dogs said as his fingers grazed the igsidian blade of his tomahawk.

Murid sighed. "Sorry. I didn't mean to be so dramatic. It's just, I miss my old life."

"I understand that as well. How did you end up with the Vikisotes then?"

"They saved me. My parents wanted me to marry

Hafoca . . ." Murid trailed off. Why was she constantly bringing up her dead husband around Two Dogs? Soon she'd be describing the details of her wedding night to him.

Actually, he may have been interested in the crick oil part. Hafoca had disrobed her and gently applied her first experience. She must have had an allergic reaction. It made her skin itch and her stomach turn. She'd thrown up on Hafoca, even getting vomit inside his mouth. He'd told her it was normal to feel sick the first time, but she'd denounced the stuff since. As she remembered the evening, she realized telling Two Dogs she'd thrown up moments before losing her virginity wasn't a suitable way to flirt.

She looked at Two Dogs. He had waited patiently as she relived her wedding night. He held a curious half smile. She internally begged him to ask a new question but somehow had momentarily lost her voice. Thankfully, he seemed to have picked up on her silent plea.

"Are your people getting ready for a celebration? I saw a lot of banners and decorations as we left . . . What exactly is the name of your kingdom?"

Murid radiantly smiled. Her excitement made her only answer the first question. "We are. The most important holiday, Celestial."

"We're literally hunting for Corlain scouts, and you're preparing a feast? Shouldn't you be preparing defenses or evacuating the children?"

Murid clenched her jaw to keep from responding too harshly. "No. Celestial is too important. Nothing, not even death, is permitted to end the sequence of events over the three days of Celestial."

Two Dogs looked at her hands. His gaze forced Murid to look down at her reins. Her knuckles were white.

"Sounds good to me. I love a party. One that lets me kill uninvited Corlains just makes it better."

Murid laughed. Two Dogs soon joined her.

"In addition to massacres, perhaps we talk about something other than religion today?"

"I agree," Two Dogs said. "You don't want to know how many Vikisotes reeking of crick oil I've punched in the face because they thought Mother Turklyo was a giant turkey."

Murid didn't even ask what he meant by that. Instead, she enjoyed her *safer* conversation with Two Dogs as they traveled the kilometers to the crick den. Two Dogs clearly enjoyed being among nature. He usually had a violent intensity, but as they traveled, he seemed to forget that, like her, he was a survivor of Corlain oppression. He asked inquisitive questions and answered without holding anything back. It was refreshing. The facades she had grown accustomed to in Vikisote society were absent from his own culture. Time passed pleasantly until Murid realized how close they were to the crick den.

"We're almost there," Murid said. "Leave the wagon here and follow me."

Two Dogs obeyed. Murid dismounted and tied the reins to the wagon. She left her shield in the wagon but nocked an arrow as she crept into the foliage on the west side of the road. Two Dogs grabbed his spear and followed. His steps were so silent that Murid could have forgiven herself for forgetting he was there. Approximately thirty minutes later, she overlooked the den from atop the cave.

"Is this it?" Two Dogs whispered.

Murid nodded with a finger held to her lips and removed a small bag from her belt, then pulled magnesium flakes from a pouch. It worked last time; Murid just hoped there wasn't a mother with a cub inside this den. Cricks were nocturnal creatures. She should be able to lure one out, assuming the den was inhabited.

Murid crept down the side of the cave. Two Dogs remained atop it with a radiant smile. She could feel the goodwill he sent her way. He pointed at her for a moment and smiled again. Murid didn't know what he meant and let the action slip from her mind. She stood next to the opening to the den. Murid crouched and peered inside.

The den wasn't too deep. Crick dens rarely were. A complex cave system would allow more scavengers to steal their meals. Besides humans, nothing was stupid enough to enter a crick den. Inside the den was the sleeping form of a single crick. It looked like a male. This was good. Males were much smaller and less ornery than their female counterparts.

Murid judged the distance to the animal. It looked to be about ten meters back. Murid checked the heft on her bag. She would mix the chemicals and throw it behind the crick. That should spook the animal into charging out. She'd likely get two or three shots before the crick either charged into the depths of the forest or turned to kill her. She'd have to make her arrows count. Thankfully, her grenade would make it less likely the crick would focus on her over its smoking pelt.

Murid placed the magnesium flakes inside the bag and gave it a quick shake. She felt warmth inside and didn't hesitate; She threw the bag over the sleeping crick, then picked up her bow and nocked an arrow as the chemical reaction began. The small bag billowed with white smoke that burned the now alert crick. It charged the exit of the den. Murid shot an arrow at it but rushed her shot and missed. It was probably for the best because the wild crick raced past her without giving her a moment's thought.

The crick rolled in the grass outside the cave. It couldn't shake the smoke that seemed connected to its fur. Murid took her time with her second shot. Her arrow lodged itself in the top of the crick's back. Murid had hoped to paralyze the animal, but the angry hiss springing from the crick's pebbled lips proved that wasn't the case. The animal turned to face her. It hissed again and charged. Murid had enough time to send a second arrow into the crick's left shoulder. It hissed a third time and increased its pace. She, out of instinct, placed Hafoca's bow in front of her moments before the animal collided with her.

The bow broke in half with the initial impact. Murid closed her eyes and cursed Two Dogs for not helping. A bright orange flash surrounded her and stopped the crick in its tracks. The animal looked dazed. It shook its head several times, standing mere centimeters in front of Murid. She didn't understand what happened, but she wouldn't waste the opportunity. She pulled her sword and plunged it into the crick's throat. The beast hissed a final time and fell over, dead. Murid slumped against the rock wall of the cave's exterior. Slow clapping surprised her.

"Amazing. I assume killing a crick by yourself will impress your countrymen?" Two Dogs said.

"No thanks to you," Murid responded.

"*No thanks to me*? Do you normally smack a crick in the face with a bow and win?"

Murid remembered the orange flash. "What did you do to me?"

"Nothing *to* you. I placed a barrier *around* you. It looks like that was a good idea too."

"So, that means it did take two of us."

Two Dogs helped Murid to her feet. "It took two of us to keep you alive. You killed that monster on your own. My shield wouldn't have lasted forever. If anyone asks, that was all you."

Two Dogs pointed with his spear at the dead crick.

"Nobody's going to ask," a stranger said. "Kill the Namerian. Take the queen."

Standing in front of Murid and Two Dogs were six men and women in green robes tightly wrapped around their bodies. Even their faces were covered. Only a thin window around their eyes exposed any skin. Murid hadn't even heard them sneak up on her, but each of the Corlain scouts had a short blade with a square guard held in front. Some held the weapons with inverted grasps. Two Dogs seemed to seethe at the *Namerian* label.

"Perfect timing, bastards!" Two Dogs shouted.

Murid watched as the Lacreechee warrior sprang at the Corlains faster than she could blink. He speared the speaker through the chest, then kicked the woman on his left. Murid thought she heard ribs crack when Two Dogs connected with her body. Two Dogs released his spear as he rolled away from a Corlain sword attack. When Two Dogs came up, he had his tomahawk and knife held in his hands. Two Dogs parried and dodged as two Corlains engaged him with attacks nearly as fast as Two Dogs' were.

Two Dogs was the obvious threat, and the Corlains clearly recognized it. Murid stood and drew her sword. She was tired of being ignored! Two Dogs charged and beheaded one of the swift Corlains. A woman near Murid turned and was skewered on the end of her sword.

Two Dogs continued to fight off the speedy attacks from the two Corlains he engaged. The wounded woman moaned on the ground as she writhed. That meant one was left for Murid to fight. She held her sword in front of her; her opponent did the same. They slowly circled each other as Murid searched for an opening. A scream behind her suggested Two Dogs had finished one of his targets.

The Corlain woman facing Murid faked a thrust, then followed with a slash. Her short sword parried Murid's down. The woman swung back at Murid's face. No bright flash prevented the dull edge of the woman's sword from slapping against Murid's face. She felt pain radiate along her jawline and took a stabilizing step backward.

Another pair of screams came from behind her. She barely got her sword in front of her before the woman could successfully slice her throat. The Corlain woman was extremely fast. Inhumanely fast, for a Corlain. She snapped a kick into Murid's chest, then changed the angle of her foot as she kicked twice more to Murid's face. She repressed the urge to vomit. The Corlain woman's sword came down, but Two Dogs grabbed her wrist.

He had hatred in his eyes. The woman yelped as he crushed the bones in her wrist. The woman screamed as she tried to pry Two Dogs' fingers with her free hand. Murid touched the blood coming from her face. She looked at the streak on her fingers. She wasn't a vain woman, but now that someone appreciated her face, she didn't want a sword wound to ruin it. Murid charged the woman as Two Dogs inflicted more pain on her. Her fingers wrapped around the Corlain's neck. Two Dogs let go of the Corlain and stepped back. Murid forced the woman to the ground and mounted her.

The Corlain woman struggled under Murid, but she wasn't strong enough to fight her way free. It felt like an eternity but likely only took a few minutes for the woman to die. As she expired, so did Murid's bloodlust. Murid panted atop the woman for several breaths.

"I'm so glad I met you," Two Dogs said.

He helped her to her feet.

"I feel the same. It looks like both of our hunts were successful."

"Was there ever a doubt?"

There wasn't. Two Dogs was the perfect complement to her.

"It'll take me a few trips to get these bodies back to the wagon. Do you feel more comfortable waiting here or by the wagon?" Two Dogs asked.

"I'll wait at the wagon. Our trophies are more likely to be found there."

"I like the way you think."

Two Dogs went about gathering the bodies. He started with the male crick. Murid helped him lift the crick onto his broad shoulders. As she let go, an odor hit her. Murid sniffed her fingers. A minty urine smell was there that made her look at the Corlain bodies. She walked toward the first body and ripped off his green hood.

"Is something wrong?" Two Dogs asked.

Murid wiped a finger along his cheek and smelled it. She sniffed again to confirm her suspicion.

"I thought so," she said.

Murid ripped open the robes covering the man. She rubbed her finger on his chest, then smelled again.

"Is this some kind of weird Vikisote tradition?" Two Dogs asked.

Murid smiled and laughed. "No, I was confirming a hunch. These Corlains fought very quickly."

"Did they? I hadn't noticed."

Was he joking or being serious? Which answer was worse?

"They were." Murid held her finger under Two Dogs' nose. "This is why. They've covered themselves with crick oil."

Two Dogs sniffed her finger and quickly moved his head away. "I know that smell. How exactly do you make crick oil?"

"Technically, it's made from crick venom. Crick venom can be mixed with a lot of chemicals to make medicine or weapons. Crick oil is a blend with plants grown on farms to make people better fighters."

"Better fighters?" Two Dogs scoffed. "It clearly didn't work."

"Crick oil is like your protector magic, though nowhere near as potent. Vikisotes use it before battles."

Two Dogs seemed to consider something. "Not just before battle. Plenty of you wear the stuff daily."

Murid shrugged. "Our warriors are always on guard."

"I guess." Two Dogs rubbed his chin. "I remember you putting some on before the Samburg battle."

Murid nodded. "The others did. It made them faster and stronger. I'm surprised to see the Corlains using it. They always acted like their muskets were good enough. We just assumed they were too scared to harvest any from cricks."

"Like I said, *it didn't work*. Don't worry about it."

"Perhaps," Murid said.

She didn't like this. The Corlains stole everything else. This shouldn't shock her, but it did.

"Are you ready? This thing isn't exactly light."

Two Dogs nudged the crick on his shoulders for emphasis.

"I'm coming," Murid said.

It took three trips to get all six bodies and the crick

back to the wagon. Thankfully nobody else, man nor animal, disturbed them. When they made it back to the ring fortress, they were practically worshipped. The honey ferm was passed with vigor as Murid had to tell the story a dozen times. Two Dogs graciously gave her all the credit. Some Vikisotes seemed to doubt the claim, but the bodies were all the proof she needed. After all, why would a man allow a woman to claim his accomplishments? Murid was proud of her true contributions but appreciated what Two Dogs did for her. More than once she had to force herself from staring at Two Dogs while sitting next to each other by the campfire.

CHAPTER 13

Two **Dogs sat** on a bench along the massive longhouse serving as the Vikisote celebration hall. All around him, Vikisotes dressed in their finest clothing, adorned with golden jewelry and mingled in various states of inebriation. A plate of roasted crick sat next to him. The meat was gamey and seasoned with pepper. It wasn't bad, but Two Dogs missed the spices his people would add to turklyo. These Northmen apparently shunned heat in all its forms. It would probably be pretty funny to trick the Vikisotes into adding spirit pepper to their crick. On second thought, considering all the honey ferm being consumed this evening, it would likely lead to a rather large fight.

Two Dogs searched for Murid. She was amid a conversation with some of her warriors. She seemed to keep her wounded cheek covered. Two Dogs didn't understand these people. Scars told the tales of strength and fighting spirit. The Vikisote men embraced them, but the women seemed to hate their scars. Perhaps Ancestors' Hand had a potion or something that could let her avoid a raised scar. Then again, it may make Murid even more beautiful.

"Really?" Swift Shot said.

Two Dogs broke from his fantasy when she thrust a mug of that sickeningly sweet honey ferm into his hands.

"No, thank you," Two Dogs said. "Come back when you have some legitimate corn ferm."

"I'm actually working on some, but it'll take another day or two before it's ready. Until then, drink up. It looks like you need some liquid courage to ask the queen to show you the ceiling above her bed."

Swift Shot laughed a drunken crow, then sipped until her mug was empty. She looked at Two Dogs' hands. Without a word, she replaced his full cup with her empty one.

"No reason to let it go to waste," Swift Shot said.

"How can you stand that stuff?" Two Dogs asked.

Swift Shot burped in his face. "It reminds me of being a kid. I get a surge of energy and my teeth buzz."

"Why don't you tell that to some of your new friends?" Two Dogs pointed at some nearby shield maidens. "They may want to *inspect* your teeth."

"That's not a bad idea. But first, I need to make sure I get the details of your date with the queen. Did you show her how your spear thrusts?"

"No."

"Why not? Bird Song is dead. There's no reason to

pretend anymore like that was going further than your fur-lined blankets."

Two Dogs swatted at Swift Shot. She almost slid off the bench as she dodged his hand. She scowled at him, more from having spilled some of her precious honey ferm than anything else. He didn't even know why he swung at her. She wasn't wrong. Bird Song was a good friend. She was also great under the blanket, but she was never wife material. No matter how much he wanted to believe she was, she was just someone to occupy his time while he looked for the right woman.

"I'm sorry," Two Dogs said.

"It's alright, but you owe me a new cup. Are you still thinking about Bird Song? Was it more serious than I thought?"

Two Dogs looked away as he shook his head. His eyes focused once more on Murid. Now she was speaking with Faida. Despite how insulting she was to Mother Turklyo's children, she was clearly an important confidante to Murid.

"Listen to me," Swift Shot said as she flicked Two Dogs' ear.

"Ow!"

"*Ow*? You helped slay some Corlain scouts after hunting a crick, but an ear flick requires an *ow*?" Swift Shot looked at Murid too. "You better hurry up and show her who you are, or I may beat you to it."

Two Dogs turned to Swift Shot and grabbed her cheeks with both hands.

"What are you doing?"

"But, Swift Shot, beautiful Swift Shot, can't you see

it's you?"

Swift Shot looked at another empty cup of honey ferm. "How much of this stuff have I had?"

"We're the last of the Lacreechee. We must wed to save our tribe. I'll bed you every night and twice on Mother Turklyo's day."

Swift Shot burst into laughter. Her face went red as tears stained her cheeks. Two Dogs laughed with her as Swift Shot shook his hands from her face.

"You almost had me, but I've heard your tipi. There's no way you can perform that much."

"I have feelings, you know?"

Swift Shot wiped tears from her eyes, but her smile remained. "You better share them with Queen Murid. I'm serious. I'll take your chance away."

"You would too, wouldn't you?"

"Would what?" Egill asked.

He forced his body between the two Lacreechee. He was drunk like the other Vikisotes but not as far gone as most. Swift Shot greedily accepted the mug offered by Egill.

"This doesn't replace the cup you owe me," she stated.

"I've heard Queen Murid regale us with her version of her crick hunt. Do you mind sharing your official version?" Egill asked.

"It doesn't differ much," Two Dogs said.

Egill smirked. "I like you. You did a good thing for the queen today." Egill slapped his thighs. "If you won't tell me about today, then how about exciting me with something else from your past?"

"What's to tell? I practice protector magic and serve Mother Turklyo. I've killed Corlains by the dozens, turklyos in pairs."

"What's a turklyo hunt like?" Egill asked.

"Unexciting from my perspective. Swift Shot has a tale she could share," Two Dogs said.

"Oh no you don't," Swift Shot said. "He asked about you. Tell him about that second eagle feather you earned."

Two Dogs reached up and stroked the three eagle feathers in his hair.

"I got the first at birth, like every other Lacreechee baby. The last one was the exciting one. I lucked into one after this woman killed a bull turklyo," Two Dogs said.

"Tell him about the middle one," Swift Shot said.

She burped after speaking. Two Dogs watched amused as she stifled a second burp and swallowed.

"Tell him about the third one first," Two Dogs said.

"I want to hear both," Egill said. "I don't give a damn about the order."

Swift Shot sighed. "Fine, I'll tell him."

"Thank you," Two Dogs said.

"About the second one," Swift Shot said with a wink.

Two Dogs rolled his eyes and slouched.

"I'm all ears," Egill said.

Swift Shot dramatically cleared her throat. "First, you need to know that Two Dogs is literally the only person I've ever heard of to *earn* an eagle's feather before puberty."

"Is earning a feather important?" Egill asked.

"Of course! Chiefs are selected by those with the most feathers. Each feather symbolizes an important feat that benefited the entire tribe. Whoever has the most is the person who can best take care of us. If someone earns more than the chief, then leadership is passed."

"I see. So, you don't believe in your Mother Turklyo selecting the best family and keeping them in power?" Egill asked.

Swift Shot shook her head. "Nope. Lineage means nothing except which tipi you sleep in at night."

"I see."

"Egill, stop interrupting!" Swift Shot shouted.

Egill held up his hands in surrender.

"Thank you," Swift Shot said. "Anyway, Two Dogs was only ten when he earned his second eagle feather. The hunters were gone. A herd of turklyos had been spotted earlier in the day. Herds are rare; rarer today because of the Corlains."

Swift Shot spat on the dirt floor. Egill laughed and tried to mimic her. His spit was thick with residue from his fermented drink. It practically clung to his face. He wiped his mouth with his forearm. Swift Shot cracked up with laughter. Egill didn't seem bothered. He simply flagged a friend to bring a pitcher of honey ferm. He quickly topped off Swift Shot's mug, then his own.

"Good man," Swift Shot said. "Where was I?"

"The hunters were gone for the day following a turklyo herd," Two Dogs said.

"Thank you. It's important to note that *hunter* and *warrior* are interchangeable terms. The only ones left in the village were the children and the softer mages."

"*Softer mages?*" Egill asked.

"You know, healers, farmers, crafters; the people who aren't very good in a fight," Swift Shot said.

"I see," Egill said as he rubbed his chin.

"Despite what you may think, not all of Mother Turklyo's children get along. Just like any family, we fight. In those days, the Esquit and the Lacreechee weren't fond of one another."

"Why not?"

Swift Shot shrugged. "Who can ever remember? We might have hunted on their land. They may have stolen an important bride. Sometimes we just want a good fight. The point is, while our warriors were gone, a few Esquits decided to attack the village. The Esquits are known for their shifting magic. Often, they'll transform into wolves, bears, or owls. They're all fierce animals but not much of a match against a protector or an elementalist. Anyway, they transformed into owls and screeched before diving on the Lacreechee left behind."

"You're telling it wrong!" Two Dogs shouted. "They didn't shift into owls; they were bears. Six bears attacked our village."

"Really? I was four. I don't remember it well. That's why you should be telling the story," Swift Shot said with a smile, indicating she knew her version was inaccurate.

"Please continue," Egill said.

He leaned closer to Swift Shot. His fresh mug of

honey ferm remained untasted in his right hand.

"A few of the women were mauled. We all gathered in the center of the village. Some of the adults tried to fight them off, but the chief at the time had foolishly sent everyone to ensure we brought back as many turklyos, and their igsidian, as possible. We gathered and waited for death."

"What did Two Dogs do?" Egill asked.

He rubbed his palms on his pants. He was truly engaged in the story.

"Two Dogs had an older brother named Proud Wall. Proud Wall was gone with the hunters, but Two Dogs idolized his brother. Proud Wall's name should tell you how strong his barrier magic was. Two Dogs tried to copy him," Swift Shot said.

"I didn't *copy* him," Two Dogs complained. "Proud Wall showed me how to do a few simple spells. I just practiced them a lot."

Two Dogs wiped a tear.

"He practiced enough that he erected a dome strong enough to keep the Esquits out. For over an hour, they banged on the barrier."

"It wasn't that long."

"Two Dogs, will you let me finish the damn story?"

"Stop exaggerating."

"Stop interrupting."

Two Dogs and Swift Shot stared at each other. He finally gave up and stood.

"Long, and inaccurate story, short, I held the barrier until the earliest hunters returned. The Esquits left, and the village was saved. Yay me."

"I can't believe the incident didn't leave him lame," Swift Shot said.

"Lame?" Egill asked.

"Thanks for the vote of confidence," Two Dogs said. He turned his attention to Egill. "Lame is what we call it when one of Mother Turklyo's children loses his or her gift."

"You can run out of magic?" Egill asked, leaving his mouth open. "Permanently?"

Two Dogs solemnly nodded. "Sometimes a mage gets his or her gifts back but not often."

"Thankfully, that wasn't the problem all those years ago. I'd be dead without Two Dogs. A lot of—" Swift Shot ended her statement abruptly. "Anyway, he passed out shortly after. It took three full days for him to wake. We thought he was dead. Magic isn't endless, but for some reason, Two Dogs seems to be able to fight longer than any of us. Honestly, his name should be Ten Dogs or Dog Pack by now. It's inspiring."

"I'll drink to that!" Egill shouted as he raised his cup. "Just another reason to prove I'm your man."

Swift Shot cheerfully clinked her mug against his. They both swallowed the full contents. Egill tilted his pitcher and topped them off.

"What exactly do you mean by that?" Two Dogs asked.

"By what?" Egill asked, then belched.

"Being our man?" Two Dogs answered.

Egill shrugged. "In Vikisoteland, honor drives everything. The gods demand that it does. To let someone help you, like save your life, then ignore them is the epitome of being honorless. I could no more turn my axe on you than I could the gods. I mean that."

Despite his deadpan delivery, Two Dogs couldn't keep himself from snickering. This forced Swift Shot to laugh. Egill looked momentarily confused but then joined the laughter. Two Dogs rose from the bench.

"I need to speak with someone," he said.

Swift Shot dismissed him with her fingers as she continued to share the laugh with Egill. Before Two Dogs got out of ear range, he heard Egill ask a question.

"Do you think he might marry Queen Murid?"

"I'm working on it," Swift Shot answered.

Two Dogs shook his head. He was the master of his own destiny, and he wouldn't be manipulated by anyone.

Two Dogs meandered through the throngs of drunken Vikisotes. A few tried to push a mug of honey ferm, but he politely declined. He looked forward to Swift Shot announcing her corn ferm was ready. That was assuming she'd share in the first place. It was never a guarantee with Swift Shot and her ferm.

Two Dogs eventually stood before his target, Faida. She seemed as sober as he, but her scowl told him she wasn't pleased he wanted to speak with her.

"I have nothing to say to you, savage."

"That's fine. I'll say what I must to you and be on my way."

Faida crossed her arms and continued to scowl. Two Dogs forced himself to relax. He had to make an ally of this woman. He would do that, whether she wanted him to or not.

"I'm sorry about what happened to your king," Two Dogs said. "I know you did everything to save him."

Faida harrumphed. "We don't need King Hafoca anymore."

Two Dogs raised an eyebrow to her blunt statement. "What?"

"King Hafoca wasn't chosen by the gods. Queen Murid was. She's the foreigner who survived a slaughter, just as the gods foretold."

"I'm a foreigner who survived a massacre. That augury is loose with details."

"Don't presume to claim to be the chosen one. Queen Murid only tolerates you because she can use you to rally the Vikisotes. Don't think I haven't seen you throwing kissy eyes at my queen."

Two Dogs clenched his fists. He had to grasp the fringe on his pants to keep from fingering his tomahawk. This woman was asking him to give her a close haircut.

"Listen, Faida, I'm trying to be civil, but don't take that as a sign of weakness."

"You don't scare me, *Namerian*."

Two Dogs' blood boiled. He violently reached for Faida's throat. A few Vikisotes nearby stiffened from his quick movement. Two Dogs gained control of his anger and closed his hands into tight fists, rather than around her neck.

"You don't realize how close you just came to death," Two Dogs said.

His voice was cold and hard. A moment of concern

flashed in Faida's eyes before her lips curled into a snicker.

"Did I hurt your feelings? I apologize. It wasn't what I intended." Faida's laugh following her words proved it was *exactly* what she intended.

"I'm going to leave before I do something I can't take back. But, before I go, you should remember one thing."

"What's that?"

"I've survived a far more recent massacre, and in my massacre the Corlains *didn't* get to go home. You assume too much about your protection here."

Two Dogs spun on his heels before Faida responded. He relished her silence. It sounded like she was about to speak. He turned to face his opponent. Before she said anything, a trio of teenagers swarmed her. They stank of crick oil and had bloodshot eyes.

"Faida! We need your help," one said.

"What is it, Isak?" Faida asked.

She sniffed and showed concern. It was apparent Two Dogs had been completely forgotten.

"We—"

"You got into the crick oil, didn't you!" Faida accused. "You know you're too young for it!"

"We wanted to help in the fight with the Corlains, but Qadira and Vadik aren't waking up."

Faida's eyes went wild with fear. Two Dogs stepped forward, but she violently threw her hands in his face.

"We don't need you, Namerian. Isak, take me. We must hurry. You stupid children."

Two Dogs stifled his anger as Faida raced away with the teens. It sounded serious, but she'd called him *Namerian* one too many times. She didn't deserve his aid. Hell, she probably wouldn't have allowed Ancestors' Hand to do anything, anyway. He wanted to find something to break. Preferably, he could find more Corlains to kill. Swift Shot's teasing and Faida's ethnic slurs had destroyed any chance of him enjoying the evening. Two Dogs was about to storm out of the longhouse when a delicate hand rested on his right shoulder.

"Are you leaving so soon?" Murid asked.

Her voice instantly washed away his resentment and frustration. He turned to face the beautiful woman who had captured his thoughts and his heart. She must not have seen Faida leave in a rush, because her eyes lingered on his face. Or maybe she cared more about him than yet another problem.

"I think I *desperately* need some fresh air," Two Dogs admitted.

"A splendid idea. Would you care to take a walk with me?"

Murid held out her hand. Two Dogs shook it.

"You're silly. You know what I meant," Murid said.

"Would it do for us to leave hand-in-hand in front of your subjects?"

"Half of them think we did the deed while covered in the blood of wild animals and dead Corlains. If by some strange chance I *am* pregnant, some will claim you to be the father."

Two Dogs allowed himself to feel the warmth that thought brought. He would make a good husband to a woman like Murid. He would gladly bounce their daughter on his knee.

"I suppose there isn't an issue then," Two Dogs said.

He accepted her hand and allowed her to lead him out of the longhouse. The night air was crisp. Even in the summer, Vikisoteland could be quite cold, at least at night. Two Dogs expected to take one of the roads and stroll toward a gate. Murid surprised him when she cut behind a different longhouse. They wove through the ring fortress until the sounds of the celebration were barely a roar. Nobody else was outside. Most were in the celebration longhouse, but many had found reasons to inspect the sturdiness of the beds in others.

Two Dogs rubbed his shoulders. "Thank you."

"For what?"

"For cooling me off."

Murid smiled. "You looked like you needed it. Faida is a dear friend, but she can be overprotective and a bit old-fashioned in how she treats strangers darker than a cloud."

So she had seen Faida, yet didn't follow.

Two Dogs snorted laughter. "I fully understand. Ancestors' Hand isn't exactly making friends either."

"What did you two speak about?" Murid asked.

"She wanted to upset me."

"Clearly. And she succeeded. Was it about the prophecy?"

"Yes. Her prophecy, Ancestors' Hand's augury; they're all turklyo shit. Nobody controls my destiny. Mother Turklyo gave me free will; I intend to use it."

"I believe in the prophecy."

"Your gods gave you free will too. I won't judge you for believing in stories I ignore."

"I didn't say *I believe I'm the chosen one*. Faida has told me I was for many years, but I feel something should have happened by now."

"Maybe we can share the title?" Two Dogs laughed. He'd expected Murid to laugh too, but she looked solemn.

"I think that's exactly what we should do," Murid said.

"Listen, I'll help you kill as many Corlains as you want. I'll live out my days in this ring fortress if I can add to my body count, but I don't give liquid turklyo shit about your kingdom or your prophecy." Murid took a step backward. She seemed upset. Two Dogs considered his words and softened his voice. "Look, I didn't mean it like that. I care about your people. I don't want any more to suffer like I have."

Two Dogs considered his words, then whether he should explain why Faida ran off, but he didn't want to lose this moment. It may have been selfish, but Murid could only help him now.

Murid nodded. "I understand. I know what you meant." She held a hand on his cheek. Two Dogs closed his eyes and relished her touch. "Will you come to my bed tonight?"

Two Dogs considered her eyes. They wavered. She looked completely vulnerable. Two Dogs couldn't hold back his feelings. He didn't care if anyone saw. He grabbed Murid in a firm embrace and kissed her. She returned his kiss and held his head in her hands.

Two Dogs didn't quite remember what path he took back to Murid's longhouse. He wasn't sure how their clothes suddenly left their bodies. He was positive it was the best night of his life.

He woke before she did and admired her body. Part of him wanted to wake her and bathe in her love, but he wasn't sure what it would do to her reputation if people saw him leave her longhouse. It was still a few hours before dawn; he suspected he could make it to a random longhouse and claim he was too drunk to find his way back to his assigned one. He left in anger; even Swift Shot would believe he imbibed some honey ferm.

Unfortunately, Mother Turklyo loved a challenge. Ancestors' Hand waited outside the longhouse. She smoked a pipe with green smoke trailing from it.

"Did you have fun?" Ancestors' Hand asked.

She cackled like the hag she was. The sound of her laughter annoyed Two Dogs more than it angered him.

"Who I spend time with is none of your business," Two Dogs said.

"Oh ho, so quick to throw insults. I was young once. I remember the thrill of a strong man between my legs."

Two Dogs stifled his revulsion. "Please spare me the details."

"Fine. I just wanted to make sure you didn't let your temper ruin Mother Turklyo's plans."

"I can't take any more talk of auguries right now either."

Ancestors' Hand stood and approached Two Dogs. He tried to walk past her, but she blocked his path.

"Listen, fool! Don't let your righteous anger complicate matters. We need warriors or we'll never do anything beyond taking on Corlain scouts six at a time."

"These aren't our people. They aren't Mother Turklyo's children," Two Dogs said.

"No, they aren't, but they are people. Not just that; they're warriors. We need them. They may not be Mother Turklyo's children, but they're still people we can use. Keep the queen happy."

Ancestors' Hand tapped Two Dogs on the ass. She cackled again and walked away. Two Dogs stared back at Murid's longhouse, then continued his search for an empty bed.

CHAPTER 14

Murid rubbed her eyes and stretched on her bed. She felt the space beside her. It was empty. Murid was briefly melancholy until the aroma of hot coffee caressed her nostrils. She sat up and rubbed sleep from her eyes. Sitting on her dresser was a silver kettle; steam rose from the gooseneck spout.

Murid rose from her bed and searched for some clothes to cover herself. She'd gladly abandon them again, but Two Dogs was no longer in her longhouse. She understood. People liked to talk, but a part of her wanted to let them. She was queen, after all.

Murid selected a green tunic with matching trousers. Her mother would have had words with her about wearing a dress, but that wasn't practical for the hunt she had planned.

After dressing, Murid walked to her dresser and grabbed a mug. She poured the hot coffee and held the cup to feel the warmth. The coffee was black, so Murid added some of the milk provided. It turned to a light brown. Murid took a sip of her gift. If Two Dogs did this every morning, he was forgiven for sneaking away.

Someone knocked on the door. "My queen, are you awake?"

"Yes, Egill, you may enter," Murid answered.

The door opened. Egill walked through and spied the coffee in Murid's hand.

"Am I interrupting anything?" he asked.

Murid smiled as his eyes lingered on her steaming mug.

"No," she answered. "I'm surprised to see you up so early."

"My head agrees with you. Unfortunately, duty calls."

"What is it?"

Murid gestured to the bench running along her table. Egill nodded and took a seat next to her.

"It's the Black Cloud. They've sacked another farm. At the rate they're going, Corlain cannonballs will slam into our walls a week from now."

"I see. What do you suggest?"

"My queen, I know you want to honor Jorosolman, but we don't have two more nights to celebrate. We need to evacuate the city. We can head farther north and prepare for the Corlains."

"That's blasphemous!" Egill looked away. Murid calmed herself. "Aren't we prepared now? We've known this fight was coming for some time. We already won our first battle."

"We lost our king at Samburg. If it wasn't for Two

Dogs, we likely would have lost more. That victory was costly, and the Corlains didn't know to expect the fight. The division heading this way isn't as ignorant. They outnumber us three to one. We must abandon the ring fortress."

"Egill, I respect your opinion, but my hold on this crown is tenuous at best. If I run away without honoring our most sacred god, I'll lose more support."

"If you lose our army to a Corlain attack, support won't matter anymore."

"We have a week; we only need three days. We'll finish the festivities, then leave. It must be in that order."

Egill pressed his palms together in front of his mouth. He looked like he was praying to Murid, but she knew he was keeping himself from saying anything he'd later regret.

"I can't guarantee we have a week. It could be much less."

"I trust you, Egill. I doubt your estimate could be that far off. In two days, we'll be done with Celestial. Jorosolman will be sufficiently honored, and we can leave the ring fortress with our army intact. Unless there's something else you haven't told me."

Egill looked away.

"There is, isn't there?"

Egill slowly looked her in the eyes. He offered a single head bob. "A week is the estimate based on the last report."

"But?"

"But we haven't received any new reports for over

two days."

"Is that unusual?"

"Yes. The Corlains are attacking our people. I've asked for constant updates, but my usual scouts are no longer sending back messages."

"What could that mean?"

Egill shrugged. "It could mean any number of things. They could be dead, they could be captured, or they could simply be lazy in their duty as they celebrate Celestial."

"Which of those sounds the most like Vikisotes? I'm sure your reports will come in today after the effects of ferm have diminished."

"I hope you're right, Queen Murid."

"If not, this place isn't called a fortress for nothing. We can fight the Corlains here. Mother Turklyo's children will help us. We have the mountains to help channel their movements or mask our escape. If your scouts report seeing the Corlains nearby, we'll change our plans, but until that point we need to show our people we don't fear Corlains more than Jorosolman."

Egill stood from the bench. "I understand. I'll inform the warriors to moderate their drinking. I'll also send out more scouts to search the roads. A Corlain division can't travel off them. If anyone's coming, we'll see them first."

"Good. Let me know if anything changes."

Egill nodded and left the longhouse.

Murid grabbed her bow. A pang of guilt hit her as she considered the poor state of Hafoca's bow. Regardless, her bow was just as ornate and deadly. She slung her quiver across her shoulders and left too. Outside was quiet. Normally, the ring fortress would bustle, but during Celestial, it was understood that work wouldn't typically start until noon.

One person stood outside the longhouse with a radiant smile.

"Queen Murid, you wouldn't know what happened to my friend last night, would you?" Swift Shot asked.

Swift Shot's grin spread far enough that it looked painful. Murid couldn't understand how the Lacreechee woman could drink so much ferm and still be this alert the next morning. Murid noticed Swift Shot had her own bow and arrow. Murid thought for a moment. She couldn't remember a time when the woman didn't have her weapons with her.

"I'll leave that topic for him to explain," Murid said.

"No need. You're walking a little funny. That tells me enough."

Murid covered her face in embarrassment. Swift Shot laughed.

"Where are you off to?" Swift Shot asked.

"Why do I have to be going anywhere?" Murid responded.

"If I was a gambling woman, I'd say you were going hunting."

"Very astute. Tonight is the second night of Celestial. It's common to serve roast squealer. I want to ensure everyone gets at least a bite."

"Are you running low?"

"I don't think so, but a squealer from the queen

will mean more."

"Really?"

Murid shrugged. "It sounded good."

"Your subjects let you hunt alone?"

"Two Dogs said something similar about my crick hunt. I convinced him that one of Mother Turklyo's children was all the protection I needed," Murid said with a mischievous grin.

Swift Shot clapped her hands. "I'm in."

"Good. I could use a companion."

Murid and Swift Shot walked to the east gate and left the ring fortress. They rode their horses for several kilometers. Murid knew it would take time to get to her favorite spot. She took the opportunity to learn more about Swift Shot.

"Thank you for coming with me," Murid said.

Swift Shot snapped a dry twig from a nearby tree and broke it into tiny pieces, then threw them alongside the road as she answered.

"No problem. I love hunting. It's a lot better than war."

Murid nodded solemnly. "I'm sure you're much better than I am. I stand out, looking like this."

Murid gestured at her red hair and pale skin.

"I wish I could stand out like that," Swift Shot responded.

Murid did a double take. "Really? Why? I wish I had dark skin like yours. It's so beautiful."

"Maybe, but your hair reminds me of igsidian. It's so bright and beautiful. Your skin looks kissed by Mother Turklyo. It's as if she placed igsidian in your flesh."

Murid rubbed the freckles on her arms. She tried to cover them, but Swift Shot moved her hands away.

"Trust me. They make you special," Swift Shot said, more forcefully this time.

Murid smiled. She could be at ease with the Lacreechee. They weren't the savages she'd heard others joke about.

"So, what's it like?" Murid asked.

"What's what like?" Swift Shot said.

"Magic."

Swift Shot's smile spread. "It's hard to describe. It feels good. It tingles throughout your body. It starts in your soul, but spreads to the tips of your fingers. The more you channel the power, the more it tingles. After you cast a spell, it's a little tiring, but it depends on how much and how often you use your power."

"That's fascinating. I don't know how the Corlains can win with you on our side."

"I wish it was that easy. We can't keep up our magic indefinitely. Doing so can lead to disaster; we could lose our power. The thought of being without magic, without my connection with Mother Turklyo, is terrifying. Even Two Dogs fears it."

"Why?"

Swift Shot gave a half smile, then looked away. "We aren't accepted into the afterlife if we die unable to cast our spells. It would mean Mother Turklyo no longer favors us. That we had done something horrible in life for her to abandon us."

"Can't you earn your place back into . . . er, where

do you go?"

Swift Shot looked at her again. "We go home, and we get to stay in eternal bliss. To answer your first question, some do earn their gifts back through sacrifice, but it's rare. Better to die than to go lame."

"I see." Murid sucked her teeth, then forced a smile. "I hope the three of you properly manage your reserves."

"I always do, though Two Dogs can be a bit reckless. Thankfully, he seems to have an infinite supply of power."

"It seemed that way in Samburg."

"He has an unlimited supply of stamina in other areas too." Swift Shot cackled laughter as she nudged Murid's elbow with her own. Murid covered her face as she giggled.

"*That* I already know."

The two women laughed again.

"So, what exactly is this *Celestial* celebration?" Swift Shot asked.

"It's the biggest holiday of the year. Jorosolman is the king of the Vikisote gods. He divided himself into three parts: the sun, moon, and planet. Through his personal sacrifice, all life was created. The other gods are his children. The animals and resources are his gifts to us."

Murid considered Swift Shot's curious expression. She belatedly remembered Swift Shot had her own beliefs.

"Those are the Vikisote stories. I'm sure Mother Turklyo had her own hand in the lands her children hail from."

"Don't worry about me. I can't be insulted that easily."

Murid sighed. "Good. My parents, before they died, wanted me to convert the Vikisotes to their religion. I tried, but you can imagine how that goes over when a seven-year-old is preaching to adults."

"Not so good, I expect."

"Exactly. The funny thing is, Faida told me stories and actually converted me. I barely remember what my parents had taught me. It was the same religion the Corlains have. That's part of why Faida got me to come around to the truth. Did you know the Corlain leader is a minister?"

"What's a *minister*?" Swift Shot asked.

"A man who speaks to God. I believe that's why they try to control everyone. Their Minister Ekundayo wants everyone to behave how his god decrees. He can't accept that people like us can believe differently and still cooperate."

"Religious zealots are always a problem, no matter the culture."

The two women rode in silence for several minutes. They moved off the road and traveled up the side of a gently sloping mountain. Eventually, Murid held up her hand and stopped moving. Swift Shot was the perfect partner. She nocked an arrow and waited for Murid to point out their targets.

Below them was a gaggle of squealers. They were small, flightless birds. Each only weighed approximately five hundred grams. The black and white birds were only thirty centimeters long. There wasn't much meat coming from an individual bird, but the meat she got was the sweetest, juiciest delicacy Murid had ever had. Roasted properly with black pepper and honey was a recipe that Jorosolman himself must have created.

"Those are what we're hunting?" Swift Shot asked incredulously. "This is a lot of effort for a single bite."

"Trust me," Murid said.

The two women dismounted. Murid nocked her bow and aimed. Squealers may not fly, but they were surprisingly swift on their webbed feet. She wouldn't have time for a second shot. She waited for Swift Shot to line up her arrow on a target. Murid nodded at her hunting partner. Swift Shot flashed a cocky smile.

Murid went back to controlling her breathing. She pointed the tip of her arrow just behind the orange beak of the closest squealer. She let out her breath and fired before refilling her lungs. The arrow sailed through the air and hit the squealer perfectly in the neck. The animal demonstrated how it got its name. It screeched a siren-like sound a second before dying. It was enough; the other squealers soon echoed the alarm.

Murid held her fingers in her ears. The birds screamed and ran away. They tried to, at least. There were fourteen birds left, but Swift Shot's arrow found the center one. Unlike Murid's regular arrow, Swift Shot's was charged with magic. Forks of enchanted lightning branched off and connected each bird. They sizzled and fell. The aroma of singed feathers and seared meat wafted over to Murid.

"How many more do we need? I don't have Two

Dogs to make trips for us," Swift Shot said.

Murid broke out in laughter. "I think we're good. Let's see if we can stuff them into our bags and head back to the ring fortress."

"Sounds like a plan. I'm suddenly hungry. Are you sure I can't roast just one?"

Murid's own mouth watered. "Considering I only expected to get eight at most, I think we've earned a special brunch."

Swift Shot slapped Murid on the shoulder. "I like the way you think, Murid."

The two women descended the mountain to the squealer aerie. With luck, they'd have eggs to complement their roast squealer.

CHAPTER 15

Githinji sat upon his horse and overlooked the grand ring fortress that served as the capital of Vikisoteland. His ruse appeared to have worked. The first southern towns, farms, and scattered hamlets in Vikisoteland were attacked, but after three, he'd skipped the rest and had his full division press hard for the ring fortress. Hafoca's death had sped up his plan but only slightly. He'd always intended to imply his desire to destroy every farm. The Vikisotes were a careless people. They wouldn't be willing to suffer discomfort any longer than they needed to. As he suspected, they waited too long to run away. He needed his prey to be in one place. He wanted a spectacular battle, and for word of it to reach Zonwalgoo. Judging by the fires lighting up the ring fortress, the Vikisotes took their time to evacuate. Perhaps they never intended to leave. Selfless sacrifice inspired some people. Githinji didn't care. He'd set the stage for the battle he wanted; now was the moment.

Githinji glanced at Zoya. She had her second brigade lined up and awaiting his signal to advance. The full division had over ten thousand men and women. He had a hundred cannons, plus a dozen trebuchets that would soon fire barrels filled with black powder and jagged metal. Queen Murid wouldn't be able to defend with the few warriors she had. Word had reached him about a handful of Namerians helping the Vikisotes. Namerians didn't concern him. They died just as easily as all his other foes.

"Zoya, are the other brigades in position?" Githinji asked.

She nodded. "Yes, sir. We await your command."

Her armor had begun to transition from black to silver. Githinji's spies had reported the previous evening had a large party for one heathen god's birthday or some fallacious victory. Githinji never bothered to learn the purpose of the celebration. He just ordered his people to prepare to attack at dawn when the men and women of Vikisoteland were hungover and tired. He had his scouts kill anyone they saw on the road. It was highly unlikely that word reached the Vikisotes about how close his Black Cloud Division was. The alarm bells and shouts indicated they knew now, but it was too late. His division had already enveloped the ring fortress. Some might escape, but only with what they could carry. Their equipment and their crick venom would be his.

The first rays of the morning sun finally peeked over the top of the mountains that surrounded the valley with the Vikisote ring fortress. Some Corlains shifted in their saddles or on their feet. Githinji understood the apprehension. He'd survived many battles, but even he felt doubt try to creep into his mind. He willed it away and slammed the door on the thought. He raised his hand to signal the attack when a messenger screamed for his attention.

"Sir, General Githinji, sir! I have an urgent message from Zonwalgoo!"

The woman placed a hand on her knee for a moment before standing at attention and giving the most pathetic excuse for a salute he'd ever seen. Her cloth uniform indicated she was from a sustainment unit, but he didn't recognize her beyond her rank of captain.

"What is it?" Githinji snapped. "We have a battle to win."

He didn't return her salute, but the woman clearly had no problem abandoning military protocol. She now had both hands on her knees as she gasped for air. It disgusted Githinji. A real soldier was tough and willing to lie down his or her life. These support personnel were soft. He couldn't trust them to hold a sword, let alone swing one or fire a musket.

The captain finally seemed to realize her lack of endurance was holding up thousands of soldiers. She stood erect once more and offered the message to Githinji.

"Just read the blasted thing!" Githinji shouted.

It was unprofessional and beneath him to berate such a junior soldier, but today was his moment of triumph. He would further ascend the ladder with this victory. His excitement to begin had allowed him to behave less than an officer should.

The captain glanced at Zoya. Perhaps she thought the female colonel would be more sympathetic. Githinji smirked. This captain apparently hadn't worked with second brigade before. Whatever the reason, the woman clearly didn't want to read the message aloud. Githinji shook his head with clenched teeth. Begrudgingly, he dismounted his horse and stomped up to the captain. His disgust grew as he watched her hand tremble before him. This woman had no business in *his* army!

Githinji snatched the paper from the captain's hand. He took off his helmet and held it out. The captain hesitantly grabbed the helmet, now fully transitioned to silver. Githinji shielded his eyes as he read the typed message. It was from the capital, and it was *not* good news. Githinji's enemies must have spoken ill of him. Ekundayo himself wanted to speak with Githinji. Githinji enjoyed as much face-to-face time with the Corlain leader as possible, but Ekundayo's tone in the letter indicated he was displeased. Githinji balled up the telegram and threw it onto the ground.

"Sir?" Zoya asked.

"It's nothing," Githinji lied.

The captain apparently chose this moment to find her courage. "Sir, I'm to escort you to our rear lines and wait for General Tosaca to arrive. He'll take you back to Corla."

Tosaca. So, that was who to blame. He and Tosaca had never seen eye-to-eye. The man was a coward. He cared more about preserving life than completing his objectives. Githinji was actually surprised. He thought the man had too little ambition to try to curry favor when Githinji wasn't present to call him on his actions. Perhaps his absence was precisely why Tosaca had chosen this moment to make his move.

"You're dismissed, Captain," Githinji said.

"Sir? I was ordered—"

"I said you're dismissed! Get your ass off my battlefield. I have an enemy to defeat!" Githinji bellowed.

The timid captain quickly spun on her heels. She dropped Githinji's helmet in her haste to depart. Normally Githinji would have chastised her further, but her comical departure made him decide against it. She must have found her stamina in addition to her courage, because she ran faster than her wheezing had indicated possible.

"Sir, shall I delay the battle?" Zoya asked.

Githinji retrieved his helmet and placed it on his head. He blinked a few times to remove the sunspots in his vision. Thankfully, his red visor quickly filtered out the harsh light bouncing off the armor of the deadliest soldiers he'd ever known.

"We shall delay nothing, Zoya," Githinji said as he mounted his horse again.

"Is there something I should know?" Zoya asked.

Githinji considered how to answer her. Zoya was his most loyal soldier. He didn't have to keep secrets from her. He definitely didn't want her attention distracted. She was a professional, but sometimes the strangest thought could infect a person, even amid battle.

"General Tosaca has whispered rumors into our leader's ears," Githinji said.

"Ekundayo?" Zoya asked. "What happened?"

"It's nothing to worry about." Githinji flicked his fingers away from himself. "Tosaca is a snake who will lie when there's no risk to getting punched in the face. I'm not the coward he is. I won't abandon my soldiers moments before a fight, will I?"

The Black Cloud soldiers in hearing range cheered as a possessed entity. Githinji smiled at their dedication and bravery.

"Ekundayo will like my gift. After the battle, I'll return, not before," Githinji said.

"Understood, sir," Zoya said.

"However, Tosaca's treachery has forced me to change our battle plan. We'll shell the ring fortress with everything at once. I want all four sides barraged. Then, we'll charge the city."

"Charge it, sir?"

"Yes, with the pachymules. Make sure the beast masters are prepared. We'll rain cannonballs on them, then have the pachymules smash through the rubble. While those subhuman bastards are dusting themselves off, we'll charge through. It won't take more than a few hours."

"No terms, sir?"

"None. People like this don't deserve them."

"It'll take time to coordinate the change with the other brigades," Zoya said.

"There isn't time to wait for confirmation the

changes were received. Observe." Githinji pointed at the ring fortress.

Zoya pulled her binoculars and watched. Githinji stared through his own. The Vikisotes wore their inferior leather armor and had their weapons drawn. Many archers were moving to line the walls around the ring fortress. It was pathetic. They couldn't reach his formations at this range, but his cannons could reach them.

Zoya pointed at the soldiers nearest her and issued orders. These soldiers galloped on their horses to link up with signal soldiers. The message would get out, but his cannons on the south side were supposed to fire last. When they shot out of sequence, Githinji was confident the others would understand their implied tasks.

"Zoya."

"Yes, sir?"

"Let it begin."

"Yes, sir."

Githinji reached down and patted his horse twice. Although a black stallion may have looked more impressive with his armor, Githinji enjoyed his white and brown painted horse. She was always calm in battle, but soothing her before the opening salvo often seemed to help.

It was only a few moments before the first cannons blasted. He had four batteries lined up on each gate. Githinji watched through his binoculars as the first cannonballs exploded. It brought a smile to his face as the archers on the south wall launched into the sky and came down in pieces. Vikisotes scurried about inside the ring fortress. Women and children hid. It was a shame they'd become victims, but today's boy was tomorrow's enemy. Githinji considered it mercy to end their lives quickly.

Next, the trebuchets launched their barrels. The brown bombs soared high into the sky. His cannons had focused on the walls and gates. They had the punch to break the infrastructure; plus, it rattled an enemy to see his protection crumble around him. The barrels, on the other hand, were for the people inside. They easily arced over the walls and exploded among their homes and streets. Jagged scraps of metal spread from each explosion and amputated Vikisotes with ease. Some barrels had short fuses. They exploded high and rained down. Others had exceptionally long fuses. Githinji delighted in picturing Vikisotes staring at an unexploded barrel with dread moments before it turned them into pink mist.

The cannons fired non-stop for over thirty minutes. The brigades on the other three gates soon realized what they had to do. Even if the Vikisotes had wanted to exit the gates and fight to the death, it would have been futile. The bottlenecks at each gate were deathtraps. Dead bodies would clog the exits before Githinji ran out of cannonballs. It almost wasn't fair. Actually, it *definitely* wasn't fair, but whoever said war was?

"Do you suppose they've had enough, Zoya?" Githinji asked.

He could hear the excitement in her voice when she responded. "I think so, sir. I want to make sure there are some for my troops to play with."

Githinji nodded. "As do I. Have the beast masters send in their pets."

"With pleasure, sir."

Horns blew. The cannons and trebuchets ended their attack. Githinji afforded himself a moment to confirm the chaos. Through his binoculars, he saw Vikisotes wail by their dead and wounded. Packs of warriors assembled and rushed to the gates closest to them. They seemed to know their best chance of escape was now. Simple people. They would learn.

Men and women dressed in bright red cloth uniforms stepped forward. They had capes that tied into their sleeves. They looked more like clowns for a child's entertainment than highly trained soldiers responsible for one of his most casualty-producing weapons.

The men and women spoke in a foreign language. Zoya had told him once which it was, but he'd forgotten. The heavy stomp of dozens of pachymule footsteps rattled his body. Murmurs from the infantry standing behind Githinji filled his ears. He understood. After all these years, even he watched in awe as the ten pachymules on this gate pressed forward.

The animals weren't the swiftest, but their exceptional height meant that even a steady pace was still fast compared to a human. The ten beasts trumpeted from their long trunks. Githinji heard the pachymules attacking the other gates echo the trumpet. Men stormed the exit of their damaged gates. Githinji had expected this. He pumped his right arm once. A barrage of cannon fire launched over the heads of the pachymules and collided into the center of the pack of Vikisotes spilling out of the rubble and craters left by the initial attack.

The cannons fired only once each, but the devastation they caused halted the rapid retreat. The survivors abandoned their wounded and raced back inside their "fortress." The lead pachymules stomped over the bodies. Githinji winced when he saw a red spray after a pachymule stepped on a wounded Vikisote who no longer had legs.

"Zoya, make sure our artillery keeps the Vikisotes penned inside their capital. One or two may slip away, but a group of more than five will be engaged," Githinji said.

"Yes, sir. They already have those orders," Zoya answered.

"Good."

Zoya was the perfect protégé.

For another hour the giant pachymules stampeded throughout the ring fortress. They crushed crops. Buildings imploded and collapsed. Occasionally, a beast master would fold his hands and move to the rear of the formation. This indicated the animal had perished or was so wounded that it no longer responded to the mental link between them. It didn't make much sense to Githinji. All he knew was only four beast masters continued to concentrate on the fortress below them. Githinji hoped the other brigades were having better luck with their pachymules. Through his binoculars, Githinji could see the giant gray animals rampaging among the people. There was a lot of dust and smoke. It was impossible to keep track of them all.

Another barrage of cannon fire drew Githinji's attention to the south gate. More bodies were added to the pile. Suddenly all four remaining beast masters left as one.

"What just happened?" Githinji demanded.

"The Namerians are engaging. They drew in our animals, but the pachymules couldn't get past a magic shield. Their elementalist finished them with her magic," the lead beast master answered.

"I understand. Zoya."

"Yes, sir?"

"Have one more barrage of cannons just to shake them up, then it'll be time to say *hello*."

"Understood, sir."

Zoya gave the orders. The cannons fired. Githinji drew his sword and pointed it at the ring fortress. It was large, possibly a thousand meters in diameter, but every centimeter had been targeted. Even with Namerian magic, there couldn't be too many survivors. Just enough to get prisoners.

"Charge!" Githinji screamed.

The cavalry up front raced ahead of the infantry. They galloped at full speed. Githinji prided himself in taking the lead. He wouldn't be one like Tosaca to wait behind his troops to gain a victory.

As Githinji neared the gate, a group of Vikisotes on horseback charged out, seven in all. His cavalry was too close to turn, so the cannons would no longer fire. Githinji considered letting them go, but the soldier in him demanded he personally see to these cowards.

"Zoya, with me. The rest of you continue through

the gate!" Githinji shouted.

Zoya followed. Conventional wisdom suggested a commander should never be alone with the next commanding officer. Githinji didn't care. He'd already won this battle. He wanted to show off how good he still was with a sword. Plus, he wanted to make sure *she* could still handle her own in melee combat.

The Vikisotes looked over their shoulders. They frantically whipped their horses to try to escape. Any fool could see their animals were in poor shape. The rear woman's horse was clearly spurting blood into the air with each step. This woman was the first whom Githinji caught up to. She didn't even look back as he swiped with his sword. Her head rolled down the left side of the horse while her body dropped to the right.

Githinji sheathed his sword. The remaining six were pushing their mounts hard to reach the slopes leading into the forest. Between the mountains and the forest, there were many places to hide. Githinji had to get them first.

He pulled his pistol and aimed at the back of the man in front of him. His hand bounced around as his horse raced. Githinji calmed his breathing as he aimed. When the moment was right, he squeezed his trigger. The ball caught the man in the small of his back. The man reflexively reached back before falling off his horse. He hit the ground hard. The man writhed as Githinji's horse passed him. A gunshot behind Githinji ended the man's screams. He had to trust that Zoya needed to shoot him rather than save her only shot for one of the remaining five.

The second death was the catalyst to get three of the remaining Vikisotes to turn around. They drew their swords and charged. Githinji relished the challenge. He pressed his horse to run its fastest. He nearly lost hold of his sword when it was parried by the Vikisote opposite him. The other two Vikisotes appeared to target Zoya. Githinji turned his horse. As the Vikisote charged again, he watched Zoya fight the other two.

The first woman was skewered by Zoya's sword as she raced past. Zoya lost her primary weapon, but Githinji knew that was hardly a concern. Githinji parried his opponent, but his curiosity got the better of him. He watched Zoya again.

She had her feet atop the saddle and squatted above her horse as she galloped for the Vikisote man she fought. He swung at her, but she dove from her mount. She collided with the man and yanked him from his horse. Githinji barely registered killing the man he fought with a blade to the chest. Zoya hit the ground atop the man and immediately stood up. She didn't look fazed, much less injured from the insane attack. She ran behind the dazed man and wrapped her arms around his neck. The man barely resisted. It didn't matter. Zoya violently jerked his head, then allowed his body to slump to the ground.

Githinji turned his attention back to where the final two Vikisotes had been. As expected, both had vanished. It was doubtful they'd find them again. That was acceptable. There always needed to be the lucky few. Legends grew from these tales. Githinji enjoyed being a legend.

Zoya, back on her horse, rode over to Githinji.

"Are you okay, sir?"

"Of course. Well done."

"Thank you, sir. We should get back inside."

"Agreed."

The screams of the dead and musket fire filled the air on the other side of the stone wall surrounding the ring fortress. Githinji and Zoya trotted their horses to the nearest opening in the perimeter. Githinji noticed yellow vapor rising from around the wall.

"Namerian magic, sir."

Githinji didn't answer. Instead, he kicked his heels into his horse and pushed the poor animal into another full gallop.

CHAPTER 16

Murid knew she should have forced the evacuation sooner. The reports had indicated the Black Cloud was still days away, but her pride and faith had told her otherwise. As the walls crumbled around her, her heart broke when she stared into the eyes of the people who called her queen.

Thankfully Mother Turklyo's children were here. Murid glanced at Two Dogs. Sweat poured from his body. He hadn't spoken in minutes. His eyes barely opened. All his efforts went into keeping a magical barrier between them and the Corlains. It wasn't a large enough shield. Only a hundred people stood under its protection. Among them were Egill, Ancestors' Hand, and Swift Shot. Other Vikisotes hid among the debris that used to be her home. Faida was with many children, but where they ended up, who knew?

Thankfully Swift Shot had killed the pachymules. She was lying on her back as she gasped for breath. Her magical reserves weren't nearly as limitless as Two Dogs' appeared to be. Egill had told her the story Swift Shot had shared about Two Dogs as a child. Seeing him struggle as he held the barrier up despite musket fire, she fully believed it.

The warriors still able to fight paced inside their confines. Many added more doses of crick oil than was wise. There were at least sixty who knew how to handle a blade. Soon they would have to for the last time. The only reason they had any respite from the Corlains was due to Ancestors' Hand.

The Intakee woman had summoned the spirits of the Vikisotes already slain. These men, women, and even children swarmed the Corlains. It would have been humorous to watch the Corlains fighting yellow ghost-like children with spiritual rocks, but the fact meant those same children could no longer play in the real world. Ancestors' Hand looked just as haggard as the two Lacreechee warriors. She looked weaker every time she re-populated the battlefield with the spirits that were killed a second or even a third time.

"Ancestors' Hand, how many times can you revive them?" Murid asked.

Ancestors' Hand only grunted. It was all the answer Murid needed.

"They can't keep this up much longer," Egill said. "We must fight our way out of here."

"What about the children?" a desperate mother asked.

Her question reminded Murid of Faida. She wished her friend help.

"They aren't focusing on us," Murid said.

It was true. Something about unrelenting spirit warriors focused an enemy's attention. Rubble filled the streets. Barely a longhouse stood, but Murid could still make out the sound of musket fire and the occasional clash of metal. There were other pockets of Vikisote resistance.

"My queen—" Egill started.

Murid clamped her fingers to silence him. She gave herself a panoramic view of the battlefield. She stood in the rubble that used to be the celebration longhouse. It no longer had a ceiling or three of its walls. The wall standing blocked her view to the east. To the north, west, and south, Murid saw a giant shifting mirror. The early morning sun reflected fiercely off the Corlain plate armor. Murid wished for clouds. That gave her an idea.

"Swift Shot, how are you feeling?" Murid asked.

Swift Shot wobbled as she stood. Murid felt immense respect for the woman as she hobbled over to her.

"I'll be better with a good ferm in hand," Swift Shot answered.

Murid laughed nervously. Even as the walls literally crumbled around her, Swift Shot was still making jokes.

"I hate to ask so much from you again, but could you do something about the sun?"

Murid pointed. Swift Shot looked confused, then understanding led to her opening her eyes wider.

"I can but not for long."

"How long can you give us?" Egill asked.

"Two minutes, three at most. In this state, I won't

be good for much more," Swift Shot answered.

"It might be a better use of her magic to keep her on the offensive," Egill suggested.

Murid considered it. Two minutes wouldn't do much beyond giving her people a chance to identify the least deadly avenue to run toward.

"What about fog?" Murid asked.

"I can do fog," Swift Shot answered with a smile. "I can get it thick too."

A plan began to form. Murid studied each cardinal direction. The south had the most Corlains fighting with the spirits of the dead. Running toward them would be suicide. The west also had thick fighting. In fact, those Corlains seemed closer to the center of the fortress where she stood. Her view of the east was blocked. Fewer buildings fell in that direction. Was that a good sign? Did it mean she could lead her people that way? Or was it a trap? The uncertainty made her hesitant to commit to that direction.

Remaining was heading north. That meant running straight into the side of a mountain. Mountains surrounded her kingdom, but the ring fortress literally used part of the mountain to make their northern wall. This meant the Corlains there could channelize her people into kill zones. It also meant *they* couldn't maneuver. If she had all four thousand of her warriors left, it would be the worst direction. Unfortunately, fate had stripped her of this constraint. The few people she had left could slip past Corlain lines. They could meet up at one of the villages on the other side of the pass.

"Swift Shot, fill this fortress with fog. Everyone,

listen up! We must make a run for it! Swift Shot will cover us with fog! We're going to head north! Take the road and stay on it! It will get us into the mountains! We'll meet in Wyrmcrest!"

Many nodded, but others voiced their displeasure with leaving the safety Two Dogs provided them.

"They'll cut us down!" someone shouted.

Murid held up her hands to calm them. "If we stay here, we're dead. The Corlains haven't been taking prisoners in Vikisoteland. We have one advantage they don't."

"Yeah, the Namerians!" a shield maiden shouted.

Murid winced. Thankfully, Two Dogs was too absorbed in his barrier to hear the disparaging term.

"No!" Murid shouted. "We know this land."

"The fog will blind us," another person protested.

"Their armor already blinds us!" Egill shouted.

"Exactly," Murid said. "The fog will give them a taste of their own medicine."

"It's too far," came yet another complaint.

Murid clenched her jaw. A glance at both Ancestors' Hand and Two Dogs confirmed they only had a few minutes left before the Corlains simply shot them where they stood.

"We have our crick oil. Rub it in deep. We'll outrun them," Murid said.

The warriors among the group nodded more vigorously. They applied even more of the human-enhancing crick oil. Egill handed her a vial. She hesitated to grab it. Thoughts of how sick it made her feel filled her memory, but the eyes of many were on her, watching intently to see what she did. If she ignored the oil, she felt it would send a fresh wave of despair through the ranks. Murid accepted the vial and poured *all* of it into her hands. She rubbed it over her face and inside her armor.

The effects of the crick oil were instant. They were the complete opposite of her wedding night. She felt like a single breath would last for weeks. Her muscles corded with potential. Even her disposition improved. She knew she could win this fight. It was as if the gods themselves had given Murid all their strength. Looking around at her warriors, it was clear they also felt the same blast of optimism. Crick oil didn't last long, but she didn't need more than thirty minutes. She had plenty of time.

"Would you like some?" Egill asked Swift Shot.

"No thanks. I'll take all the ferm you have, but Mother Turklyo provides me with the strength I need," Swift Shot answered.

"I'm sorry. After we get out of here, I'll let you sample my special reserve held in each village," Murid said.

"They save ferm for you?" Swift Shot asked.

"You never know when the king or queen might show up. Nobody wants to seem inhospitable," Murid said.

"When we destroy the Corlains, I'm going to need you to treat me to a crawl across your kingdom," Swift Shot said.

"It's a deal," Murid agreed. "May we have our fog?"

Swift Shot closed her eyes and concentrated. The ground seemed to bleed water vapor. Billowing fog rose to the height of four meters.

The shooting surrounding them stopped. Screams echoed off the destruction. The booms of cannons once more filled the air. The balls whistled as they began to explode around Murid and her people.

"Get them out of here!" Swift Shot screamed.

"Run!" Murid yelled.

Motion passed around her. Many people bumped into each other. They didn't quite know the land when most of the buildings on it now littered the ground. The glow of orange that had flared around her stopped. Murid thought she heard a body hit the ground. It had to be Two Dogs, but Swift Shot's fog was too thick, even at this close distance.

"Two Dogs, where are you?" Murid shouted.

"I've got him," Swift Shot replied. "Get your ass out of here. This fog won't stay forever!"

Murid knew she was right. It hurt her to leave Two Dogs and his friends, but she realized they were far more likely to escape than she was. With regret, she ran the way her body faced. She took comfort when her feet settled on the familiar feeling of the wood and sand that made Vikisote roads.

Regrettably, the fog didn't extend as far as she'd hoped. No more than a hundred meters past the celebration longhouse, Murid saw it dissipate. The sound of melee combat became clear as she pushed her body well past her normal limits. Murid covered her eyes from the glare shining off dozens of Corlains.

Ironically, cloud cover began to block the sun.

"The gods favor us! For the queen!" someone shouted.

Murid turned her head toward the voice. The fog was barely a hindrance at this point. What she saw was another group of survivors charge the left flank of the Corlains her group fought. The Corlains used their muskets as melee weapons. The crick oil made her people so fast that the Corlains didn't have time to reload. Murid drew her sword and joined the fray.

She leaped over a Vikisote body and came down between two Corlains. Murid surprised herself when she cleaved the head off the shoulders of the Corlain on her right. She smashed her shield into the face of the Corlain on her left. The man stumbled backward and tripped on his heels. Murid stabbed him through the throat before he could stand.

"Queen Murid!" Egill shouted.

He swung his axe like one of her father's old servants would swing his scythe during the wheat harvest. It was clear how much faster the Vikisotes moved than the Corlains. Why hadn't Murid used it before? She probably could have beaten Two Dogs in their duel.

Murid fought her way over to Egill. Each killed another Corlain who foolishly brought a musket to a sword fight.

"The north gate is only a hundred meters away, but there's a problem!" Egill shouted over the clash of metal and screams of the dying.

Cannons blasted a group of Vikisotes charging out

the hole in the wall that used to serve as a gate. The road's grade quickly shifted to a sixty-degree angle as it ran up the side of the mountain. Four cannons blocked the road about two hundred meters up the incline.

"They won't shoot us while their soldiers are engaged," Murid said. "Keep them fighting at all times. We can push our way past them."

"And once we get through the wall?" Egill asked.

He ducked a butt stroke and came up with his axe between the Corlain's legs. The man lost all fight as Egill kicked his axe free.

Murid stabbed the woman she fought with through the heart. As she freed her blade, she held up a vial of pure crick venom.

"Once we make it to the wall, we attach some of this to our arrows and clear the path."

Egill wiped his brow. He no longer wore his leather helmet. It likely laid with the bodies of her mutilated people.

"You better be a damn good shot with this bow you magically find," Egill said.

Murid spread her arms to indicate the battlefield. Bodies of all types lay in every position possible. There were weapons available.

"I'm sure the Corlains will just take a break while you grab a replacement bow, gather some arrows, attach your venom—"

A Corlain skirmisher interrupted Egill. The woman held a spear and thrust at him. He jumped backward and slashed downward with his axe. He parried the spear. Murid attacked the skirmisher from the side. Her sword broke through her right ribs and out her left ones.

"You were saying?" Murid asked.

"Thanks, but we're about to be out of options again," Egill said.

There were less than thirty Vikisotes left in Murid's group. The last of the nearest Corlains were dead, but the heavy sound of their comrades' footsteps echoed around them.

"We have to rush the cannons," Murid said. "I don't like it. It won't be pretty, but we have no other choice."

"We have one, my queen," a shield maiden said.

"What, Olha?" Murid asked.

"Let a few of us charge them first. They'll get us, but in the time it takes to reload, you can make our sacrifice count."

"No!" Murid shouted.

"Too late," Olha replied.

Olha hoisted her shield and charged the cannons with her head held low behind it. Six more Vikisotes saluted Murid and followed Olha. Before Murid could chase them, Egill grabbed her and held her in place.

"Let them honor you," he said. "Be ready to run, everyone!"

Hardened warriors nodded. Murid forced herself to watch Olha's charge. The cannons blasted, as Murid knew they would. Most of the group ceased moving, but a single warrior continued to charge.

"Go!" Egill screamed.

Murid was yanked to her feet. She shook herself

free and made sure she led the second charge. The plan worked. The Corlains were busy reloading and stabbing the last Vikisote with their swords. There were only twenty Corlains in all. Murid's group was slightly larger. The Corlains finally noticed the enraged Vikisotes. They pointed their swords at the Vikisotes and walked to stand in front of their cannons. The Vikisotes crashed into the Corlains.

The Corlains had the advantage of the high ground, but the Vikisotes were still soaked in crick oil. The battle was one-sided.

With a burst of speed, Egill passed Murid and embedded his axe into the stomach of the first Corlain. He swung the body, still connected to his axe, into a second Corlain. The second Corlain tried to slash around his dead friend and hit Egill, but the Vikisote commander kept the body between them. The Corlain eventually became frustrated and stabbed through the throat of his comrade to hit his target. The moment the Corlain's sword was committed, Egill swung his axe sideways. The Corlain lost his grip on his weapon. Egill spun as he brought his axe around. The blade landed perfectly in the center of the Corlain's back. The man's legs collapsed beneath him. Egill stomped onto the man's neck to help release his axe.

Murid's eyes widened as a Corlain sword stabbed through the wood of her round shield. It missed hitting her, but it startled her enough to curse. Her shield arm was yanked to the side as the Corlain attempted to free his weapon. Her arm twisted in such an angle she had to release her hold on her shield. With her defensive weapon stripped, she felt naked. She barely parried a thrust. She had two Corlains attacking her. One came from each side. Murid afforded herself a glance. Nobody nearby was likely to help with one of her opponents.

Murid brought her sword across her body to block an attack on her left side. The movement forced her to hug her left arm close to her body. Her fingers brushed her belt and rested on one of her vials of pure crick venom. Murid's original plan was no longer needed. Her venom had a new purpose.

"Catch!" Murid shouted as she tossed the vial toward the Corlain on her left.

The man swatted at the vial with his sword. His aim was true. The glass easily fractured and sprayed the air with crick venom. Most of it landed on the man's face. His screams redefined pain in Murid's mind. He clawed at his face; his fingers wiped away liquid skin. His head collapsed on itself. Murid disregarded him as she swung her sword back, just in time to parry another attack. With her attention no longer divided, Murid curled the fingers on her left hand into a fist and punched the Corlain. Thankfully, Corlain artillery soldiers didn't have armor. The man's nose crushed. The blow made the man stumble. He backed into one of the cannons and yelped. Murid forced him to bend in the wrong direction over the cannon. She stabbed him through the chest and felt her sword strike the cannon. When she pulled her blade from the corpse, she noticed the tip had broken off.

One of the remaining Vikisotes impaled the last

Corlain on the spear he'd acquired from a previous opponent. As the man died, the battle ended for Murid. She took stock of how many survived. Relief filled her heart when she identified Egill among the living. Besides him, she had four shield maidens and eight male warriors. The fourteen of them were a far cry from the thousands that made up her army that morning.

Egill grabbed her on the arm. "We have to go, my queen."

Murid nodded. He was right, but she wanted to look one last time at the ring fortress that had been her home for over fifteen years.

The fog surrounding the celebration longhouse was gone. So were any signs of ghost warriors. Large formations of Corlains converged on one location. Murid couldn't tell from this distance, but her instincts said Two Dogs, Swift Shot, and Ancestors' Hand were still giving them trouble. Their sacrifice gave her a chance. There were more Vikisotes who could still rally to her banner. There were other countries that hated the rules and oppression Corla enforced across Glostaimia.

Murid turned away and looked at the bodies at her feet. One brought forth the tears she'd kept at bay. Olha had apparently been the sole Vikisote to make it to the cannons. Her body had been impaled dozens of times. Her death was likely painful but brief. Many of her people had deaths like that today. Possibly, even Faida had fallen in that fashion.

Thinking of Faida brought more powerful tears. Hafoca had meant nothing to her compared to Faida. She cried for the healer and priestess more than she did after her own parents' deaths.

Egill grabbed her again. "We have to leave, now!"

Egill didn't wait for a response. He dragged Murid behind him. Her chipped sword slipped from her grasp as Egill tried to get her to run. She furiously scratched at her raw skin that suddenly felt on fire. Her crick oil must be wearing off. She would have to get more immediately!

Murid snatched her hand free of Egill. "Let's go!"

The surviving Vikisotes moved off the road and scampered up the mountain. As he passed, Egill poured concentrated crick venom over the Corlain cannons. A caustic reaction took place that ruined them as weapons.

CHAPTER 17

Swift Shot huddled Two Dogs' exhausted body against her own. The two hid with Ancestors' Hand inside the demolished longhouse Faida maintained as the Vikisotes' priestess and healer. The building, like nearly all others inside the ring fortress, was more rubble than architecture. Their space was cramped and forced them to crouch. However, it provided exceptional concealment from the Corlains searching for Vikisote survivors.

Ancestors' Hand looked nearly as drained as Two Dogs. Two Dogs collapsed from overexertion the moment Swift Shot had created the fog that covered Murid's retreat. Two Dogs hoped she and Egill made it out, but the constant blasts of cannons and muskets made him doubt anyone who wasn't Corlain would survive to witness another dawn.

Swift Shot had her bow ready and an arrow nocked, but even though some of her magical stamina must have returned, she remained silent. The last of Ancestors' Hand's spirit army had been defeated, but the Corlains seemed hesitant to move throughout the captured ring fortress. Two Dogs heard commands given to move the artillery into position. Two Dogs assumed that meant their cannons.

The nearest squad of Corlains moved farther away from the debris that hid Two Dogs and his companions. Two Dogs sighed as he suspected they were safe to speak quietly. Swift Shot let out her own pained sigh. Ancestors' Hand sat cross-legged and meditated. She hadn't spoken since Swift Shot had carried her to this location after doing the same for Two Dogs. He was thankful her powers hadn't required as near constant a cost as Two Dogs and Ancestors' Hand paid. When Swift Shot needed a rest, she could just fire her arrows as normal missiles. The cost to have them return was negligible. It meant only one dead Corlain at a time, but her arrows vanished fast enough that the Corlains often couldn't determine where the shots were coming from. The psychological effect that had on the Corlains was nearly as impactful as launching them into the air with fireballs and wind gusts.

"They're moving away on my end," Swift Shot whispered.

"On mine too," Two Dogs whispered back. "It sounded like they're going to back off until their leader shows up. I think they're bringing their cannons closer."

"Great, that's all we need," Swift Shot said.

"Any ideas on how to get out of here?" Two Dogs asked.

Swift shot shrugged and turned her attention back to the opening in the collapsed home that served as her observation post.

"What about you, old woman?" Two Dogs asked.

Ancestors' Hand didn't respond. She continued to sit and chant inaudibly to herself. The igsidian he gave her glowed brightly. He could see the orange peek out of the opening in the pouch that hung from her neck. In fact, he could distinguish a dull, orange light subdued by the green of the turklyo-skin pouch.

"Ancestors' Hand, do you have any ideas?" Two Dogs asked.

Ancestors' Hand continued to ignore him. She looked to be in deep concentration. Two Dogs opened his mouth to ask louder, then decided against saying anything.

"Can't you just give us a shield and walk us out of here?" Swift Shot asked.

Two Dogs laughed, but it came out as an exasperated scoff. He wasn't sure if she'd been joking or was scared enough to actually ask something she knew was impossible. Two Dogs had never had to use his magic for so long before. His head still pounded from the exertion. All his breaths came out deep and frantic. He was hyperventilating. This was bad. He'd seen powerful mages hyperventilate before. It had meant they went beyond healthy limits of their magic. Some never recovered. They became ostracized members of the tribe. Two Dogs would rather die than lose the gifts Mother Turklyo had given him. He suspected the Black Cloud Corlains would give him that wish.

"Isn't it your turn to come up with an idea?" Two Dogs asked.

Swift Shot offered a weak smile. Two Dogs knew she understood the situation. He was glad he'd meet his end with her. She'd always been his best friend. It was fitting.

Two Dogs looked at Ancestors' Hand. The old Intakee woman was still chanting to herself. It wasn't anything he'd heard before. Intakee and Lacreechee were similar languages, but they weren't exact copies. Ancestors' Hand made it a point to speak in Lacreechee, but she'd proven she knew many languages. She could be speaking any of them. Two Dogs wanted to be mad at her for dismissing herself from the situation, but something told him she was doing it for him. He hoped she had the chance to recover long enough to help.

"There it is," Swift Shot said, a bit louder than she should have.

Two Dogs snapped his head in her direction. "You've got a plan."

Swift Shot smiled and held up a jug. "Yeah, we finish my corn ferm. It's finally ready."

Two Dogs snorted out laughter. Swift Shot joined him. She muffled her mouth; he bit the webbing between his thumb and finger to keep from laughing. Eventually they recovered.

"You hid your homemade ferm in Faida's long-house?" Two Dogs asked.

Swift Shot smiled devilishly. "Nobody would have thought to look here. Besides, she had a lot of *holy* ferm to sample."

Two Dogs lost himself to another bout of the giggles. He envisioned Swift Shot sampling all the fruit ferms. How Faida never found out was beyond him.

Two Dogs stared at the pitcher in Swift Shot's hand and raised an eyebrow. She grabbed a cup and filled it to the absolute top. She handed the corn ferm to Two Dogs, then drank straight from the jug. Two Dogs accepted his cup and tasted Swift Shot's latest recipe.

It was amazing! It was possibly the best corn ferm he'd ever drank. Granted, knowing it was probably the last corn ferm he'd have combined with the fact he hadn't had any proper *corn* ferm in weeks meant it was a low bar to hurdle. Two Dogs leaned back his head and briefly closed his eyes while the liquid burned his tongue. He passed his cup back to Swift Shot. She refilled his mug, then flipped the pitcher.

"Back to reality," Swift Shot said.

Two Dogs nodded solemnly as he sipped his second cup of corn ferm. He looked back outside from his concealment. He didn't see any new Corlains, but his view was limited to about ten yards on either side of the road. He heard Corlains shouting commands. Men and women grunted as they moved heavy equipment. Horses clopped and whinnied. Two Dogs hated the anticipation. He wanted to charge them and get it over with. The only thing that kept him from following his instinct was his exhaustion. For every second the Corlains waited to attack, he'd be able to kill one more. He'd give them all the time they wanted. Taking a break until the next morning would be ideal, but something told him he was probably only going to get a few more minutes.

"Two Dogs, I've got Corlains again," Swift Shot said.

Two Dogs crawled over to her position. She moved to the side, and he looked through the opening. Dozens of Corlains moved on the road in front of Faida's hut. They had muskets and aimed them at Two Dogs' hiding spot. He jerked back. The sound of Corlains moving around them sounded from his old position. Two Dogs crawled back, bumping into Ancestors' Hand in the process. Corlains assembled there as well. One Corlain stood out. His helmet had a blue decoration on top. The other Corlains seemed to defer to his command. Two Dogs knew this man had to die before he did.

"Ancestors' Hand, we could use more spirits right about now," Two Dogs said.

Ancestors' Hand continued to ignore him.

"Leave her alone, I've got an idea," Swift Shot said.

"Please tell," Two Dogs said.

"It's better if I show," Swift Shot replied with a wink.

From outside, the blue-helmeted man spoke. "Namerians! We know you're in there! Surrender! We didn't give this option to your Vikisote allies!"

Two Dogs clenched his fists. Despite still feeling tired, that word still incited him to action. Only Swift Shot placing a calming hand on his shoulder held him in place. He could feel his power slowly returning. Apparently, hatred sped up the process.

"You didn't give my tribe the option to surrender!"

Two Dogs shouted.

The blue-helmeted man looked to the closest Corlains standing by him. None seemed to have an answer to what Two Dogs was talking about. This pissed him off more. How could they forget the slaughter of an entire people in just a few weeks? The black cloud on their shoulder identified them as belonging to the same unit.

"Who am I speaking with? Which Namerian tribe do you belong to?" the blue-helmeted Corlain officer asked.

"Calm down," Swift Shot whispered. "I've got an opening above us."

Two Dogs still wasn't sure what her plan was, but he'd listen to his friend. He barely registered his exhaustion anymore. He'd summon all his magic to his speed and thrust his spear straight through the man's neck.

"I'm Two Dogs of the Lacreechee tribe!"

"I see," the officer said. "You isolated Namerians have always been especially troublesome. You refuse to accept the order of things and attack without warning. Why would you expect mercy from us?"

Two Dogs clutched his spear tighter. Lacreechee only fought to defend their land. The Corlains stole igsidian at every opportunity. This man was the lowest of human beings.

"You know my name!" Two Dogs shouted. "Who are you?"

"I'm General Githinji of the Black Cloud Division. You're either my prisoners or the last to fall today. You have five minutes to decide which you'd prefer to be!"

"I have a better idea. Why don't you face me as Mother Turklyo would like?"

"Your heathen goddess means nothing to me. Your challenge reeks of desperation. I've massed my forces; I won't allow vanity to rob me of a victory."

Two Dogs looked at Swift Shot and shrugged. "It was worth a shot."

"He dies," Swift Shot said. It was a statement, not a wish. "I'll give you the diversion you need. Make sure that man chokes on his last words."

Two Dogs gripped his spear tighter. He glanced at Ancestors' Hand. The old hag was still concentrating. Hopefully she was ready because he and Swift Shot weren't waiting any longer.

Swift Shot maneuvered inside the limited space of their protection. She aimed an arrow at a cannonball-sized hole in the ceiling, then pulled as far back on the string as her taut muscles would allow.

"Three minutes!" Githinji shouted.

Swift Shot released her arrow. It flew out the hole in the roof and continued high into the sky. Two Dogs was about to question Swift Shot when he heard the crack of thunder. A slow smile spread across Swift Shot's face. Soon, Two Dogs had one that matched. Ancestors' Hand didn't react.

Outside, the Corlains stared as the clouds darkened above them. It began to rain. The rain immediately transformed into a full downpour. The Corlains seemed perplexed, then screams slowly permeated their ranks.

The cannon soldiers in clothes versus armor

screamed and clawed at themselves. The armored Corlains scanned their less-armored brethren and looked back at each other, but Two Dogs focused on their armor. It would take a long time, but the initial stages of corrosion were evident.

"I might have created a tiny, little . . . chemical-rain thunderstorm," Swift Shot said. "Give me some room to work. Once I have them panicked, get that bastard who killed our people."

Swift Shot fired an arrow out her hole, then shot another outside Two Dogs' hole. Both arrows were charged with electricity. Both Corlains were hit in their hearts and died, but magical lightning then arced throughout the wet formation of Corlains. Many fell over and twitched. Those closest to the men pierced by arrows died, but the Corlain enchanted armor meant the magic lost effectiveness after two or three people.

Two Dogs erected a magical barrier above them. He would have added sides to their magical fortress, but he wasn't strong enough. His anger consumed him. He wanted Githinji to die, which meant he needed to save his stamina.

Swift Shot continued to fire arrows of every type of elemental magic. Two Dogs could see she wouldn't be able to keep it up for long. She gave him his window; he had to take it.

Two Dogs let out a war cry as he increased his strength. Corlains fired their muskets into the debris he hid in. Two Dogs clenched his left fist and smashed through the wall. Stone and peat flew outward. Two Dogs increased his speed and added protection around himself. Githinji had several Corlains around him. That suited Two Dogs just fine.

Two Dogs launched himself at the first Corlain aiming a musket at him. He stabbed the man through the chest with the spear in his left hand. He used the tomahawk in his right hand to hook the musket and aim it away from him. The dying Corlain fired his weapon; the musket ball shattered the kneecap of the Corlain on his left.

Orange flashed all around Two Dogs. He took a knee as Corlains stabbed into his weakening barrier. He swung his spear in a wide arc and tripped many of them. He rolled across their bodies as he sliced throats. An explosion of lava landed near Two Dogs. He looked trapped inside an orange sphere for several seconds as he moved away from the burning Corlains. Swift Shot was keeping many of them away from him, but her shots were coming slower and slower. The acid rain had stopped. Swift Shot apparently decided to hit the drenched Corlains with frost-charged arrows.

"You are *tiresome*, Namerian," Githinji said.

His voice had nothing but malice. Two Dogs understood. He felt the same way for the man primarily responsible for the death of his friends and family.

"Fortunately, you're also *tired*," Githinji mocked.

He stood before Two Dogs with his sword held in salute. Two Dogs placed his tomahawk back into his belt and twirled his spear. Dozens of Corlains stood behind their general. Two Dogs charged Githinji. Githinji fell prone to the ground. The first rank of Corlains fired their muskets. Two Dogs flashed orange as his magic intercepted the musket balls.

Githinji stood and swung at Two Dogs with a sweeping slash. Two Dogs got his spear in the way, but Githinji easily broke the weapon in half. Two Dogs stared at the two halves of his weapon. Each end still had an igsidian blade. He nearly neglected to block a pair of followup swings from Githinji.

Two Dogs swung wildly at Githinji. He had to reduce some of his speed to keep his magical armor up. He forced Githinji back but wasn't able to land anything more than a glancing blow. Githinji retreated several steps. Two Dogs held both hands in front of him as the first of three volleys of musket fire slammed into him. One ball broke through his barrier and grazed his left arm. A slow trickle of blood traveled down his limb. He dropped the half of his spear held in that hand.

Two Dogs threw the half of his spear in his right hand. It flew wobbly. Githinji batted it from the air. Before Two Dogs could draw his knife and tomahawk, another rank of Corlains fired their muskets. Two Dogs was spared any further injury. He breathed heavily and was forced to direct all his magic into protection. He only had to get this last target, then he could see his family again.

Two Dogs hadn't been paying attention to his surroundings. Now that mistake was evident. He'd assumed the Corlains were firing and reloading their muskets. He knew they had multiple ranks, but that was to give the first rank time to reload and start the process over. It may have been the tactic in the past, but it apparently wasn't Githinji's plan this time. Each rank had fired and moved to the side. The last volley had been different soldiers than the first. Two Dogs fell to his knees as the reason became obvious. Staring him down was a cannon with a lit fuse.

Time seemed to slow as the cannonball flew at him. His vision filled with orange as the last of his magic surged in front of him. Two Dogs felt his body lift from the ground and fly backward. He crashed back inside the remnants of Faida's home.

Swift Shot fired an arrow back toward the cannon. The opening had a block of ice wedged inside. The Corlains returned fire with their muskets. One round hit Swift Shot in the last two fingers on her left hand. The fingers fell free as the bow snapped in half.

Swift Shot screamed as she cauterized the stubs on her left hand.

"You bastards can't kill me!" Swift Shot screamed in pain. "You keep trying, but no Corlain can kill me!"

Two Dogs was barely conscious. He hyperventilated again. It felt like he was drowning. It was a terrible feeling, but losing his magic that usually filled him was even more terrifying. He was disconnected from Mother Turklyo. Even worse, Githinji still lived. Any moment now, he would come in and kill the three of them. Two Dogs would die, and Mother Turklyo wouldn't accept him home!

"Run," Ancestors' Hand said.

"What?" Swift Shot asked.

Ancestors' Hand hadn't reacted to anything for some time. Two Dogs hadn't expected her to ever be ready with whatever magic she'd prepared.

"Run north of here. Meet up with the Vikisotes. I'll provide the distraction," Ancestors' Hand said.

She was serene. Her attitude contrasted that of both Two Dogs and Swift Shot. They wouldn't make it ten steps before being cut down, yet Ancestors' Hand was adamant they could survive.

Yellow smoke spilled in from the openings within their barely existing cover. The Corlains outside shouted their concern. Officers commanded their soldiers to prepare for more spirit warriors. Two Dogs expected to hear combat, but all he heard was preparation.

"Swift Shot, get him out of here. He *is* the chosen one. He can't fall here," Ancestors' Hand said.

"What are you going—"

"Get him out of here!"

Ancestors' Hand's voice ended any further protest from Swift Shot. She grabbed Two Dogs and threw him over her shoulders. His exhaustion began to overwhelm him. He closed his eyes, then opened them. He and Swift Shot were no longer with Ancestors' Hand. They were outside Faida's demolished hut. Swift Shot held him tightly as she ran north. Filling the surrounding air was a yellow smoke that resembled Ancestors' Hand's summoning magic, but there weren't any spirit warriors in it. It was just a thick haze. It obscured the Corlains' vision, but few seemed to be looking for people. They kept expecting another magical fight. Some retreated, like Githinji, but the junior soldiers held their weapons at the ready.

Swift Shot breathed heavily as she finally cleared the yellow smoke. Musket fire began to ring through the air, but it wasn't targeted at them. Two Dogs thought he heard Ancestors' Hand scream. Then, a wave of magical energy erupted from the epicenter that used to be Ancestors' Hand. The Corlains caught in the blast simply fell in place. They crumpled as if the life inside them had been snuffed. It reminded Two Dogs of what Ancestors' Hand had done to Hafoca.

"Is that possible?" Swift Shot asked as she tried to catch her breath. "Did she send their souls to the spirit world?"

Two Dogs didn't answer. He closed his eyes, then did nothing but sleep.

CHAPTER 18

Githinji pushed Zoya and the other three soldiers shielding him off his body. His instincts had told him to move away from the ambush the yellow smoke indicated. It wouldn't have done to have had him in the middle of a ghost army. The smoke had been different this time than earlier in the battle. It never took shape. The uncertainty that brought forced him to retreat and consider the battlefield. His soldiers had been brave. Many stayed and waited. It had cost them.

Githinji remembered the battlefield before him. The yellow smoke had become denser for several minutes. Eventually, something flashed within it. Githinji had been clear of the smoke by that point. He heard bodies falling to the ground. The clatter they made guaranteed they were Corlains wearing plate armor. That's when Zoya and others forced him to the ground and covered him. It touched him that they would willingly sacrifice themselves to save him, but it was unnecessary. They were safe from whatever savage magic the Namerians had used.

Once the flash filled the yellow smoke, it quickly dissipated. Githinji dusted himself off as he looked more closely at the effects. There was only death for at least fifty meters surrounding the pitiful sanctuary the Namerians had held up in. All the Corlains within that perimeter were on the ground. None moved.

"Look for survivors!" Githinji shouted.

His soldiers moved forward with precision. They scattered to check if any of the remaining soldiers had a pulse.

"He's still alive!" someone shouted.

"She is too!" another more hopeful voice sounded.

"Both of these guys made it!" a third person said.

Githinji scrunched his face and mouthed *what?* He took off his helmet and stared at Zoya. She also removed her helmet and gave him the same blank face he must have had. All around them Corlains shouted in exuberance that the soldiers they found were still alive. However, another common feature remained. None of them responded to their excited companions.

"Are any of them conscious?" Githinji shouted.

As he feared, he got silence as an answer.

"What is this?" Zoya asked.

"I don't know. Sleep magic?" Githinji said.

"Perhaps," Zoya said, rubbing her helmet. "I didn't see many Namerians. There might have only been two."

"I think there had to have been at least a third. Namerian mages tend to follow specific schools of magic. The man fought me like a protector. There was an archer who used elemental magic too," Githinji said.

"Those were the two I had marked . . . I see. There

was also a summoner. The spirit warriors wouldn't have come from the other two."

"Not likely," Githinji agreed. "Our soldiers may still be alive, but that Namerian witch has likely taken away any satisfying life."

"Yes, sir. Orders?"

Githinji rubbed his neck. He knew some Vikisotes escaped. He feared the Namerian archer may have gotten out as well. He needed to find the Namerians' bodies, but he also needed to secure the ring fortress. There was also the possibility that some Vikisotes were still hiding. They would have to be gathered and imprisoned.

Githinji walked closer to the Namerians' last stand. It looked to have been a longhouse, but not quite as large as most of the others. The walls were torn down, but the debris looked to have been blasted outward. Githinji took another hesitant step toward the rubble. His foot kicked something.

Githinji looked down and saw a half of the igsidian spear Two Dogs had used. He reached down and picked it up. The other half laid close by. Githinji gathered it too. He looked at each igsidian stone from several angles. He didn't understand igsidian, but it was valuable. It would be another gift for Ekundayo.

"Sir, look!" Zoya shouted.

Githinji walked around a pair of soldiers lifting one of the comatose Corlains onto a stretcher. Actions like this were taking place everywhere.

"What do you have, Zoya?" he asked.

Zoya pointed her sword at a dead Namerian

woman. She looked ancient and wore a turklyo-skin dress. She had a pouch around her neck. Zoya retrieved it after checking the woman's pulse.

"She's dead," Zoya said as she tossed the pouch to Githinji.

He snatched it out of the air. Githinji opened the pouch and saw several small pieces of igsidian. They looked like they may have once been a solid piece. Githinji sealed the pouch again and tied it to his belt. The parts of the broken spear he kept in his left hand.

"Sir! We have a survivor!" a Corlain sergeant screamed.

Githinji and Zoya immediately left the dead Namerian and raced to the non-commissioned officer.

"Where?" Githinji asked.

"Follow me, sir, ma'am," the sergeant responded.

The sergeant led Githinji and Zoya to a woman in her mid-fifties. She didn't wear any armor, but her clothing marked her as a priestess for the Vikisotes. She lay amid dozens of small bodies. Some children were only toddlers.

The woman's legs were shattered. She breathed raspy breaths as she stared daggers at the squad of Corlains aiming rifles at her. She clearly wasn't a mage, but some of Githinji's soldiers still kept their distance.

"And you would be?" Githinji asked.

The woman spat blood in Githinji's direction. He laid his helmet on the ground next to the woman and squatted. His eyes were at the same level as hers as she rested against a collapsed longhouse wall.

"The battle is over. There's no reason we can't

have a discussion from mutual respect for a worthy enemy," Githinji said.

The woman laughed. Githinji smiled and waited. She grimaced and lazily laid her hands on her belly.

"Laughter is the best medicine. You look like you could use some more," Githinji said.

Some of his soldiers politely laughed at the poor joke, thankfully not Zoya, but the Vikisote woman snarled.

"Die, bastard," she said. "The chosen one escaped. I know she did."

Githinji covered his mouth as he snorted out his own laughter. The *chosen one*? How backward were these people? This time, Zoya laughed with the other soldiers. What started as a chuckle grew in volume as the absurdity of the woman's statement mixed with her total belief in it hit the collective Corlains.

"Sure, laugh away—" The woman stopped to hack and spit more blood. "The gods decreed our chosen one will avenge all who died here today."

More laughter erupted from the Corlains. Even Githinji allowed another snicker to escape his lips.

"Exactly *which* chosen one is it this time?" Githinji asked.

A few Corlains continued to laugh; others let out a mirthful sigh. The Vikisote woman seemed enraged by their *blasphemy*, but her conviction apparently forced her to answer.

"Queen Murid! She's survived your massacres twice now. She will defeat the foreign invaders. She has powerful friends and the love of the gods!" the woman shouted.

"*The love of the gods?* Are you serious? Look around you. Your gods don't exist. If they did, this never would have happened."

Githinji stood and gestured wide with his arms. The woman didn't respond. She looked away when he challenged her with eye contact. Githinji stepped hard on her shattered legs and pressed his weight into her wound. The woman screamed throughout the duration of his attack.

"You will *not* ignore me," Githinji said.

The woman screamed. She thrashed her hands, but Githinji kept the pressure on her. Eventually, she forced herself to look Githinji in the eyes. When he saw he had her undivided attention, he removed his foot.

"That's better," Githinji said. "Would you mind telling me where your precious Queen Murid ran off to after my division defeated her army in every way?"

"Best guess, she's telling the rest of Glostaimia the reason you have to overcompensate in battle," the woman said.

Githinji clenched his jaw to keep from smiling. She had fire. He respected that. "Why couldn't you have been a shield maiden?"

Before the woman could spit anymore insults at him, he plunged both halves of Two Dogs' spear into her. The igsidian tips burrowed down her shoulders and into her hips. The hag gasped and quickly died.

"Make sure you get the igsidian back and place it in my carriage," Githinji instructed a few nearby Corlains.

"Yes, sir," they said in unison.

Githinji wiped the blood from his gauntlets onto the woman's skirt.

"Sir, Captain Kali has cleared the city," Zoya said.

Standing beside her was the aforementioned officer.

"Good, Captain Kali, good. Did you find any survivors?" Githinji asked.

"Yes, sir, but they were all wounded. They were left behind because of their injuries," Kali answered.

"I understand. How about Namerians? Did you find any more bodies?" Githinji asked.

"No, sir. The only Namerian was the one crone. Any others must have escaped."

Githinji nodded. He'd expected as much. He nearly had the Namerians, but the hag must have sacrificed herself to allow the others to leave. It didn't matter. The Vikisotes were decimated. A few dozen may have escaped, but they wouldn't even be a match for a single company.

Trumpets blared in the distance. They played a Corlain tune. Githinji and Zoya turned to face the sound. Cresting the mountain and spilling into the valley from the south were the banners of the Diamond Fence Division. Tosaca's division. Githinji squeezed his hands into fists. The bastard would gloat immediately.

"It's the Diamond Fence Division, sir," Zoya said.

"I see that," Githinji said, a bit too crossly. "Zoya, I want Queen Murid."

"Sir, I think it would be best if you spoke with General Tosaca first," Zoya said.

"I fully intend to speak with him, but the snake will

make me see Ekundayo. I'll be forced to play politician for some time. I don't want the Vikisotes to have that time to regroup and rebuild. You will hunt them down and destroy them."

"We'll have to leave immediately," Zoya said.

"I understand. I'll give you as much time as possible. I won't let Tosaca steal this victory and ingratiate himself to our leader. Our spies did well in getting us here. You can use their other reports to decipher the most logical place the Vikisotes fled to."

"Yes, sir. They breached us to the north. I think that gives me all the information I need."

"Take your best battalion and go now. Don't stop for anyone. Find the Vikisotes. Hunt them down and kill or capture them. I prefer *kill*."

Zoya placed her helmet on her head. She saluted Githinji with her sword. He stood erect and returned the sword salute. Zoya left with a few of the Corlains standing nearby. She would be clear of the city inside fifteen minutes. It would take that long for the pompous Tosaca to parade himself through the remains of the ring fortress to Githinji. He hated to play this game, but he absolutely despised losing.

Githinji walked to the intersection of the two roads moving through the decimated ring fortress. The banners of the Diamond Fence Division fluttered in the cool mountain breeze. They were white with gold trim and gold diamonds acting as fence posts. Banners were always ostentatious; Tosaca's were especially obnoxious.

Tosaca was atop a pure white mare. Appearances meant a lot to him. He seemed to spot Githinji and trotted his horse over. Githinji made it a point to stand in the exact middle of the intersection. His rival would likely try to force him back with his horse. Githinji prepared himself for the blow. Surprisingly, Tosaca didn't take the cheap shot. He halted his horse a meter in front of Githinji and stared down at him from the mount.

"General Githinji, I see you've been busy," Tosaca said.

Githinji held his arms wide. "War isn't pretty, but the Black Cloud Division gets it done. Perhaps some of your soldiers would like a lesson?"

It was an obvious threat, but the words needed to be spoken. If the Black Cloud had a reputation of being violent warriors, then the Diamond Fence had a reputation of being timid. They were the rich sons and daughters of important people who merely wanted to pretend they were soldiers. Few had likely ever engaged in a battle.

"Don't do that," Tosaca said. "I didn't come here to spar with you."

"Then why did you come?" Githinji genuinely asked.

"I came here to arrest you," Tosaca matter-of-factly stated.

Githinji scoffed. Tosaca kept a measured face. It wasn't a bluff. What had he said to Ekundayo to get him to agree to such a ridiculous course of action?

"On whose authority?" Githinji asked.

"You know whose. Ekundayo sent for you weeks ago. You can't ignore our leader and be surprised he'd take offense."

"I'm sure I have you to thank for his decision?"

This time, Tosaca smiled. "I may have shared a word or two."

"Anything you've done, I will undo. Ekundayo will appreciate this victory I've brought him."

Tosaca laughed. "You know our leader that well, do you? I may have gotten him to agree you needed to be brought back in chains, but *your* actions got him considering the option long before I spoke to him. You look at the devastation around you and see victory; I see disobedience. You've sacrificed your honor, but worse yet, you've sacrificed Corla's! This wasn't your mission!"

That wasn't true. Githinji's mission had always been to enforce the will of Corla. The Vikisotes and many Namerian tribes resisted that will. It was his duty to wipe them from Glostaimia.

Tosaca reached behind him and produced a pair of shackles. He held one end and let the other fall dramatically. It swayed in the breeze.

"Will you be obedient now, or must I do this the unpleasant way?" Tosaca asked.

Githinji could take this man. His division, though battle weary, could easily defeat Tosaca's troops. The thought was enticing, almost intoxicating, but that would ruin his legacy and the plans he'd been working toward over the past thirty years. Once he spoke with Ekundayo, he would earn his leader's forgiveness. In fact, he'd likely have a chance to facilitate a promotion. It was in his best interest to allow Tosaca this limited victory.

Githinji held out his wrists and mocked Tosaca. "I live only to serve Corla!"

A few of his soldiers cheered, but most remained silent and simply watched as a Diamond Fence soldier took the shackles from Tosaca. The soldier walked forward, removed Githinji's gauntlets, and forcibly attached the shackles to Githinji's hands behind his back. Githinji forced himself not to grimace as the soldier gave them an extra squeeze to ensure they were as uncomfortable as possible.

"Tosaca," Githinji said.

"Yes?"

"You may want to order your soldiers to sweep the area for crick venom and other precursors. With the pampered lives they've lived, most won't know the difference between crick oil and honey ferm. I could have my soldiers assist them, if you don't have a month to let your people take the lead."

A few Black Cloud soldiers chuckled. It was loud enough that Githinji knew Tosaca heard. His red face proved as much. It took the general a moment to visibly regain his composure.

"That won't be necessary. Your soldiers will be allowed to rest and recuperate without your constantly cracking whip. Shall we?"

Githinji didn't respond. His silence was now his best weapon. Any more comments would just make him look like he was posturing. A pair of Corlains from the Diamond Fence Division grabbed an arm each and led Githinji toward a caged prison wagon. As Githinji passed his soldiers, they held two fingers against the

Black Cloud coat of arms on their left shoulder. Occasionally, the Black Cloud soldier would hold one, three, or four fingers. The number indicated which brigade he or she belonged to. Githinji beamed as he returned each salute with a nod. Tosaca hadn't won anything.

CHAPTER 19

Two Dogs and Swift Shot lay prone alongside the crest of a mountain. Evening was soon to transition into dark night. It had been hours since the pair had escaped the Vikisote ring fortress. Two Dogs panted every time the pair stopped. He'd never realized how much he'd relied on his magic. He continued to search for the connection, but his igsidian stayed a dull black. The separation tormented his soul. He had no choice; if he hadn't used his magic beyond his limits, he and Swift Shot would be dead. He'd mistakenly believed Mother Turklyo would understand. She'd want him to protect the only other living Lacreechee. How wrong he'd been. For more reasons than one, he yearned for his power. It was embarrassing having to fully rely on Swift Shot to protect them.

Two Dogs reached for his eagle feathers before slowly withdrawing his hand. They weren't there anymore. Neither he nor Swift Shot escaped the ring fortress with their prized representation of their heritage. It wasn't a surprise Mother Turklyo was displeased with him. He wasn't representing his tribe properly. Thankfully, Swift Shot hadn't been deprived of her magic as he had.

Two Dogs observed her as she scanned the trails leading to them. The Corlain pursuit they'd expected had never come. A battalion mobilized soon after them but distinctly turned west and raced to some unknown destination.

"Still no sign of any Corlain pursuit," Swift Shot stated.

Two Dogs was thankful she was being considerate. He half expected her to tease him about losing his magic. He was certain those insults would pile on the moment his igsidian even showed a flicker of power. What he wasn't certain about was if he could produce that flicker.

"Shall we keep heading north?" Swift Shot asked.

Two Dogs rolled onto his back and stared at the stars. "What's the point? The Vikisotes are finished. Meeting up with them will just lead to our own deaths. We'll end up like Ancestors' Hand. I don't want to die until Corla does. I *can't* die until Mother Turklyo welcomes me back."

Swift Shot rolled onto her side and stared at Two Dogs. Her eyes were soft, but her words were fierce. "That's quitter talk."

Two Dogs turned away and shrugged. "We lost. One division ripped through us like we were children. Corla has at least a dozen divisions. We can't beat them."

"So we just run and hide?" Swift Shot asked incredulously. "Corla is greedy. They take everything. They won't stop expanding. People like us have to make it not worth their time."

Two Dogs scoffed. "Even if they stop, it won't be for long. Corla may halt to lick their wounds, but they'll recruit. They'll rebuild. A five-year break will create an even more powerful Corla. They have the people, technology, and resources to win. We were foolish to try and stop them."

Swift Shot slapped Two Dogs. He stared at her in disbelief as he rubbed the pain away.

"I don't know what it feels like to lose Mother Turklyo's gifts, but I'm *done* listening to your self-pity. You're more than your magic. Ancestors' Hand would be disgusted with you if she heard this."

"Ancestors' Hand is dead! She died because Corla is too strong! She died because the Vikisotes . . . because *Murid* chose to party instead of retreat. For those same reasons, I'm without my power. I've lost Mother Turklyo's favor!"

"Keep it down," Swift Shot loudly whispered.

"She's dead," Two Dogs repeated but quieter. "I think she'd want us to live longer than the time it takes to run across the next Corlain unit."

Swift Shot quickly stood. She stomped away from Two Dogs, heading north on the mountain road. Two Dogs stood and trotted after her.

"No," Two Dogs said.

Swift Shot ignored him. She continued to walk

north. Two Dogs ran in front of her and placed his hands on her shoulders. He dug in his heels to keep her from moving.

"I said *no*," Two Dogs said. "We're not rejoining the Vikisotes."

"You aren't my chief," Swift Shot said.

She snaked her hands between his and chopped them outward. The move pushed his hands off her at the wrists. Two Dogs didn't replace them. He stepped aside, allowing Swift Shot to walk again. He kept pace on her right.

"I'm not trying to be chief. I'm trying to keep the tribe alive," Two Dogs said.

"The tribe is dead. We can't change that. We *can* stop the Corlains from doing it again."

"How exactly? What's your amazing plan that takes a lame Lacreechee warrior and an elementalist and somehow transforms them into the deciding factor? The Vikisotes are finished. Maybe Murid has a hundred warriors left. We saw what little good they were when they had four thousand."

"I don't care," Swift Shot said. "I'm a warrior. I won't run from a war I've already committed myself to."

"Fine, but we shouldn't fight it with the Vikisotes. Murid proved how incompetent she is. We can find other tribes. Mother Turklyo's children are our true allies."

Two Dogs felt a twinge of shame. Maybe it wasn't completely fair to blame Murid for his situation, but who else could he? They hadn't been ready to face a Corlain division, but the queen had put more stock in silly traditions than practicality. He and Ancestors' Hand had paid the price of her hubris.

Swift Shot stopped walking. She slowly turned her head to face Two Dogs.

"That's the problem, isn't it?" she said. "You care more about getting your magic back than what Corla did to us. Every single one of those bastards must die. The Vikisotes are still our best chance to make that happen. They've suffered like we have. Nothing can stop a rage like that."

She was right. Two Dogs still wanted to kill every Corlain in existence, but that was impossible without his magic. Sometimes lame warriors found their connection again. He would seek these people and mimic their journeys.

"Would you feel any differently?" Two Dogs asked. "About regaining your connection with Mother Turklyo, I mean."

Swift Shot's eyes finally looked sympathetic again. She reached out and caressed Two Dogs' cheek. He closed his eyes and held his tears back.

"I wouldn't," Swift Shot admitted. "I can't imagine what you're going through. It terrifies me to think it could happen to me or that I'll fail you. You saved me. You saved all of us. Without your barriers, we would have died. Instead, you gave us a chance. If nothing else, more Corlains are dead because Vikisotes were still there to fight after they entered the city."

"You've saved me just as many times."

"This isn't a competition!"

Two Dogs took a step back after Swift Shot's

outburst.

"I'm sorry," Two Dogs said.

"No, I'm sorry. Do you want to talk about it? I know you're scared, but maybe it'll help to get it off your chest?"

Tears pooled, then fell down Two Dogs' face. Swift Shot placed a comforting arm across his shoulders. He leaned his head into hers.

"Who am I if not a protector?"

"You'll always be a protector. Even if you aren't enhanced, you're still stronger and faster than most people I know. Your magic didn't make you a competent fighter. You did that. I'll do everything I can to help you reconnect with Mother Turklyo, but until you do, I'm positive the Corlains still have much to fear."

Two Dogs lifted his head and stared into Swift Shot's eyes.

"You just won't be able to do it a dozen at a time anymore."

Swift Shot laughed after finishing her joke. Two Dogs joined her. It felt cathartic.

"Thank you," Two Dogs said.

Swift Shot smiled in response. "If you start crying again, you better get me some strong ferm first."

The two Lacreechee shared another round of laughter.

They walked for hours into the evening and took turns watching for Corlains as the other slept. They continued before dawn, always heading north. The Corlains hadn't pushed this far north, so the only people they saw were Vikisote commoners. Most ignored them. Two Dogs wasn't sure if any tribes lived in this part of Glostaimia. If they did, they weren't making themselves known.

Another day passed with the two bantering. More than once, Two Dogs slipped further into despair than Swift Shot was comfortable. Often he voiced his disgust in Murid's decisions. She'd always call him out. He'd apologize, they'd bond over how many Corlains they would still kill, then they'd laugh. Three days passed like this as the two traveled north.

Around noon on the third day, Two Dogs thought he heard several horses galloping. He and Swift Shot moved to the side of the road and hid among the foliage. Two Dogs held a hand to the ground and felt it tremble. Several riders were coming, too many to be locals. Judging by the route they took after the battle, two Dogs doubted the Corlains got in front of them. It could be the Vikisotes, but he doubted they'd be this interested in a fight so soon after nearly becoming extinct. It was possible another army lived here. Two Dogs wasn't a strong student of geography and the arbitrary borders of nations not belonging to a tribe.

"I make six riders," Swift Shot said, readying a pitiful bow she found on a corpse as they escaped the ring fortress.

She had an arrow aimed at the lead rider. Her hands trembled with the loss of two fingers. Two Dogs looked closer at the riders. Their armor was brown. It didn't shine in the midday sun.

"I think they're Vikisotes," Two Dogs said.

He sighed. He'd hoped they'd never run into any. Swift Shot would have given up once she'd remembered how much she liked ferm.

Swift Shot placed her arrow back into her return quiver. "I think you're right. Shall we announce ourselves?"

Two Dogs sighed again and held out his hand, indicating she should *lead the way*.

Swift Shot stood from behind her concealment. Two Dogs followed her to stand in the center of the road. The riders were approximately thirty yards away when they increased their pace. The lead rider waved frantically at the pair of Lacreechee.

"I think he likes you," Two Dogs joked.

"He's only human," Swift Shot joked back.

As the riders move closer, Two Dogs confirmed they were Vikisotes. He smiled when he recognized the lead rider.

"I'll be a gods' whore, it *is* you!" Egill shouted.

He jumped from his horse and grabbed Two Dogs in a fierce bear hug. After he released Two Dogs, he did the same to Swift Shot. Since she was lighter, he lifted her off the ground and twirled her once. Normally a man would have been kicked in the crotch for that, but Swift Shot seemed to be just as happy to see him.

"I can't believe you live," Egill said.

"I can't believe it either," Two Dogs admitted. "Ancestors' Hand had some magic hidden up her sleeve that gave us a chance to escape."

"Where is she?" Egill asked.

His eyes lit up with expectation. When Two Dogs

and Swift Shot stared at the ground, his eyes followed.

"I see," he said.

"Her sacrifice took many Corlains with her," Swift Shot said.

Egill nodded. "Good. I hope they all burn in the afterlife."

"Please tell me Queen Murid escaped too," Swift Shot said.

Two Dogs was about to ask the same question. A huge part of him hoped she hadn't. Under that condition, maybe he could forgive her. Her decisions cost Two Dogs his power! If she had just ordered a retreat instead of honoring some invented deity, he'd still have an army to fight the Corlains with.

"She does." Egill smiled. "We gathered in Wyrmcrest."

"How many?" Two Dogs asked.

Now it was Egill's turn to look somber. "Sixty-three."

A silence hung between the Lacreechee and the Vikisotes. Swift Shot broke it.

"Now make it sixty-five."

Egill smiled and nodded a single time.

"How far away is your stronghold?" Two Dogs asked.

"About fifteen kilometers northwest of here," Egill answered.

"How far is that exactly?" Swift Shot asked.

"You Nam . . . people and your backward system of measurement. Please join the rest of Glostaimia," Egill said.

Two Dogs sighed but allowed the barb to pass unacknowledged.

"It's about an hour's ride from here," Egill clarified.

"What brought you out this far?" Two Dogs asked.

"Queen Murid and I agreed that if you'd escape, you'd likely be on this road. We've checked it for days. I'm glad we finally found you. We've had reports that a few hundred Corlains are advancing on our position."

"We thank you for your search," Swift Shot said.

Egill rubbed the back of his head. "Honestly, I needed to get out of Wyrmcrest for other reasons too."

"Which were?" Swift Shot asked.

"Their mayor and I don't see eye to eye. Keeping us in the same room will eventually lead to violence."

"Then why ally yourself with him?" Two Dogs asked. "Can he be trusted?"

Egill shrugged. "He's a dog of a man. In our business, there's the right way and the wrong way. He prefers the *evil* way, but we're in no position to be picky."

"As long as he'll help us kill Corlains," Swift Shot said.

"That he will," Egill confirmed. "We should head back. The Corlains will soon be here."

"Why are you even out here?" Two Dogs shouted. "Didn't you learn your lesson the last time? If you wait, the Corlains will mass on you."

"We didn't want to abandon you," Egill said.

Two Dogs threw his hands up. "We aren't your saviors."

Egill's voice took a hard edge. "Nobody said you were. I told you before, *I'm your man*. We all are. Jorosolman wouldn't have forgiven me if I hadn't tried. Not after saving my life *twice*."

Swift Shot jumped between the men. "Relax, boys, let's just get off this road. I think we could all go for a tall cup of ferm."

Egill held his glare for a moment longer, then looked to Swift Shot and smiled. "I know I can go for one. We have reason to celebrate now!"

The other Vikisotes cheered in agreement. They wouldn't have if they knew Two Dogs was lame now. He shuddered when he thought of what that revelation could lead to. Egill helped Swift Shot onto his horse behind him. Two Dogs mounted behind another Vikisote. As embarrassing as it was to ride like this, he had to admit his feet thanked him for it.

The riders turned their horses north and galloped away.

CHAPTER 20

Unlike the celebration hall, this longhouse was absent of anything other than a single table with a bench on each side. A dozen influential Vikisotes in Wyrmcrest surrounded the table. They held one person at higher esteem than her.

Murid stared at the Vikisote warrior standing before her inside the longhouse. His name was Sven. A boorish man who probably just entered his thirties. He was the Mayor of Wyrmcrest and clearly upset that Murid had chosen his home to retreat to.

"I understand your worry, Sven, but this is still my kingdom," Murid said.

She added steel to her voice. Her claim to a throne was practically nonexistent at this point. The few people who survived the Corlain attack all looked at her with a new perspective. They no longer needed a reason to abandon her. Now, they simply needed the first person to walk away. Sven seemed keen to become that person.

"My *worry*? You say it like it has no merit. The Corlains know you're against them. They sent the Black Cloud to destroy you. Do you think they'll give up after a single battle? A single battle that wiped out ninety-eight percent of your army?"

Sven crossed his arms in defiance. Murid wished Egill was here. He was adamant he could find the Lacreechee. Murid knew it was a fool's errand. The Lacreechee were dead. The only reason she agreed to let him search was because he was her only ally left, and she needed to keep him happy. There was also the point of Egill and Sven absolutely despising each other. If she lost Egill's loyalty, a knife would find its way to her throat within a night.

She scratched at her constantly itchy skin. "Do you truly believe the Corlains will spare you if you turn against me?"

"Of course not, but you shouldn't have brought this to us."

"You forget your place!"

Sven took a step back. He grimaced, then stomped loudly as he took three steps forward. He was now within arm's reach of Murid.

"You need a husband," Sven whispered into Murid's ear.

That was his game. He wanted to be king. Marrying her would be the easiest way. Apparently, love was nothing next to ambition. He would seed more doubt into the minds of the other Vikisotes, then have a change of heart when she agreed to his terms. It disgusted Murid that she actually considered the offer.

She'd played her hand, but people would never accept a woman as their leader, especially Vikisotes. Murid felt she would have been more accepted as a foreign man than as a Vikisote woman. She'd never had a chance. Even Two Dogs seemed equally interested in her power as he was with her as a person. The memory of Two Dogs wounded Murid. The people would have accepted him. Now, her options were this man before her or murder in the night.

Sven stepped back and raised his voice for all to hear. "The Corlains have spies everywhere. Fortunately, I'm a man hard to lie to. I've found the spies who made it easy for the Corlains to surround your ring fortress."

Sven clapped his hands. The door at the end of the longhouse opened. Five men and three women were escorted in and forced to kneel before Murid. They all had fresh bruises, burns, and lacerations. Murid knew quite well how Sven learned the truth.

One prisoner had a scar on her forehead. It was pink and looked to have been recently covered by a scab that had been picked away. That wasn't the worst of her injuries. A sizeable portion of her scalp, approximately five centimeters, had been removed.

Sven pulled a handful of hair from a pouch on his belt. Murid soon realized the strands were attached to the missing piece of the woman's head. The man cackled as he dangled it before her.

"I'd heard once that other Vikisotes started the tradition of scalping, then the Namerians adopted it." Sven dropped the clump of hair onto the prisoner's head. It bounced off the festering wound, then fell to the floor. "I don't get the fascination." He patted the trembling woman on the head. "Don't worry, you're still beautiful."

Sven burst into laughter. His sycophants soon joined. It turned Murid's stomach to know she now relied on these *people* to reconstitute her army.

Sven grabbed a handful of the woman's remaining hair and yanked her to her feet. She struggled against his hand and whimpered.

"My queen, may I introduce to you General Githinji's spymaster."

Sven threw the woman at Murid's feet. Murid half expected the woman to grovel by her ankles. To express remorse or to complain it was a mistake. Instead, the woman curled into the fetal position and wept. Whatever Sven had done had been traumatic.

"The punishment must be death, my queen," Sven said.

This man was manipulative. Heads nodded around Murid. She would look even weaker if she ignored the suggestion. What made Murid feel sick was the fact she *wanted* to punish these people. They deserved it. She scratched her arms again.

"I suggest we line them up and serve them refreshments. We have crick venom available. The lucky ones will get that. The unlucky ones will find only honey ferm."

Murid cringed. Sven was suggesting the captives not drink their beverage but have it poured over their bodies in the hot sun. Insects would do the rest. Crick venom was merciful under those conditions.

Before Murid responded, cheers erupted outside the longhouse.

"Watch them," Murid commanded to some of her loyal guards.

Murid squirted a generous volume of crick oil into her hands. She vigorously rubbed the concoction into her skin, starting with her cheeks and neck. Endorphins surged through every cell in her body as the itchiness abated. She felt euphoric but also aggressive. Should the commotion outside be an enemy, something she almost wished for now, she was prepared to fight. It was such a pity the effects of the crick oil wore off so quickly. *Now* she understood why so many of her people constantly re-applied it.

Murid left the longhouse with Sven and a few others on her heels. She shielded her eyes as she exited the building. Once her eyes focused, a smile spread across her face. Sitting behind Egill was Swift Shot. Two Dogs jumped off a different horse. Murid searched anxiously to see if Ancestors' Hand was with them too. She wasn't, but seeing Two Dogs made her forget the man standing behind her.

She raced toward the Lacreechee and grabbed them both in a hug. She didn't care that the Vikisotes would judge this. She owed her life to these people.

"I didn't think I'd see you again," Murid said as she released Two Dogs from a hug. One he hadn't returned.

"Thank her. She insisted," Two Dogs said.

The statement hurt Murid. Two Dogs seemed different. Losing Ancestors' Hand must have hurt, but she'd lost thousands more. Surely, he couldn't be mad at her?

"These must be the Namerians we've heard so much about," Sven said.

Murid stiffened. She saw emotion fill Two Dogs' eyes.

"They prefer to be called *Mother Turklyo's children*," Murid said before anything escalated.

It seemed to work. Two Dogs hands had hovered over his weapons, but they slowly fell to his side.

"Who are you?" Two Dogs asked Sven.

"I'm Sven, the Mayor of Wyrmcrest. Perhaps soon to be much more," Sven answered.

He pulled Murid's hips into a hug. Two Dogs stared at his hands, then looked at Murid. Perhaps his stare started as pain, but it ended as betrayal. Were his eyes judging her? How dare he! Murid pushed Sven's arms away. He laughed along with a few of the Wyrmcrest warriors present.

"I'm glad you could make it," Sven said. It was clear he wasn't pleased. "You're just in time to hear Queen Murid pronounce judgment on the Corlain spies we've captured."

"You have Corlains?" Two Dogs asked.

His voice raised in volume. His shoulders heaved. Sven took a step back and stuttered.

"Y-Yes. Right inside."

Two Dogs removed his tomahawk from his belt.

"Two Dogs, don't do anything. They're prisoners," Murid said.

Two Dogs ignored her, as did Swift Shot. She drew her knife and followed her friend.

"I said *no*," Murid said.

Two Dogs and Swift Shot entered the longhouse. Murid stepped forward, but Sven's hand held her in place.

"What's going on?" he asked.

Screams from inside the longhouse were his answer. Murid shook her arm loose and raced inside.

The sight was unsettling. Half of the prisoners were already dead. Two Dogs had the head of the spymaster in his hand as he hacked it free. The two Vikisote guards hadn't even drawn their weapons. They simply watched as Swift Shot thrust her knife through the uppermost part of a captive's spine.

"Enough!" Murid screamed.

Two Dogs stared defiantly at her and scalped the last living prisoner. The man shrieked in pain as Two Dogs stood over him and taunted him with his igsidian blades dripping with the blood of the other spies.

"What's wrong with you!" Murid screamed.

She looked over her shoulder at Sven and Egill. Sven seemed amused. It probably pleased him to lose a romantic competitor without even trying. Egill looked more conflicted. On one hand, she was still technically his queen, but she knew he wanted to follow a man. Any man, it would appear.

Two Dogs yanked the scalped man's head back and allowed Swift Shot to stab him in the throat. Two Dogs sneered as he wiped his blades clean.

"We shouldn't have had to do that," Two Dogs said.

She thought this man would own her heart forever.

What she just saw was more vile than anything the Corlains had done to her. Executing prisoners was not what good people did!

"Why were they still alive?" Swift Shot asked. "If you knew they were spies, they should have been executed."

Murid considered the female Lacreechee. She thought these people were like her, but she now saw some of the savagery that others had claimed they always possessed. She rubbed the lingering crick oil on her skin.

"We aren't monsters! That was murder," Murid said.

"My queen—" Egill started.

"No!" Murid screamed. "I'm in charge here. I make the rules. I won't allow any of you to mock or manipulate me any further!"

"How else will the Vikisotes be anything other than a joke?" Two Dogs asked.

The question stole the breath from her chest.

"The Vikisotes took you in. You were the ones fought to near extinction," Murid said.

"You should have abandoned your ring fortress. You chose to celebrate. *That* is why your people died. You're a fool and you're weak. You know nothing of our sacrifice!" Two Dogs screamed.

"We celebrated because warriors have their traditions. Offending the gods would have led to more death. I would have loved to relocate, but the calendar didn't support it."

Two Dogs flinched. To him it must have felt like a

weak excuse. Murid couldn't expect him to learn and accept the *truth* in such a short time.

Two Dogs breathed louder out his nose. He constantly flexed and relaxed his fingers. Despite the connection Murid had thought they shared, she heard the pain in his voice. "You're weak. There's no other way to say it. That's why you *need* a man. It's not because you're a woman; it's because you're weak and give real women like Swift Shot a bad name."

Murid stared at Swift Shot and looked for any form of support. Swift Shot stared defiantly at her. She was fully in support of Two Dogs. She may owe them her life, but that only meant she would *spare* theirs'.

"Sven, do you have a prison?" Murid asked.

Sven smiled. "Yes, my queen. It's at your disposal."

"Good. Egill, arrest these two."

Egill hesitated. Murid snarled at him.

"I said *arrest these two*. I *am* your queen. You *will* obey me!"

"I'm sorry, Murid, but I side with them," Egill said.

Egill stood alongside Two Dogs and Swift Shot. Approximately a third of the warriors moved to stand with Egill as traitors. Sven and the rest of the Vikisotes moved behind her. Murid noticed that most of her people were from Wyrmcrest. The survivors of the Corlain fight were mostly with the people they practically worshipped now. That damn Vikisote warrior bond!

"So, that's how it is now?" Murid asked.

Her heart raced. Her anger doubled. After everything she'd been through, after all she'd lost and sacrificed, her people left the moment a man said he wanted to be in charge. The only people left did it out of loyalty to Sven, not to her. She rested her hand on the pommel of her sword. The action didn't go unnoticed.

"We have weapons too," Two Dogs said. He pulled his tomahawk and knife free of his belt. "Unlike your gods, Mother Turklyo has given us the gifts to defeat you. Leave. It's in your instinct. You're a coward. Leave."

"You're a sexist! You can't stand to know that I'm a leader and you're simply the muscle!"

Murid relished the look on Two Dogs' face as her insults landed. She scratched her arm as the pain solidified.

Two Dogs gestured at Swift Shot with his head. "Tell that to her. Or to Bright Stone."

"You can count them on your fingers. I'm utterly impressed. I see now what's in your heart."

"Don't speak ill of my chief. She died fighting the Corlains. It was a battle we *won*, but you wouldn't know what that felt like."

"We've all suffered! Namerians aren't the only people on the planet!"

Damn. She didn't mean to say that. She should have taken it back. She knew she should, but Murid had fully given in to her anger. First, she thought once more of apologizing. Next, she thought of how he should apologize to her. Murid's eyes fell on the tomahawk in Two Dogs' hand and how it was moving toward her face.

AUGURY ANSWERED

The last thing she thought was, *He wouldn't.*

CHAPTER 21

Silence hung in the air. Two Dogs looked at his fingers. Once there was a tomahawk held by them; now that same weapon was lodged inside Murid's skull. He regretted the action the moment the weapon left his hand. It felt like an eternity as it tumbled through the air and hit the unsuspecting Murid perfectly in the face.

She had tried to blame the cause of his misery on a calendar! On a holiday. He couldn't go home to Mother Turklyo because of her heathen god! Perhaps this was for the best?

As her body slammed into the table behind her, there was a moment of paralysis among the living. Two Dogs noticed Egill and his supportive Vikisotes seemed uncertain what to do. Clearly Egill was struggling with avenging his queen or maintaining his warrior's bond with Two Dogs. As Murid's body settled on the dirty floor, Sven's warriors decided for Egill and his comrades. They drew their weapons and pointed them at

Two Dogs. Swift Shot gave Two Dogs her tomahawk.

"They killed my fiancée!" Sven shouted. "They killed the queen!"

Two Dogs hadn't realized Murid had found a fiancé, but he knew that meant there wasn't a way to talk himself out of this one. He didn't care. He may have regretted killing Murid, but the rest of the Vikisotes opposing him meant nothing to him.

The Lacreechee and their Vikisote allies prepared to defend themselves from Sven and his warriors. The fight was brief. Swift Shot dropped three Vikisotes with lethal shots through their throats. Each arrow disappeared and returned to her quiver. Normally she would have added magic to each igsidian arrowhead, but the close proximity of both sides and Two Dogs' lame status made her rely on sharpened stones alone. Her accuracy was a gift, but it also identified her as a target.

The remaining eleven Vikisotes loyal to Sven flipped the table separating both groups. They held the ends and charged with their heads ducked low. Two Dogs and his allies shielded themselves with their weapons and braced for the impact. The table slammed hard into Two Dogs and pushed him backward. He only had half a dozen Vikisote supporters and Swift Shot. Thankfully, Egill was one.

Egill swung his axe at the ankles peeking below the long table. The first man had his feet swept out from under him. The opposing Vikisotes threw the table into the supporters. Two Dogs vaulted over the top and landed with his knife buried in the chest of his nearest enemy. He stood and heard a scream that stopped his heart mid-beat.

Two Dogs parried a spear with his tomahawk and cut the woman's throat who attacked him. He turned to see Swift Shot bleeding from many stab wounds. She screamed as three Vikisotes continued to gore her with their swords. Before dying, she let out one last blast of wind. It was stronger than any tornado. All survivors in the room, including Two Dogs, were thrown from their feet and landed hard on the stone floor.

Two Dogs rolled onto his back. His adrenaline waned. The ramification of murdering Murid hit him. Swift Shot paid the price for his action.

Egill was the first on his feet. He planted an axe into the heads, stomachs, and backs of the remaining Murid supporters. Two Dogs dragged himself to his feet moments before Egill could behead Sven.

"Stop!" Two Dogs shouted.

Sven scooted backward on his ass. He no longer had a weapon. His face was wide eyed and his bottom lip quivered. He held up his hands, closed his eyes, and looked away from Egill.

"Yes, yes, listen to your friend," Sven said.

Two Dogs noticed he wisely chose not to refer to him as the N-word. Egill halted his attack.

"Why? He'll claim to be king now. If you want to be in charge, this one must go," Egill said.

Two Dogs watched as the two remaining Vikisotes other than Egill barred the door to the longhouse. Next, they moved the overturned table to block the entrance further. Two Dogs laughed at the absurdity of three people expecting him to be the king of foreigners.

Mother Turklyo had a sense of humor.

"I don't want to be your king," Two Dogs said.

"You must!" Egill shouted. "You have the power to defeat the Corlains and the respect of Vikisoteland."

"I just killed your queen, so I doubt I have any respect left."

"She had to go. I loved Queen Murid, but she didn't understand how the world worked. You do."

"I don't have any power left, either," Two Dogs admitted.

Egill stared at him with a gaping mouth. The other two Vikisotes also looked shocked.

"We saw your power many times," one of them said.

Two Dogs covered his mouth and nose with his hands. He blew a frustrated breath into them. He slid his hands off his face and pressed his palms together as he spoke.

"I used up too much magic keeping the cannons from ripping into us. I've lost my connection. I'm nothing but a man with a sharp stone attached to a stick."

Sven snickered, but a hard kick to his ribs by Egill quickly ended it.

"Then, you'll help me take over," Egill said.

"I'm leaving. This rage cost me too much. I was only here for Swift Shot, and now Vikisotes have taken her from me too."

Citizens of Wyrmcrest pounded on the door to the longhouse.

"Mayor Sven, is everything alright?" someone from

outside shouted.

"Help me!" Sven screamed. "They killed the queen, and are—ow!"

Sven grabbed the ribs on his right side as Egill moved his foot away.

"Do you hear that?" Egill asked, gesturing toward the door. "You couldn't leave if you wanted to."

"We'll use him," Two Dogs said. "If he wants to be king, we can ransom his life for safe passage."

"Don't be a coward. Not now! Not after everything we've sacrificed."

Trumpets blared from outside. They sounded like they came from beyond the city limits. Egill and Two Dogs stared at the barricaded door. Only Sven seemed to understand.

"They're here! The Corlains are here!"

Two Dogs listened to the trumpets. The signal was one he remembered hearing before the battle at the ring fortress.

"We must get out of here," Two Dogs said.

Any response Egill would have given was swallowed by the sound of musket fire. The gunfire soon joined the cacophony of the terrified screams coming from the unprepared villagers living in Wyrmcrest. The two Vikisotes removed the barricade covering the only exit. They raced out and were immediately cut down by musket balls. Two Corlain skirmishers charged in with swords drawn. Egill engaged both.

He smashed the shaft of his axe into the helmet of the first Corlain and pushed him back out the door. As the man stood again, Egill chopped his axe into the belly of the second Corlain, who fell with Egill's weapon sticking out from his body. Egill reached to recover it when the first Corlain tackled him.

The two men rolled on the floor. The Corlain ended on top of Egill. The Corlain pulled a dagger and thrust for Egill's chest. The Vikisote commander threw his hands up and squeezed against the Corlain's wrists. The Corlain had the advantage of weight and position. He pushed harder. The dagger scratched at his leather armor. The Corlain was thrown off Egill with a tomahawk sticking out from the side of his helmet. Egill grabbed the Corlain's discarded dagger and stabbed the wounded man multiple times.

"Egill!" Two Dogs screamed.

Egill looked at Two Dogs moments before a sword pierced his chest. Egill looked at the bloody sword point with disdain. He sobbed as the blade wiggled itself free. Egill fell, dead. Two Dogs stared at his killer.

The Corlain was important, judging by the red decorations on her helmet.

"Stand down," the woman said.

She pointed the bloody sword at Two Dogs. He watched as Egill's blood dripped free. All he had left to defend himself with was his igsidian knife.

"Corlain bitch!" Sven screamed.

Two Dogs had forgotten about his prisoner. Apparently, the Corlains hadn't seen him either. It was a shock for Two Dogs, the female Corlain commander, and the six others who had poured into the longhouse when Sven impaled her with a long spear. One of the Corlains fired his musket. The shot was surprisingly accurate and took a sizeable portion of Sven's head off. He fell dead as the Corlain commander wheezed.

Three Corlains aimed muskets at Two Dogs while the other three removed the commander's helmet. Two Dogs dropped his knife and raised his hands. He didn't want to die without being accepted by Mother Turklyo again. If he resisted, that was the only likely outcome.

The Corlains gave water to their commander. She had dark skin and a determined look in her eyes. Two Dogs doubted she'd survive, but she looked just tempted enough to prove him wrong.

"Make sure he gets back to Ekundayo," the commander said.

"Yes, ma'am," one of the Corlains assisting her responded.

The commander didn't survive long after that. The Corlains moved toward Two Dogs as one enraged pack. Two Dogs held his hands and closed his eyes. The first blow was across the face. The next landed on his stomach and doubled him over. At some point, he was thrown to the floor. He stopped counting the number of kicks and stomps all over his body.

After several minutes, the Corlains forcefully lifted his beaten body from the floor and carried him outside. The sun was fierce. Two Dogs wished he could have covered his eyes. They were puffy. He suspected soon they'd swell enough they'd cover themselves.

"Where's Colonel Zoya?" a Corlain asked.

"She's dead," one of the women carrying him said. "Go inside and get her body. The Vikisote leadership was in there too. Get their bodies. We'll present them to

Ekundayo."

"Yes, ma'am," the first Corlain said.

"Don't worry," the new Corlain leader said to Two Dogs. "You'll get to meet Ekundayo too. Wagon!"

Two Dogs hung his head as they carried him to the prison wagon. The Corlains tossed him inside. He hit the barred walls and yelped when the Corlains *accidentally* slammed his left ankle in the door.

"Watch your feet, Namerian," the Corlain said.

A few of the soldier's peers laughed at the joke. Two Dogs nursed his broken ankle. That word no longer had power over him. He'd allowed his friends to die because of that word. Two Dogs rolled onto his side and cried in the fetal position.

CHAPTER 22

Two Dogs woke with a stiff neck, back, and everything else. Thankfully, someone must have taken pity on him; his ankle now had a splint. His prison wagon was the first of dozens. They were all in a line on the main road taking them south through Vikisoteland.

The summer sun beat down on Two Dogs and his wagon. The iron bars that made his prison gathered the heat and made it too painful for Two Dogs to lean against them. He sat on wooden boards in the center of the wagon. He was wary every time he moved of the potential for splinters.

Talking wasn't allowed for the Corlain prisoners. Two Dogs tried once to shout at the wagon behind him, but it prompted the Corlains to pull to the side and beat him. They were weak men and women, but since they'd stripped him of all igsidian, he wasn't able to ignore the blows as easily. Not that it would have mattered. His predicament was more proof Mother Turklyo hadn't forgiven him. Two Dogs hung his head and wept again.

Over the course of weeks, the road transitioned from a simple dirt road to a paved one as they traveled south. The border of Vikisoteland and the expanded Corla seemed to be the arbitrary boundary that marked this. Despite Two Dogs' hatred for Corla, he appreciated the fact that more trees blocked the road from the vicious sun. The weather and the road changes weren't the only ones that Two Dogs noted.

All his life, Two Dogs had lived in a small village. The Lacreechee tribe wasn't as large as nation tribes like the Belloots had been. A few dozen tipis were all it took to keep his people safe from weather. The Vikisotes had their longhouses, but even Hafoca's capital had been small compared to the cities that appeared when they were hundreds of miles deep into Corla.

The streets were paved and well maintained. As each day turned to night, Two Dogs saw metal poles that shined light on the top. It helped keep the city lively well past the point most should have been asleep. The homes of common citizens were luxurious by Two Dogs' standards. The stone buildings were tall with several families stacked inside.

Two Dogs watched with curiosity as Corlain civilians walked or rode their horses to another building and handed out items in exchange for the *coins* that Ancestors' Hand had spoken of. They shined either yellow or gray. They didn't look worth anything, but people protected the small pouches that held them more than they did their own children.

After a month in the carriage, Two Dogs was

relieved to be moved out of his cell for something beyond a five-minute break to purge his guts. The city was massive. Easily ten thousand people must have lived there. They looked at Two Dogs with curiosity and fear. A few children mimed executing him with either their fingers or toy muskets. Two Dogs bared his teeth; all but the bravest scampered back to their parents. It brought a rap to his knuckles by the Corlains escorting him, but it was worth it.

"Move, Namerian," the guard said.

Two Dogs obeyed. He limped but forced himself to keep from grimacing. His ankle was mostly healed, but it was still weak. He held his head high and followed the directions of his tormentors. He expected to be taken to Ekundayo. Likely the Corlain leader lived in one of the homes with windows that stacked six high. Instead, Two Dogs found himself digging his heels in and trying to keep from being thrown into the mouth of a demon.

The monster was metal, like everything else in this country. It was longer than any snake Two Dogs had ever seen. It reminded Two Dogs of a segmented bug like a millipede or a centipede. It stretched for what seemed to be miles. The monster had a long tube standing on top of the front of it. Corlain soldiers and civilians laughed at Two Dogs and mocked him. He didn't understand why they'd be so comfortable around the beast until he saw that it was nothing more than another form of transportation.

Wide doors slid open at each segment of the contraption. Two Dogs was shoved in his back by a

Corlain. His shackled hands kept him from breaking his fall. His chin scraped along the paved road.

"Get onto the train, Namerian!" the guard shouted.

Two Dogs was helped to his feet and thrown inside the *train*. The Corlains connected his shackles to a bar running along the floor of this strange vehicle. Two Dogs was thankful his arms were no longer behind him. He had to crouch because the shackles weren't long enough to let him sit straight. He feared he traded a discomfort in his shoulders and wrists to one in his back.

A shrill whistle startled Two Dogs. New prison guards laughed at him. The few Vikisote prisoners also laughed at him. None wanted to speak to him, but apparently openly mocking him was something the Corlains willingly forgave.

Two Dogs jumped in his seat a second time when the train moved. It didn't have any horses or other beasts of burden pulling it, but somehow it moved. Two Dogs tried to lean his head over his shoulder and out the window. The train was curving along a specially designed road. He could now see how it moved. The ingenuity left him mesmerized. The Corlains seemed capable of far more than the people he'd fought had shown.

Two Dogs traveled by train for another three days. He spent most of the time watching the countryside pass him by. He felt nauseous as the people outside appeared richer and richer. Two Dogs couldn't figure out why. He expected their skin to become paler the farther into Corla he traveled. Instead, he saw more diversity. People from all corners of Glostaimia walked around as equals. Two Dogs gasped and couldn't close his mouth for miles when he saw some of Mother Turklyo's children trading with the Corlains. They returned to their same expensive homes after working in their massive *shops*.

The cities became larger. Two Dogs wasn't sure what number was needed to count them all, but *thousands* would no longer do. He realized defeating Corla was impossible.

Eventually, the train stopped. Two Dogs was yanked to his feet. His back was curled and screamed at him. He hunched over as he followed his guards out. Two Dogs was forced to march through the streets of Corla. If this city wasn't the capital, then Two Dogs needed to invent a new word.

The city was a jewel by any definition. Smaller trains zipped around the city and jingled a small bell. Corlain citizens of every ethnicity got on and off. They didn't even have to walk to their shops.

The ground beneath Two Dogs' bare feet wasn't the same as the stone roads in the past cities. It was black and spongy. It burned his feet with each step. He trotted to keep up with the Corlain guards. People lined the streets on both sides and cheered. They screamed of victory against the *terrorists* and *narcos* who murdered them. Two Dogs wasn't familiar with these words, but he wouldn't have minded killing a few more Corlain guards.

Two Dogs cast a glance to each side of the road. He'd become used to seeing Mother Turklyo's children mixed with the Corlains, but now he received another surprise. The tribe before him, selling trinkets made from igsidian shavings, was Belloot. The traitors to all of Mother Turklyo's children were supposed to be extinct. Instead, here they were living among the richest of the Corlains. They were living *as* Corlains.

It seemed to take an hour of walking before Two Dogs was brought inside. His feet finally gave him relief. He forced himself to stand straight. His body hurt everywhere, but the cool indoors was refreshing enough to help him forget.

Two Dogs was dragged through the building and thrown inside a cell larger than Two Dogs expected. It had a bed in the corner with sheets, a blanket, and a pillow. The only other furniture was a strange wooden chair that had a hole in the seat. Beneath the hole was water. A small chain with a handle dangled alongside the chair. Two Dogs had never seen anything like it.

His cell was finished with a single window that had bars covering it and a light above him. The source of the light was upsetting. Embedded in the ceiling was an igsidian stone disc with a five-inch diameter. It was an affront to Mother Turklyo that the Corlains were using igsidian. The fact they were using it to simply light a cell was infuriating.

Two Dogs stood on the wooden *water* chair and tried to hit the igsidian free of the ceiling. It was too high. He couldn't reach it. Without physical contact, the igsidian couldn't be used to help him escape. That was assuming he'd suffered enough and Mother Turklyo would give him back his magic.

Two Dogs tried a few more times to reach the igsidian before giving up. He lay on the bed and closed his eyes. It was the best sleep he'd had in weeks.

Two Dogs wasn't sure how many days had passed, but eventually he had a visitor for something other than bringing food and water. They'd had fun mocking him for not knowing what a *toilet* was. He hadn't been allowed a hot meal until he cleaned up the corner of his cell he'd used before learning the toilet's purpose.

Standing before Two Dogs, through the bars of his cell, was a man with dark skin in his early forties. The man's hair was black and knotted together. His features were fair, but his muscles were impressive. This man's presence commanded attention. Two Dogs knew he hated him.

"Do you know who I am?" the man asked.

"Should I?" Two Dogs challenged.

The man sighed. He waved his hand over his shoulder. The two prison guards nodded and opened the cell door. The man entered without any hesitation. Two Dogs considered strangling the man, but something told him to speak with this man first.

Two Dogs sat on his bunk as the Corlain stood in front of him.

"Perhaps you saw my portrait as you passed through my country?" the man said.

Now Two Dogs understood. This was the Corlain leader.

"You're Minister Ekundayo." Two Dogs practically spat the title.

The Corlain religion was beneath his own. He hated how these people pretended Mother Turklyo didn't guide everything.

Ekundayo sighed again. "It's *Prime* Minister Ekundayo. That first word is important. I'm not a religious leader; I'm an elected politician."

Two Dogs didn't know what *elected* meant, but apparently it explained everything. Then again, it probably *did* explain why Corla constantly changed leaders every few years.

"You're the bastard who murdered my people," Two Dogs accused.

Ekundayo closed his eyes and shook his head. This man clearly didn't want to argue. He surprised Two Dogs when he transitioned to speaking Lacreechee. Two Dogs leaned back but continued the conversation in his native language. He would have to find out how Ekundayo learned Lacreechee.

"That was General Githinji, not me," Ekundayo said.

Two Dogs smirked. "What kind of leader blames his warriors?"

"I accept the blame in allowing him to stay in command of the Black Cloud. I don't accept any blame for his actions. I was told after my election that he'd be a problem. I thought the frontier would be good for him. I didn't know of his atrocities until weeks after they took place, then he continuously refused to return and explain himself."

"He killed my entire tribe."

"And he was punished for that and much more."

Two Dogs sat up straighter. "Punished?"

"He was tried and executed last week."

Two Dogs squinted at Ekundayo. "What's your game?"

"I know how hard life is for Namerians. I didn't want any more to suffer. If someone like you could forgive Corla, others would stop attacking us."

"Attacking *you*? You attack us. You steal our igsidian."

Ekundayo rubbed his face, then did the inexplicable. He sat next to Two Dogs on the bed.

"Namerians don't own the rights to all igsidian. It can do so much for so many. Its benefits to society outweigh your religious beliefs that only mages should be able to own it."

"Igsidian is a gift from Mother Turklyo."

"It is. I agree with you, but it's a gift to be shared with everyone. How do you think we power this city? Like all cities in Corla, igsidian is what ensures the poor have a warm room to sleep in, travel is expedited, telegrams are sent. The quality of life in Glostaimia is exponentially increased because of the turklyos. That's why we raise them. Wild turklyos die in about eight years. Domesticated turklyos live upwards of forty years. That's forty years of cutting a portion of their igsidian plate and letting it grow back."

"That's sacrilege. What about the skin and meat? All of it is a gift."

"Yes, but the stones are most important."

"Just because you've found other uses for igsidian is no reason to kill my people."

"It isn't, but usually you're the ones attacking us. A few months ago, a Lacreechee war party attacked our ranchers. Civilians were slaughtered, and they didn't even have turklyos at the time."

Two Dogs thought back to the conversation his brother and father had after his eagle feather ceremony. Proud Wall had never explicitly said which Corlains they'd attack. Then again, did it matter?

Ekundayo rubbed his face and continued. "I admit criminals like Githinji exist, but with a nation this large, it'd be impossible to have zero murderers. Your doctrine has made some tribes fanatical. I wish you'd listen to the Belloots. We've learned so much from them."

"The Belloots are traitors."

Ekundayo hung his head. "That's exactly the problem."

This man was making arguments that were hard to ignore. Still, the guards who captured him had mistreated him.

"If Githinji was the only criminal—"

"I didn't say he was the *only* one."

"Fine, but I was beaten after being captured. I was beaten in your prison wagons, on your train. Your people like to torture."

"If you know the names of your tormentors, I'll look into it, but what would you do if a single man had killed dozens of your friends? Perhaps hundreds? I've heard of you, Two Dogs. I know how strong your magic is."

Two Dogs looked away from Ekundayo. If the Corlain leader thought he still had power, it could work in his favor.

"I'm strong because of what Mother Turklyo blessed me with."

Ekundayo chortled. "Are you this year's chosen one?"

The question forced Two Dogs to sit straighter and lean away from Ekundayo.

"What do you mean by *this year*?" he asked.

"For years I've listened to various cultures speak about a prophecy and a chosen one. Haven't you ever heard other people recite the same tale?" Ekundayo asked.

Two Dogs remembered the many fights between Ancestors' Hand and Faida. "Sometimes."

"Did you ever wonder why so many cultures had the same story?"

"No."

"The simple answer is because *Corlains* made it up."

Two Dogs furrowed his brow and looked away while clicking his tongue.

"You don't have to believe me, but it's true. A few centuries ago, a Corlain prime minister came up with the idea to use his spies to infiltrate various religious groups and slowly pervert their teachings. I don't know how it worked, but it did. For the past hundred years, insurrections rise surrounding a chosen one. Since each group wants to feel special, none join forces against us. Not in real numbers, anyway. Your prophecies or auguries or fate, whatever you want to call them, are Corlain fiction. It used to be a useful strategic decision. Now, it's embarrassing. I wish we could reverse that decision, but people are fickle when it comes to their beliefs. It's hard to convince them to change, but I know in my heart it's the noble thing to do."

"If you're so benevolent, then why did you attack the Vikisotes?"

"I was waiting for this question. Tell me, what is the capital of Vikisoteland?"

Two Dogs realized Murid had never answered that question when asked.

"I don't know."

"Weren't you there?"

"I was, but it never came up. It didn't matter when Corlains were committing genocide."

"The reason you can't answer my question is because there's no internationally recognized country called *Vikisoteland*. They don't have a king. They're simply an assembly of criminals with a loose hierarchy based on religious doctrine. They just went as far north as possible to escape justice."

"Justice for what? Wanting to live their lives their way?"

"That's one way of looking at it. The other is to point out that crick venom is illegal for a reason. It can be used as a poison, a weapon—"

"Medicine!"

"*Medicine*? Is that what they called it? In school, I learned they were *narcotics*. They hurt the body more than they help. They're addictive, and more than one good man or woman has died from overindulgence."

The Vikisotes did seem to love to rub their crick oil into their skin. It always made them happier, but when it wore off, they were meaner than ferm drunks. Faida had been overly concerned when teens got some. Had they died?

"The Vikisotes didn't care about people. They used you and many other Namerian tribes to fight against us. We weren't trying to take over the world; we were trying to eliminate criminals from within our borders," Ekundayo said.

"Stop calling us *Namerians*," Two Dogs said.

Ekundayo slowly closed his mouth. The two men sat in silence for close to a minute.

"That's not who we are," Two Dogs added quietly. "We're Mother Turklyo's children."

"I apologize. I didn't realize you considered the word offensive. Why exactly is that?" Ekundayo asked.

Two Dogs blinked twice and looked around his cell. What was Ekundayo's angle? He hated the word because his father and brother hated the word. His tribe hated the word because Corlains called them that. It was *their* word for Mother Turklyo's children.

"It's just wrong," Two Dogs eventually said.

"The Belloots told us it was the preferred term. In their language, it means *blessed babes*. Isn't that close to being Mother Turklyo's children?"

Two Dogs didn't speak Belloot. He couldn't confirm it was a lie. Now that he thought of it, it sounded Bellootish.

"I can see you're taking me for my word. I thank you for that. I do want to be friends. You'll still have to do some prison time for your crimes, but if you help me bring more of Mother Turklyo's children into our community, I'm positive we can give you a reduced sentence."

Two Dogs clenched his fists. Ekundayo seemed to notice and stood. He walked a few steps away from Two Dogs.

"Perhaps that will be the start of our next conversation," Ekundayo said.

He turned and exited the cell. Two Dogs wasn't through with him. He stood and grasped the bars separating him from the Corlain prime minister.

"Don't bother wasting your time. You have a silver tongue. You use it well, but I know what you did to Queen Murid. You killed her people fifteen years ago!"

"I wasn't prime minister fifteen years ago. I was barely out of university then."

"Blaming others again?"

"No. I would have made the same decision about Murid." Ekundayo moved within inches of the bars that separated the two men. "I assume you're talking about Murid Davis?"

Two Dogs hadn't known she had a second name.

"Crick venom dealers are scum, but Murid came from a place of pure evil. Do you know what chattel slavery is?"

Two Dogs didn't. He was wary of Ekundayo's words. It seemed the man had a simple reason for why he was right and Two Dogs was wrong. He couldn't trust this person.

"I'll take your complete silence as a *no*. Chattel slavery means people are property for life; so are their children. Murid's father, Haymel Davis, was the King of

Confedera. We went to war with them to end their tyranny. Their slaves became immediate Corlain citizens. Murid would have been young, but her heritage was built on the most vile of human depravity," Ekundayo said.

Ekundayo's emotions seemed to have risen as he spoke of Confedera. Murid hadn't told him any of this, but Two Dogs could sense Ekundayo had a personal distaste for what her parents may have done. Suddenly, Two Dogs remembered how Murid had spoken about Corlains telling them what to do with their *property*. He shook his head. It couldn't be true!

"You lie," Two Dogs said.

Ekundayo offered a sympathetic smile. "As I said, I think this can be the start of our next conversation. I need you to come around. I don't blame you for the bigotry those around you placed inside your head." Ekundayo went back to speaking the Corlain trade language. "Enjoy your stay, Two Dogs."

The guards laughed. Two Dogs banged his hands onto the bars of his cell. He continued to pound them until his palms bled. Ekundayo was no longer in sight, but Two Dogs continued to scream after him.

"You lie! That's what Corlains do! You're all bastards and monsters! You won't break me! I am one of Mother Turklyo's children! You gave me igsidian! It will be your death!"

Two Dogs continued to shout and pound. Those in cells near him screamed for him to shut up. He didn't care. He wouldn't let these people win. They weren't better than him. He would prove it! His screams rang down the halls and off the walls until his voice went hoarse.

The End

Thank you for reading *Augury Answered*. As a special treat, I want to share with you the very first novella I ever wrote. Mind you, I started this story when I was twelve and finished it when I was thirteen. In other words, it's painfully bad. I admit I have two reasons for including it. First, I wanted extra pages to throw off the twist in *Augury Answered*. Some of you are smart enough to look at how much book is left to figure out the remaining plot. Second, I always wanted to hold a book with that original story. (Feel free to skip to after this story for a sneak peek at my next novel, *Zombie Walkabout*). It was originally written in a seventy-paged spiral notebook, then transferred to a typing program I doubt still exists. I had to re-type it for inclusion in this book. I cringed with nearly every sentence. It's awful (possibly so bad it's good?). If you're brave enough to give it a shot, or just want to laugh at a pre-teen's attempt at world building, then be warned of the following issues:

Grammar and spelling issues galore, I didn't correct them, despite considering it.
A lack of character or scene descriptions. I knew what I meant, just read my mind.
I frequently used exposition dialogue.
It's full of all the worst fantasy tropes.
The heroes are constantly provided a new spell or army to get them out of a jam.
Nobody needs to practice or rehearse a plan that is thought up on the spot.
A lack of female characters. I wrote characters for my

friends, few were girls in those days.

I used the conjunction "and" so many times to form run-on sentences that it was criminal.

Passive voice was a second language.

And, finally, I threw in some insta-love because "why not?"

If none of that scares you away, then you may find it interesting that this was where I created the "crick" creature. If you read (or have read) my *Bystanders* series, this was the story that Keith and Kyle planned to buy movie tickets for on their way to watching *Disorder* (which was a screenplay I wrote).

Still here? Great! Without further delay, here's *The Adventure*.

This book is dedicated to my parents who didn't help any with its production, but did bring me into this world.

CHAPTER 1
Under Attack

The beautiful village of the Sweet Water Valley was calm one afternoon. Everyone was peaceful and went about performing their daily routine, until the attack came!

"The scavengers are attacking!" someone frantically cried as people ran in all directions trying to escape the massacre that was coming.

Huge, fiery dragons armed with deadly weapons and evil black armor were carrying men. They swooped down killing many in the process. By now, the town's soldiers started to fight back at the invaders. The King watched as he put on his armor.

"My Lord," one of the King's most loyal knights spoke, "the scavengers are a deadly foe. You should retreat. I will lead the defenses and fight till I die, giving you time to escape."

"David, you are my best knight and I appreciate your concern for me, but a king who runs away from every conflict is no longer a king. He is a coward," said the King.

"But, my Lord . . ." David started.

"I shall not repeat myself. I am now going to defend my kingdom," stated the King.

"And I shall fight by your side," said David.

Both David and the King drew their swords and charged outside the castle into battle. David thrust his sword into the neck of the first scavenger he saw, dropping it instantly. The King finished one off quickly as well. Seeing this performance by the two, many of the other knights found courage and started to fight to the point where they were winning.

"We're doing it! We're doing it!" the King shouted very excitedly.

While saying this, he did not notice a scavenger sneaking up on him. The King felt the sharp point of a spear drive into his chest.

"Uggg!" exclaimed the King as he fell to the ground.

David, hearing the shout of pain, turned around just in time to parry a second blow intended for him. David ducked and slashed at the scavenger, striking it in the torso and killing it. Just as the knights gained confidence by seeing the King arrive, they lost it all as he died.

"The King is dead!!" someone shrieked. "Run for your lives! Save yourselves!"

David kept fighting to give the fleeing villagers some time and was soon hit over the head by a club, knocking him unconscious. The last thing David saw was Sweet Water burn to the ground.

"David," said a voice. "David, are you alright?"

David, slowly regaining his consciousness, looked up and saw his friend, Dawayne, over him.

"I'm surprised," David said to his friend. "I would have thought you to have been at the front of the retreat by now."

"Are you kidding? I stayed to fight off the last of the scavenger filth."

"I'm proud of you. Now, which way did they go?" David asked, testing the truth of what Dawayne said.

"How should I know? I was running . . . I mean, they went that way," Dawayne said pointing north and south.

"You're a big help," David joked.

"I try," said Dawayne.

"OK, we're going to need weapons, troops, horses, food, and shelter," David said, listing the essentials.

"What do you mean we?" Dawayne asked. "I think you mean you."

"Dawayne," David said flicking Dawayne's ear.

"Oww! OK, you mean we, but we will need horses."

"I know. How far is the closest town?"

"Gilburg is a week's travel. We can buy horses there and then go to a magical princess's kingdom. She can give us the other supplies we need."

"Good thinking, Dawayne. How far away is her kingdom?"

"It's about a month's travel and that's on horseback."

"That's a long time. Unfortunately, that's the best we can do. OK, what we'll do is buy the horses at Gilburg and then head to . . ." David said not knowing the name of the princess's kingdom.

"Gatesville is the name of Princess Lalindra's kingdom."

"I will also have to try to find the Power Sword."

"What's that?" Dawayne asked.

"It's a magical sword that is made of diamonds and can shoot off flames," David answered.

"That would help," said Dawayne.

"We better get started. We have a long journey ahead till I can claim the Power Sword and then we can attack Krag. (Krag is the leader of the scavengers.) Krag must know of the Power Sword and will, no doubt, also try to claim it for himself," David said.

As the two men were about to set out for Gilburg, they heard a soft whimper. After some searching, they found the source of the sound. It was a little girl about five years of age.

"Hello, my name is David. What's the matter?"

"The bad men killed my mommy and daddy and Christopher," the girl replied.

"We can't leave her here," Dawayne said.

"I know. We will have to take her with us. What's your name?"

"Dorris," replied the girl.

"Well, Dorris, would you like to come with my friend, Dawayne, and I?" asked David.

"Yes," said Dorris, obviously frightened to stay by herself and wanting the comfort of an adult.

"Good. We will have to walk for a long time till we get horses, but then you can ride one," said David.

"I'll fall off," Dorris informed.

"No, you won't. I'll sit behind you and hold you," said David.

"OK," was all Dorris had to say after the reassurance.

"Let's go," said Dawayne, getting impatient.

"OK, up we go," David said lifting Dorris up onto his shoulders.

While David, Dawayne, and Dorris were walking to Gilburg, they heard a scream.

"You killed my best friend. That made me sad. I guess you'll have to cheer me up again," replied a man.

"What's going on?" Dawayne asked David.

"Hold still!" the man yelled.

"I don't know, but it looks like that woman could use help. Stay here," David said to Dorris, putting her down.

"Hold her, boys," said the man.

Two other men that were watching grabbed the woman's arms.

"Let her go!" yelled Dawayne as he threw a dagger at one of the men.

"Wha . . ." was all the man could say before the dagger entered his chest.

"Alright, Dawayne!" David exclaimed as he stabbed another man through the stomach.

The last man ran into the forest like a coward.

"Are you alright?" Dawayne asked the woman.

"Yes, I am," said the woman as she kicked

Dawayne.

"Uugh . . . Uugh . . . Uugh," Dawayne groaned as he clutched his stomach.

"Ha, ha," David laughed and asked the woman what her name was.

"Maria," answered the woman.

"Well, Maria, where are you heading?" asked David.

"I am from Grassy Meadows, a nearby town that has been destroyed by Krag and his scavengers. I am heading towards Gilburg to raise an army to defeat Krag," Maria answered.

"Well, you're in luck. That's where we're heading. You can help us defeat Krag," Dawayne said.

"No, she is not in luck. She's not coming," said David.

"Why can't I?" Maria asked.

"Yeah, why can't she?" Dawayne asked.

"Yeah, why can't she?" Dorris mimicked.

"Because, she's a woman and women aren't warriors," David said.

"Neither are pigheaded men!" Maria exclaimed in fury.

"Can't she at least comes to Gilsbeard with us?" asked Dorris messing up the town's name.

"Fine, she can come to Gilburg with us, but that is as far as she goes," David said annoyed and humored at the same time.

Maria was about to argue further, but Dawayne whispered he could find a way to let her help, so she remained silent.

AUGURY ANSWERED

"And who is this sweet little angel that just helped me?" Maria asked Dorris.

"My name is Dorris and they are Dawayne and David," Dorris said introducing everyone.

The group traveled day after day until they finally reached Gilburg, finding the town full of knights.

"Why so many knights?" Dawayne asked a nearby merchant.

"You must be new or else you would have known that this is said to be the next town attacked by the scavengers," the merchant answered.

"Then we better get our horses and leave fast," said Dawayne to David.

"You're right," said David. "Where can we get some horses?"

"At the stable," replied the merchant.

"Maria, you said you would stay here. Luckily for you, Krag may attack and you'll have a shot at your revenge," said David.

"I won't break our bargain," said Maria as she winked at Dawayne.

When David, Dawayne, and Dorris went to the stables, all they saw were two bony ponies.

"You call these horses?" Dawayne asked in disgust.

"Hey, you want a horse or not?" asked a rough-looking man as he spit on the ground.

"We did, but not anymore," answered David.

"What do you mean not anymore?" Dawayne asked David.

"Trust me," was all David said.

Half an hour later, the three went to a wrestling

match.

"Not much of a challenge. Anyone else want to fight?" the winner of the match asked.

"I do!" yelled David. "I bet all my money, plus my friend's money, that I can beat you for two horses."

"How much you and your friend have?" asked the wrestler.

"Over five hundred gold coins."

"Alright, you got yourself a bet. I'll try not to hurt you . . . too much," said the wrestler with a laugh.

"Yeah, thanks," David said.

The match began. David hit his opponent seven times in the stomach with all of his force and the other man seemed hardly hurt.

"He must be made of stone," David said to himself.

"And I thought you were going to be a challenge," said the wrestler.

David rammed the wrestler against the wall.

"Ugh!" the man yelled. "That did it. No more Mr. Nice Guy."

The wrestler picked up David and threw him to the ground. The wrestler then pulled out a whip and used it on David."

"Aw! You're cheating!" said David as the whip struck him.

"Did I say no use of weapons? Huh, did I?"

"No, you didn't," said David catching the end of the whip.

He yanked it out of the man's hands and whipped the wrestler in the face. The man shrieked as David jumped and landed on the man's head. He then kicked the man several times in the stomach after David brought the wrestler's face to his knee. Finally, David picked the wrestler up and dropkicked him one more time.

"Had enough?" David asked kicking the man one more time.

"Uuuugh," was all David got for a response.

"I won!" David yelled as all the spectators cheered.

"He won't give you the horses," a man said to David. "However, he owns three in the stables."

"Could you get them for us please?" David asked.

The man ran off and soon came back with a black and a white horse. Both looked as if they were the best horses alive.

"Here," David said handing the man three gold coins.

"Thank you, sir," the man said running off into the crowd of people.

David mounted the black horse and lifted Dorris up in front of him while Dawayne mounted the white stallion. As the travelers left, Maria set two thousand gold coins on the wrestler's chest as he slowly regained consciousness and quickly took his last horse, which was brown, and mounted it. She then followed the other three at a safe distance. The party was just now taking the first steps of their quest.

CHAPTER 2
The Quest Begins

"**Well, Dawayne, you** lead the way," David said, pointing as he spoke.

"Just follow me," said Dawayne. "We just have to go south for now."

"Are you sure Princess Lalindra will give us the supplies we need?" David asked.

"Yes. She hates Krag as much as we do. She'll help us."

The three traveled further until they came upon a small forest and stopped to rest.

"I'm hungry," Dorris complained.

"Here," David said as he handed Dorris an apple. "That's all for a while though."

Dorris quickly consumed the apple. There was a rustle in the bushes nearby.

"Did you hear that?" asked David.

Before Dawayne could answer, a brown horse ran

through, followed closely by Maria. She had an arrow fitted in her bow.

"What are you . . ." David started before he was interrupted.

"Shut up and get ready to fight!" Maria yelled.

Both David and Dawayne got their weapons ready. Immediately after they were prepared for battle, a wild crick with two arrows stuck in it ran out. (A crick is a giant bear with a snake's head that has poisonous claws and can spit venom.) Dorris started to scream in terror. Maria shot her last arrow at the beast and missed. She cursed herself for missing and pulled out her dagger. Dawayne threw a dagger at the crick and hit it in the left eye. The beast roared with agony as David threw his dagger into its right leg. The crick grabbed Maria by the waist and threw her against a boulder. Maria slid down the rock and hit the ground. She didn't have the strength to get up. Seeing this, Dorris fainted.

"That did it! You shall die now!" David yelled.

The crick answered David by spitting venom at him. David dodged the venom and then, using all his strength, stabbed his sword through the monster's stomach. As the beast roared with pain, David cut off one of its fingers. The crick slapped David's hand. The blow was so strong that it sent David's sword out of his hand and into the lake.

"My sword!" said David, shocked by the force of the blow.

As the battle raged on, Dawayne climbed a tree and jumped down, landing on the crick. The crick fell over and Dawayne stabbed a dagger in the palm of each of the crick's hands. While the creature was down, David stuck his hands into the wound of the crick's stomach and pulled. The flesh ripped easily. There was so much pain that the crick ripped its paws up. The daggers pulled out. Dawayne retrieved his daggers and threw them into the crick's back. Then, he grabbed them and pulled them down along the monster's back. The crick, with its remaining strength, stabbed a bloody paw into Dawayne's stomach.

"Ahhh!" Dawayne screamed as he unconsciously fell over.

David kicked the crick in the leg. He then did a roundhouse kick across the crick's face. The crick grabbed David by the neck and then lifted him off the ground. While being strangled, David kicked his dagger through the crick's leg. The crick dropped him and David fell down unconscious. Fortunately, the crick fell backwards and Dawayne's daggers pierced its lungs instantly killing it.

"Oh what a headache I've got," Maria said slowly regaining her senses after four hours had passed.

Maria went over to David.

"Wake up, you idiot!" Maria yelled.

David groaned and then stood up.

"What are you doing here? We had an agreement!" shouted David.

"Never mind that. Where are Dawayne and Dorris?"

"I don't know. Let's find them," answered David.

The two looked, finding Dorris sleeping peacefully and Dawayne still unconscious.

"She's alright, but what happened to him?" Maria asked.

"He was cut by the crick's claws."

"Oh no," Maria said with a worried tone.

"What's wrong?" asked David.

"A crick's claws are poisonous," replied Maria.

"Then we better get him to a healer quick," David said. "Help me pick him up. Ahh!"

Maria and David both looked at David's right hand. It was twisted and broken with bone sticking out at the wrist.

"What happened to your hand?"

"The crick slapped it."

"Now we're in trouble. We lost all our horses, have very little food, and Gatesville is about a fifty day travel on foot. To make matters worse, neither of us can carry Dawayne, who is unconscious and sick from poison," said Maria.

"We better find a place to stay until our conditions get better," said David.

"Good idea. I'll go get some firewood," stated Maria.

David moved Dorris and Dawayne to a cave nearby and then washed all the crick's blood off of him. Maria came back soon after that with more than enough wood.

"Now go hunt for some food," David said.

Maria retrieved her arrows and obeyed. Two hours later, Maria came back with a wild boar and two cottontail rabbits.

"This good enough?" Maria asked.

"Excellent," answered David.

"I saw some blackberries out there," informed Maria. "I'm going to go pick some."

Later she came back with plenty of berries. David had already cooked the boar and was beginning on the rabbits.

"Here, have some," David said tossing Maria some cooked meat.

"This is great," Maria commented.

"Sure is," added the now awakened Dorris.

David fed Dawayne the best he could and sent Maria out to get more berries the next morning. As Maria walked through the forest, she spotted a wagon and an old man talking to a scavenger.

"But I don't have any more money. You took it all!" the old man complained.

"Well then, I guess you'll have to be a slave. HA HA HA!" roared the scavenger.

The scavenger hit the man as Maria fitted her only arrow.

"I mustn't miss again," she said to herself.

She aimed and fired the arrow. With great accuracy, she hit the scavenger in the neck.

"Ah!" screamed the scavenger as he dropped down dead.

The old man wasted no time by running inside his wagon. Maria walked over to the scavenger and pulled out her arrow and cleaned it off. She then knocked on the wagon door. The door slammed into her face and the old man jumped out with a cooking knife. He looked at her and then let her up.

"You're not a scavenger," the man said. "My name is Gulture and I'm a magician."

"My name is Maria."

"Maria is a beautiful name for a beautiful woman. I would like to thank you for saving me," said Gulture.

Maria blushed and asked, "Why was that scavenger bothering you?"

"He said that I owe Krag money."

"Some friends and I are forming an army to defeat Krag. There are only three of us right now, so we could use a wizard with your skill."

"Yes, I would love to help. I also have supplies and can use magic to create food," said Gulture.

"We could use those supplies," Maria said.

"Well, take me to your friends. I am eager to meet them."

"Where are the berries?" David asked as he saw Maria.

"Don't worry about it. I got us a magician named Gulture," stated Maria.

"I also have a wagon full of supplies," said Gulture.

"Could you heal my friend Dawayne and my hand as well?" David asked.

"Most certainly. I'll heal you first," said Gulture as he retrieved a staff mounted with an emerald from his wagon. "Step forward."

"My name is David," he informed. "And my friend's name is Dawayne."

"And I'm Dorris," Dorris said.

"Pleased to meet you all," Gulture said smiling at Dorris.

David stepped forward and held out his hand as Gulture said,

"Razzle Hast,

Let Me Cast,

A Spell on Land,

Repair His Hand."

David's hand was instantly healed and he could move it again.

"Now for your friend," said Gulture,

"Razzle Hast,

Let Me Cast

Life and Spirit,

Now Heal It."

At the last line, Dawayne blinked his eyes and stood up.

"What happened? Is the crick dead? Who's he?" Dawayne asked obviously confused.

"You were sick from poison and Gulture here healed you," informed David.

Gulture got to know everyone and the cast two spells. The first one made the travelers' horses come back, and the second retrieved David's sword from the lake. After that, the five ate until they could eat no more, especially Dorris. They went to bed and awoke as the sun began to rise. Then the five set out once again for Gatesville.

"Have you ever heard of the Power Sword?" David asked Gulture.

"Yes, it is very powerful. However, nobody has ever been able to pass the test. You should try to claim it," said Gulture.

"I am and I shall pass the test," David said.

"That's what they all say," said Gulture.

The five stopped and rested when they needed to until they finally arrived at Gatesville. Krag and his scavengers were attacking the city.

"We've got to help," David said.

"I'm not fighting yet," Dawayne said.

"Neither are we," said Maria.

"It's not worth fighting now and not making it to Krag," said Gulture.

"Don't fight yet, David, please," added Dorris.

"Look! Both Krag and Tor are down there." (Tor is Krag's best scavenger). "I'm fighting."

David charged down the hill and he knew he would probably die. A scavenger turned and David's sword entered its neck. David dismounted and noticed his friends fighting also. David killed another scavenger and saw the castle in flames. he was about to kill another scavenger when there was a flash of light and all the scavengers were gone. The castle exploded with Lalindra and plenty of her people inside it. When the smoke cleared, David saw the castle completely destroyed. All but thirty-nine knights were dead. They searched and found Lalindra alive, but unconscious. Gulture healed her and she stood up. Everyone bowed.

"Thank you for aiding my kingdom," Lalindra addressed David.

"Your majesty, please, we need your help to attack Krag and to find the Power Sword," said David.

"We will help with both. You must drink a potion before taking the test on an island in Death Pond," said

Lalindra.

"I will pass the test and then we will have peace!!!"

Everyone cheered at that and said it over and over.

CHAPTER 3
Barbarians

To get to the Power Sword, the small army had to go through "The Forest of the Lost."

"This is the forest where Krag used to dwell so be careful. It is filled with great danger," Lalindra said as they entered the forest. "Death Pond is somewhere in the center of the forest. I have a good estimate of where this location is at."

"I heard tales of Death Pond being in a troll's cave and watched over by a giant sea scorpion," said David.

"That is true. The troll and the scorpion are to be defeated as part of your test. You must be physically strong to defeat them as well as intelligent to notice and avoid other traps. Remember that the troll's cave is in the most dangerous area of the forest," Lalindra said.

"Then we should send some scouts ahead," suggested Gulture.

"Krag keeps his most secret magic in his home.

Scavengers will be all over the place. Unfortunately we don't have enough people to send out scouts," Lalindra stated.

"We better keep some people up tonight on guard duty," said David.

"I'll volunteer," said Gulture.

"As will we," one of Lalindra's guards said as he and three others stepped forward.

The group traveled further until they came upon a sunny plain.

"I did not know of a place like this in the forest," said Lalindra.

"Aw!!" came a loud scream as six hundred barbarians jumped out of the trees and surrounded the group.

"We do not wish to fight you," stated David. "However, we will if it comes down to it."

"Thanks for the warning," a man with a spear and shield said, "but I think it was you, my friend, who attacked us."

"We just wandered in this place and did not know of you. So please let us join forces and attack Krag," David said spying a chance to largely increase his army's size.

"Fight Krag? You're crazy! What would be in it for us?" the man asked.

"After we defeat Krag, all will get some of his treasure as a reward," answered David.

When this was said, there was a yell of joy among the barbarians.

"What do you say?" the man asked his troops.

"Should we help them?"

All the barbarians cheered and answered, "Yes!!"

"I am Borin," said the man with the spear. "And this is one of my best troops, Crusher."

Crusher was a big, muscular man who shook hands with David.

At Krag's Castle

"I almost had Lalindra under my control and then I was forced to retreat!" exclaimed Krag. "Who was that man who attacked me?"

"His name is David and he is raising an army to defeat you. He also wishes to claim the Power Sword. It would be wise to attack his army while it is still weak and small at the testing sight," finished Tor.

"Yes, they will be so excited about claiming the Power Sword that we will easily take them. Tell my scavengers in the forest to stay low. I will take four regiments (1,000 troops per regiment) to the forest to defeat them," said Krag.

"I will prepare your troops," Tor said as he bowed and left.

In the Forest

"When do you think we will make it to the testing site?" David asked Lalindra.

"We will reach it in about two days, if all is well," she answered.

The small army danced and partied in the forest

that night, forgetting about the scavengers.

"David, would you teach me how to fight better?" asked Maria.

"Sure," said David.

He started to show Maria different attacks. He would slash at imaginary enemies and then flip backwards, dodging imaginary attacks. Maria watched as she saw David gracefully execute these moves. A crowd started to form as they watched David demonstrate defenses to Maria.

"E's a bloody acrobat, that's what e is," somebody commented.

David finally finished and gestured for Maria to repeat what he had just done. She tried an easy sidekick and then attempted to jump and kick, but fell on her back.

The two practiced all night until David was satisfied with the results he saw. Then, they slept until everyone else woke up.

"You did good last night," David said to Maria.

"Thanks," Maria said.

The army began to journey once again. Borin was up front talking with David. The two rode side by side as they talked about war and women. Then, Borin shouted for another barbarian to come up front.

"David, this is Tricks, my best soldier. He is a silent warrior," said Borin.

"I noticed you showing that woman Silent Warrior Karate. You are very skilled at it," said Tricks.

At Krag's Castle

"Tor, are my scavengers ready? They should be at the testing site by now," said Krag.

"Yes, my lord, everyone is ready to attack," replied Tor.

"Excellent. They have just arrived at the testing site. All scavengers will teleport on my command," Krag said.

In the Forest

The army looked around and saw a thin stonewall.

"This can't be the testing site. Nobody could go into this," said Dawayne when they arrived at the testing site.

"You forget that this is a magical test. David, drink this," Lalindra said as she handed him a thick, blue liquid.

David drank it and gave his sword and dagger to Borin. He then looked at the wall and walked through and into it. As soon as he did this, the scavengers appeared and surrounded the army who quickly surrendered.

"Hmm, first I need some light," David said while standing in the pitch black.

David felt his hands along the wall until he found a torch. He took it and it transformed into a snake and wrapped around his hand.

"This is just a trick," David said. "I know that you are a torch."

As he said this, the snake vanished and the entire

room filled with light. David looked around and saw an island with the Power Sword on a rock. There was a bubbling green moat surrounding the island. David looked to the left just in time to dodge a mace. He looked up and saw an ugly troll brandishing the weapon. Since David had no weapons, he jumped to the island. Unfortunately the island was further out than it appeared. David fell into the moat with a great big SPLASH! He started to choke and did not know what was happening to him. Something told him to keep his eyes closed and he obeyed. He felt a sea scorpion pinch him and hold his neck. David could not bear the pain and opened his eyes. This was a big mistake. He instantly became blind. David felt around his neck until he grabbed the scorpion's claw and pulled. The claw came loose in David's hands and he realized that he had ripped it off. There was a rush of bubbles around him as he swam up on the island. When he got up there, he felt a sting in his back and was lifted off the ground. He could hear his ribs cracking as the sea scorpion squeezed him with its other claw. The pain in his back became less as he was dropped to the ground. David jumped up and grabbed the scorpion's tail by using blind fighting skills he received during silent warrior training. The troll made it over to the island and David thrust the scorpion's tail into it. As soon as this happened, both the troll and the scorpion disappeared. All of David's wounds were healed and he could see again.

"I was lucky that time," he said.

David went over to the Power Sword.

"Ha ha. You fools! Did you really think that you could beat me? Look at you. Look around you. You don't even have a complete regiment to defeat my whole army. I must admit, you are brave, but you are also very foolish. I wonder, what is keeping your brave leader? You, drink this and find out what is keeping David," Krag said to a scavenger while handing him a blue liquid.

The guard drank the potion and walked into the wall instantly exploding. Krag, as well as the other scavengers, was bewildered. Seeing the perfect opportunity, Borin grabbed his weapons off of the ground and ran. The rest of the army did the same. A scavenger threw a spear into a fleeing barbarian's back, dropping him to the ground, dead.

"No, I want prisoners!!" Krag shouted.

The scavengers started to shoot magical energy chains, which wrapped up the army as it ran. Only a handful escaped.

"I will take these prisoners back to Castle Doom. You five stay here and wait for David. Everyone else, come with me," said Krag as he, the scavengers, and his prisoners teleported away.

David reached for the Power Sword. When he touched it, he was turned and pushed backwards.

"Well, a little water will cool you off," he said.

David cupped his hands and filled them with water and then poured it over the sword. Smoke rose from it and David could hear it sizzle. He repeated this procedure a few more times. The smoke cleared and this time nothing happened. David sheathed the Power Sword and turned to face a floating spirit.

"Don't let anyone touch the Power Sword or they will be burned far worse than you were," the spirit said before it vanished.

"Wait . . . he's gone. Now how do I get back to my friends?" David wondered.

He looked up and saw some vines.

"I would never be able to reach those. I wonder how the troll got across to the island?"

David looked to his right and saw a bridge.

"So that's how he got across."

David ran across the bridge.

"Now that I'm across, how do I get out?"

He felt the wall where he came in and all he could feel was cold stone.

"Well, I guess that isn't the way out."

David tried the wall a second time and then remembered that he had the Power Sword.

"I know! I'll just use flames to burn the wall down."

David drew his sword and aimed it at the wall, but nothing seemed to happen.

"I guess that I have to say something to make it shoot flames."

David said many different things and they all failed. He then got discouraged and began to chop at the wall. The five scavengers were talking outside and the one leaning against the wall said:

"I know why Krag left us. It was because we . . .

AHH!!" screamed the scavenger.

The scavenger fell to the ground dead. The other four scavengers looked at the wall and saw a bloody blade cutting along it. One scavenger was bold enough to touch the point. When he did this, the wall collapsed and the scavenger was crushed to death. The other three scavengers drew their swords as David stepped forward.

"Kill him and get the Power Sword!" a scavenger shouted.

David held his sword firmly as the three scavengers surrounded him. One scavenger charged and swung. David ducked and swept his attacker to the ground. He then swung his sword around just in time to block a blow from another scavenger's axe. The third scavenger charged David from behind. David moved to the side, but left his sword in the way. The scavenger's momentum was too great to allow the scavenger to stop and he ran into the blade. He shrieked while grasping his stomach, which was seriously bleeding. The scavenger had also stabbed the other scavenger that was standing in the face. The two scavengers fell over dead. The first one looked at David and then at his fallen comrades.

"Just you and me now," said David. "How lucky do you feel?"

"I'm not lucky, I'm skilled," replied the scavenger.

David slashed at the scavenger who easily dodged the attack. The two walked in circles and not once did either take his eyes off of the other. David parried a blow sent by the scavenger. The two exchanged attacks for a long time until the scavenger was finally able to knock the Power Sword out of David's hand.

"I told you I was skilled," the scavenger said.

Suddenly, a spear went in and halfway out of the scavenger's body.

"Nope, just lucky," Borin said charging in as the scavenger fell.

"Borin, what happened?" David asked.

"When you went in, the scavengers surrounded us. Krag was going to bargain our lives for the Power Sword," Borin answered.

"Yes, but continue. How did you escape?" asked David.

"The scavengers captured us and when you took so long, Krag sent a scavenger in to get you. However, he neglected to tell him to leave his weapons and we tried to escape. Lalindra and Crusher were captured along with some others. I haven't found anyone except you, but I know others also escaped," Borin said.

"Well we better find the others," said David.

As Borin was telling the story, the last scavenger pulled out the spear and regained some strength. When Borin finished talking, it charged. The scavenger used laser chains to wrap up Borin. David drew his sword and aimed it.

"Flame . . . burn . . . oh come on I want some fire," he said.

As the word "fire" rolled off of his lips, a flame shot out and burned the scavenger. David cut Borin's chains and gave him his spear.

"Let's go. We still need to find those that escaped," said Borin.

The two left to search for their friends as the

scavenger burned.

CHAPTER 4
Regrouping and Recruiting

David and Borin walked for hours looking for escaped people from their army. They had no luck. It became night and the two became tired. They stumbled upon an old cottage.

"This must be Krag's old home. Maybe some secrets are still hidden inside," David said.

"I'll go around back and you go up front. If there are any scavengers, we will be able to surprise them," Borin said.

The two entered the house and found it dark and empty. Suddenly, both Borin and David were thrown to the wall and pinned. David could feel many points touching his skin. A torch came into his face and David saw Tricks.

"Thank goodness it's you, David. And Borin too!" Tricks said as he put away his katana. "We thought you were both taken."

"It is good to see you also, my friend. How much of our army have you found?" Borin asked.

The room lit up and David was disappointed that only ten people were there besides himself and Borin.

"It was hard to get away from all those scavengers," Tricks said.

David looked around to see who was there. He saw Borin, Tricks, Dawayne, Gulture, three other barbarians that David did not know, and four of Lalindra's knights.

"This is everyone," said Tricks.

"If we could only get out of the forsaken place, then we could get more soldiers," said David.

"Perhaps Krag has some magic here that I could use to get us out of this forest," said Gulture. "Everyone, cover your ears. I am about to cast a spell to let me learn all of Krag's magic that is kept here."

"But if we hear, we will know magic also," said Dawayne.

"That you would," said Gulture, "but it would cause you great pain and you would be unable to control it."

"Ah, who needs magic anyways," Dawayne said as he covered his ears.

Gulture performed the spell necessary to learn Krag's magic.

"There. I now know almost everything Krag knows. I have found a spell to let us teleport out of here," said Gulture.

The party of twelve vanished. They reappeared at a destroyed town. David saw a sign and it read "Gilburg."

"Lord Krag, I have just received word that David defeated the scavengers you left behind. He also has the Power Sword and knows how to use it," a scavenger said to Krag.

"Fools! I am surrounded by fools!! Tor!" Krag bellowed.

"Yes, master," Tor said.

"Did you leave any scavengers to guard my house?" asked Krag.

"No, I did not . . . I thought . . ."

"Idiot!" Krag yelled, grabbing Tor by the throat and lifting him off of the ground. "You will take fifty scavengers to my house and see that it has not been messed with. If it has, then I will have your head!"

"Yeeessss siiirree," Tor choked.

Krag released Tor, who went on his mission immediately and then went to the dungeon.

"I want all of you to listen now," Krag said to the prisoners. "I will free you, if you become scavengers."

"Never!!" Lalindra yelled. "We are part of the Army of Peace and will be for the rest of our lives."

"Which may end very soon!!" Krag yelled, losing his temper. "Anyone else have a different answer?"

The room was completely silent.

"Fine, but you have sealed your fates along with those of your pathetic army that was able to escape!" Krag shouted as he left the room.

"Let us find another town unharmed by Krag," Borin suggested.

"He is right," said David.

"OK, I will teleport us to another town," said Gulture.

The group teleported to a different town untouched by the scavengers.

"OK, I want to pair up in groups of two and gather more soldiers for our cause," said David.

David, who had chosen Dawayne as his partner, walked into a tavern.

"Excuse me!" David shouted. "How many of you are looking for adventure and gold?"

Everyone cheered and raised their beer.

"Then aid me in the battle against Krag. I have the legendary Power Sword and could use some troops."

David stopped talking, realizing that nobody was listening to him. He and Dawayne left. The other groups also came back without recruits except Borin and Tricks.

"This is Dogar," Borin said, introducing a man to David. "He is an archer and wishes to help us."

"I'm good at what I do and can also form great plans under stress," said Dogar. "I can also show you where the Honor Shield and Peaceful Armor are kept."

"I am told they have been lost for centuries," said Gulture.

"They are located in Skull Mountain and can only be found by the one who owns the Power Sword. I will take you to them, but first, we should eat and rest. It is only a one day trip and we can journey there tomorrow," Dogar finished.

So the group ate and then rented rooms at an inn.

In the middle of the night, Dogar got up and walked away.

CHAPTER 5
Krag's Trap

D**ogar quickly snuck** out of the town. He entered the edge of the woods and bumped into Krag.

"I did not expect you to come in person," Dogar said to Krag.

"You can't trust scavengers. They are all fools. Now tell me, was David taking the bait?" asked Krag.

"Yes, and one of his friends, the magical one, believes me and backed my story up. I told them that the shield and armor are located at Skull Mountain. I also told them that only two people can travel there and they believed me. They are very gullible," finished Dogar.

"Good, we will be set up and ready when he arrives," said Krag.

"Now where is my money?"

"It will be delivered to you after the job is done. Don't worry. I will keep my word."

"Let's see that you do."

"You should not say such things. They may upset me and I know you don't want to do that. Now, go back before someone notices that you have left."

Dogar went back to the inn, but Dawayne was waiting for him.

"Where were you?" Dawayne asked.

"I was getting fresh air," Dogar replied.

"I thought you might have, but when I looked outside, I didn't see you," said Dawayne.

"Well, maybe you weren't looking in the right place," said Dogar as he stomped off.

"David," Dawayne called.

"Yes," David replied.

"I wanted to tell you that I don't trust Dogar and we don't need him."

"Yes, we do. He is the only one who can tell us where the Honor Shield and Peaceful Armor are located."

"I caught him sneaking back into the inn. He said that he was getting fresh air, but when I looked, I didn't see him."

"Don't worry. Dogar is one of the good guys. He'll help us. You are just a little paranoid," David said as he walked away.

"You're right. I am paranoid. So paranoid that I think we are being led into a trap," Dawayne said to himself.

"Lalindra, we can't hold on. Maybe we should become scavengers. At least then we will be alive," said one of

Lalindra's guards.

"Roger, we have to hold on. We will be rescued and then we will triumph over Krag and all of his evil," said Lalindra.

Just then, Dorris started to cry.

"Not again," Crusher said in disgust.

"Be quiet. She is still young and doesn't understand what is happening," said Lalindra. "There, there. It will be alright. I will make sure that nothing happens to you."

"I wish you could be so sure," said Maria.

David, don't go. I still fear that Dogar will betray you," said Dawayne.

"Dawayne, I am going and so is Dogar. Now, leave me alone!" David shouted.

David and Dogar mounted their horses and began their journey. everyone wished them luck and then started to, once again, recruit more soldiers.

"We have finally arrived," said Dogar, after many long hours of travel.

"So all I have to do is walk inside and claim the Honor Shield and Peaceful Armor?" asked David.

"Correct," Dogar replied.

"Well then, let's go get them," said David.

The two entered the cave and were immediately teleported to the top of the mountain. David looked around and saw thirty scavengers plus Krag. He instantly knew that Dawayne was right and he had been betrayed.

"You are a spy," David said, accusing Dogar.

"You should have listened to your friend," said Dogar.

"Good job, Dogar. Here is your gold," Krag said as he tossed Dogar three bags of gold. "David, you have a choice. Either give up the Power Sword or die. What is your answer?"

"This!" David yelled as he drew his sword. "FIRE!"

A flame shot out of the Power Sword and hit a nearby scavenger. All the scavengers drew their swords and surrounded David. David drew his dagger and threw it at Dogar, who was aiming an arrow. The dagger snapped Dogar's bow wood. A scavenger slashed at David, who then jumped over the blade and kicked him in the face, breaking his neck. David jumped over three scavengers, turned around, and then kicked their feet out from under them. Next, he clashed swords with five scavengers at the same time and pushed all of them over. He twirled around to knock away all of the attacking blows.

"FIRE!" he yelled as he did this.

A circle of fire waved out of his sword and burned twelve scavengers. Most of the scavengers were shocked and confused for a moment. One scavenger jumped at David, but landed on the Power Sword and slid down to the handle. David pulled the scavenger off of his sword. He ran through an opening in the cave and came upon a white surfaced floor. David heard the scavengers coming after him and ran across the white floor. This was a mistake and David started to sink. The scavengers entered the room and one fell into the sinking surface and David stabbed him. Krag then entered the room and spoke.

"So you are trapped once again. This time, you will not escape."

"Then I guess I will just have to die trying," said David who was spitting in Krag's general direction.

"Good choice of words. As you can see, you will either fall into the pit below and starve, or you will get out and we will kill you. Either way, you die and I get the Power Sword," said Krag.

"You forgot one option," David said.

"Oh, and what is that?" Krag asked.

"This," said David. "Fiiiirrre!!"

David had dropped down and burned the ground near the scavengers. This forced the scavengers to move back. However, one scavenger fell into the pit and readied his sword. David charged the scavenger and swung at him with his sword. The scavenger put his sword in the way, but David flipped over the blade. While in the air, David twisted his body and swung at his opponent. Unfortunately, the scavenger had raised his sword over his head and sliced David's arm. David dropped the Power Sword and fell to the ground. All of the other scavengers cheered as they saw this. The scavenger pulled out a dagger and threw it at David. David dodged it by rolling to the left. The scavenger pointed his sword at David and then reached over and grabbed the Power Sword. Instantly, the scavenger was burned and he took three steps backwards. David picked up the scavenger's dagger and threw it into the scavenger's neck. The scavenger dropped dead and

David picked up the dagger and the Power Sword and sheathed them. Then, he bowed taunting Krag, Dogar, and the scavengers that were still alive.

"Krag, I hate to leave, but I must," said David.

"You forget that you are still trapped in that pit. How do you plan on getting out without us capturing you?" Krag asked.

David thought about using fire and a flame shot out and started to burn the ground. He went over to the wall and kept thinking fire. The wall burned bright orange. After about ten minutes, an opening formed in the side of the mountain where David was burning.

"Go ahead and run like a coward. You are not brave enough to keep fighting," Krag said, desperately trying to taunt David into fighting again.

"Alas, you are correct," David said. "You are too great a warrior for me to battle, so I shall flee."

When David finished saying this, he ran through the tunnel that he made.

"Quick, all of you follow me. We will still have a chance to capture him at the bottom of the mountain," said Krag.

All the scavengers left the room and teleported to the bottom of the mountain. David heard everything that was said. He had just hidden at the beginning of the tunnel and listened. When the scavengers left, he entered the room again. David climbed out of the pit and walked through an entrance at the other side of the room. He looked and saw the town where his friends were.

"I don't think I could climb down this," David

said.

He looked around and found plenty of skin and bones belonging to dead animals.

"Wait a minute. Maybe I can fly down."

David picked up one of the larger skins and jumped back into the pit. The skin worked as a parachute and gently set David on the ground. David climbed out of the pit and walked through the opening pointing at the town. He closed his eyes, clutched the skin very firmly, and then jumped down the side of the mountain. He felt himself falling quickly and his heart was beating rapidly. Then, he felt himself lift up. David opened his eyes and found himself gliding towards the town. David looked back and saw the scavengers riding on dragons, chasing after him. The dragons were swift and catching up quickly. David realized that the skins were on fire and he let go. Expecting to die, he felt himself not moving and opened his eyes. Gulture was using magic to keep David levitated. Gulture then set David down inside the town's walls.

"David, what happened?" Dawayne asked.

"Dogar was a spy and he led me into a trap. Come, we must leave before Krag destroys this town."

"Too late for that," Gulture said. "For as you can see, the town is surrounded by scavengers."

"Can't you teleport us out, Gulture?" Tricks asked.

"Yes, I could, but where would we go?" asked Gulture.

"How about to Krag's castle?" suggested Borin. "We could free our friends."

"No, we will stand our ground and let Krag think

he has us and then attack," said David.

"This isn't our town and we have no right to endanger these innocent people," said Tricks.

"Still, we are ready to fight with you," said an unknown man, "since we now know that you are serious about fighting. We have waited for this moment for a long time."

"But you would be endangering your lives," Dawayne said, about to protest.

"Like he is going to spare us if you leave," said a man.

"Good point," said Gulture.

"Well then, if you feel that way, join the Army of Peace," said Borin.

"We are all with you," the man said.

"Good. What is your name?" David asked.

"I am Brad, Mayor of Springwater, this humble town," the man said.

The people saw Krag return from a teleport with three more regiments to help besiege Springwater.

"How many people live in this town?" Borin asked.

"There are a couple thousand men who can fight well. The women and children here aren't that bad with a sword either. Krag won't take this town," said Brad.

"That is comforting to know," said David. "Right now, let's just wait and see what Krag has to say. He is very cocky and we can probably defeat him because of his overconfidence. However, just to be sure, keep your hand close to your weapon."

"Crusher," said Maria.

"Yes," Crusher replied.

"Do you think that we will ever get out of here?" Maria asked.

"Yes, we will be rescued soon enough," Crusher replied.

"David will soon free us right, Lalindra?" asked Dorris, wanting a grown woman's word.

"Yes, it's just like Crusher said. David will soon set us free and then we will defeat Krag," answered Lalindra.

"Well they better get here quick. Krag's offer is sounding better with every passing hour," said a barbarian.

"Don't talk like that," Crusher said, obviously annoyed. "Soon we will be free."

"Are all the troops ready?" Krag asked a nearby scavenger.

"Yes, Lord Krag," the scavenger answered.

"Good. Then we are ready to make demands," said Krag. "David, see reason. The town's people that you have kidnapped will die if you do not surrender yourself and your few followers. I will even make you scavengers if you like. If you do not surrender in twenty-four hours, the town will be destroyed and everyone inside will be killed. You have twenty-four hours to make your decision."

CHAPTER 6
<u>Surprise, Surprise</u>

"**Twenty-four hours, huh?**" Brad said. "That should give us just enough time to set up a little surprise for Krag."

"What do you mean?" Dawayne asked.

"This town was once a military base. It has cannons and catapults. Not to mention that we have arrows and crossbows. We are prepared to fight off Krag's attack. Call a town meeting and then I will explain everything," said Brad.

It took about thirty minutes to organize the group, but once it was done, Brad explained his plan. He said that they would place the cannons and catapults around the town. People operating the cannons or crossbows would stand by until signaled to fire. Those who had axes, swords, or spears would line up behind some cannons, which would be placed behind the only gate in town. He then told them when David yelled, "WE

SURRENDER," that those with the long-range weapons were to open fire on the scavengers. He finished by saying that if needed, they would open the gates and those with close range weapons would charge and battle the scavengers.

"Everyone get some rest. we still have about twenty hours until the battle and we want to be in our best condition," Brad said.

Everyone was dismissed and they all went to sleep. David, Borin, and Brad stayed up to discuss some flaws in the plan.

"Now that all the optimistic stuff has been said, it's time to discuss some problems with our plan. Even though we outnumber Krag's forces right now, he can still teleport scavengers inside the walls of the town and our cannons would be useless. He could also keep sending reinforcements until our supplies have diminished," said Brad. "We also have a very low food supply and the town doesn't have much outside protection."

"We have a great wizard, named Gulture, who can conjure up these items," Borin said.

"I can also make gunpowder the same way," Gulture spoke.

"What are you doing here?" Borin asked.

"I knew that you would discuss the disadvantages now and wanted to know what you thought they were. I can cast a spell that will prohibit teleporting in or out of the town's walls. Unfortunately, I can only keep this barrier up for a short twenty minutes," said Gulture.

"And what about reinforcements for Krag?" Brad

asked. "Can you help us there?"

"No, I'm sorry. I cannot," answered Gulture. "However, I don't think Krag will waste that many troops on one battle. If he did, his forces would be seriously diminished and another army would finish him off for us."

"True, said David, who was deep in thought.

"I think we are in pretty good condition. So now let's get some rest. Tomorrow is an important day," Gulture said.

"I can't wait till tomorrow when I crush the Army of Peace," Krag thought to himself.

The Army of Peace awoke and went to their positions with one minute to spare. Gulture put up the force shield and made the gunpowder supply triple. David watched as Krag approached.

"David, what is your answer?" Krag asked.

"WE SURRENDER!!!" David yelled.

Instantly, men, women, and children popped out of hiding places and fired arrows at the scavengers. A few scavengers fell before they had realized that a battle had started. David drew his Power Sword and fired a flame at Krag. Krag waved his hand and the flame vanished. Krag took away all the scavengers' magic and teleported out saying he wanted the town destroyed. The cannons started firing and scavengers were dropping dead everywhere. However, not a single member of the Army of Peace had so much as a scratch. The scavengers were running frantically. A small handful of scavengers had grouped together and charged the gates, but the doors opened and ten cannons blasted. This wiped out the group of scavengers. About ninety percent of them were dead. The rest ran for safety in the nearby forest. All three hundred of the cannons blasted, leveling the forest's edge and killing all but one scavenger. The last scavenger was teleported inside the town's dungeon by Gulture's magic since the force shield was now gone. The Army of Peace had suffered no casualties and all cheered, having known that they had just won a major battle.

"Great plan," David said to Brad.

Just then, two more regiments of scavengers on top of dragons appeared.

"Don't attack us," one of the scavengers said. "We come in peace. We are to give you this message. Krag wishes to talk of peace and will meet you at the base of Skull Mountain tomorrow at noon. Only your three leaders, David, Borin, and Brad, are to attend. Krag will only bring Tor and Dogar with him. This is not a trick. What is your answer?"

"How do we know it's not a trick?" Borin asked. "Krag could easily have a couple of regiments of scavengers attack us at the meeting place."

"You must believe us. You are to bring any prisoners you have and trade them for some of our prisoners. Meet Krag tomorrow," the scavenger said.

"I'll be there," said David.

"As shall Krag," the scavenger said as all the scavengers vanished.

"David, you know it's a trick. Why are you going to

meet with that monster?" Borin asked.

"Do not fear, for I have a plan," said David. "Come with me."

David, Borin, Brad, Gulture, Tricks, and Dawayne all walked to the cell where the scavenger was being held prisoner.

"This is our only prisoner, right?" David asked.

"Yes," answered Gulture. "I captured him."

"Well, I'll put on his armor and go as the prisoner," said David.

"Yes, but what of us who are to attend?" asked Brad.

"I can make images of the three of you," said Gulture before David could answer Brad's question.

"Great," said David. "Then when we go back to Castle Doom, I free all the prisoners, and Lalindra can use her magic to get us back."

"I don't think you should go in the armor," Borin said to David. "You are too valuable."

"I agree," said one of the townspeople.

"Tare, I told you that you were not to eavesdrop on any meetings I'm in," Brad said.

"I know, but we can argue about that later. Right now, I would like to volunteer to be the one in the armor," said Tare.

"I agree that someone else should be in the armor," said Dawayne.

"Fine, but only if Tare is qualified," said David.

"He is," Brad said.

"OK, now here is the rest of my plan. Krag kills the images and we are thought to be dead. As soon as

Tare leaves, we leave this town and fill it with images of townspeople. When we find a new base, we form our strategy on how to attack Castle Doom. Tare will free the prisoners and they will fight from inside while we attack. In a few days from now we should be free of all Krag's evil," said David.

"What if Krag keeps his word?" Dawayne asked.

"Then we get some of our army back and Tare is still able to get inside and free the rest," answered David.

"That might work," said Borin.

"I assure you that it will," David said.

"I will kill the prisoner," said Dawayne. "I haven't killed one yet."

"Go ahead, my violent friend," said Brad.

Dawayne opened the cell door and stepped inside. He then drew his daggers. The scavenger was on the floor with his armor off. Dawayne stabbed both of his daggers deep into the scavenger's back. He was shocked when he didn't hear any shrieks of pain. He flipped the demon over and saw that it had no face or stomach. Dawayne took, his daggers and left the cell.

"It was already dead," Dawayne stated.

"What do you mean, it?" Tricks asked.

"Scavengers are actually demons," Dawayne answered.

Everyone present went to look at the scavenger's body and most came out wanting to be sick.

"Well, at least we still have the armor," said David. "Gulture, make an image of me. Good. Now Dawayne, since you know me the best, leave the room and try to guess which one is the real me."

Dawayne left the room and a couple of minutes later came back in. He guessed and was right on who was really David.

"How did you know which one I was?" David asked.

"I just guessed and was right," replied Dawayne.

"Good. If you couldn't tell the difference, then Krag definitely won't be able to," said David.

"Then we will soon be attacking Krag's castle?" Dawayne asked.

"Yes, Dawayne. Very soon," David answered.

"Lord Krag, David has accepted your offer," a scavenger reported to Krag.

"Good. I will soon crush that rebellion of his. When their leaders are killed, the army will crumble. Then I will rule the world," Krag said. "Do all the scavengers know what to do?"

"Yes," the scavenger answered.

"Good, very good. Is Tor back yet?"

"Yes, he is," answered the scavenger.

"Good. Dismissed," Krag said to the scavenger.

Tor entered the room.

"Your house was in perfect order," Tor reported.

"You are lucky. Did you leave any guards to protect it this time?" Krag asked.

"Yes," Tor answered.

"Good. You are dismissed," Krag said.

Krag went to his chambers to study some magic.

"I will kill David with this," Krag said to himself as

he read a spell.

The next day, Tare put on the scavenger's black armor. Gulture made the images and then bound Tare's hands with cord to make him look like a prisoner. Tare was wished luck by many of his friends. Then, he and the images were teleported to the meeting area.

"So you have taken up teleportation? I think that the horse fits your character a bit better," Krag said.

The image of David nodded.

"I see that you have one prisoner. How unwise to give him his sword and bind his hands in front of him. As you can see, I have not brought any prisoners. This was a trap and you three will not live to tell your friends about it," Krag boasted.

The three images began to run and were shot down by plenty of arrows.

"Yes! I won!" Krag shouted. "Leave their bodies here to rot. I will teleport us all back to Castle Doom."

The scavengers and Tare vanished and then reappeared at Castle Doom. Once there, Tare went to guard the prison cell with two other guards.

"So the muck men have finally returned," said Maria.

Dorris laughed at this, finding it very funny.

"Shut up!" Tare yelled, trying to seem like a scavenger.

Maria just glared at Tare with hatred.

"I have a plan on how to defeat Krag," Brad said to

David.

"Well what is it?" David asked.

"We set up cannons and catapults all around the perimeter of Castle Doom. Then, we blast at the walls with all of our force. The castle will crumble and we will triumph," Brad said, getting very excited with the thought that the war might end soon.

"I think that your plan is too much like the last one. We should wait a little while until we think of a new plan. Something that Krag would never expect," said Borin, disagreeing with Brad's plan.

"Besides, we would kill all of the prisoners inside of Castle Doom along with the scavengers," David said, reminding Brad.

"Oh yeah. I forgot," Brad said, sounding like a child who hadn't done his job of feeding the pigs.

"What are you suggesting then?" Brad asked.

"I don't know," David admitted.

"When we move to a different location, we can make a plan," said Borin.

"You're right. We should be leaving before Krag comes to finish off the rest of the Army of Peace," said David. "Gather everyone in a town meeting and I will explain the details of how we will leave."

CHAPTER 7
Moving Locations

The entire Army of Peace was rounded up for a meeting where David explained what they were to do.

"My friends," he said. "Krag believes that Borin, Brad, and I are dead. He will probably attack this town soon and kill every last member of the Army of Peace. We must move our army to a new location. We will take all of our supplies with us and leave images behind for Krag to destroy. I expect Krag to attack in about three days. That should be enough time to escape from Krag's clutches. We need to start immediately. Everyone go home and start packing now."

"No!!" an old woman shouted. "This is my home and I'm not leaving it!"

"I have a solution for those that want to stay, but be warned. If you stay, you will most likely die," said David.

After some discussion, about a hundred families wished to stay.

"For those of you that wish to stay, defend yourselves with the weapons I leave you. This way, Krag won't be as suspicious about why the battle was far easier than the last one," said David. "Those of you that wish to stay, please see me as soon as this meeting has ended to get your supplies. The rest of you, go pack what you want to take now."

Those that wanted to leave went to their homes to pack, and those that wished to stay went to get their supplies from David. He gave them five cannons and three catapults. He left them a year's supply of gunpowder.

"Here is a month's supply of food to be divided among the families," David said to the man he left in charge. "You should be able to get your own food by then. If you last a month and Krag hasn't attacked, then either he won't or we have already defeated him."

"David," said Gulture, walking towards him, "I can't teleport this many people at one time. I will have to use a new spell called light speed travel. It will get us to our destination faster than teleportation, but it is harder to control and could end with casualties."

"Can't you just go back and forth with teleportation?" David asked.

"I could, but it would be more trouble than it's worth and I wouldn't be able to take equipment and probably wouldn't have enough time. Light speed travel is more dangerous, but I can take everyone and all of their equipment at the same time," said Gulture.

AUGURY ANSWERED

"I guess that is our only good option," said David.

"OK, organize everyone together and let's get out of here," said Gulture.

After several hours, the Army of Peace was ready to use light speed travel to find a new base. Gulture performed the spell and in a blue blur, the army flashed across the countryside. After three minutes of travel, Gulture stopped. Everyone looked around and saw a beautiful mountain spewing out a magnificent waterfall.

"This is perfect, Gulture," David said.

"Thank you," said Gulture. "Now, I shall make our base."

"Where are you going to put it?" Brad asked.

"Why, inside the mountain," Gulture answered.

"This is a beautiful place," David commented. "Everyone, move away from the mountain!!"

The people did as they were told. Gulture waved his staff around and chanted some ancient runes.

"I'm finished," Gulture said to David, very proud of himself.

"It looks like nothing has happened inside the mountain," said Dawayne.

"Well, let's see what has happened inside of the mountain," said David.

Everyone ran inside of the mountain, entering from behind the waterfall. Inside the mountain was just as beautiful as the outside. The walls and floor were made completely out of marble. As people were claiming rooms to live in, David smiled.

"Well done, Gulture. You really out did yourself this time," he said.

"Thank you. I thought you might like it," said Gulture.

"OK, now get Borin, Brad, Tricks, Dawayne, and come yourself for I need to talk to you," said David.

"Tor!!" Krag yelled.

"Yes, my Lord," Tor answered.

"Now that David is dead, I want you to take five of my best regiments and crush the rest of the Army of Peace. I want every last person in that town dead," said Krag.

"Yes, my Lord. I shall organize the scavengers now," Tor said.

Tor got the scavengers and they teleported inside the town of Springwater. The scavengers used their magic to burn the town. Tor watched as the fire burned the town down. Thirty minutes later, it was all over.

"That was too easy," Tor said to himself.

The scavengers teleported back to the castle.

"Well, what is your report?" Krag asked.

"We burned the town and killed everyone in it. Scavenger casualties were at a minimum," Tor answered.

"Good. Now we can go back to destroying small defenseless towns," said Krag. "I'm not so sure. The victory was too easy, considering how they fought last time."

"Last time, they had David's leadership and surprise."

"Yes, but . . ." Tor started.

"Shut up!" Krag yelled, slapping Tor across his

helmet with his sword. "The Army of Peace is a past menace and is no longer in existence. If I hear any more talk that any have survived, I will kill the person who talked. Understand?"

"Yes, my Lord," said Tor.

CHAPTER 8
The Plan

"Thank you, Gulture, for gathering everybody," David said. "I know that it is late in the evening, but we need to make a plan to attack Castle Doom. Does anyone have any suggestions?"

The room was silent, as nobody would speak of a plan.

"Tell him your plan," Tricks said to Borin.

"It might not work," Borin said.

"Who cares? It is all we have right now," said Tricks.

"Yes, Borin. Tell us your plan," agreed David.

"OK, here it is. At night, we use light speed travel to the forest edge near Castle Doom," Borin started. "I've been told by soldiers who have seen Castle Doom that there are vents all around it. David, Dawayne, and Tricks will sneak inside the castle and wait until morning. Gulture will use a spell to let Tare know that we are

AUGURY ANSWERED

attacking in the morning. Then he will teleport outside of Castle Doom. Everyone else will stay outside the castle in the forest and prepare for the assault. We will set up cannons to take out one wall of Castle Doom. In the morning, Gulture will make many images of strong soldiers who will be heavily armed. This will make the size of our army seem bigger. We will act as a new army ready to defeat the scavengers. While we keep Krag busy with small talk, Gulture will teleport inside the castle and signal for both David and Tare to have their teams attack from the inside of the castle. Then, Gulture will use his magic to lower the drawbridge and let the rest of our army enter the base. Krag will be very surprised and we will already be attacking from all over."

"Not bad," said Tricks. "Not bad at all."

"I liked it myself," said David. "How about the rest of you? Do you think we should go along with this plan?"

Everyone present liked the plan and they all agreed that they should put it into action the next night.

"OK, everyone go to sleep," David said.

Everyone did as they were told without any complaints.

"I am here to tell you all that David and the rest of your pathetic Army of Peace have been killed," Krag said to his prisoners. "Now do any of you wish to become scavengers?"

At hearing this, both Dorris and Lalindra started to cry.

"Never! You're a liar!" Crusher yelled, unable to accept the fact that Borin was dead.

"I don't lie and I think that you know that already," said Krag. "You were worthy opponents once upon a time."

"You are not worthy enough to eat the dirt under my fingernails!!" a barbarian shouted at Krag.

Krag did not like this comment and shot a fireball at the prisoner who spoke and killed him very slowly. The man screamed and Tare, who was standing nearby, could hardly contain his anger. He would have attacked Krag there except, he knew the battle was coming.

"I hope I don't have to do that to anyone else," said Krag. "However, in three days, I will kill one of you every hour until you decide to become scavengers."

With that, Krag left the room that was silent except for the screaming of the burning barbarian and the soft sobs of individuals.

The Army of Peace rose early the next morning. They had many preparations to make. The entire army went to a meeting hall that Gulture added to their new kingdom.

"Everyone, please be quiet!" David shouted.

The room fell silent after a couple more times of repeating this order.

"Thank you," David sighed. "Before I give the details of our plan to attack Castle Doom . . ."

At the sound of the word "attack" many men cheered. It took David a few more minutes to quiet everybody down again.

"First, I must remind everyone that women and children will stay here and guard the base . . ." started David.

Some teenagers were upset at hearing that they had to stay and would have argued, except for the fact that their fathers' silenced them. David waited until the room was quiet once again.

"I know that some of you are upset at being left behind," said David, "but we need some of you stronger men to stay here and protect the women."

The teens got the idea and realized that they wouldn't be going and that was that.

"Now, one more thing before I explain the plan. Many of you will not be coming back. If anyone is scared, you may stay behind and no discredit will come to you," David said.

Not a single man decided to step down. In fact, not one of them even thought about it.

"Good. I am happy to see that all of you still want to go through with this. Now, here is Borin's plan," David said as he explained it with the maximum amount of detail desired.

All of the women and children left to prepare a meal for the men. In most cases, it would be the last meal cooked by their families that they would ever eat. After that, David explained what each man was to do and they nodded as they got their assignments.

"OK, now everyone get your weapons, rest, eat, or do anything else you need to do before we leave tonight," David instructed.

Everyone left except David, Dawayne, and Tricks.

"I need to talk with you two," David said to them. "How do you expect to get to the sewer vents if scavengers are posted all along the wall? They can use their magic to see in the dark."

"Perhaps Gulture can cast an invisibility spell on us that would last long enough for us to get inside Castle Doom and find a place to hide," Dawayne suggested.

"Good idea," David commented.

"I get them once in a while," Dawayne joked.

"I know," said David. "But since you were the one with the great idea, you can go get Gulture."

"I knew you were setting me up," Dawayne sighed.

Dawayne ran off and came back a couple of minutes later with Gulture right behind him.

"I got him," Dawayne said.

"Thank you, Dawayne," said David as he turned his attention to Gulture. "Gulture, can you cast a spell of invisibility that will last long enough to let us sneak into Castle Doom and hide?"

"Yes, I can and the spell also allows anything you touch to become invisible as well," Gulture answered.

"Good," Tricks said. "Our plan is sounding better with each passing moment!"

"I just hope that we can defeat Krag without losing many lives," said David. "C'mon, let's go get some of that food before it's all gone. After all, this may be the last good meal we ever have."

"We will all survive," Tricks said. "Be optimistic and think positive or we will definitely fail."

"Lord Krag, I have just received word that our army

was defeated at Sweet Meadow," a scavenger reported.

"What?! How could my army be defeated?!" Krag bellowed. "Bring me the scavenger in charge of that battle!"

A scavenger entered the room very slowly and obviously frightened for his life.

"You were the captain in charge of the force that attacked Sweet Meadow are you not?" Krag asked.

"Yes, my Lord, I am," the scavenger said as he swallowed hard. "All the kingdoms are putting up teleport barriers and firing cannons on us like the Army of Peace did before you defeated them."

Krag fumed with anger then became calm.

"I understand," Krag said.

"Thank you, my Lord," the scavenger said as he released a huge breath.

"I understand that you must die!" Krag said as two other scavengers grabbed the first one's arms. "The Bloodsuckers."

"NOOOOOOOOO!!!" the scavenger screamed as his weapons and armor were taken from him. "Anything but the Bloodsuckers!!!"

The scavenger was tied upside down with his back towards Krag. Krag was handed a bunch of ant-like creatures, which he threw on the scavenger's back. The scavenger screamed in agony. The Bloodsuckers stuck their six tiny legs and head into the scavenger's back and started to drink the blood. After a while, the Bloodsuckers were fat as bumble bees and they entered the scavenger's body. There, they would sleep until the next day when they would begin to eat the scavenger's organs. He stopped screaming so he would die quicker, but he knew that it would take several years until he would be dead.

In the prison, the members of the Army of Peace heard the scavenger scream.

"He has the Bloodsuckers," one knight said frantically. "Krag will do that to us if we don't convert."

"Shut up, you!" Tare shouted to the knight, "or I will tell Krag to kill you first."

The screams came again and then stopped.

"Poor bastard," Crusher thought to himself.

"OK, everyone. We are about to go to the forest by Castle Doom," David said.

"Remember there is to be no talking when we get there or we may be spotted by scavenger patrols," said Borin.

"Yes, it is very important that we are silent. I also suggest that everybody here try to get some sleep. That is what I am going to do when I get into my hiding spot. Keep a few watches up and rotate on shifts so that everyone will be at their peak performance tomorrow. Any questions before we go?" David asked.

There weren't any questions for they had been briefed to the highest extent.

"OK, Gulture, we're ready," David said.

There was a blur as the Army of Peace flashed across the land to their destination.

"OK, everyone set up and get some rest," said Borin.

AUGURY ANSWERED

"Tricks, Dawayne, and Gulture, come here please," said David. "OK, Gulture, in the morning, make the images and then have the army march onto the battlefield. As for right now, make us invisible."

Gulture waved his hand and the other three seemed to vanish.

"Are you still there?" Gulture asked.

"Of course we are," said David.

"You sound as if you aren't very confident in your magic," Tricks said.

"This isn't my magic," Gulture said. "It's not my magic, it's Krag's. I'm just making sure it worked."

"Now you sound as if you don't have much confidence in Krag's magic," Dawayne joked.

"I don't," Gulture responded quickly in a joking manner. "When you are hidden well enough inside the castle, give me the thumbs up sign."

"But, if we are invisible, how will you know when I've given the sign?" David asked.

"I can cast another spell that will let me see you when you're invisible," Gulture answered.

"Then why didn't you cast that spell earlier? Why did you have to ask us if we were still here?" Dawayne asked.

"I forgot about it," answered Gulture. "Well, get going. Oh yeah, and good luck. You are definitely going to need it."

"Yeah, you too," David said back.

"See you when this is over," Tricks added.

"Yeah," Dawayne said.

David, Tricks, and Dawayne headed for the castle.

They used their grappling hooks to get over the moat of acid surrounding the castle. The hooks hit the wall and made a loud CLANG!

"What was that?" a scavenger asked another.

"I don't know. Let's go check it out," the other responded.

David, Tricks, and Dawayne all held their breath. However, the scavengers couldn't find the cause of the noise and gave up.

"That was close," David whispered.

The three swung over the moat to the other side. They then let go of the grappling hooks, which vanished and reappeared in Gulture's hands. They walked around the castle until they found one of the sewer vents. David opened it and the three crawled in. Dawayne closed it behind them. The three sneaked through Castle Doom, occasionally pressing against the walls when scavengers passed by. Dawayne tripped one of the scavengers once and his partners scolded him.

"This looks like a good place to hide," said David.

They walked into the armory and hid behind a big pile of cannon balls with the least bit of discomfort. David then gave the thumbs up sign and they became visible once again.

"I believe that we agreed for you to take the first watch," David said to Tricks.

"Yes, we did," Tricks agreed as he watched for scavengers.

David and Dawayne went to sleep. Tricks stayed on guard and caught himself every now and then drifting asleep. After a while, he woke David up.

"My turn?" David asked, waking back up to reality.

"Yup," Tricks answered.

"OK, you can go to sleep," said David.

"I've been waiting all night to hear those words."

Tricks went to sleep.

David looked around the room and saw some barrels of gunpowder. This gave him an idea. He started to load cannons and position them around the room. The cannons were all facing different directions. He linked the cannons to a three-foot fuse. He then spilled all the gunpowder around the room. David looked around the room and was satisfied. He went behind the cannon balls to watch again, but the rest of the night was uneventful.

CHAPTER 9
The Fall of Castle Doom

The Army of Peace woke up early the next morning and got prepared. They lined up the ten cannons they brought at the forest's edge. Twenty men stayed to operate the cannons and the rest of the men formed lines and began to march towards Castle Doom. The lookouts spotted them immediately.

"Krag! An army is approaching the front gate!" a scavenger yelled.

"It can't be the Army of Peace so who is it?" Krag asked.

"I don't know," the scavenger admitted.

"Well find out," ordered Krag.

"Who are you?" the scavenger asked the man leading the army.

"We will only answer to Krag," the man answered.

"I am here," Krag said. "Who wishes to speak with me?"

AUGURY ANSWERED

"I am Bonsker," the man answered.

"Well, Bonsker, why have you come here and what do you want?" Krag asked.

"We seek revenge for what you have done to the Army of Peace and a countless number of other armies," said Bonsker.

"You are fools, but brave ones like the Army of Peace. Since I admire your courage, I will give you thirty minutes to change your mind and go back to where you came from," said Krag.

Gulture teleported into the weapons room where David, Tricks, and Dawayne were.

"I guess it's show time," said David.

"You guessed right," Gulture said. "Are you guys ready to rumble?"

"Yeah," David, Dawayne, and Tricks all said together.

"Then let's go," Gulture said as he waved his hand. The door unlocked.

"Don't forget to free the prisoners," David said, reminding Gulture.

"I won't," Gulture said.

David aimed his Power Sword at the fuse for the cannons and shot off a flame.

"Let's go," said David.

The four opened the door to leave and unfortunately ran into two passing scavengers. David took one and Tricks handled the other. These two scavengers were tougher than most and neither David nor Tricks could kill them.

"David, Tricks, move out of the way," Gulture said.

The two men flipped backwards as instructed. The scavengers charged, but when they were directly in front of the door, the fuses were up and the cannons blasted. The two scavengers were blown away. Everyone outside was bewildered, but the cannons outside opened fire on Castle Doom, leveling one of its walls. David, Dawayne, Gulture, and Tricks charged down the hallway. Gulture used his magic to make the drawbridge disappear. Krag looked back and saw David.

"It can't be!!" Krag yelled. "You're supposed to be dead!!!"

"Yeah. Don't you just hate the Army of Peace?" said David.

Gulture teleported to the prison cells. As he did this, scavengers surrounded the three that were still there. Then the Army of Peace attacked from outside. Scavengers teleported outside before any of the attacking soldiers could get inside. The scavengers paused when they saw troops attacking the base. This gave David, Dawayne, and Tricks time to cut their way through the pack of scavengers. They killed seventeen in the process. Krag teleported to the top of a tower to watch the battle and nobody saw him do this. Nobody, except Dawayne. However, Dawayne saw Dogar run and went after him instead.

"What's going on?" Dorris asked.

"I don't know, but it sounds like a battle," answered Crusher.

"That's right," Tare said, taking off his helmet.

Tare threw his helmet at one of the two scavengers, knocking him into a pit of lava under the cages. Tare then drew his sword and stabbed it through a scavenger's face.

"Get us down so we can join the fight," said Crusher.

"Right," responded Tare.

Tare pulled a lever and all the cages opened. Gulture appeared and he, Lalindra, Maria, and Dorris teleported to the outside of the castle. The remaining troops grabbed their weapons from nearby and were just in time. Tor and plenty of scavengers entered the prison.

"Die!" Tare yelled as he cut off a scavenger's head.

Crusher picked up a scavenger and broke him over his knee. Tare was fighting tough and charged Tor with his sword pointed. Tor stepped to the side and grabbed Tare by the shoulder. Tare felt his scavenger armor evaporate and then Tor stabbed him through his back and out his stomach. Tare didn't have a chance and died. Tor then realized that most of his scavengers were dead and he retreated. However, he did have plenty of people chasing him.

Borin stabbed his spear through a scavenger's body and swung it off at another. The other scavenger got up and Maria shot it with an arrow. Both armies were losing troops by the second. Brad cut a scavenger's neck and then flipped it over his back. The scavenger landed in the acid moat. A scavenger charged Brad from behind, but Borin used his spear as a pole vault and kicked the scavenger into the moat as well. Maria took aim with one of her arrows and shot a scavenger through the leg and it stumbled backwards in the moat. Everyone in the Army of Peace started to force scavengers into the moat and some fell in themselves. Tor had taken a few scavengers and went to get the dragons. Tor and about fifty scavengers swooped down and started burning people in the Army of Peace. Maria saw this and shot an arrow into a dragon's eye. The dragon went out of control and fell down a cliff. Tor, however, escaped this fate by jumping off his dragon. He landed in the middle of three members of the Army of Peace and killed them all quickly.

Tricks and David ran through the castle with about ten scavengers chasing them. David shot a flame off and killed one. David and Tricks made a sharp turn around a corner and stopped. When the scavengers came around the front, two of them were blasted by fire. Then, Trick's kicked the next one in line and they all fell down like dominos. David and Tricks killed the scavengers before they could get up.

"C'mon," David said to Tricks.

As the two ran down the hall they were spotted by twenty scavengers and immediately pursued. David and Tricks turned around a corner, but found it to be one that the cannons had blown down.

"Whoa," David said. "Walk slowly."

David and Tricks walked across the narrow piece of ground. When the ground widened, David turned around and cut the ground. It became loose. David and Tricks then ran down the hall. When the scavengers came around the corner, the ground caved in because there was so much weight and they fell to their deaths.

Crusher turned around and swung with his mace. It smashed a scavenger's head in. Five scavengers advanced on Crusher and he killed them all with so much style that you wouldn't expect him to be so big. Crusher worked his way to the outside of the castle since this was where most of the fighting was taking place.

Dawayne was chasing after Dogar. Dogar passed a single scavenger. This caused Dawayne to stop. He had never killed a scavenger and was a bit intimidated by the sight of the scavenger's evil, black armor. The scavenger swung his sword at Dawayne, who ducked and crawled through the scavenger's legs. Then, he got up and jumped on the scavenger's shoulders. Dawayne pulled out both of his daggers and stabbed them into the scavenger's neck. The scavenger fell down dead and Dawayne continued to chase after Dogar.

Scavengers were chasing Dawayne and Tricks again. David saw an air vent and Tricks followed David as he entered it. The scavengers passed and Tricks kicked out the vent. Three scavengers were knocked over the side of the castle and Tricks battled the last one. Tricks swung at his enemy with his katana, but the scavenger blocked the attack with his shield. The scavenger swung at Tricks with all of his might, but Tricks jumped over the blade and did the splits in the air. While in the air, Tricks slashed between his legs with his katana. The scavenger dropped his sword and then fell to the ground. Tricks then kicked the body over the side of the castle.

"Not bad," David commented.

A scavenger riding a dragon passed by. Seeing this, David and Tricks hid. When the dragon had flown by, David asked:

"Do you know the commands to control a dragon?"

"Yes, I do," Tricks answered.

"Good," David said as he pushed Tricks over the side of the castle.

Tricks landed on a dragon, right behind a scavenger. He threw the scavenger off of the dragon. Tricks took control of the dragon and commanded it to attack some scavengers. All twelve were burned to nothing.

Tor killed another soldier and looked for his next opponent. Tor was fighting very well and had killed sixty-eight members of the Army of Peace. Borin saw this and stabbed the scavenger he was fighting in the neck and whipped it off at another scavenger who fell into the moat of acid. When Tor was about to kill another one of Borin's friends, Borin rammed To and knocked him over. The man Tor was fighting ran to fight an easier target.

"Coward," Tor said as he looked at Borin. "Can't

wait to die huh? Very well. I shall kill you now."

"Go ahead and try," Borin said back.

Tor swung at Borin with his sword, but Borin used his shield to block the blow.

Dawayne entered the treasury, which was where Dogar had reached a dead end.

"I see you've run into a dead end," Dawayne said.

"I shall soon kill you and then get all the gold I want. I really don't care who wins the battle, just as long as I stay rich," Dogar said.

"Then you can pay the devil at the gates of hell!!" Dawayne yelled as he threw one of his daggers at Dogar.

Dogar ducked the attack, but caught himself off balance and tripped. All of his arrows spilled out. Dogar picked up Dawayne's dagger and slashed at Dawayne. Dawayne easily dodged it and jumped on Dogar.

Tricks swooped and burned about ten scavengers. A scavenger shot a fireball at Trick's dragon and killed it. The dragon fell down the cliff. Tricks flipped off the dragon and just barely managed to grab onto the end of the cliff. He couldn't pull himself up and swung into a small cave. He was alive, but he would no longer fight in the battle.

Lalindra was pretty much watching the battle since she and Gulture had to protect Dorris. A scavenger saw Lalindra and shot a fireball at her. Lalindra formed an energy shield and the fireball bounced back and killed the scavenger that shot it. Gulture was standing next to her and killed five scavengers by firing lightning bolts at them.

"We make a good team," said Lalindra.

"You said it," Gulture agreed.

One scavenger saw David and attacked. The scavenger swung at David, who ducked and the blade went over his head. David pushed the scavenger through a window. David followed inside and saw a scavenger who was hanging upside down without any armor. He realized that he was in the throne room. The scavenger that had been pushed through the window picked himself up and charged David. David swung hard and hit the scavenger's sword out of its hand. David ran in front of the scavenger, then ran behind the one hanging upside down. David thrust his Power Sword through the tortured scavenger's belly and into the other scavenger's face. The door to the throne room opened and two more scavengers rushed in.

"Don't you guys ever give up?" David asked as he shot one of the scavengers with a flame.

The other scavenger jumped at David, but he ducked and the scavenger fell into the pit of Bloodsuckers. The scavenger screamed as Bloodsuckers began to drink to their leisure. David ran out of the room and continued to look for Krag.

Borin lunged at Tor and hit him in the chest. Unfortunately, Tor's armor was so strong that the spear just glanced off as if it had been paper. Borin paused in bewilderment. Tor took the chance and fired a fireball at

Borin, but Borin was fast to bring his shield in harm's way. The fireball destroyed his shield and knocked Borin over. Tor stabbed at Borin, who rolled to the right and dodged the attack. Borin swept Tor to the ground and thrust his spear downwards at Tor. This time Tor rolled to the right and when he got up, he used his magic to make a magical hand that went for Borin, but he dodged it.

Maria was aiming an arrow and shot a scavenger that was about to kill Brad. Then she looked up and spotted Krag. She drew her arrow and aimed it at Krag's head.

"I've got you now you son of a . . ." Maria started.

When Maria was saying this, Tor's magical hand caught her in the face and jerked her head back. Her arrow fired and went to high, hitting a dragon and causing it to crash into the moat with its rider under it. Maria took a bad step and fell over the side of the cliff. Tricks had heard her scream and just barely caught her hand. Unfortunately, both of them had bloody hands, which made Maria slip free and she fell to her death.

Tor swung with all his might at Borin, but Borin used his spear to block the blade. The sword had so much force behind it that it broke Borin's spear into two pieces. Borin dropped his broken weapon and drew his dagger. he slashed at Tor and cut Tor's arm at a spot that was not protected by any armor. Tor swung, but Borin ducked and kicked Tor's legs out from under him. Tor dropped his sword and Borin jumped after he charged Tor. Tor quickly grabbed his sword and Borin landed on the sword and slid down the blade. Tor stood and pushed the sword in deeper until the handle touched Borin's stomach. Borin's hand trembled ad he dropped his dagger. Then, Borin slid off the blade of the sword and fell to the ground dead.

Brad and Crusher were working together as they defeated many scavengers. Crusher threw a scavenger into the air and Brad used his sword somewhat like a baseball bat and cut halfway through the scavenger's body. Crusher threw another scavenger into the moat and then broke a third scavenger's neck with his bare hands. Brad saw a scavenger ready to fire a fireball at Crusher, so Brad pushed a scavenger in the way of the blast and then threw a dagger into the neck of the one that fired the magical attack.

"Thanks," Crusher said to Brad.

"No problem. Might as well kill two birds with one stone," Brad said back.

"How many times do you see anybody kill ONE bird with one stone?" Crusher asked.

"Never mind," said Brad as he slit another scavenger's throat.

Dogar and Dawayne were still rolling across the ground when Dogar kicked Dawayne off from him. Dogar slashed at Dawayne, but was only able to cut the clothes near Dawayne's leg. Dawayne kicked Dogar in the stomach and then punched him in the face. Dogar stumbled backwards and said:

"You could have killed me there you stupid fool.

You should have stabbed me instead."

"It's more fun this way," Dawayne said as he dodged a kick that was coming from Dogar.

"You think it's fun to die!?" Dogar said as he charged Dawayne.

Dawayne swept Dogar to the ground. When Dawayne was about to stab Dogar, he was kicked in the stomach. Dawayne slashed at Dogar and cut his opponents arm as he was getting up. The wound was deep and very bad. Luckily for Dogar, it was only his left arm that had been cut, so he could still fight without that big of a handicap.

"I think you should give up the dagger and go back to the bow and arrow," Dawayne joked.

"I think you should shut your fat mouth up! Anyone could take a wimp as easy as you, Dawayne," said Dogar. "Prepare to die!"

"I knew you had to be evil the moment I caught you sneaking back into the inn!" said Dawayne.

"You should have tried to kill me there. Maybe then you could have beaten me, but a girl as weak as you has no chance now!" Dogar said, insulting Dawayne.

These insults ticked Dawayne off. Dawayne kicked Dogar with so much strength and power that Dogar hit the wall, which was all the way across the room. Dawayne followed this move up by throwing a dagger into Dogar's stomach. Dawayne then kicked the dagger, forcing it to go deeper into Dogar's stomach.

"Just kidding," Dogar said, realizing that he would die.

Dogar slid down the wall dead and Dawayne

retrieved his daggers. As he passed all the gold on his way out, he grabbed a small bag and tucked it under his shirt.

The Army of Peace was being beaten and was on the verge of retreating. Then a horn sounded and an army came from over a hill and charged, starting to attack scavengers. Then from another hill another horn sounded and a different army charged down that hill and attacked scavengers. The remaining members of the Army of Peace cheered at the sight of some additional help. Brad was one of the people that cheered loudest, for he had been hit in the leg by a war hammer and suspected his leg to be broken. The scavengers whose forces were also being diminished became overwhelmed when the two new armies had shown up. The battle had turned in the favor of the Army of Peace.

David had finally fought his way up into Krag's tower.
"You're mine!" David said.
"Not yet I'm not," Krag said as he snapped his fingers.

Krag had used his magic and David was teleported to the bottom of the castle. Not only that, but now he was outside the castle. David turned to head back up, but the spotted Tor, who had just killed another member of David's army.

"David, I haven't seen you this entire battle," said Tor as he prepared to battle him.

"Well I've been inside," David explained.

"Really, I've been waiting all battle for this," Tor

said.

"Yeah. I bet you have," said David.

"I don't care where you were, now you die!" Tor shouted.

"Be my guest and try and take me!"

"Don't worry. I will!"

David slashed at Tor who stuck his shield in the way. The shield split in half. David swung again and this time Tor stuck his sword in the way to parry the blow. So Tor's sword broke. Tor was now becoming worried. He had lost both his sword and his shield. He no longer had his dagger because he had thrown it into a soldier he was fighting. David swung one last time at Tor's head. Tor leaned backwards, but the blow hit the helmet and broke it off. Tor's face was exposed. It did not look like the other scavengers or humans. In fact, it looked like a green dinosaur. Tor's magic had left him when his helmet came off and he couldn't speak either. Tor strained himself and broke off all the rest of his armor to reveal a brawny body with wings. Tor's green skin and six-inch long black claws made him look very powerful. He started to fly and grabbed David. His claws sunk into the pits of David's arms. The pain was unbearable to David and he almost dropped the Power Sword. David swung his body upwards and he landed on top of Tor's back. David wasted no time stabbing the Power Sword into the top of Tor's head and out his chin. Then David pulled back on the handle of the Power Sword. The blade came out through Tor's face. David was making his sword flame the whole time he did this. David jumped off Tor and was caught in mid air by Gulture's levitation spell. As for Tor, he fell down the cliff and landed next to Maria's body. Gulture gently lowered David to the ground. David slowly walked over to Lalindra and kissed her long and good.

"Where did those other two armies come from?" David asked, turning his attention to Gulture.

"I don't know, but they are on our side," answered Gulture.

A dragon flew by and Gulture zapped it with a lightning bolt. The dragon fell down and splashed into the moat. Then, Crusher threw a rock at the scavenger, knocking him back into the moat. The dragon's body was so big that it could be used to cross over to what had been an isolated castle.

"Cross the moat by walking over the dragon's body!!!" David yelled to his army.

The scavengers all retreated inside what was left of the ruined Castle Doom and the whole Army of Peace followed.

"I love you," David said to Lalindra and then ran quickly off to join those entering the castle.

David fought his way through the pack of scavengers and quickly worked his way back up to Krag's tower.

Dawayne entered the room where Krag was. Krag turned around and almost laughed out loud when he saw Dawayne's small body with two daggers before him.

"You're dead Krag!!! Dawayne yelled as he charged Krag.

Krag waved his hand and Dawayne's daggers

vanished from his hands and he was thrown against the wall. Dawayne couldn't move and was scared to death.

"Dawayne . . . right?" Krag asked. "You of all people should know that you would never be able to defeat me."

Krag made one of Dawayne's daggers appear in his hand. Then, he threw the dagger into Dawayne's right arm.

"You were stupid to follow David," Krag said.

Krag made Dawayne's other dagger appear in his hand. Krag threw his dagger into Dawayne's left arm.

"Ugg!" Dawayne groaned as he felt the pain.

"But everyone learns from their mistakes," Krag told Dawayne as he drew his sword. "You're about to learn from the biggest mistake you ever made, and that was following David!"

Krag pointed his sword at Dawayne's stomach and was about to kill him when David ran in and pushed Krag over.

"Now you're mine!" David shouted.

"Very well. I shall go into combat with you. After your friend watches you die, I will kill him," Krag said, referring to Dawayne.

David and Krag began to circle each other. David swiped at Krag, who easily dodged it. David tried shooting fire at Krag, but the flame disappeared when Krag waved his hand.

"You tried that one before," Krag said.

"I know, but it was worth a shot. Some day it might work," David said.

"Not likely," said Krag.

David jumped in the air and slashed between his legs. Krag raised his sword and blocked the attack. This forced David to flip over Krag. As soon as David launched, he turned around and swung with all of his might at Krag.

"You are skilled," Krag admitted as he dodged the attack.

"Thanks, I wish I could say the same about you," David taunted.

Krag fumed with anger and hit David over the head with the broadside of his sword. David literally flew across the room. David's face was dripping blood all over and he suspected that he had broken his nose. Krag made an energy net fly from his fingers at David. David used his Power Sword to cut the net to pieces. Krag shot a fireball at David, who rolled to the side and avoided it. David got up and Krag kicked him in the stomach. David started to gasp for air.

"See what happens when you mess with me?" Krag said as he kicked David in the face for the fourth time. "I'm going to teleport down and kill your troops while you hear them scream up here. Too bad that in your condition, you won't be able to help them."

David got up and swung with little force at Krag, who easily dodged the attack. David shot a flame at Krag, who teleported down to fight. David fell over, still coughing.

"You got to get that son of a bitch. Promise me you will," Dawayne said while holding on to his last bit of life.

David was too weak to say anything. He crawled

over to the window and climbed out. There was a banner hanging here and David started to climb down it. David slowly eased his way down the banner with his Power Sword gripped firmly. As he was climbing down, David noticed a scavenger that was sneaking up on Brad and David shot it. Then he shot a flame at Krag, but Krag saw it coming and he made it vanish. Krag fired a huge ball of flames at the banner, causing it to quickly burn. David started to climb down the banner a lot faster, but it was too late. David let go of the banner and forced his body to twirl while he fell. David was heading directly for Krag and David started to fire off flames. He fired flame after flame. This posed no threat to Krag, for he just waved his hands and then the flame would vanish. However, Krag had made one mistake. He was so busy defending himself from the balls of fire coming at him that he forgot about David. David was hoping this would happen and he was getting very close to Krag. Krag realized his mistake at the last second, but it was too late. The Power Sword, with plenty of power behind it, entered Krag's stomach. David had hit Krag so hard that his arms, all the way up to his elbows, went into Krag as well. Krag hit the ground with David right on top of him. Everyone stopped fighting and looked at Krag's lifeless body. The battle zone, where only seconds before was filled with the sounds that combat makes, was now silent.

"Krag's dead," Brad declared as he stared at the bloody body that was once Krag.

All the scavengers suddenly started to convulse and they dropped their swords. Their armor also fell off to reveal lifeless, naked, human bodies. The bodies all fell over to add to the number that had been killed in the battle that had just ended. Although everybody was happy that the battle was over, David still hadn't gotten up either.

"Is he dead?" someone asked.

"I don't know," said Brad. "It's hard to say."

"Lalindra, can you heal him?" Crusher asked his friend.

"No, I'm afraid not. His wounds are too severe for my magical abilities," Lalindra answered truthfully.

"How about you, Gulture?" Crusher asked his only other magical friend.

"No, I'm sorry, but just as it is with Lalindra, he has too many wounds and they are all serious," said Gulture.

"He can't die," Crusher said. "He and Borin can't both die in the same battle."

People in the crowd started to cry or curse Krag. Nobody could believe that two of their greatest leaders, best warriors, and trusted friends would die in the same day.

"Maybe if you and Gulture combine your healing powers you can revive David," Brad said to Lalindra, hoping that it would work.

"It's worth a try," Crusher added.

"You ready?" Gulture asked Lalindra.

"As ready as I'll ever be," she replied.

The two concentrated all their magic to try to heal David. After several minutes, they gave up, exhausted beyond imagine.

"I'm sorry, but that won't work either," Gulture said through heavy breaths.

While people had been worrying about David, Dorris had slowly made her way next to David. She closed her eyes and put her hands over David's heart. Dorris' hands started to glow blue and David's wounds began to heal. Everyone stopped talking and watched in awe as Dorris performed her miracle. Eventually, David opened his eyes and stood up. Everyone cheered David when he stood up and they swarmed both he and Dorris. Both individuals were smothered with thank yous, hugs, and kisses.

"We have to save Dawayne," David said as he picked up Dorris and ran up the stairs of the tower.

David, Dorris, and Lalindra entered the room where Dawayne was.

"Glad to see some people still think I'm important," Dawayne whined.

"Do your thing," David instructed Dorris.

She did as she was told and soon Dawayne was completely healed.

After more hugs and kisses and congratulations, David asked,

"Where is Borin?"

Brad shook his head. "He didn't make it. Tor killed him as well as Tare and Maria."

It took David some time, but he finally got over the loss of his friends.

David looked at the battlefield, which was now covered with dead bodies.

"Terrible, isn't it?" he said.

"Yes, but this was the price we had to pay," said Dawayne.

David picked up Dorris, kissed her on the cheek, thanked her for saving his life, and took her over to the window. David yelled out the window.

"We now have peace!!"

Everyone outside cheered.

CHAPTER 10
A New Kingdom

"**Who are you?**" David asked the men who had led the two armies.

"I am Joseph and this is Charles," the leader of the first army said. "We came to help you battle Krag and are happy to have been of some service."

"Yes, but how did you know that we were battling Krag?" David asked.

"Everyone in the world knows about the Army of Peace. We were going to join your army. My wizard, Remel, can find anyone in the world with his magic. We asked him to find you and discovered that you were battling Krag and the scavengers. So we came to your aid," Charles finished.

"Well thank you, but now I must go home. I have the unpleasant task of telling people that their fathers and husbands are now dead," said David.

"Wait. We were to bring back Princess Lalindra.

She is to rule our kingdom since our king was her father," Joseph said.

"Joseph?" Lalindra said as she came over to the group of me. "And Charles too. I thought those were your banners that the armies that helped us carried."

"We need you to come rule our kingdom. As you know, your father was sick and yesterday he died," said Joseph.

David was about to comfort Lalindra and was surprised to see that she was taking it well.

"We would really enjoy the survivors of this battle to join our army. You have some of the best men and now that you're hardly an army . . ." Charles started.

"Hardly an army?!" David yelled. "We attacked Krag while the rest of you waited for him to attack you!"

"I'm sorry. I did not mean to sound insulting. I just meant to say that now your army is smaller than half a regiment and we should combine forces. We would be honored if you would join our army," Charles apologized.

"We can't join both of your armies," Brad said.

"Our two kingdoms are one since now both kings are dead and they were brothers. We wish for Lalindra to choose a husband and rule both kingdoms. So will you join us and become part of our kingdom?" Joseph asked.

Lalindra looked at David, who nodded his head in acknowledgement that they would join.

"We accept," said Lalindra.

"Good. When we get back to our kingdom, you

can meet some men who wish to be your husband," Charles said to Lalindra.

"No need. I've already chosen one," Lalindra said as she slipped her hand into David's.

"Are you serious?" David asked her.

"I've never been more so in my entire life," Lalindra answered.

The two kissed each other.

"Great. Now David will be our king instead of the captain of the guards," said Joseph.

"You must then choose two men to be the captain of the guards for our two cities. One for Sunshine Plains and another for Sweet Meadow," said Charles.

"I choose Crusher for Sunshine Plains and Tricks for . . . wait a minute, where is Tricks?" David asked as he scanned the crowd of spectators.

"Right here," Tricks said, walking forward. "I had been trapped in a cave under the cliff and Gulture just found me and used his magic to levitate me back up here."

"OK, like I was saying. Crusher will be at Sunshine Plains and Tricks will be at Sweet Meadow," David said.

"We accept," both Tricks and Crusher said together.

It took a couple more hours, but finally the army went back to their mountain paradise. Many different men took the duty of telling families that their fathers or husbands were dead. David would have done it himself, but everyone thought that friends of the family that did survive should deliver the news. Those that had lost family members decided to stay at the mountain to live and so did a lot of other people. The rest went to either Sweet Meadow or Sunshine Plains to live. David and Lalindra lived together at Sweet Meadow where they ruled very fairly. Dorris was adopted by the two as their daughter. Of course they hand more adventures which shall be told another day. Like the time they . . .

The End

Please read on for an excerpt from my new comedy, *Zombie Walkabout.*

A woman's blood-curdling scream pierced the night sky. The beautiful and busty woman desperately stampeded over the discarded debris of an obviously abandoned city. Towering buildings looked to be mere moments before gravity would topple them. The young woman's clothes were torn in a suggestive fashion; somehow, fate had ensured all her intimate anatomy was conveniently covered.

The woman frantically looked over her shoulder. The sight behind her urged her to increase her speed, anything to defy the cruel providence of her reality.

"Please! Anyone? Help me!" she shrieked.

The woman ran down a dead-end alley and frantically banged on the locked door near the back wall. Sinister shuffling from behind made the woman jerk her head. Near the opening of the alley, several lumbering zombies slowly advanced on her position. Their bodies were horrifically disfigured. They defied logic as they lurched forward with broken limbs trailing them and entrails spilling from their stomachs. The woman panicked and continued to pound on the door, growing more terrified with each passing second as the zombies staggered forward.

Suddenly the door denying the woman rescue dramatically swung open. She fell to the ground and looked hopefully at the opening, now filled with a pure white light. Its brilliance forced the woman to cover her face and turn away.

A lone figure filled the doorway. He was dressed head to toe in chainmail armor. He held a shield and a gleaming broadsword. The hero stepped through the door and faced the woman.

"Are these gentlemen bothering you?" the hero asked her.

The woman sat in stunned silence. The hero faced the zombies, now precariously close.

"No means no!" the hero shouted at the walking dead.

The hero then promptly defeated the zombies as a cheesy 80s rock song began to play.

Sam internally scoffed as he watched the promotional video in the preparation room at Zombie Walkabout. The quality of the film was insulting. Zombie Walkabout was the dream vacation for all adrenaline-loving tourists. The cost of the tickets to get there seemed to indicate that the video could be improved. Where was the Hollywood production value? Whatever. Sam forced himself to pay attention. He flexed his corded muscles as he imagined swinging the sword that decapitated the last zombie.

Sam was an athletic man in his mid-twenties. Though his friends often stood a few inches taller, none were willing to train with him. They often told him how it was bad enough he was better looking with bigger muscles; they didn't want to confirm how much stronger he actually was.

"God this is corny! Is this really what we're spending our money on?" a woman asked.

Sam looked at her. Ava was always the downer. She felt the need to complain at everything. Honestly, Sam was surprised she even came on the trip. More than a few would have preferred her stay home in Minnesota.

"Shut up! We need to pay attention!" a man said.

Sam figured he could count on Ash to pick another fight with Ava. Although both were the same age as Sam, Ava consistently behaved several years older while

Ash acted the commensurate number of years younger.

On the television, a well-dressed, athletic man in his early forties spoke with an Australian accent as he addressed the audience. He stood among the carnage that the hero left. The owner of Zombie Walkabout, Thomas Owens, nonchalantly stepped over severed limbs as he addressed the prospective zombie hunters viewing the promotional video.

"Ten years ago this was the fate of Australia. Fortunately, the brave men and women of the Australian military were able to evacuate many survivors and isolate the plague." Thomas paused for a somber moment of silence. He then looked up with an inviting smile. "That was then. Now the pandemic of the past offers you the adventure of the future. Thank you for your interest in Zombie Walkabout. I know you will remember this amazing experience for the rest of your life. If any of you are having second thoughts, this is the last chance to bugger out and still receive a full refund. Although you may be dressed in the most state of the art armor, zombie hunting is still inherently dangerous."

Thomas paused. Nobody in the room shifted.

Like hell I'm passing on this opportunity, Sam thought.

The recording of Thomas continued. "Ace! If you're still here then I salute your intrepidness. I also remind you that in our seven-year history, we've never had a fatality or infection. Your armor is more than safe and your guides are trained in all the most advanced combat and paramedic skills. Please wait a few minutes and your guides will be out to introduce themselves and get you suited up for adventure. Good hunting, mates!"

The promotional video ended with more rock and roll blaring as the hero aggressively made out with the hot woman over several dismembered zombie bodies.

Ava rolled her eyes, and Ash stifled his anger with her. Sam ignored them as he judged the reactions of his remaining friends. The rest of the group included Eli, Kellen, Cammy, and Calli. They were all in their early to mid-twenties, except Cammy, who was only seventeen. Ava looked bored and agitated. Kellen, Cammy, Ash, and Eli just seemed relieved the video was over. Thankfully, Calli looked appropriately anxious. Eli made a good choice when he'd asked her to marry him.

"Finally!" Sam said. "Time to crush some zombie skulls."

"Hell yeah!" Calli shouted. "Best engagement trip ever!"

Ash shook his head after Calli spoke and looked at Eli to voice his obvious disapproval. "Eli, bro, what the hell? Why is your fiancée present for our bachelor party?"

"Our party?" Sam felt compelled to ask.

Ash didn't even glance at Sam. He waved him off with a flap of his hand. "Shut up."

Eli spoke before Sam could grab Ash in a good-natured, but firm headlock. "Because, Ash, it's *my* bachelor party, and I want my wife-to-be present for it."

Ash snorted. "Said no man ever."

"She cares about this more than I do. I wouldn't be getting married if I took this trip and left her at home," Eli said.

"That's for damn sure," Calli stated while firing off a pair of finger pistols.

"Which brings up my second point," Ash started. "You don't care about zombies, but I know you enjoy ogling titties. Why are we even in Australia? The money spent on this trip could have paid for a lifetime of lap dances."

Ava pushed herself up from the leather couch she'd sunk into and marched toward Ash with an accusatory finger. "You're such a misogynistic ass clown! You didn't even pay for this trip! Kellen did!"

All heads turned toward the quiet and reserved benefactor.

Kellen held up his hands to barricade himself from any glances. "Please don't bring me into this."

"Kellen, I respect you for bringing out the dollars for this," Ash began. "I'm just saying this trip seems to be taken for the wrong reasons."

Ava poked Ash in the chest with a highly manicured finger. "No one asked you to come! At least you aren't a single parent, like some of us."

Shit, Sam thought. *Not this fight again.*

Ash slapped her hand away. The *smack* sounded harder than most would consider polite.

"Bitch!" Ash yelled. "You are *not* a single parent! You're just a slut who got caught cheating and divorced as a result! Your ex can always be relied on to watch the kids, something that *real* single parents don't have."

Sam sighed. He rolled his eyes and backed away to the wall opposite the television. He leaned next to a cracked-open door. One parent or another had gifted him with excellent hearing. Sam used this ability to eavesdrop on the two Zombie Walkabout employees that had instructed them to watch the twenty-minute safety video.

Mark and Chloe were the guides for Sam's tour of Zombie Walkabout. Mark was a strong man in his fifties. He had the stereotypical outback vibe going on. His bushy beard and steely eyes added to his mystique. Chloe was a fit woman in her forties. Sam noticed she seemed to have an ever present smile. It complemented the laugh lines punctuating her face. Clearly, she was a woman who enjoyed life.

"This is just great," Mark said with a subtle accent. "We've a bunch of Yanks."

Chloe's voice had a stronger Australian accent, but it sounded sweet and motherly. "It won't be that bad."

"Not that bad?" Mark asked. "Have you looked at them? They were only here long enough to watch a short video and already we've got the earbashing Sheila going at it with that figjam."

"Yeah, but they paid in advance for the private package," Chloe responded. "Money is money. Just pile on the extra-thick accent, and we'll make a pretty quid."

Sam could practically hear Mark smile as he said, "Ace! Let's start the show."

Chloe and Mark entered the prep room and walked into a loud screaming match. Sam quickly jumped from the wall and acted as if he hadn't been invading their privacy. Mark marched straight toward the main culprits of the shouting match, Ava and Ash. Chloe smirked a little as she looked at Sam before following her partner.

"Stop screaming at my Maid of Honor!" Calli shouted at Ash.

"There's plenty of room on my shit list for you, too!" Ash responded.

Now it was Eli's turn to get into Ash's face. Sam half expected Eli to push Ash and begin their vacation with a full-out brawl.

"Bro, don't speak to her like that!" Eli shouted at Ash.

Mark cleared his throat. None of the hunters beside Sam seemed to notice. Mark blew a whistle instead and got his intended result.

"G'day, mates. I'm glad to see we have a spirited group. It always makes for a more exciting trip," Mark said.

Chloe held out her hand. "Thank you for your interest in Zombie Walkabout. Please have a seat."

The hunters regained their composure. Chloe gestured toward the comfortable leather chairs and couches. Sam and his six friends silently took their seats. Kellen pulled Ash to the farthest chair from Ava. She likewise had Calli and Cammy attempt to calm her down with soft pats on her back. After he forcefully cleared his throat, the perspective hunters gave their attention.

"Good. My name is Mark Tanaka, and this lovely lady is Chloe White."

Cammy tried to stifle a giggle, but she was unsuccessful. She covered her face as several in the room stared at her.

"Something funny?" Mark asked with crossed arms.

Cammy stared sheepishly at the floor after being called out. Still, the defiant teenager in her apparently had to share with the group.

"Nothing *Mawk*," Cammy teased. "Don't you know there's an R in your name?"

Mark sighed and shook his head. Calli nudged Cammy with her elbow.

Mark aggressively rubbed his face before speaking. "You Yanks always seem to think that only your way is right. I know my own name, but feel free to piss the guy off who *will* have a gun on this trip."

Calli stared at Cammy with pleading eyes. "Sis, please don't. Just behave. I need this trip."

Cammy offered a weak smile. "Sorry. I apologize."

Mark shrugged. "Fair enough. Let's start again. My name is Mark and this lovely lady is Chloe. We'll be your guides during the greatest holiday of your life!"

The group cheered. Sam clapped extra long. He was thankful the tense situation seemed easily forgotten.

Chloe offered one of her radiant smiles. "Before we get started, let's go over the rules of the hunt. First, Mark and I are in charge. If at any point you don't listen to us, we'll end the trip early. You won't receive a refund. It's dangerous out there, and we're not going to lose a perfect record to a bunch of cowboys."

Mark took over. The two guides seemed like they

were performing a familiar dance that they'd long ago memorized every nuance. "Rule two: You will obviously have weapons, but only Chloe and I will have firearms. The armor you'll all be issued is strong enough to protect against the blunt weapons you'll get. You shouldn't even hear a shot."

Chloe's turn again. "Besides, I know a group with such spunk young men would prefer a melee fight. See which of you can launch a ZB head the farthest."

Sam's smile spread further. His friends looked equally chuffed as their egos were stroked.

"Rule three: Never remove your armor. I don't care how heavy you think it is. I don't care how hot you are or that it's messing up your hair. The armor stays on until we're back at F Camp," Mark said.

Chloe held up a finger and firmly pointed it at each hunter. "Rule four: Never separate. We're one team. We do not search different buildings and fossick for supplies. We're here to kill ZBs . . . nothing else."

The moment overwhelmed Sam. "Hell yeah we are!"

Calli apparently decided to tap into her inner woo girl to complement Sam's affirmation. "Woo!"

Chloe beamed another smile to Sam and Calli. "I see you've already learned rule five: stay excited and have fun."

Sam led his friends in another cheer.

Mark patted his hands downward to quiet the hunters. "Alright, now follow us and we'll get dressed up for the hunt."

Kellen held a timid hand in the air. "Excuse me, do you mind if we say a prayer first?"

Sam rolled his eyes. If zombies decimating Australia hadn't proved God either didn't exist or didn't care, then what would?

Chloe appeased the request, possibly even appreciated it. "Sure, mate."

Kellen closed his eyes and folded his hands. "Dear Lord, please give us the strength to end the suffering of your children whose souls are trapped in their decaying prisons. Let us be true in doing your work. Amen."

Sam begrudgingly said "Amen" with the rest of his friends.

"Really?" Sam asked.

Before Kellen could reply, Ash defended him, "Hey, leave him alone. If Captain Money Bags want to end their suffering, then I'll help him. He can say all the prayers he wants."

Kellen smiled at his supporter. "Thanks, Ash."

Mark took a moment to look at each of the hunters. Sam got the impression he was confirming all delays were finally out of their systems.

"Well now, please follow us," he said.

OTHER WORKS BY PHILLIP MURRELL

THE BYSTANDERS SERIES

Bystanders (available now)

Bystanders II: Trophy Hunters (available now)

Bystanders III: Sleepers and Scouts (available now)

Bystanders IV: Our Contest (available now)

Zombie Walkabout (Coming late 2019)

Get updates @bystanderssaga

A NOTE FROM THE AUTHOR

All my life, I've been a fan of stories. I got so much enjoyment out of reading/watching someone else's work, I decided to start writing my own. I've already tackled gritty superheroes and fantasies. I have so much more to write. My next book will be a comedy that happens to have zombies. Grab your best friends and head to Australia for a vacation you'll never forget. My time in the military compels me to write a military sci-fi story. That will be out in 2020.

I hope you enjoy the stories I've already written and look forward to those yet to come. I love writing them for people exactly like you.

Printed in Great Britain
by Amazon